T0228654

Praise for *The*

2024-2025 Great Lakes Great Read Adult Selection
2021 Canadian Book Club Awards Winner in Fiction
2021 15th Annual Indie Excellence Juror's Choice
     Award Winner
2021 Readers' Favorite Book Awards Silver Medal in
     Fiction—Literary
2021 National Indie Excellence Awards Finalist in
     New Fiction
2021 National Indie Excellence Awards Finalist in
     Regional Fiction: Midwest
2020 Sarton Book Awards Finalist for Contemporary Fiction

"The novel . . . honors the natural world with dazzling imagery
. . . A dramatic, rewarding story about a woman reconnecting
with family, nature, and herself."
—*KIRKUS REVIEWS*

"I sank into this novel with such pleasure that I didn't want it to
end. Sally Cole-Misch is a master of language and of creating a
sense of place. I'm equally impressed by the delicacy with which
Cole-Misch handles complicated and important political issues.
This book is a must read."
—CELINE KEATING, author of *Layla*, *Play for Me*,
and *The Stark Beauty of Last Things*

"*The Best Part of Us* by Sally Cole-Misch . . . explores nature,
family, and land with nuance and patience. What hooked me
first was the utter lusciousness of the prose. . . . A beautiful love
letter to the natural world and to human connection."
—*AFFINITY MAGAZINE*

"In this mesmerizing novel, Cole-Misch draws us into the challenges of family, the rights of First Nations, and the healing power and grandeur of nature. Cole-Misch skillfully guides us to understand the perspective of each character, and we hold our breath, hoping that they can find a way through their difficulties."
—REBECCA D'HARLINGUE, author of *The Colorist* and *The Lines Between Us*

"Cole-Misch tactfully embeds . . . indigenous sacred land and our conceptions of home . . . admirable and necessary within the world of nature-fiction . . . through the eyes of an ideal protagonist . . . Her words paint the Earth as our ultimate refuge, a source of strength to draw from and live intimately within."
—*THE MICHIGAN DAILY*

"Cole-Misch draws her characters with a fine paintbrush, adding layer upon layer until each character is fully realized. . . . The descriptions of the land and water are dazzling."
—*MIDWEST BOOK REVIEW*

"A vivid sense of place permeates Sally Cole-Misch's novel, and the family itself has fissures revealed as the novel sweeps the reader along, increasing the tension until this reader was racing toward the ending. A highly accomplished novel by an author who displays compassion for all her characters as well as the natural world. I was sorry to leave this world."
—MARIAN WERNICKE, author of *Out of Ireland* and *Toward That Which is Beautiful*

"Beth made my heart sing and cry. The development of her character, how she perceives the world and her family, is phenomenal. You'll want to read this one in a single sitting."
—LINDA ULLESEIT, author of *The River Remembers*, *The Aloha Spirit*, and *Under the Almond Trees*

"Bravo to author Cole-Misch for crafting a story that takes two key political issues of the day—climate change and indigenous displacement—and weaves them into a family story that sits as close and personal as the survival of cherished summers on the lake."
—RITA DRAGONETTE, author of *The Fourteenth of September*

"This book evokes the wonder and awe we can find when we go out into nature. . . . The Canadian lake environment is almost a character in its own right because it affects the actions of almost every other character and how they define each other."
—ECOFICTOLOGY

"The tangled relationships of the family members kept me riveted to the astonishing ending. Beautifully written, with inspiring nature descriptions that made me long for time in more solitary spaces, it is a book I will long remember."
—FLORENCE REISS KRAUT, author of *Street Corner Dreams* and *How to Make a Life*

"This book turned pages in me. Drew me in slowly until I was ready to claim an island myself—a place of beauty and redemption and, ultimately, joy. Beth and Dylan and the life-giving days on the lake will stay with me."
—CHERYL BOSTROM, author of *Sugar Birds* and *Leaning on Air*

THE BEST PART OF US

THE
BEST PART
OF US

A Novel

SALLY COLE-MISCH

SHE WRITES PRESS

Published 2020
Printed in the United States of America
Print ISBN: 978-1-63152-741-8
E-ISBN: 978-1-63152-742-5
Library of Congress Control Number: 2020906920

For information, address:
She Writes Press
1569 Solano Ave #546
Berkeley, CA 94707

Interior design by Tabitha Lahr
Map illustration by *Fe Wyma*, RGD

She Writes Press is a division of SparkPoint Studio, LLC.

For every living thing

*"If the stars should appear one night in a thousand years,
how men would believe and adore.
Live in the sunshine, swim in the sea, drink the wild air.
Nature always wears the colors of the spirit."*

—Ralph Waldo Emerson

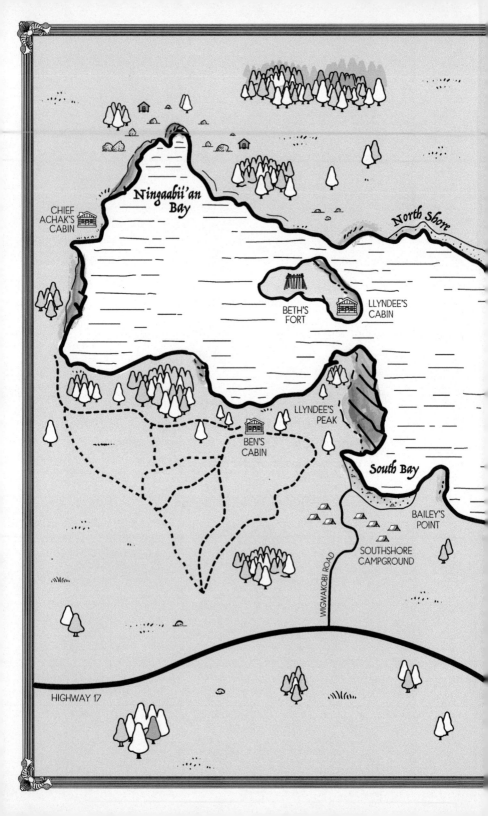

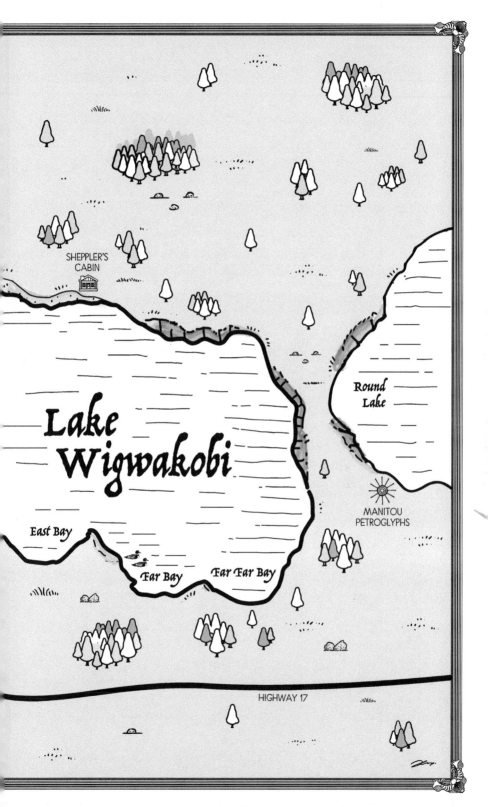

Chapter One: JULY 2004

B eth Llyndee lifts the legal envelope from the kitchen counter and grins at her grandfather Taid's still strong handwriting. He hadn't mentioned a package in either call this week, or that her mother Kate would deliver it. It isn't like him to keep secrets, at least not anymore. She scans his writing with her fingertips, as if the ink can tell her what's inside.

"Mom, juice!"

Beth jumps, sets the envelope on a week's stack of mail, and walks to the refrigerator. "Sorry, little man. I can't wait to see you in your first Fourth of July parade."

"Let's go as soon as Dad gets back. I want to wear my flag shirt and Cubs hat for sure." He stuffs half of the honey, banana, and peanut butter sandwich into his mouth, washes it down with orange juice, and bolts for his bedroom.

She picks up sandwich crumbs scattered across the floor. "We really need to get a dog," she mutters to the sink.

As Beth washes the dishes, she glances down the counter at the envelope. What was so important her mother drove four hours from Ann Arbor to Chicago and changed her flight to Arizona?

Something she wants resolved now. Kate's path is always forward, her decisions fast and right, leaving the rest of the family to fall in line sooner rather than later.

She gazes out the kitchen window at their narrow backyard, the aged cement patio a parking lot for Kobi's outdoor toys. Two Adirondack chairs, their wood succumbing to a dull, cracked gray, face the backyard and far row of maples and hemlocks. How odd that such a small space is her only sanctuary after the vast stretch of land and water she'd once called home.

The screen door's whining hinges announce Mike's return from his morning run. He hugs her from behind, the heat and sweat on his arms marking her shirt across her breasts and stomach. Beth turns to return his embrace, and they wrap each other in a tight cocoon. She inhales his aroma, maple syrup with a touch of lime—like her son's honey head with the pungency of adulthood thrown in—and runs her fingers through his dark blond curls as he releases her.

"Folks are already heading to the parade. Not much space to run between the cars and strollers, but I had a good pace, clear morning air. Where is everybody?"

"Kobi's in his bedroom, changing his clothes for the fifth time. You need to pull off your fastest shower ever."

"I'm on it. Where's your mom?"

Beth steps back, crosses her arms over her chest. "Left for the airport half an hour ago. Off to visit Maegan and her kids. For three weeks this time."

"But she got here late last night. She couldn't stay to see her other grandchild in the parade? Did she even say hi to Kobi before she left?"

"She was in the kitchen when we got up, eager to hand me a package from Taid and leave. Said I need to open it and deal with its contents as soon as possible." Beth nods at the end of the counter. "That was her real reason for coming, not to get a less expensive flight as she claimed, or to see us."

"What's in it?" Mike walks toward the envelope, but Beth grabs his arm and waves at the package with her other hand.

"Nothing that can't wait. Kobi will explode if we don't get to the parade on time. Go!"

Mike stares at her. "Don't open that without me."

She nods and pushes him out of the kitchen. When the bathroom pipes buckle as water spills into the home's lone showerhead, she walks to the envelope.

Beth turns the package over in her hands, paces the kitchen, and peeks down the bedroom hallway for signs of Mike and Kobi. Nothing yet. There's only one reason her mother would hand deliver this: something about the island, the place her family loved and had left fourteen years ago. Kate has wanted it out of their lives ever since. But why would her grandfather want to do something about it now?

She glances down the hallway again. Her brother Dylan's painting of her on the island, which she held in a tight roll as they left the lake for the last time, stares back at her. When Mike pulled it from a moving box, he'd demanded that it hang where she would see it every day. Even now, Kobi sometimes points to it and asks, "Is that really you? Smile like that for me, Mom." Beth sighs and walks back to the kitchen.

When she reaches for the envelope's corner, her body shudders. She closes her eyes and envisions one morning from the last summer on the island. She'd woken to leaves rustling above her in the early morning breeze, the silver-and-white birch branches swaying in an energetic to-and-fro as if refreshed from their own evening's rest, eager to wave good morning just to her. Chipmunks chattered as they scavenged for food, downy woodpeckers *rat-tat-tatted* in a frenetic cadence against nearby cedars and pines, and gulls cawed from across the lake at fishermen unloading their catch. A lone mourning dove cooed somewhere deep in the woods along the north shore.

She squinted to take in the brilliant sky just beyond the canopy of birches, pines, and spruce. The earth under her felt warm and comforting despite its granite base, the moss her fingers caressed without thinking offering an opposing tenderness and subtle aroma of must. She unzipped her sleeping bag and stretched. The breeze carried droplets of brisk lake water from the rock shoreline far below, where waves gathered in eager swooshes and receded in sighs. Goosebumps spread across her arms and chest.

She gathered her sleeping bag, book, and flashlight and headed down the narrow path through proud trees, sharp-jutted outcroppings, and low bushes overflowing with blueberries to her family's log cabin on the island's eastern shore. Her grandmother and father were returning from their early morning search for whitefish and trout, and her brother from drawing the sunrise, for blueberry muffins and dandelion mint tea prepared by her mother, sister, and grandfather. Like every other summer of her young life, her family had returned to the one place where Beth was surrounded by everything and everyone she loved. Someday, when she was old enough to make her own decisions, she thought she would go there and stay forever.

Her heart constricts, her breathing catches. *You can't go back, and you know it,* her mind tells her heart. *This is the world you live in now. The past is the past.*

Beth opens her eyes and rips the package open.

A handwritten letter, two stapled groups of papers titled "Last Will and Testament of Padrig Llyndee," and a deed dated June 23, 1944, slide into her hands. She scans each group and the letter. Thick bile rises from her stomach and settles in a solid block in her throat. How could Taid do this? He knows how hard she's fought to erect a solid, safe barrier between her life here and her childhood summers there. Why would he ask her to decide the island's fate?

"What has Taid sent now?" Mike asks behind her.

Beth flinches and hands the stack of papers to him over her shoulder, then clenches the counter's edge and takes two slow breaths so she can answer in a normal voice. "Guess he's decided his time is almost up and he needs to get his wills in order."

"Wills? I thought you only needed one."

She can hear him rifling through the documents behind her. "Me too. He's written two, one that passes the island to me, the other to Lily's family. He wants me to choose."

"To Lily, your brother's girlfriend?" Mike whistles. "I've never doubted that Taid has big kahunas, but that's huge even for him." He waits for her response, but Beth is too busy trying to breathe.

"What's your mother's role in this?"

She turns toward him and shrugs, resting her back and palms on the counter behind her so she can still grip its edge. "She probably saw the envelope on Taid's desk and changed her travel plans so she could deliver it right away. I can't believe she didn't open it, but the seal wasn't broken, and that's Taid's handwriting."

"What did she say when she gave it to you?"

"She was adamant I deal with whatever is inside immediately, 'so we can move on once and for all and get past whatever curse the Ojibwe put on the island and our family.' That she knows I'll do the *right thing*."

"Does she really believe Lily's family cursed yours? I've always known Kate's a control freak, but to throw her demands at you, on top of Taid's—it's too much, even for her."

Her grip tightens on the counter as she stares at the floor and remembers the intensity of her mother's anger when they left the island all those years ago, and its distant echo this morning. "You can't go home again, Beth," she said. "No one can. All we can do is stand up and move forward."

Beth doesn't have a clue how much time has passed when Mike squeezes her shoulder.

"Hey, I'm still here."

She nods and puts her hand on his chest. "Thanks, but my thoughts are in a million directions. Kobi will be out soon, the Fourth of July party will last until late tonight, and I have to catch a six-a.m. flight." She takes the package from Mike and sets it on the counter behind her. "I'll read everything more closely in Toronto, and then we can talk."

He stiffens and steps back. "You get letters or emails from Taid all the time. You talk on the phone twice a week. You must have had a clue this was coming. Are you ever going to share that part of your life with me, with us?"

"You didn't live through it all. You shouldn't have to bear the consequences."

"I live with it whether or not you talk about it, and so does your son." He paces the kitchen, turns to her after the second pass. Beth digs her hands into her pockets to guard against what's coming.

"We watch you fade away every time we're with your family. I get why your mom pushes your buttons—she's got enough anger for all of us. But every time you disappear into a polite robot, it takes days for you to come back."

Beth's not sure when the façade took over. She can sense them urging her back at holiday dinners: Taid with his sideways glances, Mike hugging her at odd moments, Kobi yanking her sleeves as if he's trying to pull down the wall she's raised between them. When the accumulation of tight smiles, controlled conversations, and going along to keep any semblance of family intact forces her so far inside that even Mike doesn't recognize her.

She could argue that he knows her in ways her family doesn't. He knows the Beth that smiles deep in her heart when she's with him and Kobi, no matter where they are. He's seen glimpses of the young Beth when they've played in the Lake Michigan sand on hot summer weekends, when she's taught Kobi about the waves, birds, and fish, and he always asks for more of that her.

But that part—the girl who lived for open skies, rocky peaks, crystal blue water, and stands of windswept pines; who craved the sweet scent of dew on the cedars on an early morning hike and the loons' wistful trills across the bays just after sunset; who shared the joy of being in and a part of nature with her brother, Dylan—could never survive living in Chicago. She shudders as she realizes how deeply she's buried her memories and that part of herself to create what felt like a contented life in spite of her surroundings.

"Sometimes the past overwhelms, no matter how hard my family tries to keep it buried. Maybe we *are* cursed."

She forces herself to look at him: he's narrowed his gaze, sharpened his navy eyes into steel arrows that pierce hers. "From what we've read so far, it sounds like your grandfather's giving us the chance to go to the island and figure out what we want for *our* family."

His words "go to the island" reverberate off blood vessels in her ears, landing nowhere.

"Why don't we celebrate the family we've created, the memories we could make there? I've seen Taid's amazing photos and paintings of the place and how you light up when you look at them. At the very least, it'd be a chance to get out of the city, which you used to say you want." Mike pauses. "Do you want to disappoint Taid, me, and your son? I bet he'd love it up there."

She knows he's pulling Kobi into the conversation to reach her deepest regret—that it feels normal to her son to grow up in a grit-filled city of concrete and steel, the skyscrapers crowding together like a forest of silver spikes reaching for the heavens in a decadent illusion of grandeur. Around people who crave cramped coffee haunts where they suck each other's energy dry through idle conversation and needy smiles, rather than open skies and full breezes that cleanse the lungs and soul. Where the constant hum of traffic and human activity whines in her ears and dulls her imagination, while Lake Michigan's waves urge her to remember another world that's alive and free just beyond her vision.

Beth matches Mike's gaze, determined to keep the rising fear and anger from escaping. "You don't understand what you and Taid are asking of me. Let me read this on my own, work through the memories and choices, and then we can talk."

Disappointment envelops his face, and she pulls him to her. He buries his hands deep in her thick auburn hair as he did after they'd said "I do" and nearly every time they make love.

"Promise me you won't decide something for the three of us you can never change," he whispers. "We deal with this together. No more disappearing."

Beth nods and tightens her grip as the panic from his demand and her grandfather's request floods through her. Mike doesn't understand that if she crosses that line, if she goes back to that part of herself and to those woods, cliffs, and water, she may not be able to return. To this city, or this life.

Chapter Two: SUMMER 1987

> *"Nights and days came and passed,*
> *And summer and winter and the rain.*
> *And it was good to be a little island.*
> *A part of the world*
> *And a world of its own*
> *All surrounded by the bright blue sea."*

—Margaret Wise Brown, *The Little Island*

"Listen to this," Kate said, clucking before and after her words. She lifted the news section of *The New York Times*, blocking the entire right half of the royal-blue sedan's front window.

"'An ABC News/*Washington Post* poll released tonight found that testimony by Admiral Poindexter and Colonel North had not helped the president's credibility. Only forty-eight percent of those polled believed the admiral's assertion that Mr. Reagan was unaware of the fund diversion.'" Kate glared at her husband, Evan, both of his hands on the narrow steering wheel like every other time he drove. "How can almost half of the American public believe Reagan didn't know, that he didn't lead the entire Iran-Contra affair?"

Beth's mother couldn't live without the *Times*, so Evan had started another subscription to the Thessalon postmaster in addition to the one that came every day at home in Ann Arbor. Who would read those editions while they were gone, the ones the weird kid flew into their front door every morning from his bike? Sometimes he'd stop and stare up at her bedroom window, just above the front door. She could see him if she sat up in bed, which she'd moved to the middle of her room so her first view in the morning was of trees and sky. Except for the mornings she'd look down and see him staring up at her. Yuck.

They'd picked up two weeks' worth of newspapers when they stopped for groceries in the small Canadian harbor town on the northern shore of Lake Huron. It was the last stop before they reached the cold, clear waters of Lake Wigwakobi—or "waters of many birches," as the local Ojibwe people called it. Her family still used that name, even though other summer residents had switched to the Canadian government's name, Big Birch Lake, many years ago. Their annual trek north to the island was as constant as the blueberries that covered it every June. Their home and sanctuary, no matter what.

Kate's stack of newspapers filled the middle of the front seat, so they had piled the grocery bags on the back floor around Beth, Maegan, and Dylan's legs. Beth hugged the bag with eggs and bread between her calves, balancing it on top of the center hump. She liked the middle seat despite its stiffness. For once, she felt bigger than her older sister and brother.

As Evan turned onto the rutted one-lane path that connected a wide center bay of Lake Wigwakobi to the rest of the world, Beth leaned to the left to see around the newspaper. She didn't want to miss the view as the path wound through the deep woods and ended at the lake's shore. Maegan shoved Beth back to the middle with her shoulder.

"It wouldn't matter if they told Reagan or not," Maegan said.

"I mean, isn't he older than Taid? He probably can't remember what anyone tells him after ten minutes."

Kate chuckled, dropping the paper into her lap. Beth smiled. "Good observation, dear. You're probably right."

Evan looked in the rearview mirror at his eldest daughter. "Don't make that comparison in front of your grandfather. Reagan's at least five years older, and I can't say Taid's showing many signs of intellectual loss."

Kate lifted the paper wall again. "You're choosing to not see what you don't want to. It won't be long before we'll have to open the cabin with them in May to make sure they don't fall and break something. At least we have the next few weeks to ourselves, just the five of us."

"We're almost there," Beth said, urging her mother to stop reading and lower the paper.

No luck. Kate straightened her back and pulled the paper closer to her face. "This part is great: 'James Dylan Barber, a political scientist at Duke University and author of several books on the presidency, said, "This has destroyed Reagan's credibility in world politics."' We can only hope that twenty years from now others will see Reagan as one of our worst presidents ever."

"Time will tell, I guess," Evan mumbled as he steered the car over the deep potholes and tree roots jutting across the path. When the tall stands of white pines, sugar maples, and silver birches surrounded them in deep shade, Kate folded the newspaper and added it to the stack. She wrapped her arms around the paper tower as if it were a fine china vase needing protection from the car's gyrations.

Beth scanned the woods with its lime-green ostrich ferns and ash-gray mounds of reindeer lichen. Everything in its place, just as she remembered. Dylan moved his long legs pressed against the back of the front seat to bump knees with Beth. They grinned at each other as the car came over the last hill and angled downward.

"Here it comes!" she yelled, catching her breath as the front window filled first with pale sand, then bright aqua water that deepened to darkest navy as the lake's bottom shifted from sand to bedrock. "We made it!" The eight-hour drive still felt as if it took days.

Evan laughed. "Never gets old, does it?"

Beth grinned back at her father.

"Nice to be home," Dylan whispered.

Evan parked in the last open spot of grass set aside for the lake's island dwellers among a small campground that rimmed the shoreline. Campers were going about their early evening rituals: eating dinner on picnic tables next to their tents or trailers; securing boats to the rickety wooden docks for the night; and preparing the nightly bonfire, now just a pile of logs, kindling, paper, and pine needles in the large fire pit near the beach.

Everyone had memorized their role long ago to move their belongings from the car to the family's maroon cast-iron fishing boat at the dock. Dylan and Kate carried the stiff brown leather suitcases, scuffed from years of transporting the family's clothes, books, and toiletries from home. Beth and Maegan took twice as many trips carrying the groceries, and Evan arranged everything on the boat's floor. Kate and Dylan made the last trip, she with the stack of newspapers and he with his large duffel bag of paints, pastels, brushes, and papers.

Beth untied the boat's fore and aft ropes from the dock and held them taut as she bounced on her toes, willing Dylan to walk faster. He kicked the dirt and sand with his black canvas Keds, his lanky frame lagging far behind his feet. He had just passed their father in height at six feet, but his brown wavy hair, deep-set eyes, and long graceful fingers mirrored their mother. Kate smiled or nodded at several campground regulars, her gait mirroring Dylan's from the weight of the papers in her arms. When Kate reached the boat, she divided them into three groups and set the piles on the two metal benches that spanned the boat's center. She, Maegan, and Evan pounced on them before the wind could send the pages lofting across the campground.

Beth tossed the ropes into the boat and jumped onto her triangle seat in the bow just before Dylan revved the outboard engine and jammed it into forward gear. Maegan and her newspaper pile slid backward onto the luggage stacked behind her. Dylan pulled the engine's lever into neutral as everyone erupted in laughter.

"Pig! I could have broken my back!" Maegan slapped at Dylan's leg.

Kate pointed at the newspapers scattered around Maegan. "Don't lose those or there'll be hell to pay."

Maegan shoved the papers under her and rotated sideways on the luggage, away from the rest of the family. Dylan turned the handle into gear again, and Beth faced forward with her legs crossed under her. She leaned over the bow to watch the water change from aquamarine to indigo as the lake deepened, and to brilliant white when the bow broke its stillness and collected it into waves. As the bay opened to the lake's wide middle, she sat up to breathe in the crisp air and feel the wind lift her long hair. Goose bumps scattered across her arms and legs.

Even in mid-July the water was still cold from a late spring thaw. Taid had taught them that the long oval lake was one of hundreds created as the last continental glaciers retreated thousands of years ago. She tried to picture the glacier digging out the humongous Great Lakes and her own lake like a bulldozer, each advance and retreat digging deeper into the earth's crust. Fishing maps showed where Lake Wigwakobi's floor dropped over three hundred feet from the granite cliffs along its shores, yet the water's clarity belied its depth—even rocks sitting fifty feet deep were easy to see.

To the right, the lake's eastern half spread out in a huge expanse of open water with forested borders and three bays scalloping the southern shore. To the north was the lake's only other sandy shore, almost a mile across and extending into the hill behind it. Beth and her grandmother, Naina, often canoed to the western end of the beach and walked its length, stopping to say hi to the Shepplers at their family cabin on the beach's eastern end. The two families had become tight friends the first summer the Shepplers arrived and often gathered for barbeques and card games. Naina and the eldest Sheppler, Aunt Betty, won every gin rummy tournament and most games of spoons.

Beth wondered how often that would happen this summer, since Maegan and Brian, the Shepplers' only son, had spent so much time together last summer—way too much time, according to their mother. Beth had hovered in the cabin's kitchen and listened to her parents argue last August after they realized Maegan was meeting Brian almost every night at the campground bonfires. Her dad had suggested that's what teenagers were supposed to do, but Kate was adamant. "She's too young emotionally, even if she is sixteen, and Brian is too spoiled and wild for her. We might adore his parents, but they let him do whatever he wants. Nothing good will come of it, for Maegan or our families."

Beth glanced back at her sister, who was staring across the lake at the Shepplers' cabin. Had Maegan talked with Brian over the winter? With four years between them, Beth was just the curious baby sister in the background, watching Maegan's many friends—girls and boys—come and go from the house and cabin. She shared the family trait of long, lean bodies and brown eyes, but Naina often teased that an Irishman must have invaded the family's Welsh gene pool for Maegan to have strawberry-blond hair and ivory skin. In family photos, her pale beauty shone next to the others' dark hair and olive coloring. To Beth, her sister felt like standing next to a winter fire: other people always wanted to be near Maegan to feel the warmth of her glow.

As Dylan angled the boat to the west, the overwhelming presence of Llyndee's Peak towered over them. The cliff rose ten stories out of the lake's deep middle, its gray, brown, and black granite glittering with quartz and vertical rows of sharp edges from shears and rockslides. The lake's summer residents and most locals had named the cliff for Beth's grandfather twenty years earlier, when he, Evan, and Ben—an American who'd moved to Lake Wigwakobi around the same time and now knew the entire lake and surrounding land by heart—had cut through the deep backwoods to build meandering paths from its north and south shores to the cliff's wide summit. Beth searched for the same faces in the rocks that her imagination had conjured up long ago, wardens standing guard over the lake and its inhabitants. Shadows from the late afternoon sun cast a dark, ominous gaze to their eyes.

Dylan slowed the boat as they rounded the north end of Llyndee's Peak, and the island's mass of bedrock and proud stands of pine, birch, and basswood came into view. Even though the lake's western half extended for another five miles, its water a rush of blues and blacks as the setting sun's rays danced across its waves, all Beth cared about was seeing their island again. Every summer, Beth asked Naina to retell the story of how she and Taid had found the island. They'd bought it in the mid-1940s, soon after immigrating to Michigan from Wales. Taid had seen things in the war he never wanted to relive, so they had gone on a Great Lakes "walkabout," as Naina called it, to let nature heal his many wounds. Once they'd hiked the kidney-bean-shaped island and fished the deep sapphire lake filled with trout, whitefish, and bass, they had found their sanctuary—their chance to return to the cliffs and woods of their homeland without traveling across the ocean to memories that didn't want to go away. They bought the entire island for $50 from the local constable, who also served as chief of the local Ojibwe or Anishinaabe First Nation.

By 1950, the couple had traveled the fourteen-hour drive from Ann Arbor to the island—which included two ferries across northern Lake Michigan and the east end of Lake Superior—a dozen times to build their log cabin. Each fall Taid borrowed a neighbor's truck to haul logs from the surrounding woods back home to their garage. Over the winters, he built the beds, couches, and tables, Evan watching and learning even as a toddler. The bridge built over the Straits of Mackinac in 1957, where Lake Michigan and Lake Huron connect, saved them two hours of travel time. Three more disappeared in 1962 when another bridge was built over the Saint Marys River, which connected Sault Sainte Marie, Michigan, with the Canadian town of the same name, only spelled Sault Ste. Marie. Eight hours seemed like a sprint in comparison. Beth knew the island was her grandparents' true home, not the bungalow they lived in the rest of the year in Ann Arbor.

When Evan brought Kate to Lake Wigwakobi for their honeymoon, her first experience in nature was overwhelming—nothing like the confined congestion of Boston, where she had grown up and attended Radcliffe for a degree in political science. The open skies, intense colors, and constant sound of waves lapping or pounding the island's edge, depending on the weather, presented a foreign world. The family still laughed when Evan teased Kate on windy days about the night they'd lain in bed and she'd screamed, "Can't you stop those waves?!"

After more visits, Kate agreed to spend a few weeks on the island every summer, the perfect refuge for Evan from the demands of teaching physics at the university, and a place where Kate could read about politics for hours, uninterrupted. Taid and Naina even stayed home with Maegan, Dylan, and Beth when they were toddlers and infants so Evan and Kate could have time alone on the island. Evan sometimes shared wistful stories with Beth as they fished together, about all the things Kate had learned to enjoy at the lake before Beth and her siblings came with them. Before every jagged rock jutting out of the island's soil became a dagger eager to stab or trip, sending her children careening over cliffs. When every heavy cloud turned Kate's imagined fears as dark and brooding as an impending storm.

Beth was always surprised by how the large cabin's beige logs blended into its surroundings in spite of the island's iridescent rocks, with their shimmering reds, browns, and golds. It looked like any other cabin gracing the lake's shores, as if nothing were happening inside, when she was certain it contained the best of her family's lives.

As they neared the dock, Dylan slowed the boat, and she jumped out to tie it to the thick wooden dock. Rubber tires masquerading as buoys moaned their hellos as she pulled the boat close to the dock for the others to get out. The family unloaded their supplies and climbed the rock steps to the cabin, a script they'd already played many times.

By now, Beth, Dylan, and Maegan knew every inch of the island by heart and traversed the trails easily to the blueberry patches, choice fishing holes, or secret hiding spots each had claimed over the years. Almost every morning, Dylan filled his duffel bag with art supplies, a banana, and at least one bag of chocolate chip cookies and traversed the island to paint in the sun's rising light. Beth had followed him enough to know his favorite haunts along the south shore's lower edge, ducking behind trees when their mother checked on him to make sure he hadn't fallen into the lake and drowned. Sometimes he'd invite Beth to join him when he heard her slip on the loose mounds of pine needles above him, but only if she didn't pester him while he was painting. She'd watch until the magical moment when he cleaned his brushes in the lake, and the paints danced their own brief scenes on the surface before fading into the navy abyss. Squirrels, gray jays, and seagulls also trailed behind to fight over the ample crumbs. He didn't show his paintings to anyone, relenting only when their parents begged him to share so they could choose several pieces for the cabin's living and dining room walls.

Maegan's days of climbing trees, building blanket forts in the woods, and fishing off the rocks had ended at least three years ago, replaced by tanning and reading on the dock in one of many bikinis. The few times she'd joined her sister on the dock, Beth realized that Maegan could tell from the sound of the boat's engine and horn whether it was Brian or the kids from shore coming to get her. By midafternoon they were all together, pushing each other off docks, waterskiing from cabin to cabin, or climbing Llyndee's Peak. Beth couldn't imagine just sitting in the sun all day or riding around with other kids doing silly things instead of hiking, swimming, or sailing, but she was intrigued when Maegan told her they'd explored the beaches at the lake's west end for new friends last summer. While many families in the lake's center section often had evening parties together, they stayed on the "tourist" side of the lake; most of the locals—Ojibwe families who had lived around the lake for hundreds of years—occupied the west end.

Beth spent her days spying on her brother; exploring every tree, blueberry bush, and bird; and canoeing, kayaking, swimming, or sailing with her parents and grandparents, reveling in all four adults' attention when Naina and Taid joined them on the island. Beth hadn't seen many places other than the island, her hometown, and a university in Chicago to hear one of her dad's speeches, but she didn't care if she never went anywhere else.

Kate and Maegan unloaded the groceries, started their dinner routine, and chatted about their plans for the summer. Evan disappeared into the boathouse to renew his ritual of restoring a 1943 Port Carling wooden cruising boat. Beth begged Dylan to help her clean several bass Ben always caught before they arrived. He'd left them floating in a tin bucket by the dock, with a latched top and tiny holes that made it look like a strainer.

Ben lived just west of Llyndee's Peak in a one-room log cabin deep in the woods. He was the oldest "tourist," as the locals called anyone who hadn't grown up on the lake, even though he'd lived there for twenty years. He knew the best fishing holes, where to find the newest eagle nests, and the name of every tree and plant in the region. Beth's parents said she was old enough to hang out with him this summer as Dylan had at her age, and she was eager to learn everything he'd taught her brother and more.

Beth retrieved their lake sneakers from the boathouse, the ones they swam in so the rocks wouldn't tear at the bottoms of their feet, but Dylan couldn't fit into his. Evan chuckled and handed his pair to Dylan. They perched on two small rocks peeking above the water in front of a wood slat table Taid had built for fish gutting. His leather-bound fish knives were long and sharp, but he'd taught each child how to peel away the skin, backbone, and innards with a specific knife. Gulls gathered on the dock as soon as they cut open the first fish, smelling an easy evening meal.

Dylan grabbed one of the smaller fish out of the bucket and wiggled it in front of Beth's face as he raised his voice to a squeal. "How could you do this, little girl? I'm supposed to get bigger before you eat me!"

Beth twisted her lips into a fish pout and answered in her most severe Wicked Witch voice. "You're the perfect size for eating, along with your brothers and sisters. I've got you, my pretties."

"Not if I can get your brother to drop me!" Dylan swung his arms in circles as if the fish had control.

Beth lunged for the dancing fish. "Don't you dare!" They wrestled for the fish until Beth lost her balance on her rock perch. As Dylan grabbed her instead, the released fish flew across the air and into the lake. They watched it swim in a small triumphant circle and then dive for safe waters.

As soon as Beth regained her balance, she shoved Dylan's arms away and pointed the bloody knife at him. "Okay, that was part of your dinner, not mine!"

"That's the thanks I get for saving you from an evening swim."

They skinned and deboned two more fish. Beth held two dissected fish eyes in front of her own and peered up at Dylan, batting her eyelashes.

"Oh, Dylan, are you coming to town to visit me tomorrow? Please say you'll save me from my boring job and show me your wonderful drawings," Beth crooned.

Dylan hissed and looked up toward the cabin. "Don't talk so loud."

"I saw you today with that cute girl who works in the grocery store," she said. "That's why you went canoeing a lot after lunch last summer, isn't it?"

"Maybe. Don't tell anyone. She lives down in Ningaabii'an Bay."

Beth looked up at her brother. "Wait, which bay?"

"We call it West Bay, but that's what everyone who lives there calls it."

"So, where did you meet her?"

"On Llyndee's Peak, and after that we met up at Ben's cabin. We saw moose last summer when we hiked his back trails."

"Will you take me next time? I promise I won't tell."

"Maybe. It's not like I want my baby sister tagging along behind me all the time." He grabbed her around the waist again and swung her as though he might throw her into the water. Beth screamed and laughed.

"Hey, you two, I need those fish," their mother called from the kitchen door. "Stop your horsing around. I don't want to eat at midnight!"

The gulls waited until Dylan and Beth reached the cabin porch before they pounced on the fish guts and skins, squawking at each other for the choice pieces.

"Who's coming with me tomorrow morning?" Evan asked at dinner. "Should be a great sunrise, with the red sky out there." The Llyndees had forecasted by the weather folklore rhyme as long as Beth could remember. *Red sky at night, sailor's delight; red sky at morning, sailors take warning.*

No one looked up from their plates. They were used to the sounds of his four-in-the-morning movements and his whistling when he returned at seven from trolling for the big fish, but the novelty of driving the fishing boat in the same triangle he and Naina had used for years was waning, even for Beth.

"I'm heading to the bonfire on shore, Dad," Maegan said. "Brian's showing me what he learned since last summer on his guitar." Beth watched Kate shoot a glance at Evan, but her father kept his eyes on his plate.

"How about you, Dylan? We haven't welcomed the sun together in a while."

"I missed my chance to start my first painting of the summer tonight, so I'm heading up to the cliff early tomorrow. Sorry."

Evan looked at Beth and Kate. "So, I guess it's up to you two to keep me company. Chester the twenty-pounder is down there, and I'm sure I can get it before Ben or the guys." As many as a dozen boats might traverse the same general path in search of the day's largest whitefish and rainbow trout each morning. The anglers knew each other's routines, who started earlier or later, and when to meet at Bailey's Point to compare the day's catch—just as the day was beginning for the rest of the lake's residents. Naina was the only woman in the group, so most mornings it was the same older men who reveled in the early morning air or fog, the vibrant sunrises, and the chance to gossip and compare catches. It was one time it didn't matter whether you were a summer or full-time resident.

"I have a date with very ripe blueberries tomorrow morning, dear," Kate said. "But, Beth, wouldn't you like to go?"

Beth stared at her plate. She and her mom usually picked berries together at the beginning of every summer. Why not this year too?

"Okay, I'll go," Beth said. She knew it had to be her since it seemed impossible for her sister to get up early anymore. Maegan would be on shore with her friends even later this summer, except for designated family nights when everyone stayed home to play gin rummy, spoons, or hearts. Dylan's flashlight was always on late in his room if she got up to go to the bathroom—he was probably reading or drawing—but he was still gone at sunrise. Maybe her mom would wait for her to pick berries.

The next morning at quarter to five, Evan and Beth climbed into the iron boat. The bright red sunset had evolved into a sparkling clear night with a hint of brisk air from the north. Millions of tiny beacons twinkled hello as Beth and Evan scanned the sky for their favorite constellations: Cassiopeia, the Ethiopian queen whose zigzag shape keeps her stuck on her throne; her king, Cepheus, who holds up his house with spindly legs; their daughter Andromeda, who reaches for her mother and father across the night sky; and of course Ursa Major, the Great Bear, the Big Dipper of the sky. Evan grinned at Beth as he started the small engine, backed away from the dock, and headed north.

When they reached their normal starting point, Evan slowed the boat to a crawl so they could switch places and Beth could steer, a skill she'd learned when she was only five. She pointed the boat toward a group of white birches on the north shore and watched her father let out the steel fishing line, his arms moving in a rhythmic ballet with the rod and line.

As the sky lightened an hour later, Beth could see the other boats, which she had recognized earlier by their engines' various moans and the men's occasional guffaws. As she turned the boat for the east leg of the triangle, she noticed that Ben had stopped and was standing, peering over the side of the boat. His net wasn't out, so it couldn't be a big strike on his line. Beth glanced back at him as she followed her dad's route. She knew the unwritten rule of pride—to only help an angler when he turned on his flash-light—was never broken.

By six fifteen, the sky had turned a pale blue, and boats were gathering at Bailey's Point. The decaying log cabin on shore peeked out from behind aging pines. The Baileys hadn't been up from Chicago in at least three years. Kate had tried to contact them last fall to see if everything was all right, with no response.

"I think I better go over with Dylan this week to check on the window shutters and make sure the squirrels haven't chewed into the cottage again," Evan said to Beth as he reeled in his line. Flying squirrels had nested in the sofa last year; who knew what damage they might have caused if they got through her dad's patching from last summer.

Beth stopped with the eight boats already floating in the shallow water, facing each other.

"Welcome back, neighbor. What'cha find this morning?" asked Ed, one of the regulars from the campground.

"Not even a nibble today, Ed. How about you?" Evan said.

"I'm actually considering a change in plotting, it's been so empty out there. John's got a ten-pound whitefish, and Carl's got a few bass. It looks like Ben's got something out there."

The men shared jokes and gossip as they waited for Ben. Beth liked listening to the old men talk, especially when they charted what type and size of fish they were catching. They thought some-thing was changing the lake, with fewer young, strong fish and more algae pulling on their lines. Some blamed pollution from the coal plant about an hour north, while others thought too many people were allowed to fish in the lake.

Beth stood and waved as Ben approached. The silver and gold lures stuck in his cloth fishing hat glistened in the early morning sun. He formed the final petal in their boats' collective daisy pattern.

"Darn algae took three-quarters of my line just before the ledge," Ben said. "I think I hit a big one just before that, but it's probably caught in the wire and weeds."

"Yeah, right, Ben, just like Evan keeps getting a tug from Old Chester," said Carl, one of the lake residents. "There's no way a *tourist* is going to catch that prize. I've got a wall waiting for that rainbow."

Evan grinned. "Time will tell. Thanks for the fish last night, Ben."

Ben nodded and smiled at Evan and Beth. "Great to have you back. Need help rebuilding your fort later this morning, Beth?"

She almost jumped out of her seat. "Of course!"

"Anybody know what happened at the bonfire last night?" Carl asked. "I heard it was quite the party."

Ed and Ben looked at each other and then at Evan. "Just some teenagers having too much fun playing a prank. The boy will be okay, but his folks are pretty upset."

"What happened, Ed?" asked Evan.

"One of the new families at the campground let their boy stay up late with the gang, and the kids told him there was more beer in a cooler back by the garbage cans. Two blackies were having a snack, and one almost got him. Tore up his jacket pretty good. I think the family's leaving this afternoon, they're so mad."

"That's a newbie for you," said Carl. "The manager better do something to store those cans, or they're going to have a real mess on their hands."

The men wandered on to other gossip, then slowly said their goodbyes. Evan told Beth to start the engine and pointed toward

Ben's boat. She was surprised her parents had let Maegan go to the campground bonfire last night after the conversation she'd overheard last summer about Brian. Even if she didn't want to hang out with the other kids all the time like Maegan, Beth still wanted to go to the bonfires to see what went on. This wouldn't help her chances to be allowed to go. The two boats traveled down the lake side by side until Evan waved for them to stop in front of the island.

"Ben, were you on shore last night? Was Maegan in on that prank?"

Ben paused. "I was there, playing cards. Brian was the one that told him to go up to the cans. Seems all the kids thought it was pretty funny."

Beth looked at her dad, then behind him. Evan turned to see Maegan standing on the cabin porch with her arms crossed tightly across her chest, staring at Ben.

Evan turned back to Ben. "No need to say more. Thanks, have a good day." He pointed to the dock and Beth steered them home, waving at Ben as he turned toward the lake's western end. Maegan was nowhere in sight.

Beth pointed at the white enamel buckets still sitting on the kitchen counter and grinned at her dad. Her mom hadn't gone blueberry picking without her. They tiptoed down the hall to the back bedroom, where Kate was still wrapped in a cocoon of sheets and blankets. Beth watched from the doorway as Evan leaned over his wife and nuzzled her ear until Kate giggled and pulled him to her. Beth turned and stomped back toward the kitchen. The berries would be mushy from the day's heat by the time her mother was ready to go picking.

She lingered over breakfast as long as she could stand it while her parents moved to the porch and talked about last night's incident. Adult conversations were filled with codes, but Beth could tell the prank brought her parents' concerns about Brian's wild streak back to life. He roamed the lake freely, his parents oblivious to his comings and goings, and stayed at the island just long enough to pick up Maegan from the dock and leave. Beth couldn't even remember what his voice sounded like. Her parents weren't sure how much Maegan was part of his shenanigans. Nor did they know how to broach it with his parents. The Shepplers were their best friends at the lake, always up for a picnic, a bonfire, a sailing regatta, or helping with the Llyndees' annual Lammas, or harvest celebration, in early August. Their cabin on the north shore was close enough that Beth could canoe or sail over when Naina ran out of sugar, but far enough to give each family time to themselves. Mr. Sheppler's frail but spunky mother was Beth's favorite, even though Aunt Betty smelled like a mixture of shoe polish and tea. Sometimes she went with Naina when the two women visited, just to listen to their rolling cackles.

She changed into a sleeveless navy shirt and plaid shorts and grabbed the four buckets from the counter. Their sturdy handles made them easy to balance even when full—as long as she spread her arms the same way that Naina had taught her to curtsy—and their solid walls kept the berries from mushing together or escaping, as they had in baskets. She marched out to the porch, letting the screen door slam behind her.

"Mom, it's almost nine thirty, and Ben will be here soon to help me with my fort. Are we going or not?"

Kate set her coffee cup on the porch railing, stood, and stretched her long, thin arms toward the sky. "You're right, sweetie, time to make a day of it. I trust we've come to a decision, Evan?"

He flung his coffee dregs onto the rocks below the porch. "Yep, I guess so. I'll hang out in the boathouse while you two head up. Is Dylan still sleeping or out painting?"

Beth remembered her promise to Dylan and didn't mention that she'd seen his art supplies on his bed when she walked by to change her clothes. "He hasn't been here all morning."

"Maybe he went to Ben's in the canoe, or somewhere with Maegan. That would be a first," said Evan. "Have fun, no stains on those white shorts of yours, Katie girl. And no eating while you pick."

Beth rolled her eyes. "Yeah, like you don't eat everything you pick before they even hit the bucket."

Evan yanked on Beth's thick ponytail as she handed two pails to her mom. They climbed the thick wooden ladder screwed into the protruding wall of granite, disappeared into the island's low wall of trees until they chose one of several patches of wild blueberry plants scattered like groundcover across the island, and settled on a surrounding bed of brown pine needles.

The rising sun warmed Beth's arms and legs as they picked the ripe navy fruit. She told her mom about the changes she wanted to make in her fort, always her first project when they arrived every summer. While Kate spent most of her days on the porch, where she could read in the shade, Beth preferred the high woods. Every year she felt enveloped into the island without question, the chipmunks, squirrels, and birds considering her only briefly before accepting her as part of their world. Even the perfect spot for her fort stayed flat and bare as if it was waiting every spring for her return, and provided enough shafts of light seeping through the forest canopy to surprise and warm her throughout the day. She couldn't wait for Ben to help her put it back together.

"I think Ben and I could make something really cool this year, since the rain the past two weeks has made all the tree branches so limber," Beth said. "Maybe I can weave them together instead of crisscrossing, like last summer."

"Sounds fine, dear," Kate mumbled.

Beth stopped picking. "You're not even listening."

"I have a few things on my mind, like your sister's safety. She shouldn't be around that boy anymore, but I have to figure out how to do it without upsetting his parents."

Why was her mother confiding in her? What did she think Beth could tell her? She turned away from Kate toward another fresh blueberry patch, and they filled their buckets in silence.

Almost a half hour later Beth stood. "My patch is empty, and one of my buckets is full. I'm moving." Kate jumped at Beth's voice.

"Okay, honey, let's try the bushes closer to the cabin along the rockslide. I'm sure those will be ripe." Kate followed Beth down the narrow path, their arms spread wide to keep the purple gems safely balanced inside their buckets. "When did you get strong enough to carry all of this? You're growing up too fast, my baby girl. What shall we make with our loot?"

"We might have enough for a few tins of muffins and some pancakes, but I'd rather make a pie if it rains," Beth said. Heavy gray and beige clouds loomed along the western horizon, inching their way east in a lazy summer breeze.

"Looks to me like we'll get a pie *and* some pancakes from what we already have."

"I don't know. Naina's recipe calls for lots more blueberries than yours."

"So? That's the beauty of mine. You still have plenty left for other goodies. Besides, Naina's not here; I am."

"But the pies we made last summer after you left were awesome." Beth had been ecstatic to stay with her grandparents and siblings when her dad had to return to work early. "They were huge. Juice oozed out everywhere."

"I guessed that when I saw the bottom of the oven last night. Naina should have taught you it's the cook's responsibility to clean up her mess, not leave it for someone else."

As they settled beside another blueberry patch, they heard the low gurgle of Ben's fishing boat idling up to the north dock.

"Sounds like Ben's here," Kate said. "I'll take three buckets down, and you can bring the last one when you come."

Beth watched her mother head down the path, not surprised that her shorts were still pristine white compared with Beth's plaid shorts, mottled with blue stains from the berries' juice. She could hear Kate's voice as she and Ben crossed on the path, and stood to look for him.

"Same spot as last year?" he asked as he reached her. He held a small saw with a serrated edge and large pruners. His closely cropped hair was growing more salt than pepper, but otherwise he was the same Ben: navy T-shirt, jeans, and hiking boots on his narrow muscular frame; his shoulders held wide and straight; and his hazel eyes gazing at her kind and true, fully open, just as he lived his life. The crow's feet around his eyes creased deeply as he smiled at her.

Beth nodded and led the way to the small opening at the island's highest peak, where five shaggy-barked white birches and tall basswoods with heart-shaped leaves formed a perfect circle. She set the pail of blueberries on top of the huge boulder behind them. After they'd inspected nearby trees for damaged or low-hanging narrow branches and picked several to prune, Ben handed her the saw.

"You get the honors this year, I'll get the smaller branches."

Beth stood in front of the thickest branch, eager to show him that she remembered what he'd taught her. She placed the saw on its lower side and sawed at an upward angle toward the tree's trunk. Once it was halfway through, she switched to the branch's top half and sawed down to meet the other incision. The branch fell easily, a clean cut.

"Perfect," Ben said as they stacked the cut branches in piles around the circle. Beth described a woven hut depicted on a blanket her grandparents had bought at the Circle Barn, a three-story, multi-sided barn restored as a gift store near town with crafts created by the local Ojibwe. She'd taken it out of the cabin's huge cedar chest that morning while her parents talked, and traced the weaving pattern with her fingers. It would be her fort blanket for the summer—what she used as a seat or a roof, if rain surprised her as she read.

Ben drew what Beth described in the shallow dirt. They used thicker branches for the vertical and angled supports between the trees, then started weaving the narrow branches loosely between the supports.

"The support bars are called the warp, and the horizontal woven branches are called the woof," Ben said.

"How do you know that?"

"Because my sister probably helped to weave the blanket you described."

Beth stared at him. He didn't look like any of the Ojibwe she'd met so far up here. His face was too narrow, his build too lean, and his eyes were pale blue, not dark brown.

"I don't get it. I thought you moved up here from Cleveland."

Ben laughed as he reached into her bucket for a handful of blueberries. "I did. I followed my sister, who fell in love with her husband, Makwa, when he was in Cleveland for a powwow. She worked at the hotel where they held the meeting."

"A powwow? Like in the movies, where they dance and chant?"

"Part of it. Different tribes or bands of a particular nation come together to plan their projects. They pass their language and traditions on to their children through their songs and dances."

He grabbed another handful of berries and walked back to Beth. "This lake used to be owned entirely by the Ojibwe that live at the west end. When many of them left to make money working in the steel mills in Sault Ste. Marie, they sold some of the land to people like your grandfather, usually for way too little money compared with the value they place on it. Makwa is one of the chief elders. He taught me everything about the lake and land that

I've passed on to your brother, and now to you. They consider this lake sacred because so many generations have lived here."

"Do my parents and grandparents know all of this?"

Ben stopped weaving branches into the second wall Beth had started. "I'm not sure it's ever come up, now that you ask. I have three nephews and a niece too."

Beth remembered her conversation last night with Dylan. "So, when your niece and Dylan go hiking on your trails, can I come too?"

"Fine with me, but you'll have to ask them."

When they finished the last wall, they sat inside the circle to inspect their handiwork. The walls were only three feet tall but gave her fort the sense of privacy and importance she wanted. They nudged several pine tufts into open areas until a metal bang made them both stop. The bucket had fallen off the rock and was rolling toward them, the blueberries splattering across the ground. A baby gull with mottled brown fluffs for feathers rolled out of the bucket and hopped from berry to berry, eating the smaller ones. Beth started to shoo the bird away, but Ben grabbed her arm and held up his hand.

"Look closely," he whispered. "That bird is alone. Gull parents don't let their babies out of the nest until they can fly on their own, which is much older than this bird. I'm guessing it's because of how it's hopping."

Beth peered at the tiny bird, smaller than the chipmunks that darted around her every summer in her fort. It held its wings slightly aloft, as if it might take off any second, but it needed them open to keep its balance. She kneeled to look closer while Ben scanned the sky.

"It only has one leg!" Beth whispered. "Can it survive like that?"

"Not likely. Its parents probably dropped it out of the nest because it's not right. I don't see or hear them flying around us, which they would do normally. They're very protective parents."

"Can we find the nest and put it back?"

Ben pondered her question. "We could, but I doubt they'd let it stay."

The bird kept pecking at the berries, stopping twice to look at Beth.

"We can't leave it alone. What if we made a nest in the bucket? Can we feed it and keep it alive?"

"We could try mashing fruit and fish and see if it will eat from a small funnel. Worth a try, I guess. If it can grow large enough to fly, it might be okay."

Beth circled the outside of her fort to reach for the pail behind the bird. They layered the bottom with pine needles and added several crushed berries. When they took turns stepping closer and closer to the tiny bird, it squealed and flapped its wings but couldn't go anywhere. Ben scooped and set the bird into the bucket.

"I have a pet gull!"

"That you do, Beth, at least until it can fly away."

Her laughter turned into a pout as she realized he was right. She pushed the bucket's handle toward Ben. "Maybe you should keep it. I cried for a week when our pet turtle died."

"I'll take it for now, see if I can keep it alive for the next few days. You get the next round of bird sitting. Deal?"

Beth grinned and nodded. "Deal."

She took one last look at her fort and headed down the path to the cabin. Before they reached the stairs, they could hear loud voices from inside.

"Maegan must be home," Beth said.

"Yep. Check in later today or tomorrow, and we'll see what we can do with this bird."

Beth waved at Ben and tiptoed into the kitchen. Her parents and Maegan were facing off across the living room. Dylan was leaning against the kitchen's pale yellow countertop in his standard white T-shirt, loose khaki pants, and high-top black Keds, eating a banana. He smiled at Beth as he raised his first finger to his lips. She joined him at the only spot where they could remain hidden but still see most of the living room.

"So, you think I caused some stupid kid to run into the bears last night?" Maegan had positioned herself in front of the huge picture window at the far end of the room, deeply shadowed from the bright sun outside.

Kate and Evan stood next to each other by the stone fireplace. It had taken three years for Evan and Taid to collect enough of the island's quartz, red jasper, and black hematite pudding stones to build the massive structure. Beth could still fit inside its huge firebox and climb on the stones to the top of its five-foot-high mantel, a thick slab of concrete. The warmth from its fires heated the entire cabin.

"That's what we're trying to figure out," Evan said.

"It was no big deal. Just a prank on one of the newbies who was stupid enough to fall for it. The kid even hung out with us afterward."

Beth heard her mother sigh. "Was Brian there? Did he start this prank?"

Dylan and Beth looked at each other and held their breath, waiting for Maegan's response. They knew this would make or break the outcome.

"He was there, and yeah, he was part of it, but so were the other guys."

"Did he start it?" Kate asked.

"I don't know, Mom. It happened so fast."

Beth could feel her mother's anger surge through the cabin. Kate turned to face Evan, impatience in her eyes.

"Look, why don't I go over to the Shepplers' to see what they've heard," Evan said. "We don't want to overreact, and I doubt Maegan was the one who told the boy to go up to the garbage cans."

Beth shook her head at Dylan. That wasn't the plan she'd overheard her parents discussing this morning. Evan was changing course on Kate, which was never a good idea. Beth had learned that lesson every time her brother and sister tried to negotiate with their mom after she'd decided what was best for them for school, sports, or just about anything else in their lives. There was no negotiating.

Kate stepped away from Evan, shook her head, and turned back to him. "That boy could have been mangled to death by those bears, thanks to Brian's antics. I'm tired of all of you taking the dangers around here so lightly, and I really don't think Tim and Barb are going to care what Brian's role was in all of this. If Brian *was* the cause, Maegan can't be around him anymore, no matter how close we are with the Shepplers. It's that simple."

"You've got to be kidding, Mom. Stop being so dramatic."

Beth squeezed against Dylan's body and waited for another wave of angry heat to rush past.

"Another word of disrespect and we will go home today. Do you want to be responsible for ruining your family's vacation?" Kate's voice rose in decibels and octave. "I know you don't see it now, but that boy will ruin your life. I will *not* let that happen. Do I make myself clear?"

Silence echoed through the cabin as the impact of Kate's words hit each of them. Beth grabbed Dylan's arm, tears already catching in her eyelashes. *No*, she mouthed to him, *we can't leave.*

Dylan leaned down to whisper in her ear. "No way Dad will let that happen."

Maegan recovered first. She moved toward Kate with her chest held high, as if she could physically match the full force of her mother's anger.

"You've made it clear all along that Brian doesn't meet your standards, Mother. But to suggest we go home early because of this is ludicrous. You really don't trust me to make the right decisions? You've raised me that poorly?"

Kate took a step toward her oldest daughter. "Don't throw

this back at me, Maegan. You're the one at fault here. No, I don't trust you to make the right decisions if you're going to make light of something like this. Either you stop going to the bonfires at the campground if Brian's there, or Dylan will have to go with you. I know he'll make the right choices."

Dylan bolted into the living room, Beth close behind. Her left cheek puckered as her teeth began to chew at its soft insides.

"Not happening, no way." Dylan aimed his anger toward Maegan even as he yelled at his mom. "Why should I have to hang out with those dorks just because she wants to?" He turned to Evan. "Do something, Dad. This is totally unfair."

Evan looked at his wife and children, their eyes pleading to give the response each of them wanted.

"I guess I agree with your mom, Dylan, at least until we figure out how to discuss this with Brian's parents. Naina and Taid will be up soon, and then we'll spend most of our nights together anyway. Maegan, you're staying home tonight. If there's a bonfire tomorrow night, your brother will go with you." Dylan dug his hands deep into his pants pockets and slouched. "Sorry, Dyl, but maybe it'll be good for you to go out with other kids."

Dylan glared at his father and pointed at Maegan. "This was about her, not me!" He turned, pushed past Beth, and left the cabin.

Beth chewed even faster as she stepped farther into the room. "Can I go too? You said I could go to a bonfire this summer."

Kate shook her head and looked down at her clasped hands. Evan turned to Beth. "We'll see, sweetie. We need to get this sorted out first."

Beth walked over to her sister. "It's okay with you, right?"

"Sure, if they decide they can trust me with you. Let's go find Dylan." Beth stayed close to Maegan as they crossed the room, her eyes glued to her sister's back. She could taste the blood oozing from her cheek.

By the time they found him, the girls had paddled around most of the island. They would have missed him entirely except for ramming into his kayak's bow as they passed a deep crevice in one of the island's steep rock walls. Maegan grabbed onto the granite to stop their rocking while Beth backpaddled to bring her end close to the rift's other side.

"Shit, it's not enough that you're ruining my life. Now you're destroying my kayak too?" Dylan leaned against its back corners, the kayak's stern wedged perfectly into the tight space. He stared at a pile of pebbles he was juggling between his hands.

"Sorry they threw that on you, Dyl. But it might actually work out great."

Beth couldn't tell if her sister was sincere or throwing their brother a line. He scowled at Maegan, clearly not buying it. "I don't want to hear anything from or about you. Just *leave* me the *fuck alone!*" He threw the pebbles at her.

Beth ducked, but Maegan only turned her face away as the pebbles assaulted. Beth studied her siblings as they stared at each other, her tongue gently massaging where her cheek's torn insides were still leaking blood. Maegan's eyes were always clear, her thoughts and intentions obvious. Not Dylan. His eyes were calm, alert but distant, as if all the important stuff was going on in a deep ocean within. He competed in Maegan's stare down as long as he could, then retreated back into himself.

"There's another bonfire most nights in the west bay," she said finally. "I've been there, and I know who's always there. You *want* to be there."

Dylan sat up slightly but tried to remain nonchalant. He scooped another handful of pebbles from a shelf in the rock wall. "Which nights?"

"Always Thursdays and the weekend, sometimes Tuesdays. Works perfectly for tomorrow night and Friday."

Beth watched her brother's face soften and the stiff hunch of his shoulders lower an inch. "I just drop you off and go? What if you fuck up again?"

"I won't. Mom and Dad told Beth that she was old enough to go to a bonfire this summer, so I'll have the perfect excuse to get a ride home if trouble starts. And you know Beth always gets what she wants." She grinned at Dylan, willing him to smile back.

"I do not," Beth said.

Maegan snorted. "You don't have a clue how easy you've got it. By the time you're my age, Mom and Dad won't care what you do. They'll be too exhausted from both of us."

"Speak for yourself," Dylan said.

Maegan scooped pebbles from the canoe's floor and threw them at him. He retaliated, and the weapons quickly turned to paddles and water. Dylan stood and pushed against the deep crevice's walls to shove his kayak into their canoe, flipping it in seconds. The girls screamed, the water's frigid cold always a surprise. Dylan threw his arms into the air. "Yes! I win!"

The sisters retrieved their floating paddles and climbed back in one at a time. "How about last one to the north shore beach has to be the first one in the cabin?" Maegan challenged him.

Dylan grabbed his paddle, dropped into the kayak's cockpit, and pushed off the rock wall into the open lake. Beth paddled on the port side to turn north while Maegan steered from the back. The race was on.

Dylan beat them easily to the north shore, where they lay on the beach, skipped stones, and stayed away from the cabin as long as possible. When thunder echoed over the middle of the west end they knew time was running out, and they reached the dock just as the ceiling of dark clouds emptied its load. They were drenched in seconds as they pulled the canoe and kayak onto the dock. Beth waved and grinned at their dad as they ran past the boathouse doorway, Maegan and Dylan laughing and jostling to push the other into the cabin first. They fell through the kitchen door, flung off their soaked sneakers, and raced to put on dry clothes. Within minutes they were back together in the kitchen making peanut butter, honey, and banana sandwiches. The air was warm, fragrant with the sweet aroma of flour and blueberries baking in the oven.

After Beth changed her clothes and wrapped a bath towel around her wet hair, she found their mom sitting in her bedroom, darning a pair of socks. She stood in the doorway, trying to gauge her mom's emotions. Had the anger subsided? Was she back to normal yet?

"Muffins smell great, Mom. Can we still make a pie?"

Kate continued sewing. "Too late today. How about tomorrow morning if you don't go fishing with your dad?"

Beth walked toward her mom and leaned against the end of the bed. "I guess. Do we still have enough berries to use Naina's recipe?"

"Not sure about that. I decided to make a double recipe of muffins instead." Kate tied the thread and pulled it to her teeth to cut off the remaining strand. "We should decide what you want to wear for Lammas, in case I need to sew anything." Kate pulled the towel off Beth's head and smoothed her hair around both ears, brushing it into place with her fingers while Beth told her about the outfits she'd brought up north. *This is what mothers do*, Beth thought. *They never simply listen. They straighten and fix, put order to everyone's lives while they act like they're listening.*

Beth watched her sister closely at dinner, Maegan's mastery of distant civility something she knew she needed to learn. After dinner, she played gin rummy with her parents, even though she could hear Maegan and Dylan talking and moving back and forth between bedrooms. Beth desperately wanted to be with them, to hear their plans and jokes, but knew if she did her parents would spy on them or, even worse, intrude and somehow ruin it all. Evan and Kate were already raising eyebrows and sharing glances every time laughter echoed down the bedroom hall, surprised that their two oldest children were sharing a closeness they hadn't had since they were small. Better to keep her parents occupied and separate from Dylan and Maegan to have a solid chance of going to tomorrow night's bonfire. Besides, she was beating them both in spades.

She feigned sleep when her father came in at four the next morning, but made sure she was up and in the kitchen, eating a bowl of cereal, when her mom got up. Two pies were cooling on the counter when Maegan and Dylan arose at ten, and by then her mom was smiling easily again. Evan took Beth to Ben's to check on the chick and to see his plans for new trails in the deep woods behind his cabin. His home was the only one on the south shore west of Llyndee's Peak.

As soon as they finished dinner, Beth ran to her room to change into jeans and a sweatshirt to protect against the evening's mosquitoes and later, its chill. As she pulled the thick top over her head, she saw her brother and sister go by her bedroom window in the powerboat. They were going to the south bay bonfire without her. She ran down the hallway and onto the porch, looking for her parents. They were huddled in one Adirondack chair on the dock, their backs to her, watching the sunset.

"Mom, they went without me," Beth yelled.

Kate sat up and turned slightly. "They're going alone tonight, sweetie, in case something happens again. We'll wait and see about tomorrow night." She folded back into Evan's arms.

Beth ran to her bedroom, threw one sneaker and then the other across the room, and burrowed under her bed quilt. It didn't matter who hadn't wanted her to go, her parents or her brother and sister. Either way she was still the baby, who was supposed to go along with what everyone else decided. She hid under the covers long after the loons' yodels and tremolos had echoed across the bays, waiting for her siblings to return.

By the time Beth got up the next morning—she was determined to stay away from everyone to keep her anger alive—the cabin was empty. Breakfast dishes were drying on the rack; placemats were stacked on the counter. Just a cloudless sky and glass-smooth lake greeted her. She sat cross-legged on the window seat that extended across the living room picture window and wrapped her cotton nightgown tightly around her legs. The powerboat was gone, so Maegan was either with Brian at the Shepplers' or in town with their mom. The boathouse door was open, so her dad was likely tinkering with his Carling wooden boat again. He wanted to finish it for a big reveal at the Lammas Day party, but Beth had her doubts. Dylan was probably on his fourth painting, if not done for the day, since the sun was three-quarters of the way up to the noon sky.

She wandered into the kitchen for a muffin and considered her options. Her dad would be the easiest to be with since he was engrossed in his boat. Maybe she could help him stain and polish, or she could talk him into canoeing to Ben's to see the chick. Dylan might tell her about the bonfire last night and whether he made it to the west bay to see Ben's niece, Lily.

No. She couldn't do that, no matter how much she wanted to know. She had pretended to be asleep when they tiptoed down the hall late last night and as Maegan slid into the other twin bed. The smell of burned cedar and oak wafted from her sister's hair and clothes, adding another layer of thickness to the sleep-laden air.

Beth had wanted to roll over, to yell at her for being such a jerk of a sister, had almost summoned the courage when Maegan started to softly snore. Now silence would have to be her best revenge. Why should she care, anyway? She had her own life to live.

Beth carried a blueberry muffin and glass of orange juice to her bedroom, something she wouldn't even consider if her mother was inside. A wave of guilt washed over her as she noticed the latest Nancy Drew book on her nightstand, a peace offering from Kate last night. "There will be other bonfires, sweetie," she'd said. Beth shook her head at her reflection in the mirror and dropped onto the side of the bed. "Get real, stupid," she whispered. Mom was probably the one who'd told Maegan and Dylan to go without her. Screw all of them.

The only person she could trust was Ben. He wouldn't ignore her, and neither would the baby gull. Maybe she could help him teach it how to fly. Muffin crumbs scattered across the wood floor as she stuffed the bottom half into her mouth and pulled clothes out of the dresser. She watched the neighbor on the north shore as she dressed, an old guy in overalls who spent hours every week fixing his ramshackle dock. It never looked any different for all his efforts. He stood and waved at a boat filled with six passengers that slowed and floated alongside. Beth ran to the window and opened its bottom panes as her grandfather yelled above the engine's hum, "See you at Lammas next Sunday, Harry. Don't be late!" Beth's anger melted into a puddle at her feet as his hearty Welsh voice echoed across the lake. She found one sneaker at the front of the closet and crawled under the bed to find the other. Naina's slender weathered arms were waiting to greet her as she reached the kitchen door.

"We decided to surprise all of you!" Naina said. "After all, we have to get ready for the party, and I have a new project for us to tackle together." Naina wrapped Beth's cheeks in her palms and lightly kissed her forehead. "You up to the task?"

Beth beamed at her grandmother. Every summer Naina seemed shorter, her tiny frame condensing as it aged, but the years didn't lessen the sparkle in her vivid green eyes or the intensity with which she lived each day.

"I'm so glad you're here."

The next several days raced by in a rush of to-do lists and anticipation. Evan and Taid headed to the provincial alcohol store for cartons of pale ale, to the grocery store for baking supplies, and to the McGinty farm on Lake Huron's north shore for their first bushels of ground durum wheat and tall wheat stalks. They spent another day circling the lake, stopping at every dock to remind residents of the upcoming celebration of the first harvest—even though anyone who lived or summered on Lake Wigwakobi would never forget the Llyndees' annual Lammas Day celebration. Maegan made sure they went to the far west end to invite the three Ojibwe families, including Ben's sister and her family. Taid had raised his eyebrows when she announced at dinner that they should be invited.

"Not sure whether this old granite rock will hold up if we add more to the list," Taid said. "We might sink into the lake!"

"Don't be silly," Naina said. "Maegan's right. Those three families are part of the community. We should include them. Don't you agree, Evan?"

Evan glanced around the table as he buttered an ear of corn. "We've gone down there a few times over the years to invite them, but either they didn't come out of their cabins to talk with us or if they did, they never showed up to the party."

Taid scowled at his dinner plate. "I know you mean well, but they don't want to come any more than some of the summer folks want them here. I'm willing to bet money on that."

Maegan refused to give in. "The past doesn't matter, and it's our party, so we can invite whomever we want. The jerks who don't like it can leave. Dylan and I met a few kids at the bonfires, and they seem nice enough. We can go with you tomorrow to invite them, right, Dyl?"

"Sure, I'll go," Dylan said.

Beth's puddle resurfaced into a wave of hurt and anger. Even with her grandparents here, Dylan and Maegan were going to another bonfire without her. She picked up her plate and walked to the kitchen.

The porch became Dylan and Maegan's work area, the kitchen belonged to Naina and Beth, and Kate bounced between both to prepare meals and deliver supplies from the boathouse. Maegan sewed old sheets together into wide streamers so Dylan could paint them for decorations. Naina and Taid always preferred traditional decorations with the Welsh flag and its red dragon, but Maegan talked Dylan into tie-dying the fabric first. Over the top he painted swirls of reds and greens, as well as yellow and gold wheat stalks.

"Your best yet," Maegan said as they draped the streamers between several trees to form a gathering circle on the island's wide flat section in front of the cabin, between the north and south docks. They added bunches of actual stalks to the bases of trees, serving tables next to the boathouse, and foldable chairs in small groupings on the porch and deck. Baking started first thing each morning with three traditional Welsh recipes: *bara brith*, fruity tea bread; Bacheldre bread with chives, sage, and garlic baked in clay pots; and Naina's secret recipe for heavy sourdough. Next came blueberry muffins, pies, and cakes.

Beth went to Ben's every day to see the chick, which was growing quickly, and to collect small onions, shallots, garlic, and chives from the woods behind his cabin for the breads. Ben carried the bird in a shallow shoebox while they hiked the woods. Twice the bird flew to low tree branches and Beth panicked, afraid he would fly away for good. When Ben put the box down on the forest floor and the bird flew back, she decided it was safe to call him Sam.

On the last morning, Naina announced at breakfast that only Beth was allowed in the kitchen for the rest of the day. "Our secret addition will make a true Welsh celebration. Evan, I need you to bring in the rest of the ale, the coolers, and all the honey, spices, and yeast you bought at the store. Dylan says you have a new project of your own." She winked at her grandson.

He grinned back at her with the same wide, large-toothed smile. "Yep, should take all day, and I'll need everyone else's help to pull this off."

"Well, I have to clear it first," Taid said. "Is this part of our normal traditions?"

"Of course. If we get it done in time, we'll try it out tonight."

"Perfect," said Naina. "We'll put sandwiches on the porch at one, and let's rendezvous at six for dinner. Now, everyone, scoot so Beth and I can get to work."

Boxes of supplies that covered the kitchen floor in the morning were slowly replaced with coolers filled with what Naina called the "secret tonic" of the British Isles. Beth's senses were overwhelmed by the aromas that filled the cabin as Naina taught her how to blend together fermented honey, yeast, and water over low heat and add cloves, cinnamon or nutmeg, oregano, and chamomile. Some batches included fruit and a bit of ale. Every time they started a new brew, the aromas evolved from wet, heavy yeast to Thanksgiving pumpkin pie to finally a rich honey wine. In late afternoon, Naina called Taid in to help so she could lie down on the couch for a short break.

"Just a bit too much taste testing, dear. I'll be fine."

Naina had let Beth taste a few batches, and Taid's versions were much stronger. He snickered and shushed her when she grimaced after tasting his last batch. "We'll keep this one separate for just the old folks," he said, winking.

"Why would you want to drink that? It tastes terrible."

"All in good time. Someday you'll love it, guaranteed." He peeked around the kitchen corner to Naina on the couch and then downed the rest of Beth's portion. "Grand idea my bride had, grand idea."

Beth was so busy she hadn't had the chance to check on what everyone else was doing outside. As she reached for the door, Taid grabbed her by the shoulders and turned her around.

"Nothing doing, *wyres melys,* sweet granddaughter. You're the inside help. Time to clean up and get some sandwiches made for dinner. Then we'll each reveal our surprises."

"Why can't I see? You know what everyone's doing."

"Of course, that's my elderly right as the *bosys.* That and your siblings are doing something nice."

"*That's* hard to believe. They've been really mean, like I'm too young for anything fun."

Taid caressed Beth's head with his burly hands and pulled her into a tight hug. "Two guarantees in life, pain and happiness. Sometimes one brings the other."

Beth wasn't sure what he meant but didn't argue. He woke Naina, and together they cleaned up the kitchen. Kate helped to make another round of turkey-and-tomato sandwiches for dinner. She clucked that they'd put away the mixing bowls and pans in the wrong places, quickly moving them to her preferred spots by the stove. Naina clucked back but didn't stop her.

Dylan came in to carry the coolers outside, then returned with a red bandana and held it in front of Beth's face.

"You need this first." As he tried to wrap the cotton fabric around her eyes, Beth pushed it and him away.

"What are you doing?"

"It's all good, Bethie, I promise."

She looked at her grandparents and mother holding the trays of sandwiches. They nodded and smiled. "Okay, but I don't see why you're keeping just me in the dark. This better be good." She turned around, and Dylan tied the fabric tightly around her eyes. He lifted her hands to the back of his shoulders, and she jumped onto his back.

Beth could smell the burning wood as soon as they stepped outside. She waited until Dylan stopped to jump off his back and pull the bandana from her face. Maegan and her dad were loading more logs onto a small fire, encircled by rows of the same pudding stones that made up the cabin's huge fireplace.

"We owed you one," Dylan said. "Now we can have bonfires here."

"And no more run-ins with bears or anything else dangerous," Kate said. "When the bonfire's here, there won't be trouble."

Beth stared at the growing fire. She knew Dylan was trying to make up for going without her, and everyone was waiting for her to be grateful. But it wouldn't be the same as going to bonfires on shore, away from the island and without her parents. She crossed her arms tightly around her chest and kicked the loose pebbles around her feet.

"Come on, Beth," said Maegan. "Everyone will be here for your first bonfire tomorrow night. What else could you ask for? Don't be a baby."

Beth glared at her sister. "That's what you always think, all of you, that I'm the baby. That I don't deserve to be included."

Maegan walked toward her. "Hate to tell you, but you are the baby, and I didn't get to go to a bonfire until I was fourteen. Try having some gratitude that Dylan felt bad about the other nights and wanted to make it up to you. I sure didn't."

Beth fought to match Maegan's stare until Evan broke the heavy silence. "We get the message, Beth. And, Maegan, get off your big-sister high horse. How about we call a truce and enjoy our first island bonfire? I call the first s'mores after dinner!"

Taid woke everyone at seven the next morning with a rousing *"Gwyl Awst Hapus,* Happy Lammas Day!" even though they'd watched the fire burn late into the evening. Beth ran for the tiny sourdough loaf she and Naina had baked for the Lammas morning's ritual and met her grandfather in the living room. The rest of the family drifted in one at a time, still in their pajamas. Maegan shuffled to the couch and lay down again.

"I'll just watch from here," she muttered and closed her eyes.

"Forget about her, Taid. I'm ready," Beth said and handed the loaf to her grandfather.

"Naina and I are so grateful to be here for another year of harvest celebration with our family. For others, a high mass might be their religion. Our Welsh traditions provide our rituals and faith in family and heritage. Let us break this bread in thanks for the bounty of our health, wealth, and happiness, and may it protect us and bring magic to our lives for another year." He broke the loaf into four even pieces, which Beth took one by one to each family member for a small bite. She handed them back to her grandfather, who placed the pieces into a stiff, cracked bowl made of woven wheat shafts Naina had brought with them when they left Wales more than forty years earlier. "Off you go, wyres melys."

"Just me?"

Evan pointed toward the kitchen door. "The torch is passed, Beth. Better hurry!"

She ran outside and saw Sam sitting on the fishing boat's bow at the south dock, looking west toward Ben's cabin. During the last three days of Lammas preparations, she'd met Ben at her fort to help Sam get used to her and the island. Sam explored a wider range every day but always flew back to Ben's boat as he was leaving. She had decided the bird would never separate from him.

But here he was on her island, standing on his one leg on the front of her boat. She whistled at him, and when he flew toward her, she turned and ran to the cabin's farthest northwest corner. She placed a piece of bread on the ground against the wall's edge, covered it with a pile of pine needles, and whispered, "*Bendithia 'r cartref a 'r teulu hwn*, bless this home and family." Sam squawked from a tree above her, then hopped across the treetops to follow her to each of the cabin's corners.

"Don't eat any of these," she pointed and yelled at him, burying the bread under deeper piles of needles to hide its scent. At each corner she whispered the Welsh prayer of protection. When she returned to the living room, Naina had poured seven small glasses of her honey wine.

"Here's to a magical day of laughter and celebration," Naina said. Beth pretended to sip the evil-tasting concoction while everyone else drank heartily. Maegan grabbed Beth around the waist and pulled her onto the couch between her and Dylan.

"Now I get to say no fair! I'm seventeen and drinking my first glass of mead, and she already knows how to make it."

Beth's grin stretched across her high cheekbones.

"We've only got a few hours to get all the final preparations done," said Kate. "I need some breakfast to wash down this wine. Who's going to help with the pancakes?"

Maegan and Beth spent the rest of the morning weaving individual sheaves of wheat into hearts and halos or tying them into small bouquets, while the others loaded the tables with fruits, breads, juices, ales, and coolers of the honey wine, or mead, each marked with its percentage of alcohol for fair warning. When the first boats arrived at one, the family divided to greet guests at each dock: Naina, Evan, and Maegan to the north and Taid, Kate, Dylan, and Beth to the south. The men dropped off their wives, children, and contributions of food or drink at a dock and then tied their boats next to each other in the open water. The huge arc of boats connected from the north to south docks was one of Beth's favorite sights of the summer, as if the vessels were having their own party as they floated together on the waves.

Kate and Beth were amazed that Taid could still remember every guest's name and where they lived on the lake, greeting each woman with a kiss and every man with a hearty handshake. The buffet table quickly filled with casseroles, platters of meat and cheese, salads, and cookies. Beth tried to count heads but quickly lost track. Kate pointed to the local residents and vacationers who gathered together around the beverages table, the only day of the year they would spend so much time together.

"Somehow Taid pulls it off," Kate said. "I don't know what he says to them, but they all want to come."

Just as they thought the last of the guests had arrived, Ben rode up with two women. Taid said he was the last guest, so Beth tied the boat to the dock. She did a double take at the younger girl with Ben and ran up the steps to find Dylan, who was helping Aunt Betty find a chair on the porch. The Shepplers had arrived just before Ben, Kate and Barb Sheppler greeting each other with stiff smiles. Brian wasn't with them. Clearly the conversation about the bonfire incident hadn't gone as well as her dad had hoped.

Beth cupped her hands around her mouth. "Dylan, c'mere, fast." He turned, and Beth pointed to the end of the dock. He grabbed the nearest chair for Aunt Betty and sprinted to the dock next to Taid.

"Let me help you, Mrs. Akeene," Dylan said as he reached for the older woman's arm. Taid stepped back and waited as Dylan helped both women onto the dock. Ben followed with a huge wooden bowl filled with greens.

Kate leaned down to Beth. "Does Dylan know these women?"

Beth whispered into her mother's ear. "From the end of the lake, Mom. Lily works at the grocery and the Circle Barn."

"Ah, seems I've missed something. Thanks for the heads-up."

The older woman, tall with light brown hair that flowed almost to the small of her back, had Caucasian features but wore a brightly colored dress and woven sandals. Her daughter's features were clearly Ojibwe—jet-black hair in a long thick braid and deep, round ebony eyes—but she was dressed in cutoff jeans and a red T-shirt.

"Taid, Mom, this is Mrs. Akeene and her daughter Lily," Dylan said.

Taid hugged Lily as Kate stepped forward and shook Mrs. Akeene's hand. "So nice to have you join us. Welcome. How do you know our dear friend Ben?"

Ben laughed and put his arm around Lily's mother. "This is my sister Anna. She's married to Chief Makwa Akeene, Lily's father. She invited me up here to heal after my wife died in Cleveland's 'sixty-six riots, and I never left."

All four Llyndees were struck silent. Beth had told her family that Ben's sister was married to the chief at the west end, but she'd never considered that Ben had gone through something horrible. She'd learned in school about the 1967 riots in Detroit but didn't know they had happened in 1966 in Cleveland too.

Anna wrapped her arms around Ben's waist. "Best day of my life when my little brother came here to live."

"Beth shared that your sister lived here too, Ben. How nice. But we're so sorry to hear about what happened to your wife," Kate said, then looked at Dylan standing next to Lily. "How do you know the Akeenes, Dylan?"

Dylan looked at his mom, then at Beth standing slightly

behind her. He shook his head slightly as he looked at Lily and back at Beth, and she nodded back. "Lily overheard us say something about Ben while we were at the Circle Barn. That's how we met."

"Yes, that's right, Mrs. Llyndee. I've helped your family several times there and at the grocery store."

Kate smiled. "Oh yes, no wonder you look so familiar, Lily. Welcome. Welcome to you both, and thanks for coming." She turned to Lily's mother. "Is your husband joining us this evening as well?"

"No, unfortunately not," Anna said. "This lovely invitation is a bit of a stretch for a tribal leader to accept, but for reasons I'm just starting to understand, Lily and Ben were adamant about coming." She smiled at Dylan and Lily standing next to each other.

Taid stepped forward in the renewed silence. "Well, this is simply grand to meet both of you. Now I need to get this party officially started, so let's join everyone else. Dylan, you're in charge of explaining our Lammas celebration to Anna and Lily."

Beth watched Kate follow him up the steps and engage Anna in conversation while Dylan and Lily bounced nervously against one another and into the crowd. She skipped up the steps. The magic of Lammas Day had begun.

Taid met Naina on the porch, where she was waiting with a long brass horn. His tall frame and barrel chest towered over their guests, his thick white hair fluffing in the breeze like the feathers of a baby loon. He played three short bursts of the horn's flat notes, and the crowd stilled. "Welcome, neighbors and friends, to our eighth annual Lammastide celebration. For those who are new to this event, we're glad you've joined us and hope this will be the first of many." He found Anna and Lily in the crowd and nodded at them.

"As most of you know, this is a Welsh tradition that goes back centuries to celebrate the first wheat harvest of the season. Our thanks to the McGinty family"—Naina and Taid pointed and led the crowd's clapping for the couple and their four children—"for once again providing us with their first bushels. Lammas is about family, friends, shared bounty from shared labor. As our ancestors have proclaimed before us, I say to you now: the winter looms ahead, but today the fields are full, and our table is surrounded by those we cherish. We are grateful for nature's gifts on this precious earth and the immense beauty of this beloved lake, which once again gives us so many reasons to be thankful together. There is something profound in the knowledge that people all over the world are celebrating the enduring wonders of nature today, the universal spirit that no man can create. May we each harvest love and kindness in ourselves and others in the year ahead and, most important, shield the joy. *Iechyd da!* Cheers!"

The crowd cheered and moved toward the tables of food and drink. Beth and Maegan joined Kate and Naina to cut and serve the loaves of bread, while Taid and Evan poured glasses of mead. Every time Beth ran to the cabin for plates and silverware, she searched the crowd for Dylan and Lily, who sat on the rock landing's edge with their legs dangling over the side, their backs to the crowd. Once the line of guests waned, Beth filled her own plate with food. She pondered Ben's bowl of greens, lifted the fiddlehead of a bracken fern, and held it in front of her face.

"Not sure what to do with it?" Ben whispered from behind.

Beth jumped. "Is this for decoration, or are we supposed to eat it? I recognize the other plants from your woods, but it's too late for a new fern to be sprouting."

"Of course you can eat it. I found it the other day. Lammas also means second growth for nature, when plants and trees shoot new leaves and stalks to replace the ones damaged by weather or insects. You can usually tell them apart because of their slightly different color or texture." He took the fern from Beth and folded it into his mouth. "Delicious."

"That's so cool. Can we go hiking so I can see the Lammas plants?"

"Anytime." He lifted a piece of each plant from the bowl and waited for Beth to name it: wild onions, red clover, dandelion leaves, arrowhead, rose hips, and violets. He pointed to Dylan and Lily, still huddled together on the island's granite outcropping. "Maybe we'll invite them too. Lily knows more plants than I do."

Beth looked at them and back at Ben. "I just realized something. If Lily and Dylan get married someday, we'll all be related!"

"Hold on, let's not jump the gun. They're way too young for that."

Beth looked at her brother. "I betcha. You just wait." She reached for a spoonful of her own Lake Wigwakobi salad. This was an awesome day.

After the guests had eaten their first helping of food, some settled into group conversations, while others followed Dylan for tours around the island with Lily tagging along. Maegan and Beth taught some of the women and children how to weave the wheat sheaths into designs and watched as Dylan left with a group of several excited teenage girls, who returned looking dejected.

"Guess those girls know he's off the market," Maegan whispered to Beth as they tried to help a slightly intoxicated woman from the campground weave a sheath without breaking it in half. "They were all over him the other night at the south bay bonfire. He couldn't wait to leave."

Beth scowled at her sister. "Why did you guys leave me behind? That was so mean, Maegan. I've missed it all. Did he go to the Ojibwe bonfire all three nights?"

"Of course he did. Can't you tell by how they're acting with each other?"

Beth looked at them standing next to each other by the dessert table, his fingers hovering around hers like the monarch butterflies who flit into the tall milkweed their grandmother had planted by the boathouse. She finished weaving another set of sheaths into a wreath and handed it to the woman.

"You said I could go."

"He never would have gone down to the west bay bonfire if you'd come with us. Don't tell Mom and Dad, but the campground crew in the south bay gets really rowdy. You're too young to handle what goes on there. Trust me, it wouldn't be fun for you."

"I know things."

Maegan laughed. "Whatever. I'll take you next week, well before we leave for the summer. I promise."

Beth pointed at Maegan's face. "You better, or I'll tell Mom how much you talked with Brian over the winter. Where is he, anyway?"

Maegan looked toward the north dock, where Naina and Evan had gathered the youngsters for a fishing competition. Excited squeals pierced the party's constant hum as the kids reeled in smallmouth bass or perch. Brian was pulling the hooks out of the fishes' gasping mouths and rebaiting them with a fresh chunk of worms.

"He showed up a few minutes ago. We figured it was better to keep our distance today, or at least until the chill thaws between Mom and his parents."

Beth scanned the crowd for her mom, who was deep in conversation with Mrs. Sheppler. "Yeah, well, it looks like Mom's gotten past it."

Maegan followed Beth's gaze and grinned. "All right. See you later, Sis." She dropped the wheat into the bucket and jogged down the hill toward the dock. Beth watched her sister greet Brian with a hug. Just like always, Maegan had all the luck in this family.

Beth wandered through the crowd and talked with a few kids her age who had gathered around the fire pit. Most of them hung out all summer together and had asked her to join them a few times, but she liked to hike alone or with Ben. He taught her cool stuff and laughed at her jokes. She searched the crowd and walked toward him, then stopped a bit behind when she saw the serious looks on his, her mom's, and Mrs. Akeene's faces.

"My wife, Mary, was helping to feed folks that summer in Cleveland," Ben said. "A gang drove by and shot into the crowd. She was the only one hit."

"I knew this place would get Ben away from that ugliness," said Lily's mom. "And that it would revive his soul the way it did mine. I don't think either one of us would know how to manage the dangers of city life anymore."

"Nor would we want to," Ben said.

"Maybe I need to spend a few weeks with both of you so the dangers of *this* place don't scare me so much," said Kate. "I grew up in downtown Boston, and I understand how to deal with that lifestyle much more than the bears, cliffs, and weather up here." She looked out toward the lake. "I get so claustrophobic when I'm up here. I know it sounds crazy, but the trees and water keep closing in on me. Like the disasters they could cause are going to swallow up each of my kids, one by one, and I can't control anything or stop it from happening."

"Your kids know this place as well as they know their own hands," Ben said. "You and Evan have taught them how to be safe on these rocks. I've seen it firsthand every time Beth and Dylan come for a hike."

"I've learned that nature always has the last say," Anna said. "Once you accept that, you can relax and start to see its magic."

Kate turned to look at Dylan and Lily, who were perched back on the island's edge. "I thought I was keeping track of my kids, but I guess not."

"They're welcome anytime," Ben said. He leaned around Kate and waved at Beth to join them. "Beth included. I'll have to start making up things pretty soon just to keep her interested."

She blushed. "Can I come over tomorrow to see where the new ferns are growing?"

"Beth, remember what I told you about waiting for others to invite you?" her mother said.

Ben ignored Kate. "Of course you can. Bring your grandfather too. I'd like to show him some spots on the north trail of Llyndee's Peak that need some work."

"That's very nice of you, Ben," Kate said. "Now it's time we get the desserts out. Beth, will you help me, please?"

She followed her mom to the cabin for the last of the breads, cookies, and pies. The guests migrated back to the tables for a second helping of dinner and dessert as dusk settled on the horizon. Evan and Dylan lit the logs and brush they'd built into a large triangle pile that morning in the fire pit. Beth yanked one of the huge wooden Adirondack chairs close to the stone circle, next to Maegan and Brian, who had already positioned themselves to watch the annual end-of-the-party show. They bet how many of the men in various levels of sobriety would fall into the lake as they climbed between the tied boats to get to their own. Each splash into the lake's chill brought a split second of silence before the fallen man rose to the surface and howled, and the crowd responded with its own shrieks of laughter. Brian won the bet at five, as well as another bet that Mrs. Akeene wouldn't let Lily stay. They watched Dylan reluctantly help the women into Ben's boat, then plop on the ground next to Beth's chair as the boat headed west.

"No luck tonight, dude," Brian said. "I thought the mom was really grooving on you too."

Dylan gave Brian a sidelong glance and sulked in silence.

Ben returned just before dark with his guitar and joined the remaining guests—the Shepplers, the morning trolling crew and their families, and the McGintys—around the fire pit. Dylan added new logs to the bonfire and pulled an open chair toward its warmth. Beth couldn't believe how fast the day had gone. She sank deeper into her chair as Ben played his guitar and others sang or hummed along.

A collective "Look!" jolted her awake. Everyone was standing, staring at the night's sky. The Milky Way was splattered in bright strokes of white and silver directly above them. Then she saw it—a sudden curve of fluorescent lime green dancing across the northern sky. They pointed and cheered at each new wave of green, pink, violet, and white as the aurora borealis burst across the blackness. The waves turned into curtains flowing into and out of each other in a magical rhythm that Beth's body instinctively tried to mimic. She swayed with the beams as they waltzed across the northern sky, slowing as they slowed and then retreated from view. Final bursts of green and white shot across the sky like flashing headlights, as if nature were giving them a grand finale. They clapped and yelled "Cheers!" and "*Iechyd da!*" to the midnight sky.

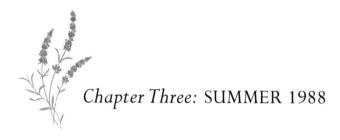

Chapter Three: SUMMER 1988

"Okay, spit," Ben said as he held the inside of the swimming mask in front of Beth's chin.

"Spit? Where, in there?" Beth pointed at the mask's glass. "How am I supposed to see anything? That's gross."

Ben leaned against the side of his fishing boat and absorbed the boat's floating rhythm in the late afternoon waves. "Those loons swim fast down there. Even with their summer tuxedo colors and the water's clarity, you'll need the glass to stay clear. You doing it, or you want to look through my saliva?"

Beth wrinkled her nose, grabbed the mask, and pushed a glob of spit out of her mouth with her tongue. A small puddle fell onto the glass; the rest drooled down her chin. She waited until most had slid off, then swiped her mouth with the back of her hand.

"Swirl it around and let it dry. Now the mask won't fog up while you're underwater."

"You could have told me that first."

"Yeah, but what fun is that?"

"Are you always this nice to children?"

Ben lifted his eyebrows and chuckled. "Only the smart ones."

Beth reached for her black swim fins to hide the flush sweeping across her face. She'd spent at least three days a week with Ben this summer after he assured her parents she wasn't intruding on his life. He'd told them she was a welcome change from the singular life he maintained the rest of the year, that he enjoyed teaching her how to live off and in nature as he had with Dylan two summers ago. So far, they'd kayaked and mapped the shoreline and hiked the web of deep woods trails he'd cut behind his cabin. The paths covered at least six miles from the base of Llyndee's Peak to the west bay, where Lily and three other Ojibwe families lived.

Everything seemed even more alive and vibrant after he taught Beth about the water, fish, and plants; the nesting patterns of birds, otters, and deer; and how each was an essential piece of nature's puzzle. She caressed every leaf, frond, and rock as if her hands could absorb their energy, and she picked baskets of wild onions, clover and violets, milkweed, and goldenrod to add to the family's dinner as salad or tea. Dylan and Lily sometimes joined them for hikes or swims. The days passed in a flash, not like in school, where the endless sitting made Beth burrow into herself or pretend she had wings to escape the boredom.

As she climbed onto the stern's edge, the rumble of a power-boat's engine echoed across the bay. Maegan was standing in the boat, pointing at the fallen water skier, her high-pitched laughter bouncing across the waves. Beth wondered why she ever thought it would be cool to go with Maegan and Dylan to the bonfires every night instead of playing cards with her parents and grandparents or reading a good book. Watching boys chug beers and throw up in the woods was stupid, almost as idiotic as the Kelton twins boasting that all the boys wanted to go to second base with them. Her brother and sister made her pinky swear to secrecy the first night she went with them to the campground bonfire, adamant that nothing be shared with their parents.

Last night Dylan was ready to leave the bonfire and go down to Lily's after ten minutes. He let her tag along once she promised not to pester him. At least people played guitars and drums at the west bay bonfires. Lily's cousin Amik had talked with her for at least an hour, the first time anyone besides Lily had noticed her. She'd spent the rest of the night pretending she had to use the bathroom so she wouldn't sit in the same spot, and to spy on Amik with his friends as she walked between the bonfire and the house. She'd dawdled among the artwork and photographs in the living room until one of the elders asked if she needed help, and she ran out of the house.

Beth and Ben had been tracking two broods of eaglets on their daily hikes when they found a group of loon families nesting in a small cove. She was sure it was the same family hooting between bays last night when she and Dylan rode down to Lily's, and she'd run to Ben when they'd arrived to ask if they could find them today. He'd nodded and told her to bring her new snorkeling gear.

She dipped the fins in the water and yanked a heavy rubber triangle onto each foot. What felt cumbersome on land would give her wings in the lake. She pushed off the boat and slipped into the lake's soft embrace. Her body knew instinctively how many quick breaths to take to recover from the rush of shivers from toes to brain. "Better than electroshock therapy for clearing the head and heart," Naina pronounced every summer before her first skipping dive off the dock. Kate had told Evan to stand watch this summer, sure that Naina's elderly heart would stop as soon as it hit the water. When he decided to join Naina in her midday swims around the island, Kate took over the vigil, the crease in her forehead growing deeper and the contented smiles on Naina and Evan's faces wider. Beth thought they should yank her mom in with them one morning so her head and heart would stop being so afraid. Could her mother even swim?

Beth leaned her head back to listen for the loons' high-pitched, rhythmic hoots. "Which direction are they swimming?"

Ben lifted his olive-green cap to scan the shoreline with binoculars. He pointed toward the cove's east end. "Looks like they're all out, chicks too. Go slow. Head to the northeast about thirty yards. I'll whistle when to stop. The chicks will piggyback before the parents dive as long as they don't see you."

Beth grinned and waved before flipping onto her back. Three plump clouds provided bearings to swim backstroke until she heard Ben's whistle. As she turned with only her head above water, two light gray chicks plopped from grass nests just above the water's edge onto their parents' backs—conspicuous pom poms against the adults' black-and-white checkerboard wings and ebony heads. *Oo-AH-bo, oo-AH-bo* echoed across the cove as they swam toward the third family. Beth swallowed a mouthful of fresh lake to silence her giggles and followed far behind, using only her fins to propel her forward.

When the two loons reached the others, they circled and hooted at each other before the adults lifted their wings to slide their chicks into the water. Beth lowered the mask over her eyes and dove. Even from several yards away, she could see the loons' legs and bellies, their heads jutting underwater every few seconds in search of food. As soon as a school of small perch appeared underneath, silver scales shimmering even in the navy depths, the birds dove. Flashes of black and white torpedoed through the group of fish once, twice, three times, magically flipping and turning by extending one foot to the side and using the other as a brake. Once they clasped several fish in their long, pointed bills, they popped to the surface to share their catch before diving again.

Beth had watched the loons yesterday from shore as Ben explained how their legs, perched so far back on their bodies, could propel them so fast underwater. They barely moved when they dove, yet they swam faster underwater than most birds could fly. The adults shared their catch with each other like one happy family—unlike the eagles, who fed only their own brood. She realized she'd floated too close when a sharp staccato of high piercing notes rang across the water. *Oo-ee-oo-ee-oo-eeee-oo.* The adults stretched their white banded necks and glared at her, the chicks hovering behind.

Beth dove and turned toward Ben and the boat. She stretched her body and kicked hard with her fins, then tried to spin and turn like the birds. It wasn't the graceful dance she'd just watched, but she didn't care. She rose to the surface for air and dove again, delighted to pretend she was flying underwater.

"Okay, that was so cool," she yelled as Ben helped her back into the boat. "They spin and turn to keep up with the fish, almost like they *are* fish! You didn't tell me they could flip around that fast. Wow!" She jumped in circles as she talked, laughing and swinging her arms before she fell on the bow's bench. "Just wow."

Ben grinned and scanned the cove with the binoculars. "They're done eating; chicks are piggybacking back to the nest for a nap. Pretty awesome, huh?"

"Let's come back tomorrow with Dylan. Maybe Lily can come too. He hasn't done this yet, right? He would have told me." She turned toward the island two bays away, still bouncing on the seat as she pulled off the mask. "I can't wait to tell everyone. What time is it?"

"Time I got you home, giddy girl." He pulled the engine's cord and pointed the boat toward open water. She *was* giddy, like someone had tickled her insides with a loon's feather, and her body was as light and fine. Her heart beat wildly in her chest, excited to experience nature's magic. Beth turned and lifted her face to the wind.

Evan came out of the boathouse to wring out a rag stained with oil and paint as Ben edged his boat up to the dock. Beth grabbed her clothes and gear and ran to her father.

"Dad, Dad, wait until you hear what I did," she yelled as she ran up the rock steps. He waved at Ben, then mimicked Beth jumping in front of him.

"Something amazing to make you this excited. Tell me while I clean up before dinner." The loons, the diving, her spectacular, vivid day spilled out as she followed him into the boathouse, to the docks to retie the boats, and behind the cabin to check the natural gas tank. "And the best part is we can go again tomorrow, and the day after that, and the day after that!"

"We warned you, don't hog Ben's time. He has a life too, you know."

"But he said we can go back with Dylan tomorrow if the weather holds. You should come too!"

"Naina has to go into town, but maybe I can take her first thing. I'd like to see those loon babies on their parents' backs."

When they entered the cabin, a wall of thick air stunned Beth and Evan. He stopped in the doorway as if he'd run into a real wall while the tension made Beth dizzy, as if she could feel the planet rotating. Kate and Maegan were setting the last bowls of salad and potatoes on the table. Dylan was already eating, his elbows wide across the table, head drooped over his plate. Evan swatted at both elbows as he walked to his seat across from Naina.

"Thought you two might miss dinner this evening," Kate said as she sat at one end of the table. "Where were you?"

Beth and her dad shared a confused look as she slid into her seat between Dylan and Naina. "Believe it or not, the last coat of varnish is on my wooden boat," Evan said, "and Beth was just telling me about her adventures watching the loons with Ben." He looked around the table, but only Kate and Beth returned his gaze. "I don't know what's going on in here, but we both had a grand day." He nodded at Beth. "Why don't you—?"

"That's wonderful. Can't wait to hear about it," Taid shouted from the table's far end. His shoulders curved forward as he dropped his fork onto the china plate and pushed both away, his head shaking as he laid his crossed arms on the table. Beth didn't know this hostile man—so different from her grandfather's usual buoyant energy—and had never seen his body fighting not to explode in rage. She froze as he lifted his head and stared at her with eyes the color of agony. Her molars crushed the inside of her right cheek.

Taid's voice and posture rose as he slowly pronounced each word, his glare switching from Beth to Dylan. "After she tells us about the supposed Ojibwe artifacts she found by her fort. Dylan here is sure they must make this island some sort of hallowed ground."

She turned toward Dylan. When Sam had unearthed pieces of wooden bowls and painted sticks by her fort yesterday, Beth assumed they were leftovers from her grandparents' early camping days. She'd shown them to Dylan as he crossed the island, but he'd acted like they weren't important and told her not to say anything. Why did he tell everyone *her* surprise? And what the heck did the Ojibwe have to do with this?

Dylan stopped eating. "All I'm saying is we should show Lily's dad what's up there. If they're nothing, it's no big deal. If the stuff is theirs, they have a right to know and decide what to do with them. If it's a burial site, they consider that sacred ground."

"Wait a minute, back up," Evan said. "What stuff, and where did you find it?"

"And why is Dylan the only person in this family who knows about it?" Kate said. "You could have shown me the other day when we picked blueberries."

Beth shook her head at her mom and scowled at Dylan, who crossed his arms over his chest and stared out the picture window across the room. "I was reading in my fort, and Sam was tapping on something," she said. "He was in the crook of the huge boulder right behind me, pecking under the moss and pine needles, and pulled out a piece of a wooden tube. It has stuff engraved on it, some birds and the sun, I think."

She turned to her mom. "I just found them yesterday. I figured Naina and Taid had forgotten them when they were camping a long time ago, and I wanted to surprise everyone. I was putting the stuff into a pile when Dylan showed up." She stared bullets at him. "Guess he wanted the honors instead."

Taid grunted, and Evan shook his head at his father to stop him from saying more. "How is it possible to find anything new on this island?" Evan said. "We've walked every inch hundreds of times. Are you sure your gull didn't bring them from someplace else?"

"What's the big deal?" Maegan said. "Whether they're from Naina and Taid or the Ojibwe, why not just bury them again? No one has to know. Who cares if there's old stuff up there?" She reached for the bowl of green beans.

The family sat in stunned silence. Finally, Naina took Beth's hand and looked at Maegan. "I don't think it's that simple, Maegan. I don't remember camping that far up on the island, so I doubt it's anything we left behind. Whether they're decayed or not, if the items belong to someone else, they deserve to at least see them. Given how long the Ojibwe have lived on Lake Wigwakobi, Dylan may be right. There's right and wrong here, I'm afraid."

"Exactly, Naina," Dylan said, sitting up. "I looked at the carvings and art at Lily's house last night, and some had the same sun engravings."

Beth grabbed her seat as the air's thick energy swirled around her. That was the last thing he should have said. Blood drained from her cheek into her throat as her molars chewed.

"Wait a minute," said Kate. "I thought you went to the camp-ground bonfire last night. We never agreed to you going down to the west end."

"I go down there all the time, Mom. The people are nice, and they don't play stupid games on each other like the kids on shore. It's no big deal."

Kate looked at Evan for support, but he shook his head. "Let's stick to one issue at a time. Are you sure the markings were similar, Dylan?"

"Yes. I mean, I think so. We need to show someone so they can decide if the stuff is theirs. I'll ask Lily and—"

"You'll do *what*?" Taid yelled as he stood. He reached over the table to point a shaking finger with its curved arthritic joints inches from his grandson's face. "This is *our family's* sacred ground, the land your grandmother and I bought with the few pounds we had left from Wales. I bought it fair and square from the clerk, who, by the way, was probably from the same clan as your precious Lily. If he wanted to sell it, what's up there didn't matter to them then, and it shouldn't now. End of story."

Evan stood and pulled Taid's hand away from Dylan's face. "Wait, Dad. No one's saying anything about ownership rights. Let's not get carried away." He held his father's arm until Taid sat down again.

Kate leaned forward and set her elbows on the table's edge, her hands clasped together under her chin. "Well, first we have to show respect by calling them by the correct name. I believe that's Ojibwe or First Nations, according to the latest articles I've read." The forced lilt in her mother's voice whined through Beth's ears like a clarinet out of tune. "They call their collective group in this region the Anishinaabe, with seven clans named after animals or birds. I wonder if the families that live on Wigwakobi are part of a loon clan. Wouldn't that be appropriate, Beth?"

Beth nodded slightly and stared at her plate. When no one else replied, Kate continued.

"I've gotten to know Lily's mom, Anna, a bit since she came to the Lammas festival last year, just brief conversations when we go to town. She's a lovely woman and might be willing to look at them alone, since she agrees that it's better to keep our two families separate. Your future is much different than Lily's will be, Dylan. No need to have anything more than a friendship."

Dylan started to speak, but Evan, who was still standing, held up his hand. "Stop, Dyl. And Kate, you're getting off track again. Let's get back to what Beth found."

Kate narrowed her gaze at Evan. "Fine. We can deal with the other issue later. But the Anishinaabe or Ojibwe have a right to their items and maybe part of this property. I've read about several cases like this in North Dakota and Manitoba, where the governments are considering supporting the First Nations' land claims."

Yesterday Beth thought what she'd found would be fun for her grandparents, something to remind them of their first visits on their island. How did this go so wrong?

Taid glared at Kate as he threw his napkin on his plate. "*Rydych yn ffyliaid!* You are fools! No one's telling anyone what's up there, you hear me? Dylan, you mark my words, you tell that girl and they'll be all over this place, wanting to take it from us for their precious ancestors. Like they did with the McGintys at their farm a few years ago. Remember that, Evan? Just because they found a few silly relics, the family had to give up five acres of their land to keep the community peace."

Taid stared out the picture window and swallowed hard enough that Beth saw his Adam's apple lift and fall. "They'll have the fight of their lives, because I'm not giving up this island to anyone. Not now, not ever." He stood and strode stiffly out of the cabin, the wood screen door slamming behind him. Naina hugged Beth's shoulders and followed her husband outside.

Minutes earlier Beth had floated into the cabin, filled with the magic and beauty that nature had given to her. Now a quicksand of anger and fear consumed her heart and muscles. This wasn't supposed to happen. She started to shiver and pulled her legs to her chest to contain the quicksand's spread. If she closed her eyes and remembered the baby loons on their parents' backs, the freedom of diving deep into the lake, this would all disappear.

Maegan stabbed at her food. "I've never seen him that mad. Good going, Dyl."

"I'm not the one who found it. Beth gets that honor."

She turned to face her brother, only inches away. For the first time in her life, she wanted to pour his precious paints over his white T-shirt, to make him feel her hurt. He refused to return her gaze.

"You told me not to tell, so why did you? You're that jealous of my hikes with Ben?"

Dylan laughed, mean with a cold edge. "Ben already showed me everything he's showing you. I told you not to say anything so this wouldn't happen to *you*. I knew Taid would explode."

"No, you didn't," Beth yelled back. "Besides, I wouldn't have told him we have to show it to precious Lily so *her* family gets to decide. I found it, not her, and it's on *our* island. It doesn't matter who it belonged to before. It belongs to us now. Tough luck for them. Right, Dad?"

Evan and Kate exchanged a long glance. "The cat's out of the bag. It doesn't matter who opened it," he said. "Now we have to figure out the right thing to do."

"Beth," Kate said, "Taid might feel threatened, but he expects everyone to respect and honor his Welsh heritage and traditions at the Lammas party every year. Surely we should do the same for the Ojibwe."

"No!" Beth screamed at her mother. "They're just a bunch of stupid sticks and bowls and stuff. Even Lily and her family won't care about it. You're using this as an excuse to stop coming here all the time because you can't deal with all your silly fears, and you can't control our lives up here like you can at home. You don't even try to do anything up here with us. All you do is sit on the porch and read your stupid papers."

She was as shocked by her words as everyone else. The inside of her right cheek had turned into crabmeat, the blood mixing with bile rising from her throat. She slumped into her chair, pulled her knees back into her chest, and mumbled through her legs. "We can't tell anyone. We can't. Please."

"Enough, Beth," Evan said. "You owe your mother an apology. I get that you're scared and angry, but enough accusations. No one goes anywhere or says anything until you show us everything tomorrow, and we discuss this with consideration for each other. Dylan, that means you too."

Dylan nodded, picked up his half-eaten plate of food and carried it into the kitchen, then walked past them to his bedroom—without even glancing at Beth. How could he do this to her?

Kate and Maegan escaped to the kitchen to wash the dishes while Evan went to the rock landing where his parents sat in the Adirondack chairs, facing the lake. Beth crouched on the living room window seat and watched her grandfather occasionally sit up to yell and wave his arms. Naina rubbed his shoulder each time until he calmed. When Evan and Naina walked up to the cabin arm in arm in the gray dusk, Beth ran to the back storage room for Taid's jacket and a flashlight and snuck out the back door and down to him. She hesitated when she reached the back of his chair, suddenly afraid of the rage she'd seen earlier.

"Aye, wyres melys, come to keep me company?" Taid said. "Look at Andromeda light up the night sky."

Beth wrapped the jacket around his shoulders as his long arms welcomed her, and she fell into his lap. "This is all wrong.

I was so excited to show everyone what Sam and I found, and now I've ruined everything. I never thought the stuff might not be ours."

Taid reached for her face, his huge hands covering her cheeks and ears. "You listen to me. You did nothing wrong, and *no one* will ever take this place away from us. This island is a part of us as much as your long fingers, brown eyes, and love for this lake make you a Llyndee."

She smiled and tried to block the anguish still hanging in his eyes. He kissed her forehead. "Now remind me what constellation is next to the North Star. I need a refresher course if I'm going trolling with you and Naina in the morning. Will be good to fill these old lungs with early morning air."

As he pointed, she listed off the summer sky's constellations, watching his face to see if his normal cheer was returning. When they'd run out of stars, Beth leaned back and felt her grandfather's chest rise and fall beneath her. She'd never seen him so angry or scared, but he was right, and Dylan was wrong. Their family owned this island and everything on it. They should be able to choose whether someone else saw any part of it. Dylan had double-crossed her, betrayed her secret. She expected that of Maegan, but never Dylan. She wrapped her hands around Taid's, her teeth now focused on the inside of her left cheek. Taid would fix this mess, or she would. No one was taking this away.

Beth woke up coughing the next morning, surprised by the dull electricity still hanging in the cabin's air.

"What time is it?" Maegan moaned, throwing the covers over her head.

Beth reached for her Timex watch on the nightstand between them. "Almost nine. Why is it still so dark?" She pushed aside the blue-and-yellow-checkered curtains and peered outside. "Yuck, the sky's like cement. No wonder no one else is up."

Maegan buried deeper under the covers.

Glutinous fog hung over the lake, the low hum of fishermen's boats trapped in its blanket. Beth opened the window a bit and lay down again. The damp air fingered its way through the narrow space and hovered above her until it collided with the indoor air's tense voltage and dropped in a mist onto her face. She crossed her forearms over her eyes and tried to remember the lilting serenades of the loons last night as she'd gone to bed. They'd helped her to relax until Maegan came in, and they ran through possible scenarios for what their parents and grandparents might do with the stuff Beth had found. They even considered grabbing their pillowcases and flashlights and hiding all of it in the old outhouse until they could scatter it by Lily's house or along Ben's trails.

Beth remembered using the outhouse once when she was little. Her dad had clutched her in his arms in the middle of the night, only the moon lighting their way. He'd followed a well-worn path behind the boathouse along the island's north shore, counting aloud the one hundred steps between the cabin and the tiny wood shed between two stands of jack pines. A scar still ran the length of his right forearm from the jutting granite that had sliced a deep gash when he tripped, his arms taking the brunt of the fall as he kept her safely embraced. Naina had given her a bucket to use at night after that, but Kate had been adamant they wouldn't return for another summer without a proper indoor bathroom.

The thin bedroom wall of plywood and studs shook behind her as Dylan rolled into it on the other side. He was already too big for the twin bed stuffed into what was essentially a closet, most of his original bedroom taken for the bathroom. No windows, a sliding door, a small light tied to the metal headboard, and a high shelf for his clothes. Sometimes she tried the bed when no one was inside, slid the door shut to see what a cocoon felt like. It fit Dylan, always comfortable in his own space, while she preferred deep breaths and open air. Whenever she walked by lately she covered her nose, the space reeking of his teenage scent.

She counted as the bathroom door shut and opened one, two, three times, but it was the lack of kitchen sounds and aromas—pans and plates retrieved from the side cupboard with its squeaky hinges, silverware pulled from their drawers and placed on the dining room table, the greasy sweetness of fried bacon and pancakes—that brought her to full alert. Was everyone else avoiding the inevitable too? She pulled the covers tight around her as her mind raced. If Taid and Dylan fought again, what would her brother do? Taid might have a heart attack if Dylan brought the Ojibwe leader here—or worse, get out the shotgun he used last summer on flying squirrels that had invaded the attic over the winter. Would Dylan betray the whole family and honor Lily's instead?

Beth flinched as three urgent knocks hit their bedroom door. "Time to get up, girls," Kate said as she opened the door and walked to the end of the twin beds. "Everyone's up and has had breakfast, just muffins or cereal. We're waiting for both of you, so please dress quickly. You can eat your muffins on the walk up. Beth, please bring your Instamatic camera with you."

Both girls lay still. "Now, please. Don't expect me to come back here again." Kate strode out of the room. They grabbed shirts and shorts scattered on the floor and walked to the bathroom to brush their teeth. Beth stomped into her Keds as she ran down the bedroom hallway while Maegan grabbed the blueberry muffins waiting for them on the kitchen counter. They found the rest of the family as they were climbing the ladder to the island's interior. Kate hovered behind Naina, and Evan followed Taid in case either lost their balance on the steep stairs or the narrow trail. Dylan led; Beth and Maegan followed behind.

Taid stopped twice along the path's first curves to scan the clearing sky and take in the lake's western end, the others jostling to avoid bumping into each other. "We should take this walk every morning, *fy nghariad*, my love. Good for the heart and soul."

Naina took his hand and pulled him forward, and Taid reminisced out loud as they walked. He and two buddies from the Ford plant where they worked in Detroit had come up every fall in the late 1940s to hunt and build the pathway that wove across the island. They had dug between boulders, shrubs, and trees, searching for the gentlest path to get to the other end.

"We froze every night in our tents." Taid laughed. "They were as happy as we were when we could afford to start the cabin. Helped build that too."

"Which guys, Dad?" Evan asked.

"Eddie and Pete, both lost in the Korean war. Never got to see the cabin done, dammit."

The family listened as the couple identified the northern white pines and eastern red cedars they'd moved as seedlings from the cabin site forty years ago, now at least fifty and thirty feet high, and the other spots they'd considered for the cabin before settling on the island's eastern edge. Sam followed them up the path, perched high in the trees at each stop. Beth's shoulders and stomach relaxed as her grandparents told more stories.

"We thought we would lose our jobs the first summer we asked for two weeks off to come up here and build it," Taid said. "Then Pete had the brilliant idea to ask our supervisor to come with us." Taid stopped again and laughed, a rolling chortle that echoed through the trees and bounced off the rocks. "Old Stan kept calling in for us, he liked it up here so much. We were gone almost a month. Great times back then."

Naina grasped Taid's hand. "And now too, dear. We have our family here, and it's a gorgeous day." She turned to Kate and asked her to remind them where the best patches of blueberry bushes were located, which were sweet and which tart.

When the tree canopy opened and the sun's rays reached the island's floor, Naina stopped to inhale the fresh, sweet fragrance of lavender poking out among a low stand of junipers. She tore off a handful of the pale purple and blue blossoms, rolled them between her hands, and extended them to Beth and Maegan.

"I brought the seeds for these plants from Wales. *Lavendula* covered the entire hill behind my naina's place. Made the entire town of Penarth happy in July and August. We haven't made satchels or oils from it yet, have we, girls?"

Maegan took the blossoms from her grandmother's hands and rubbed them in her own.

"Perhaps we'll pick some tomorrow. Boys love the scent behind your ears," Naina said.

Beth giggled, Maegan grinned, and Kate lifted her eyebrows. "The boys need no more encouragement than they get already, thank you." She looked up into the trees' canopy, the birch leaves swaying in the steady breeze. "How about we get to our destination? All these trees are giving me the willies."

The rest of the family erupted in laughter, and Sam squawked in response. "You're fine, dear," Evan said. "Pretend they're skyscrapers instead, if that helps. They won't attack you. Only Sam, a few bears, and vengeful beavers to worry about."

"Yeah, Mom, keep a lookout. Those beaver teeth might get your ankles any minute," Dylan said as he squatted above them on a gray boulder speckled with white gummy moss. Kate shoved at his knees and waved the group forward.

Beth walked with her grandmother, eager to point out her favorite places to explore in the island's deep center. Maegan and Kate walked far behind, united in serious conversation. When they reached Beth's fort, Taid inspected the branches she'd woven into makeshift walls. He gave her a thumbs-up, but his smile disappeared as he noticed the brightly colored blanket patterned with human figures and bears that hung at a slight angle across two large silver birch limbs—a partial roof she'd used the other day to block the hot sun, its edges swinging in the light breeze.

He turned away and scanned the eastward view of the lake's wide center and Llyndee's Peak to the south. Several sailboats were scattered across the far bay, their tall white sails tight against the wind. Beth was surprised the sun was almost at high noon. That meant the path that usually took her twenty minutes to travel had taken them more than an hour. She clasped her hands behind her and tried to spy her grandfather's face out of the corner of her eyes. He took several deep breaths, his eyebrows and lips pursed, as if he were willing himself to enjoy the view in spite of what was to come. The family stood behind him until he shook his head, turned, and ambled past Beth's fort toward their destination.

The wood cylinders, bowls, and sticks were in the same place she had left them, scattered around a flat oval space between the island's highest peak and a wide rockslide that fell all the way to the water's edge. Ben had taken Beth and Dylan to the town's historical museum last summer to see pictures of the island before Taid and Naina owned it, when settlers had used dynamite on this and other local cliffs in search of gold prevalent in the Canadian Shield. Other than uranium and ore, they had come up empty.

Evan had taught them how to maneuver up, down, and across the slide's jagged or loose boulders in the first years on the island, claiming if they could traverse these, the rest of the island was a cinch. Dylan still climbed the slide to get to his favorite perches for painting in the late afternoon sun, and Beth sometimes followed him to fish off the bottom boulders or bug him to teach her to paint. He hadn't agreed yet, but she was determined. Perhaps she would use his mistake telling Taid about all of this to get him to give in.

Beth jumped as Evan patted her on the shoulder. "Okay, kid, you're up. Let's see what you found."

She looked back at her dad as he pushed her toward the center of the open space. "Those are what Sam was pecking at," she said, touching the wooden tubes and sticks with her sneaker. The young gull watched from the top of the boulder behind her. "I think there's six or seven scattered around. I only dug up a few sticks; they're painted with initials or animals." She stepped over the items and moved closer to the boulder. "Here are the bowls, which have a few engravings. Do any of these look familiar, Taid?"

She grabbed one of the sticks with a bear painted on it and wrapped it in the bottom of her shirt with both hands. As she watched her family consider her finds, she rolled the stick in her shirt against her hips with her palms, the same way she and Naina used a long wooden rolling pin to flatten pie dough. The pressure of her palms rolling over her stomach calmed its roiling.

Dylan dug around the exposed pieces, some of their shapes decayed or fraying. Kate and Maegan joined him while Taid and Naina circled the area, and Evan inspected the items.

Kate handed Evan an intact cylinder, about a foot long and wide. "These might be bowls or some containers," he said. "Looks like birch bark was on the top and bottom. Cool construction to make such a thin, round piece of wood like this. They might be several decades or just a few years old."

He handed one to Naina. She ran her fingers over the engravings. "I recognize this combination of bird and sky symbols from the other blanket we have in the linen closet. We bought it in town when we brought the beds up that second summer. Remember, Taid?" She held it up to him. Taid nodded and looked away. "I suppose anyone could be on our island when we're not here, and we wouldn't know the difference," Naina continued. "But I can't imagine them leaving this behind. It's lovely."

Dylan held up an intact stick and another partial one, curved on one end with hints of colored rows. "If these pieces go together, they almost look like parts of a drumstick." He turned and rubbed his hands along the bottom half of the boulder, then stood and moved back a few steps. "Does anyone else see red paint on the bottom of this rock? It's faint, but they look like the same images on lots of things at the Circle Barn. They must mean something."

The family moved toward Dylan and shared guesses about what they saw, except for Taid. He stood next to Beth, and they watched the family on their treasure hunt. She hadn't noticed the paintings, but now they were obvious. Beth rolled her T-shirt tighter with each find and dug in the shallow dirt with her sneaker, as if she could dig a hole deep enough to fall into and disappear. She liked that the thin white rubber of her sneaker's toe provided little protection from the force of her kicks on her big toe, as if the pain could numb the rest of her. The sadness in her grandfather's eyes last night had shifted to a piercing stare, a mixture of fear and anger spreading from his eyes to his clamped jaw. He grabbed Beth's hand and squeezed it. As much as it hurt as her fingers turned numb from his clasp, she held on tight.

Evan stood and cleared his throat. "Okay, so we know what's up here. Let's take this one step at a time. Beth, hand me your camera."

Beth pulled the long leather strap holding her camera over her head and handed it to her dad without letting go of Taid.

"I think I should take pictures of all of this and then drive to the Sault to get them developed. That should take about a week. In the meantime, let's visit the museum the kids went to with Ben and see if they have any information. Maybe—"

"They don't, Dad. There's nothing about the Ojibwe," Dylan interrupted. "It's filled with stories about the French settlers and how the town developed, mainly mining and fishing stories. We need to go to the reservation museum and talk with Lily's dad."

Taid coughed as he lifted his chest and spat his words at Dylan. "You do that, and you're no longer welcome on this island, Grandson."

Dylan stumbled backward against the boulder, and the rest turned from Dylan to Taid. Beth stopped kicking as tears welled in her eyes. She crossed her legs and leaned against Taid's arm.

"Taid, we agreed to take this one step at a time," Kate said. "There's no reason for such harsh words."

Maegan kneeled to trace the rock paintings with her fingers: a sun, a triangle-shaped bird, and a person with their arms raised to the sun. "I mean, this is cool stuff, but why should we care about it? Why don't we wash these off and throw the rest of the stuff away? It's not like anyone's missed it." She picked up a few sticks, and they broke into several pieces. "See? No one will know what's here, let alone care. You can't even tell what they are anymore."

Beth watched her parents and grandparents look at each other, as if sizing up the others' stances. She tried to remember anything Ben had told her about Chief Akeene and the Ojibwes' customs, anything that would help everyone to calm down, but her mind was blank.

"Maybe we need to look at this another way," said Kate. "We could do what Maegan suggests and bury it again or leave it all alone, forget anyone ever found it. If someone finds them without us, they would be on our island illegally, and we could charge trespassing as well as claim ignorance. The more important question becomes, are you comfortable fishing with Ben or the Ojibwe folks every morning and not saying anything? Obviously, Dylan wants to tell Lily, but I don't think I'd mind keeping it from her mother. She's very nice, but it's not like we will ever be friends."

Dylan stood and walked toward her. "Why not? She's not good enough for you, since she married an Ojibwe?"

"Don't suggest I'm a racist, Dylan. Blood has nothing to do with it. Our lives are too different, that's all."

Evan stepped between them. "Stop making this about something other than it is. I'm not sure how to answer your question, Kate. I would be fine keeping it from Ben and the others, except we ask the entire lake to honor our traditions every summer at Lammas. How can we not honor theirs?"

Taid grunted. "You can't compare the two. We work for days so they can come together and share in an honored Welsh tradition. What Dylan's suggesting might turn the entire reservation against us and threaten our home. If the McGintys felt forced to give up some of their farmland, put two and two together. Every family has its secrets. This will be ours."

Naina looked at the engraved piece still in her hands. "I honestly don't know." She looked up at Taid and Beth. "Of course I don't want to do anything that would jeopardize our right to this precious place, but look at this. It must have historical significance to someone. Can we not share what we've found? Won't they be kind to us since we've been a part of this community for so long?" Her eyes pleaded with her husband.

Taid let go of Beth's hand and walked over to his wife. He grabbed the wooden tube and threw it down the rockslide. The others gasped and leaned forward to watch it bounce off a huge boulder and fly through the air before it splashed into the lake and disappeared. "That's what they'll do to us. They'll stake their claim and throw us out. Even if the province doesn't side with them, no one on this lake will want us to stay if we don't honor their supposed rights. You want to see the best in everyone, but I know I'm right. We can't risk it, not for these few decayed trinkets."

Naina nodded, and Taid wrapped her in his arms. Dylan stared at his grandfather, then turned away and slapped the huge boulder with the palm of his hand. Beth wanted to do what Taid had just done—throw all the stupid stuff in the lake and stop this fighting. She'd found it; she could get rid of it too.

"Dad, we have to accept that Dylan might be right that these are Ojibwe," Evan said. "But we don't know how and when all of this got here. Let's take the photos and get them developed, then do our own comparison at the Circle Barn between these markings and the drawings there. In the meantime, we own the island, so this stays between us. Are we agreed?"

Maegan nodded. "So no one talks with anyone about this. That includes Lily or anyone in her family, or her friends."

Beth stepped toward her father. "What about Ben? I'm sure he wouldn't tell anyone."

Maegan laughed. "Don't be silly. Ben's part of Lily's family. Of course he'll tell them."

"She's right, Beth," Kate said. "Even if he's not Native American, they are his family now. Besides, he might not know any more about this stuff than we do."

Beth was sure he would if she asked him, but she kept silent so her grandfather wouldn't get mad at her too. Her parents would believe Dylan once they compared what was here to pictures at the barn, and then they would think they had to tell Lily and her family. She might too. Especially to Ben, Lily and Amik. But give up the island? Never. If only Dylan hadn't told everyone else first.

"Okay, we're agreed," Evan said. "This stays with the family." He extended one arm with his fingers outstretched, and one by one everyone except Dylan united their fingers into a Celtic knot— the shape Beth had learned to weave with her siblings' fingers before she could even talk. They stood together, waiting. "This is so wrong," Dylan said as he trudged up to the group and made the final circle in the family's bond.

Their collective effort to be jovial on the walk up the island dissolved into pensive silence as they returned to the cabin. Beth glanced at each person as the group marched in line rather than in pairs, their eyes glued to the path. Only Dylan's emotions were obvious, his anger sharp on his face and his stride controlled as he paced himself well behind the rest of the family. The silence lingered through lunch.

Beth pretended to pick out a book from the dozens stuffed onto the living room bookshelf as her family slowly dispersed: Kate and Evan went to Sault Ste. Marie to drop off the film, at least an hour's drive each way; Brian picked up Maegan to waterski along the calm north shore; and Naina fell asleep in the rope hammock tied between two parallel white birch by the fire pit. Taid sat next to her in his Adirondack chair, his beige twill hat pulled low over his eyes. Dylan had disappeared as soon as they returned.

She wandered through the cabin, too scared to go back to her fort. The remains of a solitaire game covered the small round log table in front of the sofa. The piles of suits were messy, helter-skelter, a sure sign that Maegan had been playing. In her grandparents' bedroom, clothes were piled on a corner chair, the bedspread still askew from when they rose. Three books were stacked on the table next to Naina's side of the bed, and a small flashlight perched on top of the headboard's log post. Across the hall, Kate's clothes hung in the narrow bedroom closet according to color and type, her brush and comb placed parallel to each other on the dresser, and the marriage quilt Naina had stitched for Beth's parents on their tenth wedding anniversary was tight and smooth across the bed. At least a week's worth of *The New York Times* lay on the floor. Every Monday and Thursday, Kate or Evan drove into town for her beloved paper— often a week late by the time it arrived, but she didn't care. All relevant reading, her mother said.

Beth sat on her father's side and thumbed through *All the President's Men*, the top of several books stacked on his nightstand. For the past week, her parents and grandparents had debated at dinner whether Nixon should have gone to jail for the Watergate scandal ("Of course," her mother and Taid had said, while Naina and her father felt it was better for the country to move on) and whether President Reagan and some guy named Poindexter should be charged for lying about the Iran-Contra affair. Why was it so important to them to blame someone for everything that happened? She tossed the book back on the pile and went to her bedroom to get the newest Nancy Drew mystery, *The Secret of Mirror Bay*. The stories were getting predictable, but she still liked Nancy.

Beth stopped at her brother's room and slid open the door. His box of acrylic paints and crayons lay on his bed, but the watercolor tray and brushes were missing. If he was painting with watercolors, that meant he was somewhere on the island, close to the water. Maybe today he would teach her to paint, especially if he felt guilty about the trouble he'd created. They could talk about everything that happened—just them, without everyone else butting in with their opinions—and come up with a plan. She left her book on the kitchen counter, grabbed an apple, and headed outside. As she strode back up the island path, she stuffed acorns and small pinecones into the pockets of her denim shorts. This would be fun.

She veered off the path when she reached the first spot where Dylan might be painting, tiptoeing to the edge to peer down toward the lake. Nope. The next two spots on the north side were empty too, so she crossed the island and followed its southern edge to the middle of a small bay. She crouched and slid down a short decline to a landing, then leaned over its edge to scan the rock shoreline. Dylan was about thirty feet below her. His wavy hair bounced as he switched his gaze from the paper covering his lap to whatever he was painting on the horizon. His bare feet hovered just above the water's edge, his toes dipping toward the water to a secret tune. A perfect target.

Beth pulled the acorns from one pocket and sat with her legs dangling over the landing's edge, her stomach on her thighs. She aimed at the small bowl of water next to his left arm, the one he dipped his brush in after every group of strokes. She missed wide at first, hitting a young birch tree. Her next attempts hit his satchel leaning against the tree. Dylan continued painting, oblivious. She rolled onto her knees to aim with more of her body and focused on the bowl. The acorn hit dead on. She jumped backward and covered her mouth to block her giggles as Dylan looked up. Maybe he thought it was a squirrel, but he'd figure it out with one more shot. Time to go for the big arsenal.

She pulled three narrow pinecones from her back pockets, cupped them in her hands with the rest of the acorns, and leaned over to position her arsenal above his head. Just as he looked to his right, she opened her hands and watched the barrage of nature's weaponry fall onto his head, arms, and back. Dylan chuckled and looked up at her. She raised her arms in triumph.

"Knew you were up there," he yelled. "You made a mess of my painting." He ripped the paper from its stack and held it up. Smears of green, blue, and brown drooled down the page.

Beth stood. "I'll come down and fix it, if you show me how."

Dylan stared straight ahead for what seemed like an eternity before nodding his head. "Yeah, okay, get your butt down here. Path's up and to your right."

Beth scampered back up the hill and found the narrow path that meandered down the island's side away from Dylan and switched back toward him. She ran around the last curve but stopped short as he came into view. Beth looked up at her point of attack—she wouldn't have seen Lily sitting next to him from her angle above. She must have been here all along, what Dylan was looking at when he turned to the right. Beth shoved her hands into her pockets and took a few steps back.

Lily turned and smiled at Beth. "Hi, come join us." Beth stood her ground.

Dylan stopped painting a wide swath of watery blue on a blank sheet of paper and waved her forward. "Come on, you've bugged me

forever to teach you how to paint with watercolor, and so has she."
Dylan smiled at Lily. "You can both learn today. Get over here."

Lily stood and grabbed Beth's hands to help her around another
stand of protruding birches on the narrow rock ledge. Beth stepped
over Dylan and sat between him and the satchel. He ripped a sheet of
thick paper in half and handed it and a brush to each of them. They
listened as he demonstrated various brush strokes, paint choices, and
how to make the paint dance across the page as he added more or
less water. The girls laughed at their awkward results, even as Dylan
took turns placing his confident hand on theirs to guide them. When
they'd filled their sheets, he gave them each a full sheet.

"We'll make the same painting. Just follow my strokes. Let's
paint the horizon across the lake in three sections of color across
the page, only make believe it's night so the hues are stronger. The
key is to let the brush and paint do the work; don't try to control it."

Beth followed Dylan's lead but couldn't keep up with his
pace. She peeked across his lap to Lily's painting—much better
than hers—and at Lily, whose furrowed brow showed the frustration Beth felt. She reached to clean her brush in the bowl leaning
against Dylan's stomach and watched the blue and green tornado
swirling in the water. Beth jumped when Dylan tapped her brush
with his. "Let's go, no stopping."

Lily swatted at Dylan's brush with hers. "Don't yell at your
students or we'll take revenge." She dipped her brush in the water
and ran it across his white T-shirt, leaving a muddy green stripe
across his stomach. "Oops."

Beth laughed as Dylan stared at his shirt. "Two against one,
Dyl," she said as she flicked her brush in front of his chest. Splat-
ters of blue sunk into the fabric.

"Good one, girlfriend," Lily said. "I like it, kind of a tie-dyed
hippie thing. Suits him."

Dylan put his hands over the water bowl. "Okay, I can tell
I'm losing both of you. I better get to the last step, even though

neither of you are anywhere near done. Beth, grab the salt shaker in the front pocket of my bag."

She reached into the pocket and held her hand over the top's holes as she pulled the shaker out. "No wonder I couldn't salt my eggs yesterday."

Dylan showed them how to fill their brushes with globs of phthalo blue paint and a touch of water and spread it across the top third of their paintings. When their skies were a consistent shade of indigo, he handed Lily the salt shaker.

"How many stars do you want in your sky? The more you shake, the more stars."

Lily stared at the shaker, then at her painting. "What happens to the salt?"

"You'll see."

The girls oohed and aahed as Lily sprinkled her sky and the salt soaked up the paint wherever it dropped, creating sparkles of white. Beth spread the salt in an angle across her sky to recreate the Milky Way.

"Crap, I put too much on. It's all turning white," she said.

"So you wait until it's dry, brush the salt off, and start over. That's the beauty of watercolors," Dylan said.

"How long does it take to dry?"

"Longer than we have now," Dylan said as he pointed to the east. The family's blue powerboat was heading across the lake toward the south dock, their parents done with their afternoon task. "I'll keep it in my stack, and you can try again later tonight."

Beth pushed down the panic rising from her stomach and tried to mimic Dylan's nonchalant calm.

"Aren't you two coming to the bonfire tonight?" Lily asked. "I know Amik would love to hang out with you again, Beth. He didn't shut up after Tuesday's bonfire; told me all about your conversation together."

Beth blushed, surprised that he'd say anything about her and embarrassed that he'd told Lily all the stupid things she'd said that night. "Really? I thought I acted pretty dumb."

"Not to him. He said your life in a college town sounds exciting."

Dylan stood and reached across Beth for his bag. "We'll come down if we can; not sure if Mom and Dad will free us or not. I'll explain later."

Beth grabbed Dylan's arm and shook her head at him. He yanked it out of her grasp and added her painting to the others in the satchel. "Something about not having our annual card tournament yet, but I doubt Maegan will go along with it. So we'll probably be there," he said. "Wouldn't want Bethie to disappoint Amik, would we?"

Beth jumped up and shoved at Dylan, who tossed his bag at her before he fell backward into the lake. She watched him resurface, relieved that he hadn't hit an underwater chunk of the island but pleased with how forcefully she'd pushed him. Was it because she was still angry at him and worried that he might tell Lily later? Or irritated for teasing her about a boy?

Lily laughed and hugged Beth. "Big brothers can be such a pain; mine drive me nuts. Nice comeback."

They embraced for a few seconds, Beth happy that Lily was taking her side until Dylan's hand gripped her calf. She knew better than to fight what was coming or have Lily try to hold her to the land, where they both might fall onto the ledge. Instead, she jumped off the rock away from his grasp and pulled her knees to her chest, cannonballing next to him. As her body sank, she saw Dylan reaching for her from above. She extended her hand to his and let him pull her back to the surface. They treaded water and stared at each other, Beth determined to match his gaze, until he nodded and smiled.

"You know you soaked Lily and all my paint supplies up there," Dylan said, nodding toward Lily. "It will take days to dry all that paper, and I'll have to buy some new paints."

Beth looked at Lily and back at her brother. "Sorry, Lily, but Dylan had it coming."

Dylan swam to the ledge and looked back at Beth. "Looks like my baby sister has decided she won't be ignored anymore, especially by her big brother."

She dove underwater to hide her triumphant grin. Yes.

By the time Dylan and Beth returned to the cabin, Naina and Kate had prepared a fish casserole and salad. Beth changed out of her wet clothes and woke Maegan from a nap. Everyone was quiet at dinner to avoid reopening the tension of the last twenty-four hours. Beth watched her sister play the adults perfectly, testing and confirming their collective wish for a peaceful evening. Before they'd finished their meal, she had approval to go to the campground bonfire.

Hanging with a bunch of kids seemed better even to Beth than staying home with her parents and grandparents. Maybe the space was good for everyone. The longer they didn't talk about the stuff she found, the more it all might disappear. She changed into a new blue-and-green-checked shirt, jeans, and clean sneakers. Maegan loaned her a light blue sweatshirt and showed Beth how to tie it around her neck.

An hour after dinner, they joined Dylan in the powerboat and headed for the south shore campground. The last bursts of a setting sun were fading above Llyndee's Peak, and the dull thickness of dusk was descending, turning the sky and water steel gray. Brian ran to the dock and tripped as he was about to grab the boat's bow. He rolled from his knees and hands onto his butt and laughed. Maegan climbed out of the boat and knelt to hug him.

"Hey, beauty, I thought your parents wouldn't let you out tonight," he said.

"My powers of persuasion convinced them. Did I miss anything?"

Beth rolled her eyes at Dylan, who was still sitting by the steering wheel. She walked to the stern to tie down the boat.

"Of course not, party never starts until you get here. Did you bring it?"

Beth turned in time to see Maegan pull a square bottle with golden-brown liquid out of her jacket pocket and hand it to Brian, who wrapped his jacket around it. She'd often seen her grandfather take the bottle from a top kitchen shelf and pour a small amount in a glass with a lot of ice, right before dinner. Maegan looked back at Dylan and Beth.

"You guys are coming, right?"

Dylan slumped in his seat. "I'll stay here, wait until it's safe to drive past home, and head down to Lily's. You staying or going with me, Beth?"

Maegan walked back to the boat. "I don't think you should go down there tonight. Who knows what you might say if you have a few drinks, and we agreed we wouldn't talk."

Dylan didn't move, so Maegan tried another approach. "I definitely don't think Beth should go. Mom and Dad are already on edge. Can you imagine what they'd do if they found out she was down at Lily's again, let alone you?"

"Taid will be more upset than Mom and Dad, once he sees that you've stolen his prized whiskey."

Maegan waved him off. "He never drinks it anymore. Besides, Brian can buy more in town with his fake ID."

Dylan looked at Beth. "Up to you. I'm going, because it's Mrs. Akeene's birthday."

"So their whole family will be there?"

"I assume Ben will be there. That is what you're asking, right?"

Beth frowned and looked toward the campfire. The kids were laughing at something, including a boy who looked like another of Ben's nephews, Amik's younger brother. Why would he be down here?

"Isn't that Keeme?" she asked. "Why would he be here if they're celebrating his aunt's birthday?"

Dylan stood and scanned the group of kids. "I don't know. Let's go find out."

They followed Maegan and Brian to the group closest to the beach, where Keeme was talking to the twin girls Beth thought were stupid beyond words. Dylan reminded him of his aunt's birthday.

"Crap, forgot all about it. I guess I better go." He bent his wrist toward the fire to look at his watch. "They won't start for another half hour at least. Can I catch a ride with you guys?"

Dylan nodded, and Keeme turned back to the twins. Maegan waved them over to her group and handed Dylan a beer and Beth a can of 7-Up from a cooler. "Wrap your hand around it. No one will know the difference," she whispered to Beth.

The fire pit was at the far corner of the campground, close to the shoreline and separated from the open area where renters parked their campers or pitched their tents. Smaller logs were piled against the outside of the low brick wall outlining the pit. A boy Beth didn't know kept reaching into a bucket of pine needles and flinging them at the fire. The flames spiked and the needles hissed as they burned, the fire receding until he tossed another pile at the flames.

A group of younger boys was already rowdy, daring each other to jump over the fire. At least a dozen teenagers were sitting on huge logs circling the fire or standing in groups, most with beer cans in their hands. Beth scanned the campground for adults who might be upset that the kids were drinking alcohol. One couple sat on a picnic table outside their white aluminum camper playing cards with the help of a flashlight, and the campground owner kept his normal perch on the deck outside his office. Neither seemed to notice or care.

Brian and Todd, one of the usual crew Maegan hung out with every afternoon, were comparing waterskiing stories from earlier in the day. For the first time, Beth liked the feeling of standing with the group, being part of their conversation, even if she said nothing. She sipped her pop and tried to seem relaxed. A few girls who looked around her age were sitting next to the fire, separate from the rowdy kids, looking nervous but excited. She'd say hi in a few minutes, once she was sure Dylan was staying for a while.

"Who was the guy who almost ran you over?" Todd said. "Man, he didn't see you in the water until the last minute, when you stuck your skis up in the air. He's probably some redskin from the other end. Those guys are all blind."

Brian snorted. "No shit, dude. No shit."

Dylan stared at Maegan, waiting for her to step into the conversation. When she pretended to focus on the whiskey in her glass instead, Dylan downed the rest of his beer, threw the can toward the cooler, and walked back to Keeme. Beth waved at Maegan and followed him. He yanked on Keeme's shirt, even though he was making out with one of the twins, body locked against body.

Keeme spun around, angry at the interruption. "We're leaving now," Dylan said and strode off toward the dock. Beth watched Keeme look from Dylan back to the twin, trying to decide between the girl and family obligations. She tossed her pop can into a nearby garbage can and ran to the dock. Dylan had the engine running and was untying the boat's stern. She untied the front and jumped into the boat as he put the engine into reverse, then fell onto the seat that faced backward behind him as he floored the engine. Keeme was running down the dock waving his arms. She yelled at Dylan to turn around, but he didn't or wouldn't hear. Keeme and the campfire faded away as the boat sliced through the bay's light chop and into open water.

Dylan kept the engine at full speed all the way down the lake, except as they passed the island. Beth asked him why he always slowed to a crawl. "Dad knows the sound of the boats by heart. If Mom notices he hears us going past the cabin, she's sure to catch on that I go down there every time."

"Do you think Dad always knew you went to Lily's?"

Dylan smiled and shrugged. Beth assumed their parents knew nothing her brother and sister did at the bonfires, or they wouldn't let them go. All these secrets her family pretended to keep from each other. What hope did they have of keeping the one they'd promised each other that morning?

As Dylan accelerated the engine to full speed again, Beth slouched in her seat. Flickering constellations hung in the air above her, each with its own personality and wattage. She swept her gaze over her favorites and tried to remember the names of the ones on the horizon's edge. How many billions of years would each star live in the same spot? Safe, secure, no one trying to push them out of the way. Why did some leave their homes, shoot across the sky into oblivion, and others just fade away? She'd ask Ben. He'd know.

She was glad she had come with Dylan, just in case he was tempted to tell Lily. Part of her was sure he wouldn't defy their family's Celtic pinkie knot. But another part had watched him with Lily earlier and had seen how he looked at her, how much he wanted to impress and please her. Maegan's idea from the other night in bed still made sense, even if her family figured out she had taken everything. Dylan would forgive her, sooner or later. She wondered if she could do it, if it came down to her family or the Ojibwes' rights to the island. If she could remove the items, none of this would matter, and they could go back to being the family they'd always been, on the island that was and always would be a part of them. Safe and secure, just like the stars.

"Bethie, someone's waiting for you," Dylan said as he slowed the boat.

Beth swung around to look at the dock, where Amik was waving. She turned and huddled in her seat behind Dylan.

"Come on, he's a nice guy. You'll have fun, not like the idiotic bullshit at the other bonfire. And there's cake too."

What kind of cake did they bake for birthdays? She peeked at Amik, who was catching the rope Dylan threw to him. Suddenly her bright shirt felt garish. She pulled Maegan's sweatshirt over her head and shoved her arms through the sleeves.

"Are we in time for the birthday celebration?" Dylan asked.

Amik smiled and pointed toward the cabin's porch. "Just starting. Lily sent me down since she's putting the candles on the cake. Hey, Beth."

She stood and lifted her hand in a meek wave. Amik extended his hand, and she took it to step out of the boat. "What kind of cake do you have for birthdays?" she asked.

"Same kind as you. I saw the chief buying it in the grocery store yesterday. Vanilla is my guess."

Beth turned her face toward Dylan behind them to hide her embarrassment. What a stupid question.

They walked past the fire and up the long trail to Lily's family cabin. A wide porch extended its entire length, stained in the same dark brown as the rest of the log home. From the lake it was almost impossible to see, even in daylight.

Lily's mother sat at a corner table in front of family and friends, who filled the porch. They waited on the steps as Lily walked through the crowd with the huge cake. Dylan grabbed Beth's hand and pulled her to the back of the porch while everyone sang and cheered.

Lily's dad stood behind his wife. Beth had pictured him as larger than life, with a huge headdress like in the movies. Instead, he wore a black shirt and pants and a belt with a large beaded buckle, his long gray hair pulled into a ponytail. He looked a lot older than she expected, but his deep-set eyes held a youthful glow, just like Taid's. Ben had told her that the elders had accepted his sister as the chief's spouse almost at once when they saw how he looked at her, how his strict, serious demeanor softened. Beth understood as she watched the chief look at his wife and daughter with a tenderness she'd rarely seen in her own father's eyes.

"*Boozhoo.* Greetings. Thank you for coming," he said as Lily and three other women cut the cake and handed pieces to waiting hands. "We are blessed to have so many loyal, loving relatives and friends to celebrate Anna's day. You are what keep our family and heritage strong. Our ancestors would be proud of our dedication— to each other, to our history on this lake, and to the values and beliefs of our Anishinaabe. Have a happy heart, my beautiful bride. *Miigwech.* Thank you."

The crowd spread out, plates in hand, the elders inside while the rest headed down to the bonfire. Beth saw Ben walk down the steps with a large group, unaware they were there. She waited with Dylan until Lily joined them with three plates of cake.

"Hey, you two, I saved us the best pieces. Let's head down with everyone else."

Dylan stopped at the top of the steps to wave to Lily's parents and wish her a happy birthday. The chief nodded with a tight smile while Mrs. Akeene grinned and waved back. "Thanks, Dylan, nice to see you here. You too, Beth."

Beth waved and followed Dylan and Lily down the path. Two large tubs with beer cans were close to the blazing fire. Ben was still talking with the same people, too large a group for her to intrude. She ate her cake.

"Watch out for the secret Native ingredient," Amik said to her. "Might turn your hair black."

Beth stared at him before she realized he was joking, and

shook her head. "Yeah, that was pretty stupid of me to think you'd have a different cake. Sorry."

"No worries. So you've been to a few of these; how do they compare to the bonfires in the south bay?"

"There aren't many adults at the other one, just kids getting drunk and stupid. Why?"

"Just curious how the other half of the lake parties. Not much difference then, only here the adults are the ones getting drunk."

"Yeah, my parents do the same thing when they get together with the Shepplers and McGintys." She kept one ear bent toward Lily and Dylan to make sure he wasn't telling her anything and stepped closer to them when two men started playing guitars. Amik watched her move away from him but stayed in his spot.

She took small bites of her cake to make it last while she tried to hear what Lily was saying. When she finally caught bits of conversation and realized they were talking about Lily's job at the Circle Barn, Beth relaxed and tried to talk with Amik again.

"At least you guys all have fun together. No one seems to argue or play dumb tricks on each other."

"Don't be too sure of that. I've heard stories of some nasty fights late at night. My folks always leave before any of that happens, so I don't get to see them."

"Really? I have trouble imagining that. Everyone always seems so happy. I like the music and the dancing." Several people had started a line dance, chanting and moving in ways she'd never seen her family dance. "But I only know Lily and Ben, and I'm sure they'd never be unkind with anyone."

Amik turned to face her. "You're sure about that?"

Beth looked across the crowd at Ben. His eyes were dark and intense, as though the man he was talking with were suggesting they shoot the loons because they made too much noise at night. There had to be a good reason he looked mad. She shuffled her feet and found a soft spot in the dirt to dig with her toe. "Well,

Ben is great when we go hiking or follow the loons and eagles. Maybe you don't know him that well."

Amik looked across the crowd at Ben. "Maybe you don't either. Everyone has secrets."

Beth looked at Dylan and Lily arm in arm next to her, then turned and stepped toward Amik. "What do you mean, everyone has secrets?"

He raised both hands and stepped back. "Woah, chill. I didn't mean anything by it. Just conversation."

Beth blushed, realizing she'd overreacted. "Yeah, sorry." She watched the dancers while she tried to compose herself. It was just conversation, as he said. There was no way he could know anything bad about Ben. And he didn't know about her family's secret. She was rude and stupid. She tapped her foot and tried to move to the music. "Hey, will you teach me how to dance like that?" When she turned, Amik had disappeared.

A north wind blew into Lake Wigwakobi early the next morning and settled there for four days. Obese clouds gathered long enough to release a torrent of rain before the wind shoved them south and carried in another collection to flood the area again. The rain collided with white-capped waves and flew over the north dock, filling the boat hulls several times a day. Beth pulled every sweatshirt she had out of her dresser drawers, even the ones from earlier summers that were tight now, and added her wool pajama bottoms as a base layer under her jeans when she helped her dad pail out the boats. Even her bright yellow rain slicker was water-logged by the second day.

Naina and Kate filled the bathtub to rinse clothes and hang them over the shower curtain rod or across the makeshift line Taid strung in front of the stone fireplace. Everyone took turns running to the woodpile under the cabin's back corner to keep the fire going. Her parents had picked up a full tank of natural gas when they went to the Sault to have the film developed, so the oven, fridge, and lights kept working.

Beth adored everything about the storm. She watched from the picture window as the clouds bounced off each other like bumper cars at a summer fair, fighting to be the last one in the sky. She stood on the deck with her arms spread as the storm's energy surrounded her. Its urgency turned her this way and that, and she giggled at the feel and sound of the huge raindrops landing on the hood of her slicker. When her dad called for tools to fix whatever the wind had pulled loose on the cabin or boats, she grabbed trees to stop the wind from blowing her backward and to keep from slipping on the wet rocks between the cabin and boathouse. After they finished the latest chore, they'd run to the back storage room door and peel off their wet top layers, laughing at how fast the other tried to get them off and be the first in a hot shower. If Beth lost, she burrowed under her bed's thick blanket and quilt to wait until it was her turn.

By the third day, the wind had calmed but the rain persisted. The smiling daisies in Naina's gardens closed into themselves, fighting to prevent their pollen from washing away. Even Beth couldn't bear to go outside and be soaked again, but the hours stuck inside seemed interminable. Games of gin rummy, hearts, and poker became deadly dull. Maegan and Kate turned impatient first and retreated to their bedrooms unless it was time to prepare a meal. Naina and Taid stayed by the fire, reading and filling out crossword puzzles together, while Evan brought in his huge fishing tackle box and restrung trolling rods.

Dylan had closed his bedroom door the day before and only came out to get a plate of food and take it back to his room. Beth assumed he was reading or drawing, the light on even in the middle of the night when she got up to use the bathroom. In the afternoon, when everyone else was napping or reading, she wandered down the bedroom hallway and listened outside his door.

"Are you ever coming out of there?" she whispered through the plywood door.

"Not until the storm stops."

"No one wants to do anything. Can I come in and watch you draw?"

"No."

"I promise I won't bother you. I've read all my books, and it's raining too hard to go outside. C'mon, Dyl, please?"

Silence. She slid the door open just enough to show half of her face. Dylan was slouched against the back wall, sketching Lily in the woods with charcoal.

"You've seen what I'm doing. Now you can leave. Scram, Bethie."

She grinned, knew he didn't mean it as soon as he said her name like that. She opened the door a touch more and knelt in the opening.

"Wow, when did you start using charcoals? Is it hard?"

Dylan sighed, pursed his lips, and drew in silence. Beth watched his long fingers move around the page, his left hand drawing and his right hand smudging the charcoal to create shadows or fill in tree trunks. Lily's face was delicate, her smile glowing off the page.

"You didn't tell her anything the other night, did you?"

Dylan stopped drawing, sat up, and looked down at her. "No. I keep my promises. I will change Taid's mind, though. He needs to let the chief go up there and tell us if the stuff is theirs. He's a fair man. He won't make us leave the island."

"But what if you're wrong? He seems serious; at least he did the other night. We can't take that chance."

Dylan's brows lifted, and he put his first finger in front of his mouth. "Shut up," he hissed at her. "Do you want everyone to know where we went and ruin everything?"

Beth looked down the hallway. Their grandparents were reading in front of the fire, and their parents' bedroom door was closed. "No one's around. We're fine," she whispered back.

Dylan pointed at the wall next to him. "These walls are too thin to say stuff like that."

"Well, I don't see why they should be mad anyway. She's much nicer than Brian. I don't get why they're letting Maegan be with a jerk like that and don't want you to be with Lily."

He shook his head. "You don't get it, Bethie. Just leave it alone."

She leaned against the door wall and pulled her knees to her chest. "The only good thing about this rain is it might wash away all that stuff I found."

"Or Sam's dug a hole big enough to hide from the storm, and he'll bury it."

Beth jumped up and grabbed Dylan's arm. "Sam! He's been out there all this time!"

"Yeah, he's a gull. He's supposed to live outside, remember?"

"He's only got one leg. He can't get around in this mess. How is he finding food?" She ran to her bedroom and threw on a pair of jeans and another sweatshirt, grabbed her slicker and rain boots out of the storage room, and sprinted to the kitchen. Two almost moldy muffins in the bread bin would have to do. She pulled her hood up and headed up the path toward her fort.

The pine needles were more slippery than the rocks, and her rubber boots made it hard to climb the path's steep sections, but the trees provided enough leverage and cover that she wasn't drenched by the time she reached her fort. She called for Sam and followed his peeping until she found him hiding under a pale pink blanket she'd added to one of the fort's walls. When she lifted the soaked, heavy wool, Sam's head popped up and shook in circles as if it had been frozen in place, his body shivering the water from its top feathers. She broke off a tiny piece of muffin and tossed it at him. He grabbed it with his beak and peeped for more.

His nest on a middle shelf of the boulder was in shambles from the rain cascading over the rock. She walked around to its north side and poked at the spot where they'd buried the wooden tubes and sticks. They were still there, as were the red ochre paintings. This was the perfect time to get rid of it all, say the rain washed them away. She lifted pieces out of the shallow dirt and pine needles and piled them in the corner. She would wrap them in her coat and put them in the outhouse, just as she and Maegan had planned.

The more she dug, the more her heart and brain tugged in opposite directions. She stopped and looked at the paintings. Even if she got rid of the drums and bowls, they would still be there. Weren't they as or even more important?

Beth stepped backward, and Sam squawked to stop her from stepping on him. He flew up to what had been his nest. Beth dug for more artifacts while Sam's squawking became a constant squeal.

"Hush, Sam."

He alternated between squawks and squeals until she stopped again. Even he looked drenched, if a bird could be. She relented.

"Fine, I'll leave this here for now. But you can't live there anymore, silly bird. Your nest is ruined." She looked up at the sky, the brooding clouds gathering for another explosion. "You don't have time to build a new one either. Come on, let's get you to the cabin, and we'll figure something out." She broke the muffins into tiny pieces and dropped them behind her on the path as she walked. Sam followed. As she climbed down the ladder, she told Sam to go to the boathouse. He bent his head sideways from the top of the rock.

"You know what I'm saying." By the time she reached the boathouse door, Sam was perched on the roof above it. She found a box large enough for the bird and carried it to the woods by the sagging outhouse to fill with pine branches and needles. When she brought it back to the boathouse doorway, the skies exploded in a solid wall of rain. Sam squawked and dropped into the boathouse with her. She took off her raincoat and shook the pockets over the box to deposit the last morsels of muffin, and Sam hopped onto his makeshift nest.

Beth grinned and put her slicker back on. "Now you'll stay dry." She stood in the doorway waiting for the rain to subside, pleased that Sam was safe. She'd decide what to do with the artifacts tomorrow.

A massive chattering of birds woke her early the next morning—gray jays, killdeers, gulls, and mourning doves all eager to chat and sing after the storm. Beth opened the curtains a crack. The air was soft and clear, the last of the stars disappearing into the pale morning sky. She ran to the living room window to see if Sam was still in the boathouse. The box was there, but Sam was not.

"Naina fed him some of last night's leftovers when she left to troll with your dad, and he flew away," Taid said from the couch behind her.

Beth sat next to him. "Then he must be okay."

"I'm sure he's fine, thanks to you." Taid wrapped his arm around Beth, and they watched Naina and Evan glide up to the dock. Evan tied the boat, and Naina handed him the rods, followed by a huge rainbow trout to put into the floating bucket by the dock. Taid raised his arms and cheered.

"Woo-hoo! We'll have a feast tonight. Finally, fresh food!"

An hour later everyone crowded into one car, and Evan drove to town for groceries. While they shopped, he and Beth walked across the street to the post office to see if the film had arrived from Sault Ste. Marie. They picked up the photos and Kate's latest pile of *The New York Times* and waited in the car for the rest of the family.

Beth sat next to her father on the front seat. "Are we going to look at them?"

"Sure. You can have the honors. Let's hope they turned out."

She ripped open the large manila envelope. A dozen photos fell onto her lap, each with a clear shot of the boulder's paintings or the objects on the ground. They divided them into three piles, one for each of them and one for Naina. When the family and their multiple bags of groceries were loaded into the car, Evan handed four photos to Naina.

"Okay, here's the plan. Let's go to the Circle Barn and divide into pairs. We're shopping like any other day. Maegan, you stay with Beth; Mom and Dad, you stick together; and Kate's with me. Rotate around to the honey, the moccasins, all the things we would normally shop for. Don't pore over the books, or they'll wonder what we're doing. Dylan, your job is to keep Lily occupied so she doesn't notice what we're doing."

Dylan nodded, his eyes revealing his excitement to see Lily. Beth liked knowing something about Dylan that no one else fully recognized. Maybe what she thought about getting rid of the drums and that no one would care was right, even if no one else saw that either.

By the time they reached the massive round red barn with its black octagon-shaped roof, their car was smothered in dust from the mile-long dirt road off the highway. Four other cars were parked haphazardly in front of the barn's wide-open doors, which meant there were other customers. She took one last look at the rock paintings in her photos and shoved them in her jeans pocket. The family tried to seem nonchalant as they entered, all of them waving at Lily, her aunt, and her cousin. Dylan walked straight toward Lily, while Maegan stopped at one of the front tables with jars of fresh honey.

"What are you doing?" Beth whispered at Maegan's back. "We're supposed to go to the bookshelves first, remember?"

"I pick up a jar of honey every time I'm here. We have to act normal." She grabbed a small jar and waved Beth forward. They meandered their way around tables of dreamcatchers and another stacked with brightly colored blankets. Beth opened a blanket with human figures in its design. It looked like one of the rock figures—a stick man, front leg straight and the back bent as if walking, its arms raised at ninety-degree angles in the air. Her initial elation that she'd found a match in their treasure hunt turned to panic. She folded the blanket and stuffed it under the others.

Maegan had already found a book with red paintings on rocks in Ontario. Beth picked up another one and flipped through the pages. "Stop reading so closely. You will give us away," Beth hissed. Instead, Maegan turned and called to their father. He and Kate were across the room, trying on moccasins.

"Hey, Dad, can I get a few of these books? I think I have to study this stuff in history class next year, and some of this is pretty cool."

Beth stared at their parents, stunned that Maegan was going so far away from their plan. Their mom looked equally shocked that her daughter would yell across a busy store. Evan regained his composure first. "Sure, honey, whatever you think looks good." Taid and Naina wandered over to the girls and scanned the books, suggesting several to Maegan. This was working out better than anyone imagined. Leave it to Maegan.

Beth picked out a book and moved to the gallery, a small side room with paintings and sculptures. She looked at the table of contents and found a chapter that looked as if it might tell her what the symbols meant. She peeked at the gallery's wide entry a few times, which was still clear of people, so she pulled out the photos and compared the images with the book's drawings. They were identical. The chapter's last page included a photo of a site with a rock wall filled with paintings, and deep holes in the soil in front. The caption read, "Ojibwe believe the manitou rock spirits will take back what they know is theirs if their sacred space is disrupted." She better put the drums back in place, fast.

"Can I help you figure something out?"

Beth jumped, and the book slammed to the rough wood floor. That was Ben's voice. She shoved the photos into her pocket as she reached down to pick up the book. Her teeth gnashed at the inside of her cheek.

Her hands trembled as she shook her head and handed the book to Ben.

"You okay? What's up?" he asked.

Beth stepped back and tried to laugh, but it sounded like a high-pitched whine instead. "Nothing, I was just helping Maegan pick out a book. No big deal. What's up with you? I mean, how are you?" She looked past him toward the doorway, wishing she were there instead of in front of Ben.

"I'm fine, thanks. Can I help you figure out an Ojibwe sign or saying? I've learned some of their history."

"No, no, I don't want to know any of that stuff. Just Maegan."

Ben stood in front of her, waiting for her to meet his eyes. She could feel them piercing through her eyelids, but she didn't dare look at him. He'd know she was lying. She needed to get away from him, fast.

"I see," he said. "Now that the rain's stopped, the woods should be teeming with Lammas ferns that will make a sweet salad. Want to join me for a hike later? I'm taking Lily home, so we should be back by one."

Beth ran her tongue along the inside of her cheek to soothe the ripped skin. She wanted to go, but she couldn't today or any-time soon. Not until she and her family decided what to do with the stuff on the island.

She heard her mother before she saw her. "Beth, are you in here?" She couldn't remember the last time she'd been this happy to see her mom.

"Right here. Do you need me?"

Ben turned and nodded at Kate, who returned the greeting. "We're getting ready to go. I wanted to make sure you didn't want to buy anything before we left."

"No, I'm all set."

Kate put her arm around Beth's shoulders and looked at Ben. "Well, we're off then. Nice to see you again, Ben."

He waved at them as they left the gallery. Beth whispered, "Thanks" as they walked to the counter. Lily slid Maegan's books into a large paper bag and handed them to her. As the family walked out of the barn, Beth turned toward the gallery. Ben had the book open to the same page she had been reading.

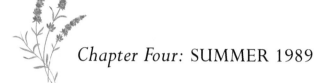

Chapter Four: SUMMER 1989

I t happened in an instant, but like every other momentous event in life, the actual seconds lingered.

Naina had taken the powerboat and a pie to have tea with Aunt Betty, who rarely traveled up to the lake anymore with her son and his family. Beth's grandmother hopped lightly on her tiptoes while they made breakfast.

"Why don't you two have a good long hike," she'd told Taid and Beth. "You know Aunt Betty. I could be there until next Sunday!"

Taid had followed her to the north dock and watched with his binoculars until she arrived at the Shepplers' dock. Beth watched him from an Adirondack chair by the fire pit, where she was reading *Walking* by Henry David Thoreau, a new book her grandmother had given her when they arrived. "It will help you feel right at home in the world," Naina had said. After Taid plodded to the cabin, to the deck, and back through the cabin to the porch by the kitchen, Beth laughed and peeked around the chair's tall back. "Looking for me?"

"There you are. I haven't been to the top of Llyndee's Peak in years; what do you say we take a long hike like Naina suggested?"

"I'm not sure she meant something that strenuous. Are you sure you want to climb that far uphill?"

Taid scoffed at her concerns. She'd come to the island with just her grandparents right after school let out for the summer to help them open the cabin and to "keep Taid happy and away from the Ojibwe items"—her mother's whispered command as Beth climbed into Taid's royal-blue Lincoln Continental. It was a huge, ugly boat of a car, but she could stretch across the entire back seat and not have to fight for space with her brother and sister.

The first days were awkward without her parents and siblings until everyone's natural rhythms and habits synced together. They kept busy with cleaning tasks, and Beth rebuilt her fort, this year without Ben. She'd hiked with him only a few times at the end of last summer, and always with Dylan and Lily so he didn't have a chance to bring up the Ojibwe art book. She missed going to the west end bonfires and exploring with him, but if Ben came anywhere near her fort, she knew she'd fold and show him what she'd found.

Beth had laughed when her grandparents asked her two nights earlier, as they sat on the porch mesmerized by a huge pack of sparkling fireflies, if she missed the rest of the family. The unease she'd felt when they first arrived had been replaced by a mixture of elation and resentment: finally, someone listened to her *and* wanted to spend the entire day together. Naina woke her every morning to go trolling or fish off the dock, and she even shared her Welsh secrets for perfect homemade bread. Taid rowed around the island while Beth swam to match Maegan's feat at thirteen, and they didn't hesitate to let her sail on her own. At night they built a playing card castle that covered the entire dining room table. After it was finished, they moved to the porch to eat meals and tiptoed past the table so the structure would survive until the rest of the family could see it. When they listened to news on the radio, they even discussed politics together. She couldn't remember her parents ever asking her opinion in those conversations.

"Are you kidding?" she'd replied. "I haven't had this much fun in forever. You both treat me like a person, not the baby who doesn't know anything."

Her grandfather had pointed to the glowing lightning bugs. "We're all like one of these fireflies," Taid said. "We shine a million times in our lives, but we may not recognize when it happens unless we shine so brightly that others notice and celebrate our good fortune, our kindness, or our success. But we have to believe that, just like these fireflies, our glowing has value and meaning. Even if no one sees it but us."

Since Naina had taken the powerboat to visit Aunt Betty, they had to take the fishing boat to the south side trail on Llyndee's Peak—a much easier climb than the north trail's terrain. They bounced across the open water like a pogo stick, the small engine's top speed of twelve knots unable to power the boat over the midday waves. There was nothing to do but endure the sheets of pelting water as they plummeted between the rolling whitecaps.

They had separated only briefly on the trail to the top of the cliff, she to photograph a flutter of monarchs swarming a luscious milkweed, and Taid to pick wild raspberries down a small slope from the path—a long-held secret stash the animals rarely bothered with since it was perched so close to the rock wall's edge. She'd heard him yell his customary "Hooray!" when he reached it, but when she yelled back about the butterflies, he didn't reply.

As much freedom as they'd given her, Taid hadn't left her alone in the woods because the spring drought had forced the bears and moose to search for food in places humans didn't expect. Either might attack if cubs or calves were nearby. Taid's solution was to carry a spoon and small cooking lid on their hikes to alert the animals they were coming. She hadn't heard the ringing of tin or smelled the pungent aroma of wild animals. Why didn't he answer?

"Taid? Wait for me. Did you find lots of berries?"

She started down the slope toward the raspberry bushes that hung off the last fringe of land, as if reaching for an escape into the sky. He wasn't by the bushes. Her heartbeat already echoed the pounding of breaking waves on the huge rocks below. As she inched to the slope's edge in desperate hope that Taid had found a new stash she didn't know about, she yelled his name again. Nothing. Beth ran back to her starting point, where she could see down to the rock wall, her voice shaking as she yelled for him, for anyone to hear and reply.

As she turned back toward the cliff, the afternoon sun sparkled off the metal cooking lid, hovering about ten feet below her in a small birch growing sideways from the rock. Beth knew exactly where it was on Llyndee's Peak, since Dylan had climbed to a nearby ledge last summer when they'd hiked with Lily. Like a stupid jock, he had dived into the water at least fifteen feet below. Lily was thrilled, but Beth had been terrified he'd hit one of the thousands of jagged, knife-sharp rocks that lurked just under the water's surface.

She threw her backpack aside and shimmied her way to the edge, grabbing every tree and bush to hold her to the land. Beth wrapped her ankles around a narrow birch as she lowered onto her stomach to peer over. Her grandfather lay splattered on one of the lower boulders. One arm jutted out at an odd angle, and blood covered half his face. Both legs dangled over the rock as if he might jump any second.

"Taid, can you hear me?" Beth screamed.

His left leg rose in response. Relief waved through her.

"I'll be right down." She sprinted back up the hill and down the trail. Within minutes she reached the lake, a distance that had taken them almost an hour to traverse. She threw her backpack in the boat, yanked the steel anchor's sharp spokes out of the rock's cracks and roared the engine into reverse, then shot forward at full speed. The propeller careened off the cliff's underwater shelf, the boat lurching and swaying in response. She rounded the cliff's curve and Taid appeared, balanced at a perfect forty-five-degree angle on the huge boulder as if he were lying on a recliner in the sun.

Beth steered into the lake, turned the boat sharply, and rammed it onto a small pile of rocks below Taid. The boat held for a few seconds and slid back into the water's grip. She scanned the rocks for other options, circled again, and shoved the throttle to full speed. The boat jumped over the lowest rocks and held between two chunks of granite, but for how long she wasn't sure.

Taid lifted his head just enough to watch her. Blood drooled down his cheek and into the folds of his neck. "Good thing . . . fishing boat . . ."

Beth held her breath as he spoke. "Thank God you're awake. Are your legs okay?"

He tipped his head.

The cliff wall between them was a solid mass of granite, quartz, and limestone, without fissures or peaks to climb up to him. She stepped onto a seat bench and stretched to reach Taid's feet. She missed by inches, pulled back, stretched again. This time she could barely touch his heels. He'd have to jump. She dug under the benches and bow and flung every life jacket, seat pad, and windbreaker onto the boat's open floor.

"Okay, I'm piling stuff so you can jump. Hold on."

"That's my firefly," he said.

Beth took a wide stance to balance herself on the seat bench.

"Taid, I'm ready for you. I'll break your fall as you come down."

Taid lifted his chest an inch, and his body dropped in a huge mass. Beth reached for his legs to steer him toward the padded mound and twisted her body under him to take the impact on the boat's iron hull. He screamed when his broken arm hit the bench, and his legs, body, and head collapsed on top of her. Beth gasped for air as the boat under her and her grandfather's weight on top compressed her lungs. She reached for his neck to find a pulse.

"*Iawn*," he whispered. "Okay."

It could have taken minutes or hours for Beth to inch herself out from under him, shifting his weight as she moved so Taid was lying fully on the soft pile, his arm resting on a seat cushion by his head. Beth reached into his left pants pocket for the cotton handkerchief with the red, green, and white Welsh flag that was always with him and wrapped it around his forehead. The cut wasn't deep, but it was bleeding a lot. Beth fell onto the bench. Her ribs throbbed, and her heart was seized into a fist, but her grandfather was alive and safe.

The sun's yawn over the adjoining bay signaled late afternoon. The whitecaps would punish Taid if they tried to return to the island, and she wouldn't be able to lift him out of the boat by herself. She pushed off the rocks with a paddle and stayed as close to the cliff's edge as possible without ruining what was left of the propeller. Her eyes focused on the north point of Llyndee's Peak and the one place she knew she'd find help.

The farther they plodded, Taid's motionless body lying on the life jackets in front of her, the more the shock of what had happened settled in her, and she shivered in the afternoon sun. After they rounded the cliff's north point, she turned west and followed the shoreline. Beth waved one arm when she saw Amik and Ben walking down from his cabin for their early evening troll, rods in hand. Her ribs burned for her to stop, but she kept waving until both men started running. She yelled, "Llyndee's Peak, Taid fell" as she steered up to the dock. They jumped into the boat, and someone grabbed her forehead to hold her steady as she leaned over the side, unable to stop the rush of bile, food, and panic from her stomach.

They dressed Taid in his brightest long-sleeved shirt to give him color and hide the cast when Evan, Kate, and Dylan arrived three days later. His hair wasn't long enough to comb over the stitches along the right edge of his forehead, but Naina puffed her foundation powder over his face to lessen the cut's deep crimson tones and the surrounding black-and-navy bruises. Ben volunteered to pick up the family on shore, since Taid was still a bit unsteady on his feet, and Kate's alarm bells would surely go off if Naina or Beth picked them up alone. They spent all afternoon preparing a traditional island dinner of baked whitefish, pansy-and-spinach salad, blueberry muffins, and pie. Ben brought an Adirondack chair from the fire pit to the porch for Taid, where they waited together, along with a pitcher of Tom Collins cocktails and bottles of root beer, homemade cheeses from the Circle Barn, and a collection of canvas deck chairs.

Beth intended to stay with her grandparents on the porch as Ben's boat rounded the peninsula, to show her parents how confident and comfortable she felt on her own. She didn't anticipate that Dylan would bounce out of his seat and wave wildly when he saw her, or that her body would deceive her and run to greet them at the dock.

"Guess you missed me, huh?" she said to Dylan as they hugged.

"Excess energy from the ride; don't let it go to your head. Hope your month was better than mine. Jesus, I'm glad I'm not an only kid."

Kate stepped onto the dock and pulled Beth away from Dylan. "My turn. How's my baby girl?" She kissed Beth lightly on the forehead and held her by the shoulders. "You look happy and healthy."

Beth squealed as her dad grabbed her from behind and spun her in the air. "She looks better than that! Can't wait to hear about all your escapades."

"So much great stuff, Dad, and I found a ton of new places for you to paint, Dyl."

Ben helped with the luggage and followed the family to the porch. Naina met Kate at the stairs while Evan and Dylan went to Taid.

"*Dim pryderon*, son, no worries," Taid said. "Wait until you hear about our brave Beth."

Dylan hugged his grandfather and stared at Beth as he sat on the porch railing next to her, his eyebrows raised and demanding an explanation.

Ben sat on her other side. "Impressed me, that's for sure. You should be proud of her."

Kate covered her mouth as she saw Taid's face. "My God, what happened?"

Naina sat next to Taid and took his free hand. "The raspberry bushes on Llyndee's Peak are officially off limits. He stumbled and fell, but all is well. Nothing to concern you, Kate dear."

Kate and Evan dropped into the open chairs as Naina handed drinks to everyone. "Okay," said Evan, "let's hear it."

Taid pointed at Beth and smiled. "I'd be much worse if it wasn't for her fast thinking and skill with the boat, I'll tell you. You know the stash I always visit halfway up the trail?"

Everyone nodded.

"The earth gave way as I reached for the berries. I slid off the ledge and landed on a boulder a ways down; don't honestly remember much of that. Beth had the boat under me in minutes, caught me as I came down. Knew to pile the life vests to cushion our fall and wrapped my head in the Welsh colors." He pulled a fresh handkerchief out of his pocket and waved it. "She lived up to her full potential *and* our family's that day. My hero."

Beth dug her hands between her thighs and stared at her shoes to avoid her parents' stares. Ben wrapped his arm around her. "Couldn't have done it better myself. Lily's uncle was home and stitched Taid up, and then we went to town to cast the arm."

"Lily's uncle, the Ojibwe doctor?" Kate said. "Why didn't you take him to the hospital?"

Beth shook her head at her mother. "Because we needed to stop the bleeding. Besides, he had all the ingredients for the yarrow poultice Ben showed me how to make last summer. I mixed them together, and the bleeding stopped as soon as he put it on the cut so he could stitch it. There was no reason to wait for someone else to put in the stitches."

"He did a fabulous job. Lovely pattern," Naina said as she swept Taid's hair away from the row of sutures. "Adds character, don't you agree?"

Taid batted Naina's hand away. "She's a celebrity, that daughter of yours. Everyone on the lake's talking about how fast she sprinted down the trail to save me. They've been stopping by all week to hear the story. Even folks we don't know, right, wyres melys?"

Beth nodded, dug her hands deeper between her legs.

"Only casualty is part of the propeller, but with all the fish these ladies have reeled in, we won't need to troll for at least a week while it's fixed." As he rambled on about visiting the boat harbor in town, deep concern settled on her parents' faces. Beth waited for her mother to explode in her usual diatribe of fears, all the places and things she couldn't control at the lake to keep her family safe. Dylan glanced at Beth, and they both knew it was worse when their mother didn't say anything. Finally, Taid ran out of words, and Evan spoke.

"We hoped you were having an adventure with Naina and Taid, but we had no clue you were the family's shining hero as well," he said. "We're so proud of you, Beth."

Taid lifted his glass. "Iechyd da! Cheers!"

Dylan panicked in Beth's bedroom later that night, after Taid and Naina had gone to bed. He paced the perimeter of the room, shooting glances at his parents and Beth on each pass, as Kate demanded that Beth tell the story again. She interrupted with questions to confirm that the accident had been as dangerous as Kate imagined it, and didn't hide her tears by the time Beth was done.

"Between this and the hostility those Ojibwe artifacts have created in our family, I don't know how to feel safe or happy here," Kate said.

Evan wrapped his arm around her shoulders. "We have to look at all the positives. Beth did everything right when she saved Taid—her instincts told her exactly what to do in an emergency."

Kate shook her head and turned toward her husband. "I can't help but think of how we'd feel right now if something worse had happened to Taid, or to Beth. How many emergencies do we have to have before anyone listens to *me*?" She pulled away from Evan and rubbed her hands back and forth along her thighs. "It's not just all the regular dangers from the rocks and the water. What about the Ojibwe belief that those rock spirits will take back what they think is theirs if their sacred space is disrupted?"

"But it didn't happen on the island, Mom. It was on Llyndee's Peak," Beth said. Kate's fears negated everything that Beth had done right in Taid's emergency—her mom was looking for any reason to see the worst.

Kate stared at Beth, then at Evan and Dylan, who had stopped pacing to hear their mother's response.

"I'm not sure that matters," said Kate. "If there's a curse or someone wants revenge, they'll do it wherever it's possible. I feel silly even suggesting that some rock paintings have powers, and at home I could convince myself it was all nonsense. But this incident terrifies me."

Last summer, the family had collected several artifact pieces from the pile Beth had created and taken more photos of the red paintings on the boulder. The pieces and photos sat on the dining room table at home, where everyone took turns comparing the items to the artwork in the books from the barn. At Thanksgiving they'd agreed that the stick figure paintings on the rocks with their arms raised depicted medicine manitous, the Ojibwe spirits who inhabited special rocks where the sky, earth, water, and underground came together. The decaying wood and birch bark cylinders were drums, the beating sticks engraved with birds, moose, and suns that matched the rock drawings. The books said that members visited the spirit rock to sing and ask for guidance, to bring fish to the lake or health for their people.

Dylan was fascinated by the artwork and mythology, excited that an important Ojibwe relic was on their island. He felt their research proved that they had to reveal what they'd found, but Taid was even more convinced they'd lose the island forever if anyone told Lily's father. The family's arguments had grown dark and angry at Thanksgiving and Christmas, Evan trying to mediate between Taid and Dylan's demands without success. By Easter no one dared bring it up and ruin another holiday meal. Beth could hear her brother and sister talking late at night throughout the spring, when Dylan's occasional raised voice sent Taid's name through the wall she shared with Maegan. The one time she'd tried to join the conversation, they'd shooed her away, claiming they were talking about school stuff.

Beth knew her grandfather had met with his attorney and had some kind of papers drawn up, but he refused to discuss it further—the war had taught him that once a decision is made, you stick to it, right or wrong. "That's the only way to survive," he'd said. She wondered if Taid's war nightmares ever left him, even on their beloved island.

Evan stood. "Taid's accident has shocked and surprised us, and our imaginations are running wild. Let's go to bed and get a fresh start to the summer tomorrow."

Beth's parents filed out of the room, and Dylan followed. She watched his bedroom door slide closed and collapsed onto her bed, her knees and arms pulled tightly to her chest. She stayed locked in position long after the loons had ended their mellow wails across the bays.

The next morning the cabin felt claustrophobic, like a vacuum had sucked out the air and filled it with thick human energy. Even without Maegan in the bedroom—she would arrive later in the week after summer semester was over—the frenetic air woke Beth early. She needed refuge in her fort. Was it because of her mother's reaction to Taid's accident that she wanted to escape? Or was it simply the mix of personalities after such a relaxed, loving time with her grandparents? Taid would be fine, and he and Naina were fighting any residual fears they might harbor for their safety at the lake, especially at their advancing ages, as best they could. If they could resist the urge to panic and celebrate that everyone was okay, why couldn't her mom do that too?

Beth dressed and tiptoed to the kitchen. She was making a sandwich when Dylan came in to load cookies, an orange, and a banana into his canvas satchel. He grinned when he saw her and pulled her into a tight hug. She'd grown used to him disappearing early in the mornings and again at dusk to paint, and now with Lily in the afternoons. After spending time with them last summer, she understood why—they had a connection, a bond, something entirely different from what Maegan had with Brian. He would likely escape to see her every day this summer, where he would feel safe. Beth squeezed his taut middle.

"You did good," he whispered. "No matter what she says or does, be proud."

"It was so scary, but Taid's okay. And now Mom's making it into something so much worse. How do we stop her from ruining the summer, Dyl?"

"We'll figure it out. If Dad can't reason with her, we'll make it right for each other. You, me, and Maegan. I promise."

She nodded. "Where are you headed?"

Dylan released her and hung his bag across his body. "The south shore. Nice shadows over there in the morning. Lily works until two, so I'll be around until then."

"I'm heading up too. I'll meet you at the stairs." She glanced at her parents and grandparents still sleeping in their rooms as she collected her books from the bedroom nightstand and used the back door to reach the island's interior. Strange how she was always more comfortable now on the island than in the cabin, just as Dylan had been all along.

They shared the main trail until it led steeply uphill. Dylan turned south toward a rockslide and its lowest stretches to catch the last of the sunrise. Beth watched him stroll over the wild array of rocks as if they were a smooth sidewalk, his memory and hips easily leading the way. She veered off the main path to hike in a Z pattern up to her fort, Dylan's words energizing her. She crisscrossed the island's width to collect blueberries, check out nearby shore residents' activities as they started their day, and watch the colors change on Llyndee's Peak as the sun rose higher in the brightening sky. Everything would be fine. It had to be.

When she arrived at the island's top, she walked past her fort to the rock paintings. The dull red figures kept their proud poses like every other time she'd looked at them, but this time her mother's fears rang in her ears. Could these really bring pain and retribution to her family, just because she'd disturbed the drums? Every member of Lily and Amik's family had been polite with her, if not kind. Would ancient members really want to do her family harm? Could they?

"They can't. They wouldn't," she murmured, shaking her head.

Sam's head popped up from his nest, which he'd rebuilt in the same small depression in the boulder where it was washed away last summer. He hopped toward her and waited for her to sit down and open her bag.

"You know, you're going to get fat on all this bread," she said as she broke up several tiny pieces of her sandwich and tossed them toward his foot, knowing he'd squawk endlessly until she fed him. Once Sam was content, she settled on the blanket to read her grandmother's literature textbook from primary school with Welsh writer Dafydd ap Gwilym's poems and Dylan Thomas's short stories. Naina's schoolgirl notes in the margins were as enlightening as the poems themselves.

She stopped reading when Dylan walked up a few hours later with paints and paper in hand, struck silent by his request. Dylan had never drawn any of them, not once. She pulled her knees to her chest and crossed her arms loosely over them as he painted her and the surrounding cedars, pines, and silver birches, the rocks and moss she knew as if they were a part of her. She was amazed at what he created—that he captured her so completely, from the subtle freckles on her nose and specks of gold in her dark chocolate eyes to the still pink scar on her right knee from shaving her legs for the first time. He laughed when she pointed to the addition of her right hand caressing the moss next to her blanket, a habit when she read.

"I've watched you a few times, which makes up for the hundreds of times you've spied on me."

Sam had flown away as soon as Dylan appeared, but he added him in the background, just a few strokes of white and gray but clearly her silly bird. Her jaw dropped when she handed the painting back to him and he told her to keep it. He never shared his paintings willingly.

"Don't want to keep a painting of me, huh? So why'd you paint it?"

"I'd love to have it to remember how you look when you're here, when you're home. But you should keep it."

Her gaze jumped from the painting to his face. Fear filled his eyes, but there was anger in his scowl. "She has to know how much all of this means to us, Dyl. She has to."

Dylan grabbed handfuls of pine needles and threw them down the hillside. "Mom's always sure she has the right to control everyone because she knows best. You heard her. She'll do whatever it takes to keep her family together and safe."

"This is the only place where we *are* together anymore. Taid's accident should prove to her that I can take care of myself. We all can now."

Dylan shook his head. "She doesn't know how to trust something she's so scared of losing. But it's her *and* Taid's ridiculous fears that will ruin it all if they don't listen to me."

He threw more piles of pine needles as they sat in silence. When he stood, his eyes had regained their normal calm. "You've always been the one who believes in our family no matter what, Bethie. You look out, but the rest of us look in, not always in a good way." He squatted in front of her, covering her knees with his long fingers and wide palms. "If this gets ugly and it takes a while for Maegan and me to make it right, look at that painting. Look in to remember, Bethie, look in."

He stood and turned for the north shore, following the sun and shadows.

When Beth returned to the cabin, she expected to find her parents and grandparents following their normal early afternoon habits: Evan working on his wooden boat, Kate reading on the porch, and her grandparents parked in the Adirondack chairs for their afternoon naps. Instead, raucous laughter echoed through the trees as she reached the lower trail. She followed the sounds to the north deck, where they and Aunt Betty were sitting around a circular card table. Thick brown bottles of Red Cap ale sat at each person's elbow, along with small plates of cheese and grapes. Stacks of red or white plastic poker chips filled the table next to Taid. He had to be the dealer, given the smirk on his face.

"How many cards would you like, my love?" he said to Naina. She stared at her cards and lowered three to the table. He nodded to Kate, who rapped the table with her knuckles.

Taid didn't let that go by. "Ooh, look out, Kate's hot again. No cards? I fear for the rest of you."

Beth looked at the neatly piled stacks of chips in front of her mother, almost twice as many as were scattered in front of her dad, grandmother, or Aunt Betty. She didn't know her mom knew how to play poker.

Kate drank from her beer bottle, intent on her cards, and didn't notice Beth until Taid waved her over.

"You want in? Your mom's running the table. You may be sharp enough to beat her."

Beth watched as her mom and Aunt Betty called and raised each other until the older woman had put in all but two of her chips. The group roared as they finally turned over their cards: three kings for Aunt Betty, three aces for Kate. She reached across the table with both arms to slide over her winnings and stack them into a new pile.

"Gee, Aunt Betty, do you need a temporary loan? I have a few extra chips I could head in your direction, for a fair price," Kate said. She winked at Beth as the group howled.

"You in or out, Beth?" Taid said.

She looked at the lake and the perfect sailing ripples that had brought her back to the cabin. "Tough choice, but sailing wins." She looked at her mother, expecting her normal list of safety instructions and demands.

"Please wear your life jacket, dear, and have fun."

Beth waited, assuming she would tell Evan that he had to go with Beth or that she could only sail where they could see her. When Kate simply smiled at her and picked up the cards Taid dealt to her, Beth looked at her dad. "What gives?" she mouthed at him.

Evan stood. "Count me out this hand; I'll help Beth get the sailboat out." He wrapped his arm around Beth's shoulders, and they walked into the cabin together. Once they were safely out of earshot in the bedroom hallway, Beth turned to her dad. "So?"

"We talked late last night, and I have your mom's promise that she will try to put aside her fears and enjoy this summer with her family. I know we can help her have fun up here again, just like Naina and Taid and Aunt Betty are doing with the card game. If we include her more, I think she'll come out of this negative maze she's built around herself."

"What about the Ojibwe stuff?"

"That's where you come in. Dylan has to keep his promise and not tell Lily or anyone else. I think if we can keep that quiet this summer, we can address it over the winter with Taid and make some progress. We need one good summer to get back on an even keel."

"They deserve to know what's up there," Beth said. "You know that as much as I do, even if it scares me."

"Yep, but let your grandfather heal and your mom have fun up here again. Tiny steps this summer, bigger ones next year. Deal?"

Beth hugged him. "Thanks, Dad. I knew you'd figure something out."

Evan pointed to her bedroom. "Get your suit on, and I'll help you raise the sail."

Beth changed, grabbed a beach towel, and ran to the dock. Evan had raised the mainsail and held the boat at the dock, pointed into the wind. She hopped into the sailboat, threw the life jacket from the boat's hull over her shoulders, pushed the tiller to the right, and pulled in the mainsail. The wind billowed through the sail and she was off, headed southwest.

Within minutes, she passed Ben's cabin. He was sitting in a low canvas chair on his dock, reading. They waved and Ben yelled, "Ferns are almost ready for picking."

"I'll be over tomorrow," she yelled back. She was headed straight west now, the steady breeze a taut, full pressure on the mainsail. Beth lifted her face to the sun and wind and closed her eyes. Everything would be fine now, thanks to her dad. She and Dylan could go to the bonfire tonight, and the rest of the summer would be perfect. She breathed deeply, her body relaxing for the first time since her parents arrived.

As she tacked to the northwest, she noticed a gray canoe in the distance. Whoever was in it seemed to be paddling in her direction. After she glanced back several times, she recognized Amik's dark hair and wide bright smile and came about so their paths would cross. She let out the sail and turned into the wind as they reached each other. He grabbed the bow of the sailboat and pulled himself alongside until he sat next to her.

"I wasn't sure if I'd see you again after you and Taid showed up at Uncle Ben's," he said.

"Yeah, that was pretty wild. I'm amazed he wasn't hurt worse, with how old he is and how far he fell, but he'll be okay." She pulled her thighs together and looked at her feet. Why hadn't she headed east, and why hadn't she worn her new bikini? Suddenly, the one-piece suit she had on felt way too small. And tight. She fought the urge to pull up on the shoulder straps.

Amik waited until she looked at him again. "Why haven't you and Dylan been to the bonfires? Why such a stranger?"

Beth tried to smile and wave him off. "I was up with just my grandparents, helping them open the cabin, so we were really busy. Dylan came up yesterday. He's probably with Lily now."

"Of course he is. I saw them walking the trails behind our cabin an hour ago. That's how I knew this must be you sailing." He switched hands to hold the two boats together and put his left hand over hers. "*Aaniin* Beth, nice to see you again."

Beth hid her blushing by turning her head so the wind blew her hair across her face, and used it as an excuse to pull her hand from Amik's to twist it into a high bun. She'd forgotten how his voice had affected her last summer, low and as smooth as a silk scarf she kept in a drawer and took out only for special occasions. "Great to see you too, Amik. What's new?"

"Not much, same old stuff. My dad worked in the Sault all winter at the mill, so I was stuck cutting logs to keep the cabin warm." He raised his right arm and flexed his bicep. "Paid off though, don't you think?"

Beth tried not to stare at the bulging muscle. "Impressive."

"Oh, and Ben and the chief met last week with some researcher from Toronto who found a bunch of rock petroglyphs over on Round Lake. It sounds pretty cool. Maybe you can come with us to see them tomorrow. I bet Dylan will come with Lily."

Beth sat up to stop her stomach muscles from clenching as she tried to sound nonchalant. "I think I read about those in a book Maegan bought last summer."

"They're usually on high cliffs, away from people. I guess they're considered sacred by the elders, part of our heritage and all that. My grandfather said his family used to go to one nearby all the time, but he can't remember where."

Sweat exploded through every one of Beth's pores. It settled on her skin and cooled in the steady breeze. She shivered. "Why would they go to one?"

"That's the cool thing. These engravings and paintings were done maybe hundreds or thousands of years ago, right? And you can still see them. They're on specific rocks that hold healing powers. My great-grandmother was cured of some illness after her family went to a rock on the lake every day for a week. My grandfather can't remember where it is now, but he swears it's on Wigwakobi, not Round Lake."

Beth watched Amik as he talked. His belief in the spirit rock's ability to heal was clear. "So, singing and playing drums to some rock really worked?"

Amik paused. "How'd you know about the singing and drums?"

Beth looked away again, pretended to tighten the mainsail's sheet. Crap. "Maybe it was in the books. I don't remember. Everyone's always pulling out drums at the bonfires when they play music, so I guess I figured that's what they did there too. Sorry, go on." *Shut up*, she yelled to herself, *shut up!*

She listened as Amik told her about the paintings at Round Lake, silently comparing them to what she'd found. The same circles, moose with lines going straight up from their backs, thunderbirds, and turtles. Double crap. As he stood up to replicate the stance of the men on the rock, a gust of wind caught the sail and whipped it toward him. She grabbed for the sheet but didn't catch it in time, and the metal boom hit him square in the stomach, hurtling him backward into the water.

"Oh my God, I'm so sorry!" She waited for him to come up and grabbed the end of the canoe so it didn't drift away. "Amik? Where are you?"

The other side of the sailboat angled sharply downward. She turned in time to see his laughing eyes looking up at her before the boat's lean was too steep and she slid sideways into the lake. As she came to the surface, she reached for the sailboat and splashed Amik with the other hand.

"No fair, that was an accident!"

"Right. Anything you say, Beth Llyndee."

"I'm telling the truth, Amik—" She didn't know his last name.

"Akeene, just like Lily. We're cousins, remember?"

"I know, but I didn't know how." She swam to the other side of the sailboat and rested her forearms on top, mirroring Amik. "So do your names mean anything in Ojibwe?"

"The old tradition is to name children after things in nature. My uncle's name, Makwa, means bear. I guess his parents must have known that he was going to be a big guy. My first name is embarrassing. It means beaver. My parents claim the animal is revered for its tenaciousness and strength, but my friends tease me about it. Maybe I'll change my name to Tom or something when I'm older."

Beth laughed. "I like it. Amik Akeene sounds good together." They floated on either side of the sailboat for a few minutes, until she tried to fill the empty space again. "Did you say hello earlier?"

Amik nodded and reached across the sailboat to cover her hand again. "We say *Aaniin*, or *Boozhoo*, for hello, but it really means 'I see your light.'"

Beth blushed but squeezed Amik's hand back. "My grandfather always tells me I'm the one living up to our last name, which sort of means 'lake goddess' in Welsh. That's just as dumb."

He pointed to his canoe floating along the south shore. "Now's your chance to prove it, lake goddess, and take me to my canoe. I'm not swimming that far."

Beth lifted herself into the sailboat and leaned to the other side while Amik did the same. Her wet, tight bathing suit was probably exposing her as much as his wet T-shirt and jeans, so she reached for the towel in the hull. Amik leaned in, and she held her breath as his lips pressed on hers. She stayed still, waiting until he pulled away. When he did, they smiled briefly at each other, and Amik pointed at his canoe. Her first kiss, and Maegan wasn't here to talk about it.

She avoided looking at him as she wrapped the towel around her body and pushed the tiller to the right to head in the canoe's direction.

"I've never sailed before. What do I do?"

Beth pointed to the front of the hull. "Sit there. I can do everything."

Amik switched seats and watched as she adjusted the tiller and sheet until the wind caught. She came close to the canoe on her first pass but decided to come about once so Amik could see how well she could sail. On her second try she steered it perfectly to the canoe's windward side.

Amik grabbed his canoe. "I'm impressed. You are a lake goddess."

Beth shook her head. "Dad taught us how to sail. Maegan's even better."

"Glad we ran into each other. Let's do this again. Soon." He leaned toward her, and Beth lifted her head slightly to meet his kiss. Amik reached his hand around the back of her head and kissed her harder, longer. When she felt his tongue pushing on her lips, she jumped slightly, and he pulled away.

"You and Dylan are coming to the bonfire tonight, right?"

Beth looked at his hand holding the canoe. He had long, thick fingers, huge knuckles. The ones that had just wrapped themselves through her hair. She shook her head to regain her composure. "We may have to stay home if Maegan's coming. I'm not sure when she's supposed to get here." Maegan wouldn't arrive for two more days, but Beth didn't know how she felt about going tonight. Scared, excited, nervous. Amik was almost two years older than she. What if he wanted her to do things she didn't know how to do? She needed to talk with Maegan.

"Come if you can. My uncle's going to tell everyone what they found, and then we're going to celebrate."

She nodded, and he squeezed her hand before climbing into the canoe. He watched as she adjusted the sail and tiller again, grabbed the wind, and sailed away. She was glad her back was to him so he couldn't see her huge smile as she steered toward her island in the distance.

Dylan and Beth went to the bonfire that night and the following. Amik was by her side, held her hand often, but only kissed her a few times when they walked in the dark by the dock. Ben hovered nearby. She tried to tell herself it was out of a sense of paternal responsibility rather than how she had reacted to the Ojibwe art book last summer, or to what Lily's father had told everyone at the bonfire.

"Tonight, we celebrate, for our families have been reunited with loved ones from long ago," Chief Akeene said. He held up two boxes made of birch bark and beads. Amik whispered that the boxes carried loved ones' remains, and by searching their records, they identified who would have lived by Round Lake almost a century ago. The chief handed the boxes to two women. Beth smiled, relieved that they hadn't found any boxes on the island. Maybe the stuff she found didn't mean anything.

"How blessed we are to find this home of the manitous, where we can pray for their protection and guidance. It holds the great paintings of Kitchemanitou, the sun and all that is good; Miship-izheu, the protector of our precious waters; and our most powerful manitou, the Thunderbird. With our medicine drums we offer songs to the manitous as gifts, and they will answer our prayers."

Several older men raised large versions of the drums she'd found on the island and beat them with the same decorated sticks. The crowd cheered, and Amik wrapped his arms around Beth and lifted her into the air. She grinned and pretended to be excited even as her guilt and fear deepened. Dylan looked even more conflicted. His brow stayed tightly furrowed as he listened, staring at the ground or looking sideways past Lily and Amik to Beth. Every time their eyes connected, he shook his head.

She stayed near Dylan both evenings in spite of Amik's interest in moving away from the crowd. Taid and Evan had kept

Dylan busy both days helping to repair the docks, but she feared he would tell Lily everything when they were alone. The first night was easier because of the dancing and celebration. The second night the bonfire was subdued and relaxed, and she couldn't find enough excuses to keep Lily and Dylan from wandering off. When they stood again to leave the bonfire, she jumped from her log seat and suggested they go with them. Dylan yanked her from the crowd, his back to the bonfire. She could see Amik and Lily watching them, surprised and confused by their actions.

"You're fine, and so am I," Dylan hissed into her ear. "I have *everything* at stake here, remember?" His stare challenged her, demanded that she be as strong as he had to be. "Don't blow this. I know how to make this work out in the end, but you *have* to act normal and do what I say." His hand tightened around her elbow.

"But, Dylan, I don't know what you're planning. Amik—"

He grabbed her other elbow. "You're fine with him. He won't do anything you don't want him to, I promise. Just don't let him bring up what we heard last night. Promise me, Bethie."

She nodded several times and swallowed hard, frightened for the first time by her brother.

He wrapped her in his arms and held her until she stopped shaking. She fought to relax the fear out of her face and was relieved when he released her, and the calm she was used to seeing in his eyes had returned. They walked back to the fire. Lily and Amik were standing next to each other.

"Sorry," Dylan chuckled. "Just a small sibling spat. Lily, you ready?"

She nodded and touched Beth's arm lightly as she passed. Within seconds they disappeared into the woods. Amik kept his distance when they sat down on the log again, and even invited Ben to join them. They talked about a new trail they were building to connect Ben's cabin to the row of Ojibwe homes surrounding Lily's family, at least three miles apart. Ben was paying Amik to help him, and for the first time Beth wondered how Ben made a living. She listened, worried that Amik was ignoring her.

By the time Ben left, she'd decided to make the first move and inched closer to Amik, hoping he would take her hand again. Instead he glanced at her in surprise and reached for a stick to poke at the fire. She tried to fill the space by telling him about loon diving with Ben the previous summer, the huge whitefish her grandmother caught trolling earlier in the week, anything to get him to talk. Nothing worked. She slumped into herself, dug her hands between her thighs, and chewed on the inside of her cheek.

Amik turned to her a few times as if he was going to say something, but he stopped every time he looked at her. Her heart imagined the worst, that somehow he'd learned about what was on the island, overheard her and Dylan's conversation, even if her mind knew that was impossible. It had to be something Dylan said to him—that she was too young and inexperienced. As she reached for his arm, a group of Amik's older male cousins walked up.

"Dude, better party's going on over at Nootan's place. You in?" Amik stood. "Yeah. I'll catch up."

The boys turned and walked along the shore, disappearing in the darkness beyond the bonfire. Amik turned to her and shoved both hands deep into his jeans' pockets.

"I guess I better go. You'll be fine here until Dylan gets back, right?"

Beth stood and stepped closer to him. "Can I come with you?"

He shuffled his feet backward and grimaced at her. "They're older. Probably better not."

"So that's what this is about? I'm too young and naïve? You didn't think so a few days ago on the sailboat, or last night. What did Dylan say to you?" She wrapped her arms around her chest and let her anger, fear, and disappointment shoot from her eyes to his.

Amik raised both hands and stepped farther back. "Whoa, take a break, Beth. Dylan didn't say anything I didn't already know. But blood's thicker than water, you know?" He shot his own anger back at her. "You and Dylan know that, and so do we."

Beth looked at him, confused by his words. What was he talking about?

"Whatever, I'm out of here. Thanks for the good time. Let's try it again sometime." He waved slightly and walked into the night.

Early the next morning, Beth sensed that Naina was standing by her bed. She didn't want to go trolling, didn't want to see or talk with anyone. Dylan had refused to tell her everything he'd said to Amik as they tied the boat to the south dock last night, only that he'd told him to take things slow with her or he'd scare her away.

"So, nothing about our parents disapproving of us at their bonfires? Nothing about how I'm stupid and naïve about boys?"

Dylan shook his head.

"You don't need to tell anyone to go slow with me."

Dylan howled, "I didn't mean it *that* way. I said that you're independent, used to doing what you want. If he put demands on your time, you might run the other way."

Beth stopped short, considered what he was saying. "So, what did he say back?"

"Not much." He grinned at her. "Great night for me, by the way. Everything's coming together just like I want." He spun around and hopped up the rock steps toward the cabin.

She'd run after him, poked at him to tell her his plans all the way to his bedroom, where he'd smiled and slid the door closed.

Her head had spun with crazy thoughts the rest of the night—dreams of being with Amik, of his grandfather remembering it was the island he'd come to as a kid to pray to the manitous, of the look on her mother's face if she knew her first kiss had been with an Ojibwe boy. It wasn't out of prejudice, her mother had explained long ago, when she'd first found out about Dylan spending time with Lily. "They are destined for separate lives, and I don't want either of them to be hurt," she'd said to Beth. "Lily's mother agrees with me; she sees reality." How did their moms know what kind of life they would or should have?

She was exhausted by the clash between her mother's perceptions and reality, and by the vividness of her dreams. Just this once, she'd pretend to be asleep and let her dad go with Naina. After a few moments, Naina lightly patted her shoulder and walked out of the room.

When an odd horn woke her, the high sun and quiet in the cabin told her she'd slept much later than she intended. She went to the north deck and saw her grandparents and mother on the dock, cheering as Dylan helped Evan and his Port Carling wooden boat slide into the lake from the boathouse floor. The rich mahogany her dad had covered with a dozen layers of stain and polish glistened in the sunlight, the brass horn on the front bow gleamed, and the small Canadian and American flags on either side of the stern sashayed in the light breeze. He turned the key, and the inboard engine's deep rumble rose out of the water. Beth waved and cheered, and he beamed at her with a thumbs-up.

By the time she ran to the dock, he'd idled to its end to pick up Kate and had taken off for the north shore. "Where's he going?"

Taid and Naina stood arm in arm watching the boat's high back spray. "Just checking out the engine to make sure it's set right," Taid said. "Probably swing by the Shepplers' so they can have a peek at it before they pick up Maegan on shore. That boat's a beauty, isn't it? Our son did us proud."

Maegan! She couldn't wait to tell her sister everything so they could figure out why Amik had been so weird last night. She ran inside to clean their bedroom and found Dylan in the hallway.

"They'll be back with Maegan in a half hour. You staying?"

Dylan waved as he walked past her. "Nope, Lily's waiting. See you tonight at dinner."

"Tell Amik he's wrong about whatever he thought happened last night," she yelled at his back. He waved again as he turned into the kitchen and disappeared.

The family spent most of the next two days together, parents and grandparents questioning Maegan about almost every day of her freshman year at Northwestern University—her classes, Chicago, her friends and professors. Kate was elated that her eldest daughter was attending a challenging college, and even happier she'd broken up with Brian the summer before. "Enough of that wild boy in our lives," she'd said.

Dylan stayed home to play the family's traditional first-night-of-vacation game of hearts around the dining room table. He and Maegan took off in the powerboat the next two days. Beth tried to go the second time, but they waved her off, said they'd be back in a few minutes after they dropped Naina and their mom on shore to go to town for groceries. That had been two hours before. She'd never seen them willingly spend so much time together, couldn't imagine what they were doing or why no one else had noticed what was happening. When she'd tried to tell Maegan about Amik the first night in bed, Maegan hadn't stayed awake long enough to talk. Beth had thrown a pillow at her, but she'd just moaned and rolled over, hugging Beth's pillow. "Too tired," she'd said.

Beth waited for them to return on the deck, where she was finishing the Lammas Day invitations for Taid and Evan to deliver that afternoon. When she was done, she helped to decorate the wooden boat with red, green, and white streamers and to tie the Welsh flag over the bow. While the two men rambled on about Taid's ideas for a bigger, grander Lammas Day celebration,

Beth used the binoculars to try to spot the powerboat. Where had they gone?

She gave up and lay down on the dock. Maegan always sunned on the south dock and got lots of attention—maybe Amik would ride by and notice her. She breathed deeply and let herself enjoy the sun warming her skin. The men kept talking as they moved from the boat to the boathouse to tinker with something, walking by Beth as if it were nothing new to see her sunning on the dock. Everyone had gone crazy in this family.

She heard the low hum of Ben's boat engine moments before the twang of the powerboat mixed in. Ben was coming around the island's north side. She forced herself to lie flat when the powerboat idled up beside her, as if she didn't care where her siblings had gone. Maegan laughed as the bow's rope thwacked Beth in the stomach.

"Don't think you can take over my spot," Maegan said. "Tie us up, will you?"

"Thanks for leaving me, once again," Beth said as she pulled the rope to the forward ring.

Maegan got out of the boat and patted Beth on the head. Beth shoved her sister's arm away from her. "Don't be nasty," Maegan said. "What we're doing has nothing to do with you, at least not right now. Don't make it a big deal."

"But it is. Before you got here, I was part of everything, including the bonfires. You don't know about anything I've done this summer. Tell her, Dylan."

Dylan wasn't listening. His face was ashen as he stood paralyzed in the boat, looking toward the north dock. Beth and Maegan swung around and saw Ben and Lily's father standing together by the fire pit.

"Welcome back, Maegan," Ben said. "Can you find your grandfather and father for us, please?"

Taid and Evan walked out of the boathouse and stood about five feet from the men. Beth felt as if she'd been hit by lightning—electricity whipped up her spine, through her brain, and to every nerve ending. Only her fingers twitched as the current tried to escape. No one in her family moved.

Ben filled the void. "Padrig, Evan, I'd like you to meet Chief Makwa Akeene, my sister's husband."

Dylan rushed past his sisters. "Dad, Taid, this is Lily's father."

"Yes, I see, Dylan," Evan said, stepping forward to shake the chief's hand. "We've met your wife at our Lammas Day celebrations, and as you can see by the decorations on the boat, we were just about to deliver our annual invitations. We hope you'll join us this year. Beth, do you have their invitation?"

Maegan's hand pressed on Beth's back, forcing her to move. She ran to the porch to her stack of invitations sitting on the railing, held in place by a large rock. Several fell on the ground as her shaking hands rifled through the pile. As she bent to grab them before the wind could carry them away, Maegan crouched next to her.

"You go. I'll clean these up," Maegan whispered. "Act like you don't know anything, and it will be okay."

Beth looked at her sister and nodded, relieved that Maegan was there to lead the way. She ran down the hill and handed the invitation to the chief.

"It's for your whole family, of course," she said.

Chief Akeene tipped his head at Beth. "Thank you. We appreciate the invitation." He turned toward Evan and Taid, who still stood just outside the boathouse door. "I apologize for intruding on your day, but we've learned of a possible healing site on this island, and we believe you know where it is."

"What right do you have coming here to claim something like this?" Taid said as he walked forward.

Dylan jumped at Taid's words. Beth stepped next to her brother and tried to show him the same confidence Maegan had given her. He glanced at her but missed her intent, his panicked eyes jumping from their grandfather to the chief.

Evan grabbed his father's arm to stop him from walking any closer to Ben and the chief. For the first time Beth realized that the chief was the same height as her grandfather. She'd never seen anyone else as tall as Taid.

"We've recently discovered a healing site with rock paintings and petroglyphs on Round Lake, and it reminded some of our elders that they visited such a place on this lake as well, on an island," the chief said. "We've searched the other islands but haven't found significant rock structures that would befit the home of medicine manitous."

He glanced at Beth and Ben. "I also understand your family has shown a rare interest in Ojibwe history lately."

While she was shocked that Ben would tell the chief about the books they'd purchased, she realized she already knew he'd figured it out. How could she have expected him not to wonder why she was looking at those pages so intently last summer and avoiding him this summer? He'd been to her fort many times and had seen the huge boulders at the island's top. He and Amik were building the trails together; certainly they'd talked. Was that why Amik mentioned blood and water the other night?

Ben returned her shocked stare with a gaze of kindness and apology. The guilt of what she'd hidden from him overwhelmed her, that her and her family's fears had stopped her from doing what was right with such a good friend. Their best friend up here, who also knew how much this island meant to her and to her family.

Dylan stepped between Evan and the chief and was about to speak when Evan shook his head at his son. Maegan had joined Beth and pulled Dylan to them. She kept her arm tightly around his waist.

"We recognize that this site must be very important to you, since you've come when you've chosen not to in the past, even when invited," Evan said. "I don't know if we have what you're looking for, but we've always been good neighbors on this lake and consider this our precious home, just as you consider your land sacred for your family. Before this goes any further, we need to agree on one point: my father and mother have legal ownership of this island."

Taid moved forward next to his son, crossed his arms in front of his chest, and waited. The chief took a step back and switched his gaze to Taid. Beth felt as if the waves, the breeze, even the birds had stopped moving, waiting for his reply.

"I respect your rights as owners of this island. I ask that we be allowed to see what of ours is here, so that we can determine how to move forward. Surely that is also fair."

"And if we tell you there's nothing of yours here?" Taid said. "Will you leave us be?"

The chief's back stiffened, and Ben stepped forward. "I wouldn't have brought Makwa here if I didn't know that he and his family are honorable, as I also know of you. I stake my friendship both ways, knowing both families will be honest and fair."

Evan looked at Taid, who nodded to his son before pointing at Ben. "I'm taking you at your word, and I will be honest and fair. But I'm telling you right now that I will not relinquish one inch of this island. I don't care what's up there or how important you think it is to you. Your people sold it to me over forty years ago, and it's not my problem if you didn't care enough to keep it."

The chief looked at Taid, taking in his words. "Perhaps after we've seen the site, we can all get the answers we seek," the chief said. Taid waved the men forward to the porch. Beth, Dylan, and Maegan followed until the chief stopped and whispered to Ben. The four elder men circled together on the porch, then turned in unison toward them.

"Dylan, you come with us," Evan said. "Maegan and Beth, you need to pick up your mom and grandmother on shore. They must be back from town by now."

"But that's not fair. I—" Beth stammered.

Maegan grabbed her arm. "That's fine, Dad," she said. "We'll go get them."

Beth watched the men slowly climb the steep stairs, Dylan leading the way.

By the time they returned from shore, Ben and the chief were gone. Maegan kept reassuring Beth on the boat ride that Dylan would know how to get Taid and the chief to agree, but Beth's gut told her otherwise. At dinner Evan confirmed that the rock paintings were of the medicine manitous, the same ones they'd found at Round Lake. They didn't disturb any of the drums and sticks, saying to do so would show disrespect to the medicine men.

"I knew we made a mistake moving those items," Kate said. "It terrifies me all over again, but I have to admit that I'm glad it's out in the open, and we don't have to carry this dreadful secret around anymore." Naina agreed, while Taid was as adamant as ever that he wasn't giving any part of the island to anyone.

"I'll give him this, though," Taid said. "A straight-up kind of guy, that chief. See why you like him, Dylan."

Dylan wasn't paying attention to anyone. He stayed in his room until dinner and left as soon as they were done. Beth knew he was going to see Lily and find out about her father's plans. She read with a flashlight late into the night, waiting for her brother to come home and tell her what was happening. When she woke at four, the book and lit flashlight on the bed next to her, Dylan still wasn't home. When Naina woke her to go trolling, Maegan was closing his bedroom's sliding door and walking back into their bedroom.

"Is everything okay?" Beth whispered.

Maegan nodded and waved Beth away. "I told you, we've got this. Stop being a pest."

As much as she wanted to believe her, Beth wasn't sure. She peeked through the crack between the door and the wall as she left with Naina. Dylan wasn't home.

When she and Naina returned without even a nibble, Dylan was walking out of the cabin with his art bag. Beth tried to stop him, but he turned and headed to the other dock. By the time she helped Naina out of the boat and ran toward him, he was paddling away in the canoe.

The rest of the family wasn't saying much either. "They can come get the drums, but that's it," Taid said. "We've got a Lammas Day to prepare for, and I've got great plans." Her parents said it was up to Chief Akeene and his First Nation to decide what they wanted, and the best the family could do was go on as though nothing had happened.

But Beth knew they weren't right. Dylan must be planning something. That neither of her siblings would tell her anything scared her, brought back all the ways she'd felt left out when she was younger. She was old enough to help, and they were shutting her out again.

Naina and Beth started their normal routine of making pies and breads. By midmorning, Beth told her grandmother they needed some fresh herbs for the bread and left to find them along Ben's trails. The lake was glass calm, and a quiet haze hung in the air. She reached his dock in minutes in the kayak and ran to his door. Ben or Amik would know what happened, and she needed to explain her side to them.

Ben didn't answer. He and Amik were probably working on the new trails. She walked along the shoreline to the first trail, thankful to be out of the cabin and by the water. She waded calf-deep to pick up a long stick floating near the shore, driftwood that had been caressed by the lake to a silky smoothness except for a few sharp nubbins that even the endless wash of waves couldn't wear down. She wanted the stick to be hers—to carry it along the trails, to the top of Llyndee's Peak; to keep it in the corner of her cabin bedroom and take it back to Ann Arbor, to reassure her that she would always be a part of everything here. But she knew Ben would tell her that the stick wasn't meant to be indoors, wasn't meant to be her promise of a safe future. She set it back down in Lake Wigwakobi and walked into the woods.

She saw Amik before he saw her and hid to watch him pull out and chop the shrubs and underbrush. She felt an instant attraction to the power and look of him at work. When the sensation became too strong, she stood, and he saw her.

"Come to help me on the last stretch?" Amik waved and smiled.

She jogged down the hill, relieved that he seemed happy to see her. "I was trespassing for some of Ben's ripe herbs."

He stared at her, and she alternated between the ground and the space just past his eyes. When he stepped to the left to meet her gaze, she tried to smile but grimaced instead.

"Did you know what we were hiding?"

Amik leaned on his shovel and nodded.

"I'm so sorry, Amik." She couldn't stop herself. "I just found them last summer and didn't realize how important the rock paintings were until I heard Chief Akeene talk about the other place. Dylan and I freaked out, and he couldn't get my grandfather to agree to show anyone. It was horrible, and—"

He pulled her body against his, his heat shivering through her. When he kissed her, she responded, relieved that he wasn't angry with her. His hands roamed her back, in her hair, and down to her thighs. She mimicked his moves.

As abruptly as he'd reached for her, he pulled away. "Shit," he whispered as he turned and walked down the path, his hands wrapped around the back of his head. She waited, afraid she'd done something wrong. When he turned, she tried to hide her confusion, but he saw it.

"I'm sorry. It's this whole thing. I don't know how it's going to turn out."

"I don't either. Have you heard anything?"

He walked back to her. "Just that the tribal elders are meeting this weekend to discuss their options. What you've got up there is probably older than the healing place on Round Lake. This could get really bad."

Beth frowned. "I wish I'd never found the stuff."

"Really?" His eyebrows rose, and he took a step away from her. "That place means a lot to my family. My grandfather can't wait to go back there, where he thinks the manitous saved his mom."

Beth kicked at the ground with her toe. "Of course you're right. But my grandfather's sure he doesn't have to let anyone onto his property, no matter how sacred the place may be." Tears started to well in her eyes, so she kicked harder to focus on the pain to her toes in hopes the tears would stop.

"Hey," Amik said as he reached for her hand.

Beth looked up at him. "I can't lose this place, Amik. My family and I couldn't bear it. Please don't let them take it from us." The tears ran down her face.

"It's not up to us. I wish it was. But no one really owns any of this land, you know? The manitous may decide for us, if your grandfather and my uncle aren't willing to bend."

Chapter Five: SUMMER 1990

" D ad, can't you drive faster?" Beth stared at the speedometer and sighed. Sitting in the front seat with the endless pavement in front of them made the hours driving north feel like days compared to when she sat in back, where her mother was now stretched out, sleeping.

"Not with the number of highway police out today. They must be preparing for the rush of Fourth of July travelers," Evan said. "Only fifteen more minutes and we'll reach the border. We should be there by three."

Beth had been anxious to get up to the island for three weeks, ever since Dylan left with Taid and Naina to open the cabin. She'd asked to come up early like last summer, but her parents had been adamant that Dylan go alone. "Good for them to spend time together, to talk and reconnect," Evan had said. Beth wasn't convinced.

The family may have found a conflicted sense of unity after the chief saw the Ojibwe relics and rock paintings on the island last summer, but that didn't mean Dylan and Taid agreed on what should happen next, or hesitated to remind the other how wrong he was. Dylan had researched Ojibwe rights in Canada and the United States over the winter and was shocked at how little recognition either country gave to Native Americans to own land that had been part of their heritage for generations. Where items of historical significance were discovered, the land often became a national park or preserve. What if the province of Ontario claimed rights to the island? What would the government do with it?

Taid had gone into overdrive, meeting with every attorney who knew anything about property rights in either country. Every possible deed and claim to the island was created in case the chief or province claimed rights to at least the island's west end. At the same time, he maintained his positive first impression of Lily's father and the respect he showed the family and its place on the island.

"No anger, no accusations, just wanted to see what was there," Taid had said. "Of course, that doesn't mean I'm bending on any of this. He and his clan can say whatever they want. It's our island."

That they hadn't heard from Taid or Dylan over the past three weeks made Beth even more on edge. Usually her grandparents called from the post office when they were in town for groceries, but not this time. What if Taid and her brother had argued to the point of no return, or her grandparents were realizing how close Dylan was with Lily? Taid's anger might spill into that relationship, and then Dylan would run away even faster, stay away from the family as much as he could. Stay away from Beth, then, too.

At least her mother's focus was elsewhere. Maegan and Brian had reunited, and Kate was adamant that her daughter was making a mistake. Beth wasn't sure they'd ever been apart. While Mrs. Sheppler was thrilled with the nice time Maegan showed her son whenever he went to Chicago—"Maegan's such a good influence on Brian, don't you think?"—Kate didn't hesitate to express her alarm and disappointment. "You're studying at one of the top universities in the world, and Brian can't even hold a steady job," she'd said to Maegan over Christmas break. "You must meet all sorts of great guys at college; why can't you focus on one of them instead?" Beth agreed with her mother on this one. She'd never understood what Maegan saw in Brian or why she would want to be with someone who just wanted to hang out all the time.

Maegan wouldn't join the family on the island until mid-July, after the early summer semester was over, so Kate had focused instead on getting Dylan to finish his college applications. Beth wasn't sure how Dylan felt about college anymore, since he'd dodged most conversations by telling their mother to do whatever she wanted and he'd decide later, when he knew his options. Kate had chosen three universities because they had excellent architecture schools, which she felt was how he should use his artistic ability. "You'll be a pauper as an artist," she'd claimed.

"Thanks for your confidence in me," he'd replied.

Beth's first priority was to find Dylan painting alone, when he could tell her how he really felt—about college, about Lily, and what his plan was to make everything work out between Taid and Lily's father. Then the conflict she'd created could finally be over.

She was impatient to see Amik too, to find out how he felt about the island now. Everyone knew something was up at last summer's Lammas celebration, a nervous curiosity hovering in the air. But her family had been enthusiastic hosts like always—Taid even more boisterous in his laughter and charm—and Lily and her mom hadn't shown signs of tension with Beth's family. Amik had even stopped by.

That last day on Ben's trails, she'd told him she would be back early this summer. Did Dylan tell him why she hadn't come? Would Amik even care anymore? He'd laughed at her suggestion that they write to each other over the winter. She'd written him four letters and gotten one brief note back.

Taid was waiting for them on the campground manager's porch, the old men sharing stories over ale. He sauntered down when they'd finished loading their belongings into the boat.

"Ah, the rest of my lovely brood has arrived. Ready to head back to heaven, Llyndees?" Beth relaxed when she saw his broad smile and twinkling eyes and folded into his waiting arms. From her perch in the boat's bow, the wind and lake's spray washed away the winter's worries. The faces on Llyndee's Peak gleamed in the midafternoon sun, almost smiling in spite of their piercing stares.

Dylan was sitting on the porch when they idled to the dock. Beth jumped and waved in wild circles as he had the previous summer, and he nodded and came to meet them. He smiled but avoided everyone's gaze.

"I trust you helped Taid around the cabin, rather than run off and paint all day," Kate said as he helped her out of the boat.

"He's done just fine," Taid said. "Three perfect grandchildren, a joy to have around."

Kate patted Dylan on the chest. "I brought all of your college applications."

Dylan lifted her bag out of the boat and set it in front of her. "Nice to see you too, Mom."

"Okay, let's have at least one day of peace, shall we?" Evan said as he hugged Dylan. "Where's Naina?"

Dylan nodded toward the cabin. "They're inside, making dinner. Beth and I will get the bags. You guys go ahead."

She watched the three adults walk up the steps before turning to her brother. "Who's 'they'?"

"Maegan. She's been here since spring term let out in early May. I'm guessing Brian was with her until we arrived."

"But she's supposed to be at school for summer semester."

"Yeah, no kidding. Taid and Naina told her they wouldn't cover for her, but they didn't make her go back." Dylan climbed into the boat and lifted another bag onto the dock. "We've actually had a pretty good time together. Brian's an okay guy, I guess; just drinks too much."

Beth couldn't believe what he was saying, about Maegan or Brian. No wonder no one had called to check in.

Dylan sat on the boat's back bench. "I'm in no hurry to go up there, are you?"

She wanted to hear Maegan's explanation but didn't want to absorb the tension and anger that had to be bouncing off the cabin's walls. She sat on the dock and turned toward the sun. "Taid seems happy."

"He's okay as long as no one brings up the artifacts. The few times I've tried to talk with him about it, he just nods and walks away. He's still adamant there's nothing to talk about and won't go to the Circle Barn or agree to meet with Lily's dad."

"What is the chief saying?"

"He's telling the elders to be patient until he and Taid can talk again, but they're pissed we didn't tell them right away, when we found the stuff."

"That's what I feel the worst about, especially since it was Amik's grandfather who remembered the place. Do they still welcome you at the bonfires?"

"For the most part. The chief's brothers don't like me much right now, but they've always been kind of standoffish. Amik's looking forward to having you back."

Beth tried to contain the grin erupting across her face. At least that part of her summer might work out. She looked up at the cabin and glanced at Dylan to gauge his mood, decided to take a chance. "And your plan?"

Dylan looked toward the lake's west end. "I've still got to put some key pieces in place. I know how to get Taid to talk with Chief Akeene, but I may need Ben's help to make it happen. Then the rest of the plan will fall in place. Mom's demands for college will be the last hurdle."

Beth was confused. "What does one have to do with the other?"

"They both decide my life, Bethie, that's all."

She peered at Dylan, but her chance to ask him to explain further evaporated as Maegan slammed the kitchen door and marched down to the dock. Dylan threw the remaining bags out of the boat, anticipating Maegan's next move. He climbed out as she hopped in.

"I'll be back for dinner, let them cool down," Maegan said as she pulled the engine's cord. She backed the boat away from the dock and turned to the east toward the Shepplers' cabin.

"I thought you guys were going to make everything right," Beth said.

Dylan sighed, his hands on his hips. "We will. It just doesn't look that way yet. Let's put the bags on the porch and canoe over to Ben's. Lily and Amik are waiting for us."

The days flew by. Dylan left early every morning, Maegan spent most afternoons at Brian's cabin, and Evan and Kate took long rides every afternoon in his Carling wooden boat. Beth trolled most mornings with Naina, read in her fort after breakfast with Sam hovering in his nest behind her, and spent afternoons swimming and sailing with Taid and her dad or hiking with Ben, Amik, Lily, and Dylan. They'd gone loon diving, climbed Llyndee's Peak several times, raced in their canoes and kayaks, and hiked to Round Lake to see the petroglyphs. The family returned to playing cards at least a few nights a week after Evan demanded a ban on island or college discussions when the cards came out. So far, it was working.

Every other night she and Dylan went to the west end bonfire. She sat with Amik and soaked up the exquisite moments: the lake's calm evening hum, constant and reassuring even in its blackness just beyond the blaze; the laughter, songs, and warmth of Amik's voice; the echo of barking gulls and trilling loons; and so many stars, as if the galaxies were holding a grand, illicit celebration after they thought the humans had gone to bed.

Dylan still hadn't told Beth his entire plan, but she'd gotten enough out of Naina on their morning trolls and from Amik at the bonfires to know that Taid and the chief were talking through Dylan and Lily. Taid still wanted to keep rights to the entire island, and the chief thought the western end should be given back, but he'd promised he wouldn't go to the local or provincial government until after they'd talked in person. When Lily's mom mentioned at a bonfire that she was concerned the elders might demand that the entire island be returned to them if Taid didn't step up soon, Beth chewed through at least three layers of her left cheek. Dylan had to make something happen soon.

She was heading up to her fort after breakfast in late July when her mother stopped her. "Beth, dear, can I ask for a favor today?"

Beth was surprised that her mother even noticed her. Between trying to convince Maegan that college mattered and Brian didn't, and chasing Dylan with college applications as he ran out the door every morning, Beth assumed she was the last thing on Kate's mind. "What's up?"

"You and Naina have such fun fishing every morning. Will you take me?"

Beth paused, trying to hide her shock. "Sure, but we can fish right off the dock for smallmouth bass or perch."

"I'd rather go someplace where no one will see me trying to worm my first hook."

Beth snickered at her mother's turn of phrase. Taid had taken all three grandchildren fishing along the southern section of Llyndee's Peak when they were little. They'd sat for hours and watched the rock bass and perch circle the hooks, then finally give in to temptation. "If you don't mind riding around the peak, there's a great rockslide on the south side where the smaller fish hang out."

"That sounds perfect. I'll get my sneakers and hat."

"You want to go now?" Beth wanted to finish her book and see how Sam was feeling. He had seemed off yesterday and didn't squawk hello or goodbye.

"Your dad went into town with Taid to refill the gas tanks and get my newspapers, and Aunt Betty just picked up Naina. So no one will know what we've been up to." She tapped Beth's shoulder as she walked toward the bedrooms. "I'll meet you at the boat."

Beth scanned the kitchen as if the walls and windows could restore her freedom. Silence. "Great," she mumbled. She threw her book on the counter, then reconsidered—maybe she could finish it while her mom fished. She collected her first fishing rod and her grandfather's tackle box from the boathouse and dug up a few thick, gooey worms with some soil from Naina's daisy and milkweed garden and shoved them into a small paper bag. Her mother was sitting with her normal perfect posture on the center bench, her large white cotton hat tied tightly under her chin to shade her entire face.

Kate watched Beth maneuver around the fallen rocks, idling to find the underwater crevices where the fish would hide. She asked Beth why she didn't anchor the boat ("easier to float and paddle back to our spot than get the anchor out of these rocks"), how deep they could see into the lake's depths ("probably forty or fifty feet"), why they used worms instead of bait for small fish ("because that's what Taid taught me"). Kate scowled at the worm's slimy black excretions when she stabbed it with the hook.

"You've wormed your first hook, Mom."

Kate's eyebrows shot up as she realized her mistake and laughed. Beth chuckled with her, then stared as her mother kept laughing, as if she were releasing months of pent-up energy. The last time she'd heard Kate laugh this freely or this long had been years ago, when they'd ridden bikes to Beth's first day of second grade. The elementary school was just three blocks away, and Kate had challenged her to a race. As they made the last turn, the bus Beth was supposed to be on turned in front of them—a massive yellow wall with hot exhaust that smelled like putrid rotten eggs. Kate had turned sharply in front of Beth to prevent the bus from hitting her and forced them into the only escape, the roadside ditch. Their front tires stabbed the deep trench, and both fell forward into the thick mud on its far side. Beth looked at her drenched new outfit, close to tears, but her mother was laughing—loud and with a vigor her reserved nature rarely allowed.

"Why are you laughing?" Beth had demanded. "My clothes are ruined, I'll be late for school, and everyone on the bus probably saw us."

Kate had waved away Beth's concerns, scooped up two chunks of mud, and plopped them on their heads. "I don't remember the last time we played in the mud. Do you?" She'd slapped her hands together, the dark brown goo flinging across the air onto their faces, and Kate had howled again. "Guess you'll need to call in sick today. Let's have a grand last day of summer together."

And they had—they'd waved at everyone staring at them on the ride home, sprayed each other with the garden hose to clean up, biked around the Huron River, and shopped for a second first-day outfit. They'd even stopped for an ice cream cone at the local Washtenaw Dairy before dinner. A carefree, remember-forever kind of day.

If her mom could laugh like this, maybe her dad's plan to help Kate relax on the island really was working.

After she explained how to lower the fishing line into the water and Kate understood the next step was to sit and wait, Beth opened her book and read, glancing up at a particular boulder as she turned the pages. Kate asked if that was where she'd saved Taid. Another surprise—she never expected her mother to phrase it that way.

Beth nodded and shuddered as she remembered his arm dangling at an ugly angle. Then she saw them: three eaglets hanging on to the edge of their nest, mother and father standing guard on nearby cliff landings. The parents' massive white heads flicked from the babies to the boat, alert for danger and ready to protect if needed. The eaglets peered over the nest's mound of twigs and thick sticks with round beady eyes, the tufts of fine gray fluff on their heads flopping up and down as they paced to gather their courage.

"Look, the eaglets are getting ready to fly for the first time," she whispered.

Kate followed Beth's gaze. "Those are eagles? Their heads aren't white."

"Yeah, they're gray until they're adults. These guys are only two months old. Ben and I have been tracking the parents for three years, and this is the first time all three chicks have survived. They build their nest there to keep raccoons from eating the eggs, but we think either the horned owls or ravens have gotten them before. The mom's stayed around more this summer, and she fights off the other birds better than the dad."

Beth pointed to the female, a head taller and wider than the male.

"How do you know they're the same eagles as last year?" Kate asked.

"They mate for life and use the same nest every year."

The female eagle leaned forward, lifted her wings, and chirped in a high rolling staccato at her young. One peeped back at her, spread its wings, and jumped. Beth and Kate held their breath as it seemed to sink toward the water. The father swooped, its massive wingspan creating a draft for the young bird's smaller wings to catch the air. The eaglet followed its father as he circled above the water twice before landing on a low boulder just above the lake.

Beth grinned and looked at her mom. Kate was mesmerized by the birds, the fishing rod forgotten as it hung loosely in her hand. They watched the other eaglets take their turns, one landing in the lake and hopping back to the cliff, while the other flung itself far enough into the air to catch the breeze. It flapped wildly in a wide circle and bounced off the nest's front wall before disappearing into its deep insides. The parents chirped and hooted their encouragement from rocks below the two eaglets as they flew in short bursts back up to the nest, then joined them. The babies took one last glance at Kate and Beth before their parents stood over them on top of the huge nest, nodding back and forth at each other as if they were comparing notes about their children's first foray into the world.

Beth told Kate to reel in the line so they could check the hook. The worm was gone. Her mom shoved another onto the hook and tossed it back into the lake, promising to focus on her line. Beth read.

After several minutes Kate looked up at the nest and sighed. "When it comes to children, parents are just instinct and hope and fear. Even for those majestic birds."

Beth waited.

Kate played with the reel, pulling the line up a bit and back down. Her lips were puckered together, which usually meant she was about to make what Kate thought was an important point. When she finally spoke, Beth had to lean forward to hear her mother's voice.

"When I came to Michigan for graduate school, I never intended to get married, let alone have children. Politics was fascinating, especially then with all the protests going on for civil rights, women's rights, and against the Vietnam War. The university was at the center of a lot of those demonstrations, and they created positive change in the political culture. I was thrilled to be part of it."

Beth closed her book. "So you were one of those people I read about in history class, standing up in front of rows of police and yelling for Nixon to stop the war? Did you burn your bra too?"

Kate laughed and nodded. "I did both, but in Ann Arbor the university and the police kept everything pretty civil compared with other places. We got a lot done, moved the national conversation forward enough that Nixon finally started to feel the heat to stop the war."

No wonder she always read political articles out loud. Why hadn't she talked about this before; how did Beth not know this about her mother? "So why'd you stop working in politics?"

Kate nodded slightly. "Because Maegan, then Dylan, then you came along. I met your dad when he was watching one of our peace rallies and got him to join in. We were married a year later, and I watched Nixon resign and leave the White House from the hospital, two days after Dylan was born."

"Did Dad make you quit working?"

"I can't blame it on your father. It was just what a woman did back then, I guess, and somehow I thought I'd go back to that work after I raised all of you and sent you flying off to your own successful lives." Kate looked up at the eagle's nest and back at Beth. She'd never seen her mother look at her like that—with questions and regret, rather than confidence and determination. Beth didn't know what to say, so she watched the eagle parents preening their young.

Kate leaned over the boat to see if the worm was still on the hook and then looked back at the nest. "After you've tried to protect your children for so long, made them your entire life, it's hard to go back to who you were before, or to try new things. Once a parent, always a parent, I guess." She wiggled the reel as if she knew what she was doing. "I just don't want your brother and sister to give up any of their dreams for silly young love. They have lots of time for that."

"Maegan's nuts to want to be with Brian."

Kate jumped. "Exactly! She could have a brilliant life ahead of her, but she won't with him. You see that too, don't you?"

Beth nodded, surprised that her mother asked her opinion. The rod moved up and down as Kate repeated, "I can't let that happen, I can't."

"Maybe you just need to listen to what they want, Mom. Talk rather than tell."

Kate squinted at Beth, shifted her shoulders up and back, and raised her fishing rod. "Yes, well, it took years for us to stop the Vietnam War. Maybe I need to be more patient for my children to see their right paths to success."

Was she pushing so hard for Maegan to go back to school and for Dylan to go to college because she hadn't realized her own dreams? Her mom wasn't old; she could still take chances, do new things. Beth rubbed the hull with her sneaker's toe to gather her courage.

"You and Dad have taken a lot of boat rides this summer, and now you're fishing. What's next, swimming?"

"What do you mean? I'm a great swimmer!"

"I've never seen you swim."

Kate's eyes popped open as she stared at Beth. "What time is it?"

Beth looked at her Timex. "Almost noon. Why?"

"Fishing is boring. Let's go have some real fun."

Kate reeled in the line and faced forward on the bench. Beth hugged the shoreline to avoid the open waves, but Kate yelled above the engine's hum to take the most direct line back to the island. Why the crazy rush, and what was her mom planning now?

As they tied up to the dock, Evan walked out the kitchen door. "We're making sandwiches. Want one?"

Kate nodded. "Is Naina back yet? Aren't you going for your prelunch swim?"

"She's still with Aunt Betty, so I was going to skip. Why?"

"What about me? Beth, you joining us?"

Evan walked to the edge of the porch. "What have you two been up to?"

Beth raised her arms and shrugged. "We watched the eaglets fly on Llyndee's Peak, and now we're here. That's all I know."

Kate tossed her hat onto the ground and kicked off her shoes. "Am I going by myself?"

"No, wait, I'm coming," Evan yelled. Beth watched as her parents grabbed each other's hand, ran down the dock, and jumped into the lake. Was that really her mom, laughing and hollering in the water in her white T-shirt and navy shorts? Kate had changed rhythm in a matter of minutes, and Beth couldn't keep up with the tune, if she even knew the song. She followed them from shore as they swam from the south to north dock, Kate beating Evan by at least one body's length.

"Think you can keep up with me?" Kate yelled to Beth.

Beth threw off her shoes and ran off the dock toward her parents.

The entire family watched the next day at noon as Kate jumped off the dock again, this time with Naina too. Taid asked Dylan and Beth to go with him in the powerboat and follow behind, just in case Kate got cold halfway through their swim around the island.

"Don't want her to stop the other two from their normal routine," he said.

Ben was kayaking nearby as everyone gathered on the dock, and Dylan invited him to join them. Maegan and Brian cheered from the canoe but turned south toward Llyndee's Peak as the three swimmers rounded the north dock and headed down that side of the island. Dylan steered the boat, Taid and Ben watched from the back seats, and Beth stood next to Dylan, using the top of the windshield for balance so she could take pictures. Naina and Evan kept a steady pace side by side, while Kate swam two or three lengths ahead, stopped and waited for them to catch up, and took off again. As much as it looked as though she was trying to match their strokes, Kate kept barreling ahead.

While their mother hadn't pestered Maegan about Brian the previous night at dinner, she'd demanded that Dylan finish the last college application before he left for the bonfire. Beth was beginning to believe that Dylan didn't intend on going to college at all, but she couldn't imagine what he would do instead or that he could avoid their mother's demands forever. Why wouldn't he want to go to college, experience that freedom, and spend every day drawing for his classes? He could always change his major from architecture to art once he got to school. Beth glanced at Dylan and made a mental note to suggest that when they talked next. She needed to find him alone soon, before the summer and his options slipped away.

But what if Dylan really did have another plan for his life? Didn't he have a right to pursue those choices instead? She thought her mother's swimming showed that she was trying to relax and take part in the family's interests, and she wanted to believe that Kate could enjoy the lake again, as Evan claimed. That her mother had the best of intentions to protect her, Maegan, and Dylan all these years. But were those intentions about her own life choices or theirs? The more she watched the strength and determination of Kate's stroke, the more Beth's instincts screamed that her mother couldn't stop herself from trying to force Maegan and Dylan to do what Kate thought was right for their lives—even if she did learn how to relax enough to enjoy the beauty and joy of this lake and island.

As the swimmers edged the rockslide, Beth saw Sam perched on the top. He swooped toward her and circled, squawked loudly, and returned to the island's peak. She hadn't made it up there yet today, and he was probably wondering why he hadn't gotten a muffin yet. Dylan looked up the steep wall of fallen rocks and turned toward Ben.

He nodded slightly at Dylan. "Looks like Kate might have changed her view of this place," Ben said. "What do you think, Taid, time for you to change your view of things too?"

Taid grunted. "Should have known you'd try to bend my ear again. Don't bother, Ben. I'm not giving up anything to anyone."

"I don't think anyone's suggesting you do that, Padrig. But by refusing to even talk with my brother-in-law, you're guaranteeing this will end up with the province. Do you really want that to happen?"

Beth turned slightly so she could see her grandfather sitting in the back seat behind her. His left hand was twitching, which had started after his fall last year and grew into a full tremor whenever he was angry or upset. He grabbed the shaking hand with his other one and buried them in his lap.

"Look, my friend, I know you mean well. I'm trying to be the person you expect me to be by keeping my thoughts about your sister's family and their supposed rights to myself."

Ben wasn't deflected. "So as you watch your family enjoy this beautiful lake and you traverse your island, you're still willing to risk it all?"

Taid shook his head and a finger at Ben. "Every attorney I've met with has produced another document to prove my rights. Your brother-in-law's out of luck, and so is the rest of his so-called nation."

Dylan shoved the boat throttle into neutral, stood, and turned toward the men. Beth tried to jump out of the way and fell onto the other front seat. "So-called nation?" Dylan said. "You're not being fair, Taid. They deserve your respect, and I know they'll do the same, if you'll just let me take you to meet with them. I know we can find a solution that respects both families."

Taid stood and faced Dylan. "Dylan, tell me, is your name still Llyndee? Or do you want to switch it to Akeene?" His voice stayed measured, but the strength of his threat was clear. "You're either with us or against us, my boy."

The boat was floating toward the sharp granite blocks at the bottom of the rock fall. Beth reached for the oar stored along the boat's side and saw her father swimming to them.

"Dad," he yelled from the water. "Stop your threats. Ben and Dylan are trying to help you see reason."

Taid sat back in his seat and crossed his arms. Kate and Naina were swimming to the rockslide's bottom boulders. Beth felt the boat lean as her dad climbed onto the boat's back ladder behind Ben. She paddled toward Kate and Naina, glancing behind at Taid and Ben between each stroke.

"Your family loves you and this place more than anything else in this world," Ben said. "They don't want to cross you, Padrig, but you're putting them in an untenable position if you won't at least talk with Makwa. Didn't he treat you with respect when we came to the island last year?"

Taid nodded. "I've said that. Seemed like an honest man."

"And hasn't he given you plenty of time to consider his request to meet, which Dylan conveyed to you when you first arrived this summer and again last week?" Ben asked.

Taid nodded again.

"And if you're sure that you have the necessary paperwork to protect this island, what's the harm of showing the same consideration back to him?"

Taid leaned slightly to the left to look at his wife. She nodded. "It's time, dear."

Beth turned back to Taid as he faced Ben and Evan.

"There's nothing your brother-in-law can say that will change my mind. But I will accept your argument and give him the respect he's due. On the provision that only Evan and I meet with him and whatever one person he wants." He turned to Dylan. "No one else."

Dylan stepped toward his grandfather. "But I know both of you. I'll be able to read his reactions and help you find common ground."

"I'm not stupid, Dylan. You have divided desires. No."

Dylan threw his arms in the air, turned away from his grandfather, and leaned over the windshield. Beth wasn't sure, but she thought he had started to cry. Evan pointed toward Kate and Naina. She paddled next to them and shoved the oar between two rocks until the women could step into the boat, then pushed away from shore. Evan and Kate shared the seat behind Beth, and Naina sat behind Dylan, who dropped into the driver's seat and started the engine. The family and Ben rode back to the cabin in silence.

Beth leaped out of bed a week later when her grandmother tapped her on the shoulder, eager to take Naina trolling in the damp early morning air and get one minute closer to finally ending all the nonsense she'd started with the Ojibwe artifacts. Ben was taking Taid and her dad to meet with Chief Akeene at ten, and Naina and Kate would go too, supposedly to visit with Anna but actually in case Taid's anger erupted in the next room. Dylan was still campaigning to go, sure he could get the two men to agree, but Beth knew their grandfather wouldn't change his mind. She pulled jeans and a sweatshirt over her pajamas, stepped into her rubber boots at the kitchen door, and ran to the boat.

Naina dropped her fishing line as soon as Beth steered toward open water. The horizon was crimson red, but the top of her universe was clear. Cassiopeia, Andromeda, and Cepheus glittered back at her from their wide Milky Way bed. Just where they were supposed to be, a family together through the eons.

She'd never dreamed Dylan and Taid could argue the way they had over the past two years. Taid's quick rise to anger was normal, but he'd fought Dylan with an intensity and heat usually reserved to defend the family and its traditions against outsiders, not one of its own. Dylan's rage had stunned her even more. Before this he had backed away from conflicts, kept his thoughts and opinions to himself—as he was doing with their mom about college. He wasn't backing down this time when it came to the artifacts. The whole fiasco felt like a massive boulder rolling faster and faster downhill, destined to send them hurtling into the water to be pinned forever on the lake's floor.

But not today. Today a huge chunk of the boulder would disappear. Ben and Lily had outlined her father's proposal last night: picket fencing around the Ojibwe artifacts with a sign summarizing their history, another sign at the island's west end with a trail map to the site, and No Trespassing signs scattered in a north-to-south line connected with roping, just past the site's fencing. Full ownership of all but the artifact grounds would stay with the Llyndee family, with rights of survivorship to the Ojibwe First Nation if at any time the family didn't want the island. Taid listened but didn't say anything, at least not to the group. She'd heard his and Naina's voices through the walls long after everyone had gone to bed.

"Woo-hoo, give me a hand!" Naina's rod arced sharply, and she leaned backward and locked her reel to stop her catch from taking off with the thin steel line. Beth put the outboard engine into neutral and held on to the boat's low sides to climb up to Naina's bench. She straddled behind her grandmother, as Taid had done for her when she landed her first big catch when she was ten. They leaned forward as one to give the line some freedom, release the pressure, then pulled back quickly to lift the rod into the air and crank in the line as fast as they could. Beth held the rod above and below the reel and pulled with all of her strength while Naina spun the wire line onto the reel, then helped her hold the reel in place as they leaned forward again. They kept the angler's dance going for several minutes until the trout's silver belly popped to the surface, twisting and fighting as it rose from the lake's depths.

Beth grabbed the large fish net, waited until Naina yelled, "Now!" and shoved it underwater. Its round aluminum rim shone in the navy water as she scooped, the huge fish eluding her until the third try. Naina dropped the rod to help her lift the thrashing fish into the boat. The trout was too big to fit into any of their buckets, so they filled the middle section of the boat's floor with enough water to keep it alive until they could get back to the island.

Ben and the other early morning anglers cheered as Beth steered the boat up to the morning circle and she and Naina held up the huge rainbow trout. A few suggested she'd caught Chester, the infamous thirty-pounder that roamed the deep waters of Lake Wigwakobi. Naina waved them off, sure hers wasn't more than twenty-five pounds, but she grinned and bowed all the same.

Ben followed them back to the island, said he'd be back in an hour, and turned toward his cabin. Taid and Evan stood on the dock with their metal coffee mugs, tight in conversation until Naina showed them her catch.

"Now that's a good woman!" Taid said.

Naina waved him off as she had the other guys. "Thank goodness Beth was along to get it in the boat. It's her catch too."

Kate and Maegan were putting the last batches of French toast, Canadian bacon, and scrambled eggs on the table. Beth inhaled the sweet aromas, the first time she felt she could breathe deeply inside the cabin the entire summer. After last night's meeting with Ben and Lily, a wave of fresh air had swept through the cabin, carrying away the ugly molecules of fear, anger, and doubt that surrounded them whenever the family argued.

"I made muffins to take with us to the meeting with the Akeenes," Kate said. "Dylan, is there anything else Lily's parents might like?"

"Just don't be late. Her dad hates that."

"How'd you find that out?" Maegan said. "Bring Lily home late, and he was waiting on the porch with his hunting rifle?"

"Yeah, something like that." Everyone chuckled, including Dylan.

"Her father's right about being on time. Good practice to get you ready for your classes next year," said Kate. "You mailed your applications when you went into town yesterday, right?"

Dylan and Maegan stared across the table at each other. Beth reached for her orange juice so she could study their gaze: determined, serious, just like the last two times she'd caught them sitting shoulder to shoulder at the end of the dock with their feet dangling in the lake, long after they'd returned from the night's bonfires and everyone else had gone to bed. The last time she hid behind the pines and watched their intense exchange: the long pauses, the occasional fits of angry words, and their eventual nodding in agreement. Something was up.

"Dylan, you did mail them, didn't you?"

Maegan tipped her head an inch. Dylan dropped his fork onto his plate and let the ringing of metal on china reverberate as he drank half of his juice. He leaned forward and stared at the table. "I mailed the damn things. That doesn't mean I'm going."

Kate's eyes widened, and she looked at Evan. He shook his head. "Not now, Kate. Stop pushing. Besides, we have something more important to focus on this morning." He lifted his coffee mug. "You ready for this, Dad?"

Taid nodded slowly, staring at his plate. When he didn't respond, Naina jumped in. "My worry is that visitors won't honor the signs. I'd hate for the girls to run into a stranger if they're picking berries or Beth's at her fort."

"Beth can move it closer to the cabin," Kate said. "Dad and I can help you move everything this afternoon when we return. You can pick a new place by then, can't you?"

Beth didn't want to move it, wouldn't find another spot that felt right. Every time she sat somewhere else on the island, Sam visited but flew back and squawked at her from the fort.

Kate glanced at her watch. "We better get moving. Ben will be here in five minutes."

Dylan stood but didn't carry his plate to the kitchen with the others. Beth watched from the doorway as he blocked their father's path to the bedroom hall. "I really think I should go with you. I can sit in the other room with Mom, Naina, and Mrs. Akeene, just in case. I know Lily's parents; you guys don't. You know I'm right, Dad."

"You may be, but it was Taid's request for just the four men, and the chief agreed."

"But Lily will be there. She'll feel responsible if she can't get her dad to agree with Taid about the sign and the ropes. "

"That's not your responsibility, Dyl. We all know what's at stake here."

Dylan grabbed his father's forearm. "No, you don't, or you'd let me come."

"Then tell me what I'm missing." Evan stepped closer to his son, waited.

"What happens today determines my whole life. You have to include me. I know I can make it work. Please, Dad, listen to me."

Evan stared at Dylan for a moment before patting him on the shoulder. "It will be fine. You'll see. I know what this means to you, to all of us." He stepped around Dylan and walked to the bathroom.

Beth turned to clear the last plates from the table as Dylan strode past her and out the kitchen door. She carried the stacked plates to Maegan, who was filling the sink with soapy water. "Let's soak the dishes. I think Dylan and I are going for a sail," she said.

Beth looked out the window at her brother standing at the end of the dock, then at her sister. "Since when does Dylan want to go sailing with you?"

Maegan shrugged.

"I was going to kayak over to get my book I left on top of the cliff yesterday, but I'll go with you."

"We need to go just us. Besides, you're probably meeting Amik up there again, right? Mom's going to have a heart attack if you fall for an Ojibwe too, you know."

"I'm not falling for anyone." Beth looked away to hide her rejection.

"You'd be surprised where your heart leads you, even when your head knows it's wrong."

"Like you with Brian? You're not going to save him, you know."

"Save whom from what?" Kate interrupted as she and Evan walked into the kitchen. "Those dishes will be done when we get back, correct? Let me wrap the muffins, and I'm ready. Where are your parents?"

Evan pointed toward the dock, where Dylan and Ben were helping Taid and Naina into the aluminum powerboat. Evan gave Beth a quick hug and whispered, "Almost over" before he followed Kate outside.

Beth turned back to Maegan. "Fine. I could care less what you and Dylan are planning. I'm going to get my book, and you can finish cleaning up." She pointed at the dishes as she walked out the door. "Have fun with those."

Beth wanted to kayak to the next bay to check on the newest nest of baby loons, but she didn't know how long her parents would be gone. Instead she paddled to the north trail that led to the top of Llyndee's Peak. She wrapped the zippered sweatshirt she'd thrown into the kayak around her waist and jogged up the winding forested path, every step and lunge over rocks and plants memorized deep within. Without thinking, she caressed the smooth orange-brown bark on a scattered row of cypress trees as she passed, their overlapping puzzle pieces so different from the craggy skin of the oaks and pines. She stopped to hug the massive chestnut tree that stood proudly in the middle of the trail, one of the last in the region according to Ben. She looked to the west when she reached the cliff's top and its wide-open landscape. Ben, her parents, and her grandparents were almost to the western shore.

She turned east toward the cliff's front edge and walked to the collection of rocks and low junipers where she'd read yesterday. Amik had surprised her, and after they'd made out for a while, he'd asked her to take him sailing again. Another fun, perfect day.

Her book was where she'd forgotten it, the pages flapping indiscriminately in the breeze. Her skin tingled as she picked it up and felt the black granite's heat radiating off the book's cover, the rock already warmed by the summer sun like a stove's burner left on too long.

The eaglets were peeping in their nests, eager for food. She found a spot partially hidden by grasses and a tree stump so she wouldn't scare the adult birds when they returned. From her perch she could see all of the lake's eastern half and part of its western side. Shoreline residents were swimming, canoeing, sunning on docks. Several large sailboats were racing in the far eastern bay, traversing the same triangle marked with buoys every spring. Taid had bought their heavy wooden sailboat before the cabin was even done, something to take out when they needed a break from "creating our magical home," he'd said. It was an old, grand relic, not like the lightweight fiberglass sailboats that had popped up around the lake in recent years. "They'll never cut through the big waves with the elegance of ours," Taid claimed.

Beth stood to see their south dock. Maegan was talking with her hands as Dylan raised the sail and checked the rudder. She handed him a life vest, which he threw on the boat's floor. He put his hands on his hips and turned away from Maegan, toward the water, and shook his head. She strode toward the end of the dock and pointed at him, then toward the west end of the lake. They had to be arguing about Lily or the meeting.

Suddenly Dylan climbed out of the boat and stomped past Maegan toward the cabin. She leaned forward aggressively and yelled at him before he disappeared inside. Beth chuckled as she watched her sister climb into the wide sailboat and push away from the dock—she'd known they wouldn't make it sailing together. They might have been spending a lot of time together plotting something, but they were still like oil and water. Their molecules just didn't blend.

Maegan was the best sailor in the family after their dad and found the wind within seconds. The huge white sail arced and filled as the boat barreled east toward the far bay and the other sailboats. Beth checked the west end, where their boat was a tiny speck tied to the Akeenes' dock, and returned to her spot to read her grandmother's book of Welsh poetry and wait for the eaglets' parents and hers to return. She glanced at the sailboat occasionally as Maegan tacked across the lake's wide center, the steady wind creating waving ribbons of blues with tips of white. A gorgeous, glorious day.

A potent burst of wind grabbed Beth's book out of her lap. She woke in time to see it careening over the cliff, even as she lurched forward to try to retrieve it. Another angry gust wrapped her long hair around her face, blinding her. She tripped and fell into the grass just inches from the cliff's edge. The adult eagles below watched with their broad ebony wings partially extended, ready to escape or protect their young if she fell—she wasn't sure which.

The east bay was still bright and vibrant with activity, the sun just past noon. Maegan was almost to the far bay, the boat leaning hard to port, her body leaning backward over starboard for counterbalance. Beth knew her sister was grinning, maybe even laughing as she raced with the wind. She peered down the cliff wall at her grandmother's book lying on the bottom ledge just before the water, as Taid had teetered on the brink last summer.

Taid, the meeting—were they still down there? Beth searched both island docks for the powerboat. Nothing. Dylan was drawing by the fire pit, in his own world as much as Maegan was enthralled in hers. The western sky had turned dark, crouching, with heavy rolling clouds brooding over the horizon. Their heavy shadows enveloped the western part of the lake in an eerie film. Pinpricks of people were walking onto the Akeenes' dock and climbing into the boat. They were too far away to see body language, whether they were happy or mad. Either way, they'd be back soon. Maegan needed to head home, and so did she.

She scanned the western sky, now pulsing eastward in a massive frown. Waves were slamming into one another in a raucous mishmash of conflicted energy, striking the shore in angry booms and receding in thick foam before the next surge advanced. At least one storm came through every summer, each with its own personality. If from the north, the rain lasted several cold, dreary days. Southern storms were brief, impish, filled with heat and lightning. The north shore still held the remains of the last eastern storm's powerful winds, which had flattened several cottages and turned a wide swath of forest into grassland. A western summer storm usually ripped across the lake in a matter of hours.

From her view on the cliff, the lake seemed split in half. To the west the water was churning, its hue matching the cloud's hanging underbellies, and the waves jumbling and swelling as the power of the encroaching storm gained steam. Beth cupped her hands over her eyes to shield them from the contrast as she looked east, the high sun still floating in a vivid blue sky and reflecting in diamond bursts off the lake. Maegan was farther east, but she had tacked to face the island. Could she see the looming darkness beyond Llyndee's Peak? Was she heading home? Dylan was safely ensconced on the rock shelf by the fire pit, the island's girth blocking the wind and clouds.

Ben was struggling to keep the boat from lurching in the rising waves, trying to balance between the crisscrossing whitecaps like a cowboy on a wild stallion, even though he was hovering near the shore and away from the strongest currents. She studied his path, knew Ben would opt for the safety of land if he thought they were in danger. As long as he didn't panic, she wouldn't either. Maegan was still heading west, so she must have seen what was coming. Beth peered over the cliff's ledge again and pondered whether she could get to her book with the kayak before the storm arrived.

A dense gust whipped across the cliff, then another and another, each one lifting the oak and birch trees' leaves to expose their pale undersides. A wall of rain extending across the entire width of the lake's southwestern end was approaching the boat with Ben, her parents, and her grandparents. He must have realized they couldn't outrun the storm, because he was steering toward the south shore to wait it out under the forest's canopy. Beth spun to check on her sister, who was heading east again, away from the island. Shit, Maegan, turn around! That old wooden sailboat was sturdy, but it wouldn't make it home if she didn't come about soon. Beth ran to the cliff's north edge to see how rough the waves had become between her and the island. Even if she could run down the trail in a few minutes, could she get across the three hundred yards of now unruly lake in her tiny kayak and get to Maegan in time with the fishing boat?

The storm was moving fast, rain and lightning pelting the lake's western third. Dylan was futzing with the fire pit, shoveling out old ashes and adding new logs. Beth waved her arms and yelled at him. Nothing. He had to notice the wind getting stronger, even in that protected space. She paced as she gauged the storm's speed and Maegan's path. She'd come about and was heading west again, toward them, but that was almost worse. If she stayed near the far bay, she could find land—now she was heading back into open water. Beth jumped up and down to try to get her sister's attention and point her toward the east bay, but she knew it was pointless. The distance was too far, and the mainsail kept blocking Maegan's view.

Dylan. He was the closest option, the only one now. Beth grabbed two long sticks to wave in circles as she yelled down to him. He looked up but not at her. She'd stayed too long, damn it. The eagle mother lifted its enormous body and flew over her, calling in a weak staccato, *kleek kik ik ik ik*. It hovered in the growing power of the wind and then flew toward the island and circled high above Dylan in dips and climbs, reveling in the storm's gusts. She tried to mimic the eagle's call, but he was taken by the real bird. Maegan was still heading west, now in the widest section of open water.

The rain was halfway across the west end. She had to do something fast. The eagle had caught his attention. What else would do that? What had Ben taught them that Dylan would recognize? She cupped her hands around her mouth and leaned over the cliff's north edge. *Oo–AH–bo, oo–AH–bo–oo–oo–oo*, she yelled over and over. Her vocal cords strained to hit the loon's night-wailing notes as best she could to span the distance. Sam appeared and landed on the boathouse roof, staring up at her. Great, maybe he could help to get Dylan's attention. She waved the sticks again and pointed at Dylan, but Sam just angled his head to the side and stared at her.

She tried again, another series of six loon calls, and at last Dylan searched the air for the wail's source. Beth waved and wailed again until finally their eyes connected. She pointed west and mimicked rain, then pointed toward Maegan and formed a triangle with her hands above her head—the warning sign Naina taught them to express fear or danger whenever they were on or in the water. Dylan ran to the south dock and saw the impending storm, then looked east toward Maegan. She was still in open water, losing her battle against the rising whitecaps and strong crosswind, almost in irons. He looked at Beth and pointed at himself, then at Maegan, to Beth, to her kayak, back to himself and the kayak again. After he got Maegan, he'd come for her. Beth shoved both thumbs into the air.

Dylan took off for the north dock, blocked from Beth's view. She hopped on her toes, alternating between watching for him to reappear and watching Maegan, who was a bit closer, though the sail was still blocking her view of Beth and the western sky. Finally Dylan came around the island's point in their dad's Carling wooden boat. What the hell was he doing in that? It was faster than their or Ben's fishing boats, but would it hold up in the pounding waves? Beth jogged back and forth across the clearing, anything to release her frantic energy as Dylan sped over the waves.

She could tell Maegan saw him when she lowered the mainsail and secured it and the boom to the rudder. As Dylan reached Maegan, she climbed onto the bow to grab the front of the powerboat and push it forward so she and Dylan were side by side. The two boats careened off each other with each monstrous wave. Beth screamed, "Faster!" even though she knew only the eaglets could hear. Lightning loomed, and they had to get home before the metal mast made them an easy target.

Maegan pulled the wooden boat farther forward so Dylan could tie both back ropes to the sailboat's bow. As he floored the throttle to spin the sailboat around behind him, Maegan dove into the back of the boat. He finished a wide arc to face the island just as the first pellets of cold rain hit Beth's back. Dylan pointed to the cliff, and Maegan waved with both arms. Beth grinned and returned the gesture, heavy drops already soaking her head, back, and thighs.

A bolt of lightning lit the sky just west of the cliff, and its thunder rumbled the ground underneath her. As much as she wanted to stay until they reached the island, Dylan would get her next, and maneuvering the path's rocks and carpet of pine needles—as slippery as ice from the rain—would demand extra time.

Her brother and sister huddled together in the driver's seat behind the low windshield of her father's prized possession, the sailboat bucking across the angry waves as they advanced by inches toward the island. The sailboat might not make it back in one piece, but at least they were safe. Beth took one last look at the nest. The mother had covered the eaglets with sticks and brush before she'd disappeared high above the clouds to avoid the rain. Beth escaped into the safety of the forest canopy as another round of lightning and thunder exploded above her.

She traversed the trail quickly, slipping only once. Her feet flipped into the air, and she fell on her back so hard that she bounced a few times before the slick layer of wet pine needles sent her sliding down a steep section of trail. She regained her balance and breath in time to dig her heels into the loose soil just before a steep drop-off into the deep woods. As she straightened her legs to stop from sliding over the edge, a protruding corner of granite sliced through several layers of her calf like a chunk of cheese. Tiny beads of blood erupted into ugly rows as they mixed with the dirt and dead pine needles already stuck to her leg. She rolled onto her hands and knees and patted down the thick section of skin hanging from the top of the cut, where the rock had dug the deepest, screaming at the fierce pain. Dylan would come to get her soon; she had to keep going. She hobbled back to the trail and stayed close to one side so she could grab nearby trees for balance. The blood drooled down her calf, soaked her sock, and congealed inside her sneaker.

When Beth reached the lake, she grabbed a downed birch branch for support against the waves and walked in up to her knees, eager for the cold water to numb her calf's spurting blood vessels. The lake was still at war with the shore, the wind and rain shoving wave after wave into the tall grass, stones, and boulders in wild bursts of attack. She buried her feet between the underwater stones for balance against the raging lake and lifted the long patch of loose skin. The water swirled around and into the open wound and turned red, then maroon as the blood from her sock and shoe escaped. Streaks of exquisite pain pulsed through her leg and up to her heart as she held the cut open so the waves could lift the dirt out and freeze the open blood vessels. She counted thirty quick breaths before the numbness took hold and she could hobble a few steps to look to the west. The rain still pelted the lake, now an odd shade of greenish brown, but the sky above the far western shore was clearing. Their southern dock was still empty. Shouldn't Dylan and Maegan be back by now?

Once she'd crawled onto a grassy portion of shore, she folded the sweatshirt in half, wrapped it around her calf twice, and tied it to her leg with the sleeves. Huddled next to her kayak, her calves pressed tightly to the back of her thighs in a low squat, she positioned herself under the tree cover but still kept the south dock in sight. Within minutes she was shivering uncontrollably. Every time the waves seemed to subside, the lake taunting her to try to kayak home, she'd stand, and the lake would respond by pummeling the shore again in a booming pulse that pounded deep in her eardrums. Even the spray from the strongest waves tasted different—uglier, harder, without oxygen. She buried her head between her chest and knees and rocked from heels to toes in a desperate attempt to control her shivering and panic. "Please let the storm stop," she whispered. "Let everyone be okay. Please let Dylan come soon."

She didn't know how long she'd rocked and prayed when the echo of a gurgling engine bounced off the rocks above her. She stood and screamed her brother's name as her father's wooden boat careened into the dock. Maegan fell onto the dock as the waves crashed the antique Carling over and over into the unforgiving pylons, hiding her from Beth's view. Finally Maegan sat up and reached for the bow's rope, pulling what was left of their father's five-year project around the wide dock's end to its more protected, shallow side. Blood matted her hair on one side, drooled down her left arm and thigh, wiggled around her knee and down the front of her shin. She tied the boat to a metal ring, turned to see Beth, and pointed east before collapsing on the dock.

Maegan didn't move no matter how many times Beth screamed for her. Waves were consuming the wooden boat's stern, filling the hull until all but the tip of the bow had been swallowed. Beth pushed her tiny kayak into the snarling water and tried to paddle through the whitecap waves to her sister, but the crosscurrents between the cliff and the island made it impossible for her to move forward. The ugly brown waves seemed to rejoice in sucking her out into the deep, then throwing her back against the rocky shore. When one smothered the kayak's front end with a swift crack, she paddled backward and let the boat slide back onto land. The front end hung like a huge teacup off the end of the shore, which the lake was happy to fill. She pounded on her thighs as she hovered on the shoreline, beating herself for not bringing a life jacket as her mother had always demanded. If she had, she was sure she could have swum to Maegan, gotten the fishing boat, and gone for Dylan and the sailboat. That had to be why he wasn't with Maegan.

Again she huddled and shivered, alternating between staring at Maegan lying on the dock and burying her head. She'd never learned the right way to pray, since they didn't attend church like some of her friends at home. What if she was doing it wrong? She tried to remember the Welsh prayers Taid recited at holidays or the chief's solemn messages to Mother Earth at the bonfires, but her mind was a thick fog. "Please let the storm stop," she repeated over and over and rocked in time with the waves still breaking in anger against the shore. Her teeth quivered against each other so powerfully from her body's shivering that she feared they might crack. She wrapped her arms more tightly around her legs, her knees crushing her chest, and dug her molars into both of her cheeks. At least her teeth would stop vibrating.

When the hum of another boat's engine registered in Beth's mind, it was well past her. She saw Ben's back first, then her parents and grandparents. The storm had passed, the lake was calming as if it had found its senses again, and the far western sky was washed clean to a bright clear blue. The sun was well to the west, which meant she had hovered there for at least an hour.

As they reached the dock, her parents jumped out and leaned over Maegan. Evan lifted her into his arms as Ben helped her grandparents out of the boat, and they moved together up the cement-and-rock stairs toward the cabin. Suddenly Evan stopped and turned in the direction Maegan was pointing. Beth stood as they looked across the lake at her, their faces filled with the shock and fear she'd been trying to hold at bay. When Ben ran to the north dock for his boat and drove toward her, she fell back to the ground. Finally, this day could be over.

Neither Ben nor Beth spoke when he arrived. He stepped out of the low fishing boat into the shallow water, held it with one hand so it straddled the shore, and wrapped his other arm around Beth's waist to lift her onto the middle bench. He pulled her broken kayak and its paddle off the rocks and laid it crosswise between them. She'd rather he threw it in the lake and let it sink for all the good it had done her today, but she knew that was against everything Ben believed in, to not leave a trace of yourself in nature. Not even today.

She scanned the lake for Dylan and the sailboat as they rode back to the island, even though she knew he couldn't still be out there. Either he had come home while she was crouched and asleep, or he had floated with the waves to the north shore so the sailboat wouldn't be destroyed in the storm. Her calf pulsed and screamed for attention. Beth pulled the blood-stained sweatshirt tighter and hugged the wound with both hands so it didn't bounce in the light chop. As they reached the end of the south dock, she climbed to the bow to tie down Ben's boat. Her father's prized possession lay battered on the other side of the dock. Only the bow, steering wheel, and driver's seat sat above the water. She stared at the remains. How could their lake destroy something so precious?

Ben moved in front of her and reached for her hand. "Let's get you inside to take care of your leg. How deep is the cut?"

"Just a scrape except for the top part. I slipped at the trail's curve. I'm okay."

He wrapped his arm around her waist and lifted her every time she stepped with her right toe. Taid met them at the kitchen door and pointed to the dining room table, where Naina was waiting with wet towels, gauze, and Band-Aids. She could hear her parents talking to Maegan in their bedroom but not her sister's voice.

"Is Maegan okay? The cross currents were too strong, and my kayak cracked, so I couldn't get back to her. She's okay, right?" She winced and squeezed her right thigh to block the pain as Naina unwrapped the sweatshirt and inspected her cut.

"Doesn't look too bad except for the top. Let's go clean it in the bathtub, and we'll wrap it up tight," Naina said as she gathered the first-aid items and started down the bedroom hallway. Beth figured Taid and Ben must have gone to get Dylan, because they weren't inside anymore.

Her bedroom door was open a crack, and she peeked through before turning into the bathroom. Kate was lying tightly against Maegan's back in bed, and it looked like every blanket in the house was on top of them. Evan sat on Beth's bed, leaning over so his head was close to Maegan's, and he was murmuring something. Maegan's eyes were squeezed shut. Beth couldn't tell whether she was unconscious or didn't want to hear what their father was saying.

"Come in here, dear," Naina called.

After Naina cleaned and bandaged Beth's calf, she returned to her bedroom. Maegan and Kate were sleeping, but her father was gone. She found him on the south dock, scanning the shoreline with binoculars. He pulled her into a tight hug.

"Maegan said you got Dylan's attention to go get her from up on the cliff," Evan said. "How'd you do it?"

Beth told her dad what happened, how Dylan and Maegan were in the Carling boat together, headed home, when she left the cliff. She couldn't tell if he was proud of her or not because he didn't look at her. He'd pulled away and lifted the binoculars back to his eyes while she talked. She realized no one had really looked at her since they returned, not even Naina.

"Is Maegan all right?"

"She's scared and in shock, maybe a bit of a concussion."

"Where are Taid and Ben? They found Dylan on shore, right?"

Evan turned to look in another direction. "They're down by the Shepplers'. So far I've seen them stop a few times and put something in the boat."

Beth stepped in front of her dad and pulled on one of his elbows, forcing him to look at her. "Why wasn't Dylan with Maegan? What did she tell you?"

Evan lowered the binoculars and finally gazed at Beth. His eyes were serious, reserved, like at home when he had a meeting with the university's trustees. "Just that he took the sailboat. My guess is it was too much of a drag behind the Carling, so he decided to ride it to shore so neither boat would be ruined."

Beth glanced at the remains of her dad's boat. "Why would Dylan take your boat?"

"It was a good choice, actually," Evan said from behind the binoculars again. "The fishing boats with their low sides never would have made it out to Maegan in that storm."

Beth scanned the shoreline, waiting for her dad to announce

that he could see Dylan climbing into the powerboat with Taid and Ben. When the hinges creaked on the kitchen's wooden screened door, they turned to see Naina walking to the edge of the porch. She had the same stern, closed look as her son. Evan barely shook his head, and Naina turned and walked back inside. The same rush of panic that had consumed Beth on the cliff rose from her stomach to her throat.

"Why did Naina look at you like that? Didn't Taid and the chief agree?"

"No, they didn't, but that's not something to discuss now, Beth," Evan said, again avoiding her gaze. "Your sister's in shock, and we need to find Dylan." He tried to chuckle, but it sounded more like a grunt. "He's probably sleeping somewhere in the woods, wherever he went to get away from the storm. You stay here, take care of your leg. I'm going to walk the north shoreline and find him."

Evan strode to the north dock, and she followed, hopping and limping behind. By the time she reached the dock, he was driving toward the north shore. For the first time, the water, sky, and trees closed in, overwhelming her as her mother had been claiming for years. What if Dylan wasn't okay? Why hadn't the chief and Taid agreed? What if everything had gone wrong because of those artifacts she'd found, and they had to leave? She stood in the middle of the dock, arms wrapped around herself, frozen in place.

Her father returned at dusk. Beth was sitting on the edge of the dock, waiting. She jumped up, forgetting the cut until her calf throbbed, and grabbed the bow as he pulled the engine's gear into neutral.

"Hold the boat for me; we need some flashlights from the boathouse," he said.

When Evan returned a few minutes later, Beth asked if she could come with him. "No. I don't want to have to worry about you too."

Beth couldn't hide her panic as tears filled her eyes. "Dad—"

Evan held up his hand to stop her. "Dylan is fine. We just have to find him. Go inside and help your mom, and we'll return with him soon." He backed away and disappeared into the encroaching night air.

By seven the next morning, the fishing crew's boats were parked helter skelter by their docks. Ben had met them at their normal starting points and directed them to the island. Beth watched from the picture window as her father told the group where they'd searched and where they thought he'd be, based on the storm's winds. Long chunks of the wooden sailboat's sides and bottom sat next to the steps to the north dock. By nine, ten more boats had tied up end to end around the island's point, just as they did every year at Lammas parties. Two more boats arrived filled with men, one tied up, and they all climbed into the other boat to head to the north shore. As news spread around the lake that Dylan was missing, almost every person Beth had ever met either rode by to gawk or stopped to ask how they could help. Everyone except the Ojibwe. Not even Amik or Lily came.

Somehow none of that mattered anymore. The most important thing was convincing everyone that her leg was fine so she could join in the search. After all, she knew Dylan's favorite hangouts for painting or hiking better than anyone. He must have gone where he knew he'd have the best cover from the storm, and maybe he hit his head or broke his leg. Something so he couldn't get back to the shore so they'd see him. She knew she could find him, if she just had the chance.

By noon everyone would return to the island to check in. Naina made two batches of muffins and put Beth in charge of making as many peanut butter, honey, and banana or turkey sandwiches as she could pull together. Kate came out of the back bedroom to get some orange juice, hoping Maegan would at least drink something, and yelled at Naina.

"Two of my children are fighting for their lives, and you're concerned with feeding people?" Kate reached past Beth to grab a banana and stomped out of the kitchen.

Naina rubbed Beth's back and pointed at the sandwiches. She stacked them on a tray with the muffins, helped Naina carry them onto the porch, then asked her to redo the bandage on her leg. If it was tight enough, it wouldn't hurt as much, and she wouldn't limp in front of her dad.

As the entire group of searchers sat on the porch and docks eating their sandwiches, three provincial police in medium brown uniforms, stiff black boots, and wide hats rode up to the dock. Beth was shocked to see them, to think that anyone thought Dylan was really missing. As she fought back tears, Taid wrapped his large hand around hers. "Just a precaution, wyres melys, not to worry."

Beth nodded but leaned into Taid, and he wrapped her in his arms. She waited there until the police and her father returned to the maps, and listened while the police described how the search would go from there. When everyone had their directions, Beth forced herself to walk in a normal gait up to her dad.

"Let me go with Ben and Carl, Dad," she said in the most confident voice she could muster. "I know where Dylan's normal spots are to paint in that section of the shore. I know I can find him."

Evan hesitated and watched as she fought to put full weight on her leg. "You won't last ten minutes hiking with that cut, as much as I know you want to try. You can go, but stay on shore and tell them the specific spots to look. Deal?"

Beth nodded, and Evan reached for her, holding her tightly to him for a few seconds longer than his normal hugs. When he let her go, she hopped to the dock and climbed into Ben's boat, and they were off. She would find him.

By daybreak the next morning, Beth had written up a list of new places where Dylan hung out on the north shore. She'd stayed on the beach yesterday afternoon and evening to direct everyone who landed by her where they should look in their section. When Carl arrived with another piece of the sailboat from his bay, which was farther east than they had focused the search, she'd expanded her list. Evan and Taid discussed the storm's wind speed and direction with the police, who thought it was unlikely he'd gone that far but ruled nothing out. They'd brought three dogs with them and asked for pieces of Dylan's clothing. Beth ran inside, the pain in her calf irrelevant at this point. She grabbed three of Dylan's T-shirts and emptied the contents of his painting satchel onto his bed. Her mother stopped her in the hallway.

"What do you think you're doing with those?" Kate yelled. "Those are Dylan's. You can't take those."

Beth took a few steps back. "The police have dogs, Mom. They want stuff with his scent."

Kate grabbed the bag and pressed it to her chest. "No, they can't have this. I will put the items back in his bag. His bed needs to be ready for him when he returns." She walked past Beth, sat on Dylan's bed, and slid the door closed.

Two dogs covered the areas where they'd looked the day before, and one went to the new spots farther east. As Ben headed toward the north shore, Beth asked him to stop. They floated in the water, and he looked at her new list—all the places they'd hiked with Lily and Dylan. She wondered whether he could have ended up to the west even though the storm's wind had blown east.

"What if he was trying to get back to the island and not to shore?" she asked. "We have to think how Dylan would think, not how the police or my dad would respond."

Nothing was impossible, Ben said. They split up, each with three sites or trails to cover, and agreed to meet back at the boat in two hours. Her calf was better, but she walked slowly, calling Dylan's name and stopping to inspect beneath and around any underbrush. The first trail was empty, as was the broken-down shack her brother had painted several times, so she headed farther west toward a huge arched rock among a stand of silver birch. It wasn't far from the water, and the trees created a huge umbrella—a perfect place for Dylan to go in the storm. As she got closer to the huge boulder, she saw something moving.

"Dylan!" she yelled, then stopped cold when Lily stepped toward her instead. They fell into each other's arms.

"I was sure this was where he would be," Lily said. "I've looked everywhere we've ever gone, even though my father ordered me to not leave the house."

Beth stepped back. "Why?"

"Because of what your grandfather said, all the threats and horrible names he called our family. I don't know what they're going to do. The elders have decided the gods are punishing your family for taking the island and defaming our people. But they have to be wrong. Dylan can't be taken from us."

Beth couldn't believe what she was hearing. "What did my grandfather say?"

Lily shook her head. "I can't repeat it. Ask your parents. My father asked about the original purchase of the island, and every-thing went wrong from there. He shut down at a certain point, no matter what Ben, my mom, or I said to him. When we find

Dylan, he will be devastated. We have no chance to be together now, at least not here."

They hugged again and cried until Beth's overwhelming fears for her brother and her family forced her to move. They circled the rock in larger and larger circles, calling Dylan's name with even greater urgency. Lily told her where she'd look next, and Beth doubled back to the beach to meet Ben.

When she and Ben returned to the island for flashlights, their search of the western part of the north shore void even of clues, Maegan was lying in her pajamas on a woven cloth chaise on the north deck. Beth took the outside back stairs and sat in the chair next to her. She was still pale, her hair limp around her face.

"The last spot I saw him was right there," Maegan pointed into the lake's wide middle. "He promised me he could get to the island or north shore and keep the sailboat intact."

She paused. Beth waited.

"If we hadn't had that last argument about how to convince Mom he didn't want to go to college, if I hadn't tried to talk him into doing something he didn't want to do, he would have gone sailing with me. And we'd both be sitting here, and everyone would be having another lovely summer." Maegan closed her eyes and shuddered.

"That storm came from nowhere. You couldn't have known how bad it would get. Besides, how would it have helped if he was sailing with you?"

Maegan grabbed Beth's hand and squeezed tighter with each word. "Because he would have sensed the storm way before I did and tacked back sooner, or raced for the south bay instead of trying to get home. I've never paid attention to the signs, and he always has."

They'd all counted on Dylan's strong intuition over the years, except when it had mattered most. That was why he'd wanted to go to the meeting with Taid and the chief—he must have known, somehow, that it would end badly otherwise.

Beth wrapped Maegan's hand with both of hers. "We'll find him. We just have to think like he does. Where would he go, if he was hurt or confused? I've tried all his favorite spots to paint or hike along the north shore, but I must be missing something."

Maegan shook her head and held on to Beth's hand, the tears slowly falling down her cheeks and into the creases of her neck.

Another day, more searching in new spots and returns to old ones, more search dogs, more tears. Now that Maegan was up and moving around, albeit slowly and with little ability to reason or think because of the concussion, Kate spent most of the time lying on Dylan's bed. When she came out, she questioned whoever was near or paced from the north to the south dock and back with binoculars. She'd jump at the slightest noises—gulls cawing, waves splashing on the rocks, leaves rustling in the breeze—and didn't stay long, claiming she needed to get everything ready inside for Dylan when he arrived home.

Beth and Ben were finishing their second search in the nooks and bends along the base of Llyndee's Peak when a large Ontario police boat passed them and stopped about a hundred yards east of the island. They watched as two men in scuba gear came out of the boat's enclosed cabin and prepared to jump overboard.

Beth lost her breath, her sense of balance, and for a second her eyesight. She felt Ben grab her from behind and hold her upright. "No!" she yelled. "Dylan didn't drown. He's too good a swimmer. They're wasting valuable time. We need to tell them to stop." She turned to Ben. He looked back at her with a resigned sadness she'd never seen in his eyes. "No! You're wrong. All of you are wrong. Take me back to the cabin. I'll search on my own if I have to."

As they tied up to the south dock, the police captain was explaining to Evan and Taid that diving was standard procedure after four days' search in any body of water. "When I interviewed your older daughter, she showed me where she last saw your son, Mr. Llyndee. We have to follow all leads and protocol."

Beth sat in Ben's boat and listened to her father asking them to hold off for another day. "My family is frantic. My wife can't bear much more. This will be devastating if she sees them out there."

The captain shook his head. "I'm sorry, we have to follow our procedures. The dogs will be called in after today."

Taid stepped forward, in front of Evan. "Take your silly divers and leave. Our friends will help us from now on."

"They have to dive for a minimum of twenty-four hours according to provincial law. You'll have to sign a release form, Mr. Llyndee, as parent to the child, to get them to stop after that. Otherwise they stay out there."

Evan saw Beth sitting in Ben's boat and waved her to him.

Beth strode past the captain. "They're crazy, Dad. I have lots of new places to look. There's no way he's out there."

Evan nodded and grasped her shoulders. "I need you to keep your mother and Naina inside, at least for the rest of the day while they're out there. Do you understand?"

"But I came up with new possibilities this morning. What if he wasn't with the sailboat when it crashed? What if he tried to swim to a different shore? He might be at the old farm just west of Ben's cabin, the trail between Wigwakobi and Round Lake, the cave in Settler's Bay, or . . ."

Evan shook her shoulders. "You must do as I say. Now. I need to count on you for this, Beth. Do you understand?"

Beth swallowed, nodded, and ran into the cabin. Her mother was in Dylan's room, her sister and Naina lying down together in Beth's bed. She went back to her mom, who was looking through Dylan's portfolio cases. She sat next to Kate and watched as her mother tried to mirror Dylan's brush strokes with her fingers. Beth had no clue how she was going to keep her mom from going outside once she'd looked through all of Dylan's paintings, but she'd figure out something. Her dad was depending on her.

The sound of pecking woke her first. Not the sound of boats trudging through their normal fishing routes well before daylight, just like any other morning on Lake Wigwakobi, or the sun rising over the horizon, winking through the birches and pines. She wondered if anyone caught Old Chester yesterday. If there even was an Old Chester. Nothing was certain anymore.

There was that odd pecking sound again. Beth rolled over in her sleeping bag to face it. After spending all day inside with her mom, sister, and grandmother, she'd escaped late last night to her fort. She had to think clearly, where the walls weren't closing in on her. Was it the new folks on shore repairing their rotting dock? No, much closer. A squirrel pounding a nut against the granite? No, too slow, methodical. Beth squinted just enough to see Sam staring back at her, a small piece of metallic paper in his beak and the webbing between his long toes spread across her granola bar's bright-blue-and-silver wrapping. She'd thrown it in her backpack before leaving the cabin last night.

"Let me undo it." She reached for the bar, and Sam hopped to a nearby rock, waited for her to free it from the wrapping, and bounced back to enjoy his breakfast.

Beth rolled onto her back, crossing her arms over her eyes and forehead. Like every other morning in the past four days, the tightness in her chest came first, followed by tears, then sobs as her heart swelled with the pain of reality fully returned. Her mind replayed the same scene for the thousandth time, searching for another ending: she'd thought they were safe, that it was okay to run for cover from the storm.

As she lay there, the questions all began again. She knew he wasn't gone, or she would sense it, wouldn't she? If what she was feeling was loss, why had she been so defiant yesterday when the officer talked about the futility of the search? Dylan was the essential piece in her family's entire puzzle. She'd known that since she was little—how he could listen to anyone and make them feel special. Even her mom, who didn't listen very often to anyone, always in her own head, opened up to Dylan when they were home. Maybe their lost connection when the family was up here was another reason Kate didn't like the island.

The last time Dylan visited her fort, he'd painted her portrait and told her to look in rather than out. She closed her eyes and tried to picture him—where he was, where she believed he would be. It had to be some place like this, somewhere familiar. Beth had come to crave this space the same way Dylan had to paint every day, where she could think on her own and sleep under the star-studded sky. She'd escaped up here almost every night this week, when the cabin and her family's silence became deafening, or they had finally passed out in exhaustion. They'd grown quieter each night, unable to fathom what might have happened but giving in to it all the same.

"No!" Beth bolted upright, pounding her fists into the ground. Sam squawked and jumped to safety. Beth cried and hit the ground, whispering, "No" over and over again while Sam chirped softly in response. Slowly the rhythm of his chirping calmed her, and she started to breathe in the forest's aromas and focus on the dozens of familiar knots on the birches that looked like eyes staring back at her. She considered all the places Dylan loved on this lake, in the woods and cliffs surrounding it, the places only the two of them had hiked.

"He's still here. I know it," Beth said to everything around her, everything that felt as much a part of her as the family in the cabin down the hill. "He's not gone. The lake wouldn't take him; it wouldn't betray us like that. Not when this is where he's most alive. We have to keep looking." Sam chirped back at her, then let out a loud *squeee-wawk* before flying east, over the cabin and above the lake. Beth picked up her flashlight, pillow, and sleeping bag and headed down the path to the cabin.

She heard the high whine of the powerboat approaching the island before she saw it. As she rounded the edge of the forested high ground to the wooden steps that took her over the steep granite cliff to the cabin, the Ontario Provincial Police boat with two sheriffs pulled up to the dock. Ben was sitting on the porch railing, sipping a cup of coffee. He looked exhausted, his eyes bloodshot and a gray stubble of beard spreading across his chin.

"Looks like you spent another night up top," he said to her.

"Best place to clear my head and see into my own heart, just like you taught me," Beth said and nodded at the officers as they climbed the steps to the porch. "I'm glad you're here. I have some ideas for where we should look today. Let me see who's up inside."

One of the officers cleared his throat and stepped forward. "Actually, miss, we've come for another reason. Can you see if your grandfather's up and about?"

Evan opened the cabin door just as Beth reached for the handle. "Beth, I was just coming to get you." He extended his arms, and she fell into his embrace. As they stood in the doorway, her father spoke to the men outside.

"Are you here with the diving search release form for me to sign?"

"Actually no, we have official paperwork of a different nature to give to your father, the senior Llyndee. Is he available?"

Evan looked at Ben, who shook his head. He didn't know what they were talking about. "Sure, come on in. We're just gathering in the living room. Join us, Ben."

Beth followed her father into the living room and sat next to Naina on the couch. Kate and Maegan huddled together on the picture window seat, their bodies silhouetted against the early morning sunshine outside. Evan stood next to Taid in front of the stone fireplace, her father's hands buried in the pockets of the khaki pants he'd worn for days. They were still stained across the thighs with Maegan's blood.

The police officer handed Taid a folded sheet of paper. "Mr. Padrig Llyndee, I regret to inform you that we are here to serve you with this temporary eviction notice." The officer stopped, cleared his throat, and continued. "I'm sorry to have to do this at this time, given all your family is going through. But the Ojibwe tribe of the Anishinaabe First Nation has filed a specific claim on this land, in recognition of the discrepancy of measurements used in the Robinson Huron Treaty of 1850 and the significant value of the artifacts found hereon. You are hereby required to leave this island no later than twenty-four hours from now or by eight a.m. on July 28, 1990."

Beth stared at the stones jutting out of the massive fireplace that she or Dylan had often used at night as steps to climb to the top and read on the thick cement mantelpiece while everyone else played cards. This couldn't be happening, not now. No matter what Taid said, the Ojibwe people wouldn't be this cruel. Besides, she'd thought of at least five places they hadn't looked yet that Dylan loved. He was out there, waiting for them to find him.

Taid unfolded the paper and read slowly. Evan did the same. They both turned and looked at Ben. He shook his head. "I'm as surprised as you that this is happening."

Taid threw the paper into the fireplace's massive opening. It hovered briefly, then fluttered to the floor. "This paper means nothing to me. I have full rights to this island, and I have at least half a dozen papers in the other room to prove it."

The officer stood firm. "That may be true, according to US law, but you'll have to go to court to prove it here in Ontario. Until then, the district judge issued this for the safety and concern of everyone. For now, you must leave."

Beth felt the same frozen panic that gripped her that first night of the search. She didn't dare look at anyone but her father, even though she could hear Maegan crying, her mother mumbling, "Oh, dear God," and feel Naina heaving softly next to her.

Beth jumped up. "We can't go. Whatever my grandfather said, he'll apologize. He didn't mean it. We have to stay and find Dylan. They have to understand that. Please, Officer, you can explain that to them."

"Given the situation, we can extend the search without you for three more days, in the water and along the shore," the officer said. "If you have other places you'd like us to look, show us on the map, and we'll try there as well. We will notify you of our findings daily."

Her father wrapped his arms around his chest and shook his head, tears streaming down his face. Taid looked at her with the same agony that she'd seen when he'd first heard about the Ojibwe artifacts. If she hadn't found them, none of this would have happened. Dylan and Taid wouldn't have fought. Their island would be safe. Dylan would be here, and they'd be preparing for the Lammas party right now, just like every other summer.

Kate stood slowly and walked with her back straight as a pole to Taid, even as her shoulders sagged. She glared at him, then turned to the officer. "Please tell the Akeene family and the Anishinaabe First Nation we are very sorry for the problems we've caused. Their gods have spoken clearly. You have my personal promise that my family, what's left of it, will never return to this island and lake again. It has taken more than enough from us already, and we have no need of it anymore." She walked down the hallway to her bedroom, and the door clicked closed.

Brain waves disconnected, and bolts of lightning darted through Beth's head. She squeezed it to try to stop the voltage, then spread her arms as the cabin pitched beneath her, like a tectonic shift in geological plates had forced her world askew. She fell onto the couch, and Naina pulled Beth tight to her chest.

No no no no no, this wasn't happening. Not now, not when they were so close to finding Dylan. She clung to Naina as the others stood and walked toward the bedrooms, and Evan went outside. Beth could hear him talking to Ben and the officers, but everything seemed muted and in slow motion. She wanted to run to Ben, knew he would agree with her to go talk with the chief, explain the new spots they needed to search. But her body stayed wrapped with Naina's. She buried her head in her grandmother's bony shoulder and matched her quiet heaving with her own. Naina's sweet smell, like the lavender she'd brought from Wales and planted on the island, pulled Beth to her. She wanted to run but didn't dare let go.

Her father returned to the family room and dropped another set of official-looking papers on the table in front of them. Kate came out of her bedroom with her clothes, books, and newspapers packed in two large suitcases and took them out to the porch. When she returned, she told Beth to start packing and collected books and other items around the living room to stack on the dining room table. Naina led her from the couch to Beth's bedroom, and together they packed her belongings in whatever suitcase or box they could find. Maegan followed silently behind but kept disappearing into Dylan's room. Every time Beth passed his room, her sister was digging through his satchel, separating each piece of paper as if one contained the answers to all their questions. Beth pulled Maegan into their bedroom and demanded that she tell her what she was looking for.

"Nothing, I guess," she said. "I thought we had a plan, but I don't know anymore."

Kate found them and pointed toward another drawer to empty. The last time Maegan snuck back to Dylan's tiny room, everything was gone. She lay on Dylan's bed and turned her back to the door.

When Beth had packed her clothes and books, she went outside to find Evan and Taid. Surely they weren't really leaving. They had pulled the boats into the boathouse, returned the folding chairs and barbeque to their respective spots in the storage shed, and stretched out the long ladders to nail the winter shutters over the windows. Beth ran to her father and grabbed one end of the ladder.

"Wait, Dad, we're coming back, right? Why are you putting up the shutters?"

Taid answered. "I'm going to fight those crazy Indians with all I have, but I'll be damned if they can come here and see or get into my home."

Beth's mouth opened, dumbfounded at her grandfather's words. She yanked on the ladder to get her father to pay attention to her. "Dad, make him stop!"

Evan dropped his side and walked to Beth. "I know this doesn't make sense right now. As soon as I get the rest of you home, I'll come back up. Dylan's strong. He's out there somewhere, waiting. We will find him, and Taid will get the legal situation resolved. I don't want to go either, but we have to, for now. Please don't argue with me."

Her dad looked at her with an anxious intent she hadn't seen in days. "Promise me, Dad. Promise."

Evan nodded.

Beth watched Taid hand Evan a shutter, and he climbed up to the small window on the living room's north wall. Inside, Kate and Naina rushed to empty each room as the shutters killed the sun's warmth and glow. When the last shutter sealed shut the huge picture window, an immense silence joined the darkness through-out the cabin. Beth stood in the middle of the family room, willing her eyes to see Dylan's paintings hanging around the room—the ones their parents had begged for and he'd finally agreed to share.

She ran to his bedroom and used the flashlight on the high shelf to find the large black leather case that held Dylan's unframed paintings at the end of his bed. She'd put his painting of her from last summer in the case for safe keeping—the one he'd told her to look at to find the answers she needed. She had to find it now.

Kate stopped at the doorway as Beth pulled the small sheet of paper out of the case. She pushed Beth aside, zipped the case shut, and handed it to her as she pointed to the south dock where they were filling Ben's fishing boat. Beth rolled the painting into a tube and held on to it with one hand as she pulled the huge flat case outside, down the uneven rock steps her feet had memorized by the time she was six, and onto the thick wooden dock. She stared at Ben, pleading for an explanation. He looked back with her same fear and confusion and reached for the bag. Maegan followed behind with another load, handed it to Ben, and pulled Beth back to the porch. No one looked at her; no one said a thing.

She watched from the porch as her father locked the bolt of the boathouse door and leaned his head against its thick log wall, the one he'd shellacked for at least the twentieth time a few weeks ago. Taid put his hands on Evan's shoulders, and they stood together until Kate slammed the porch door, jolting them back into reality. Beth jumped as they turned and walked toward her, surprised by even their sudden return to emotionless movement. They joined the four women on the porch and started to load their arms with the last bags and boxes.

"Wait," Naina said. "We can't leave like this." Beth turned toward her grandmother, relieved someone was ending this mad-ness. Naina grabbed her husband's hands. "Taid, please."

"All we can do is pray, my dear."

Evan reached to pull Kate, Maegan, and Beth into an embrace with his parents. The girls joined in while Kate stepped backward, away from the rest, and stared out at the lake.

"We leave with broken hearts yet thankful for all the love and joy this glorious part of the world has given us," Taid said. "We pray for strength in the coming days, weeks, and months so that we may find our lost son and our own peace and understanding, so we can come together again and share the love and light within ourselves and for each other, and revel in the beauty of this land once again. Though so much has been taken, let much be reborn in time."

He and Naina started to recite the Welsh prayer spoken by generations of Llyndees, and everyone but Kate instinctively joined in.

Grant, God, Thy protection;
and in protection, strength;
And in strength, understanding;
And in understanding, knowledge;
And in knowledge, all light and truth;
And in light and truth, justice;
And in justice, love; And in love, God;
And in God, all goodness.

As soon as Taid uttered the last word, Kate picked up a box and walked toward the dock. She handed it to Ben, climbed into the boat, and sat at the far end of a bench. The rest of the family slowly made their way to the dock and filled the boat. Beth took her position at the bow and pulled the rope from the dock's metal ring. Ben steered the boat around the point for a full view of the cabin and then followed alongside the island's full north and south lengths before heading across the lake toward the south shore. The seconds flew by in hyper-speed as Beth tried to memorize the island's every tree and blueberry bush, every ledge where she'd watched her brother paint, the smell and feel of the water, the sound of the birches dancing in the breeze and of the boat cutting through the lake's shimmering sapphire waves. Her eyes darted everywhere, sure she would see Dylan standing somewhere, waving for their attention. As Ben turned away from the island, she saw Sam perched on one of her fort's walls. She pointed, yelling for Ben to stop, but her father pushed her back in her seat and once again shook his head. He leaned toward her and held her free hand in his, gently rubbing his thumb over hers.

As the island fell farther behind and her back faced the oncoming shore, she looked at what was left of her family. Her mother was staring into some distant place only she knew, while her father scanned the lake and shore. Maegan sat next to their father and watched her hands roll over each other as if she could wash away the pain of the last days. Naina and Taid sat together as one, their arms around each other, their eyes focused toward shore. Every part of her felt diminished, as if she were melting or fading into an empty shell. Only Ben returned Beth's gaze with a small nod and a frown.

Beth wanted to be absorbed by this lake, this place that had meant everything to her and to her brother. It wouldn't, couldn't betray them. Even if the manitous were talking, they wouldn't take Dylan like this—he was as much one with them as Ben.

How would she navigate the world without him or this place, even if it were for just a few days, a week? She squeezed the small painting tighter in her palm to grab both sides of the boat. *He's out there somewhere*, she screamed from deep inside, but the words wouldn't come out. *We can't leave. We have to find him. Please don't do this. Don't make me do this. We can't leave. I can't leave. I can't.*

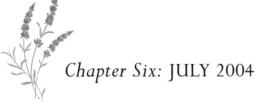

Chapter Six: JULY 2004

Rising heat from Toronto's sidewalk hits Beth like a force field as she emerges from the subway station into the midmorning sun. Frostbite ravaged the tips of her ears last winter in the same eleven blocks between the station and the hotel where Environment Canada and the US Environmental Protection Agency held their meetings, but today the heat presses her navy silk blouse to her skin. She slides into an empty elevator and holds the Close Door button so she can grab a breath mint and brush her hair before she reaches the correct floor. Meeting attendees are circled around the coffee pot in the hallway. She shakes hands and greets each of them before entering the room and walking to her usual spot where her metal nameplate reading Dr. Beth Llyndee, Director of Limnology, US EPA Region V sits at the head of the long rectangular table next to Harvey Metzger, her counterpoint in the Canadian agency. She was promoted to the job two years ago; he's held his for almost eighteen.

Harvey sits down next to her. "Nice of you to join us. Now we can begin. Will everyone take their seats, please?"

Beth studies Harvey's face, an open book for the day's mood: relaxed, charming, a colleague, or filled with partisan protectiveness and pride. That he knows she will voice her agency's position that several aging wastewater treatment plants along the north shores of Lake Ontario are not meeting the latest quality standards probably isn't helping his perspective.

She scans the room and realizes everyone is seated and waiting for her. "Since the water effluent assessment is first on the agenda, shall I begin?"

"Certainly, the floor is yours."

As she stands, Harvey grabs her elbow to whisper in her ear. "Two agenda items to add this afternoon, so we'll need to have lunch to discuss. *Comprenez-vous?*"

Beth nods slightly and walks to the podium. Is he throwing the agenda items, lunch, and French at her as a show of control, since she's in his town, or because of what she's about to present? She pretends to organize her notes at the podium until she can look up without signs of irritation, and then she clears her throat and begins.

Three hours later, with a commitment from Harvey's agency to begin upgrades to the treatment plants and renew weekly water-quality reporting, Beth follows Harvey to a sidewalk stand to buy sandwiches. They sit on a bench facing Lake Ontario in Harbour Square Park, beside other workers reveling in the noon sun. Occasional drafts of mist waft across her face from a nearby fountain whenever the breeze shifts in their direction.

As Harvey rambles on about the afternoon's agenda, Beth closes her eyes under her sunglasses to listen to the lake's gentle rolling. Chicago and Toronto are so similar—humongous urban centers on a Great Lake with vibrant economies and residents from dozens of cultures—and yet she thaws on Canadian soil. Her heart calms, her breathing eases, and it feels safe to open that place deep in her gut and relive a few memories with the affection they deserve. She's glad she decided to read Taid's letter here. Away from her other life and who she is in Chicago, she can remember what her family had been, who she was on the island, and consider the betrayals and guilt locked away with her memories. She vows to leave the evening reception early and try to recall this sense of calm before she reads Taid's letter and wills.

"Wow, you've pretended to listen to me for the last ten minutes," Harvey says. "Where do you go when you disappear like that?"

Beth lifts her shoulders and chuckles. "Sorry, too much on my mind these days."

He stands. "Everything okay?"

Beth smiles, stands, and turns to face the lake and its fresh breeze. "I'm fine, everything's fine. Something I thought was buried long ago has resurfaced, but I'll figure it out."

He matches her gaze at the lake and waits. When she doesn't offer more, he clears his throat. "Life can throw some crappy curveballs. Remind me to tell you a few of mine sometime."

His earnestness surprises her. She turns to him and nods toward Bay Street. "Thanks, Harvey. Do I have time for a quick walk before we start again?"

"Sure, I have calls to return. See you shortly." He turns and strides back to the hotel.

Toronto's sidewalks teem with locals and tourists. For five blocks Beth mirrors the pace of two men debating the Blue Jays' chances of winning a pennant; then she turns to wait at a cross-walk and head back to the meeting. At the island, Naina listened to Detroit Tigers games on the huge citizens band radio. When was the last time they took Kobi to a Cubs game?

Life after her grandmother's death changed in subtle but significant ways. At family gatherings, her kindness and humor are missing, something the rest of them lack or can't muster without her. Has Taid written about her in his letter? Does he want his ashes scattered on the island, as Naina asked in her will? What would Naina say about Taid's letter and two wills, if Beth could ask her?

She jumps as two women walk into her back, when the streetlight changes and she hasn't moved. She steps away from the curb.

"I'm sorry. I'm going in the wrong direction," she says. The women watch as she backs up a few steps, and resume their conversation as they cross the street. Others jostle around her as she stands in the middle of the sidewalk, frozen by all the possibilities in Taid's letter. What if she can't do all that he asks of her? How will she deal with his disappointment and the regret she will feel in response? Beth turns and strides back to the hotel, willing the questions out of her mind. The meeting will be a welcome relief.

At quarter to six, Beth closes the door of her hotel room. She tests the king-sized bed and bolts upright an hour later, when a nearby room's door slams shut. Only fifteen minutes to freshen up before the evening reception. Beth hangs her dress on the back of the bathroom door as she showers quickly, grateful that the knit fabric's packing wrinkles will relax in the steam.

The banquet room is already filled with people in small groups around high-top tables, one long bar, and a table of hors d'oeuvres. Beth moves around the room's perimeter until someone approaches her. She scans the crowd for the newest EPA administrator, Mike Leavitt—the third person in the post in just four years under President Bush—who is standing in front of a wall of windows overlooking Lake Ontario. She's encouraged that he wants to enhance water protections in spite of the president's derision for environmental management, a point her mother makes every time they talk. Harvey and his boss are introducing Leavitt to several Canadian dignitaries, and she's grateful for Harvey's skill at schmoozing so she has time to get something in her stomach before joining them.

As she moves from one conversation to the next, Beth reminds herself to focus, smile, engage as Mike would do if he were here. He's off work tonight and waiting for her call, wondering what's in Taid's envelope. Long after her usual patience for idle chatter has waned, however, she is still talking. Harvey notices and pulls her to an adjoining terrace. She leans over the railing, both hands wrapped around her wine glass, and takes in Lake Ontario's calm expanse of navies and blacks.

"Even I couldn't stomach the bullshit coming out of those two guys' mouths," Harvey says. "Like either of them care, eh?"

"I haven't heard you talk like that in a while. What's up?"

"Just tired, I guess. Tired of fighting the good fight with so little reward. I bet they'll negotiate the new air emission limits until the next election so they don't have to do anything."

Harvey's secretary knocks sharply against the floor-to-ceiling windowpane, points to her watch, and waves him inside.

"Time to return to the show. Stay out here; I can handle the rest of the night."

"Are you sure? I can go to dinner if you need me." They're both shocked at her offer, since she rarely joins in after-hours social events with work colleagues, and her boss has been glued to the administrator's hip all evening. She looks down at her glass to hide her surprise and shame, knowing that her offer is more to avoid reading her grandfather's letter than to support Harvey or their work.

"Just promise me you'll figure out the answer to whatever is bothering you," he says as he backs his way toward the door.

"Thanks for the reprieve."

He nods and disappears inside.

202 THE BEST PART OF US

The envelope stays in her briefcase until she's ironed her blouse and slacks for the next day and changed into her pajamas. She turns the package over in her hands as she sits on one corner of the bed, moves to the side chair next to the window, then returns to the bed. Is she more afraid that she will do as Taid asks and defy her mother and perhaps her father, or that she'll choose not to go back and disappoint the two men, maybe three if she counts Kobi, who she cares about most? Who she would never want to disappoint?

Where do her desires lie? The realization that neither question asks what *she* wants—only what others want of her—hits Beth like a boulder dropping on her stomach. She tosses the envelope on the bed and walks to the small refrigerator in search of alcohol.

She turns the side chair to the window and looks at the city's lights as she chugs two small bottles of chardonnay. Shock is still what she feels after all these years, that a wisp of one day's events could change everything, that lives so connected and sweet could unravel on such happenstance. How many minutes, days, and weeks of her life has she spent missing Dylan? He's been the biggest hole, deep in the middle of her soul. Or was he just the start, and the cavern is as much about everything that happened afterward and since?

She assumed all these years that the battle was between her mother and Taid. One determined to put that part of her life behind forever, to forget she had a son or spent summers on an island in Canada, and expecting everyone else to do the same. The other celebrating the memories and all they once were to each other—even if they couldn't be where the family's love shone brightest because of his own error in judgment. Beth tried to balance between them to preserve whatever sense of family she could find, for herself and her son. At a certain level, she knows she focused on preserving the family's status quo to avoid dealing with her hurt and anger toward all of them and even nature itself. They all betrayed her.

For the first time, the loyalty her mother has asked—no, demanded—of the family galls Beth. She respects that Kate could make a conscious decision to flip a switch, accept what is and move on, as she seemed to accomplish that last day in the cabin. In many ways, Beth knows she's mirrored her mother in terms of looking forward, not back. But she also wants her mother to pay a price, to understand how much her demands have cost the rest of them.

Neither Maegan nor their father would fight her then or now; they've made that clear. Evan promised he'd find Dylan and Taid would win the island back in court. But Kate told him she and their marriage would not survive if Evan went back to the island, forcing her to hope for something that would not happen. Dylan was gone, she said, and the island and the Ojibwe manitou curse were to blame. He gave in but dealt with Kate's demand by pulling away from the family. Beth can't imagine giving up on Kobi. How could her father give up on Dylan and the place he cherished, just to appease his wife?

Naina's stroke a week after they left the island derailed Taid's intentions. Certain the stress and sadness of the island fight had caused the stroke, caring for his wife became Taid's single focus. He healed her enough to eat and read and laugh, but never talk. When she died six years ago on the same July date that they'd left the island, Taid saw it as completing the circle. "Now I wait for the gods to decide it's my turn to go," he said.

And then there is Maegan. She and Beth waited every night for good news from the Ontario police. With their fingers crossed and hands clasped together, they stood in the hallway and listened as their dad took the call in his office. For a month they hugged and cried when he hung up. "It can't be. It just can't," Maegan whispered in Beth's ear. She didn't go back to Northwestern when

Beth went to high school in September. Instead, she focused on getting their mother out of bed. Kate may have pushed the whole family forward, but it took months of grieving for her to accept her own decision. Once she did, her entire focus was on Maegan and her future.

"You will go back to college for the winter term," Kate commanded, "and be everything you're supposed to be." Maegan suggested she transfer to the University of Michigan and live at home, where she could still be there for their mom—and, Beth thought, help herself to heal as well—but their mother was firm.

"Time for all of us to start over, Maegan. That includes you."

A month after she moved to Northwestern, Brian joined her, and three months later she was pregnant. The night before their shotgun wedding, Beth tried to talk Maegan out of marrying Brian—now an obvious alcoholic. Maegan shrugged, said he was probably all she deserved and someone it would be impossible to disappoint. They escaped to Arizona, where Brian got a job on a landscaping crew, and two more babies followed.

By the time Beth was a junior in high school, Kate claimed she'd learned what her demands had wrought. "It may have taken two children to learn that I can't control their destiny," she said to Beth, "but it won't take a third. You are free to do what you want with your life, and I will not interfere." Beth felt her mother had given up on her, was happy to rid herself of any responsibility for her youngest daughter.

Instead, Kate became a devoted grandmother to Maegan's children. When Brian left soon after the third child was born, Kate spent even more time in Arizona, where she felt useful and needed and could escape the family dynamics at home. Maegan admitted she needed Kate's help so she could work enough hours to pay the bills, and she considered it her penance for "all the ridiculous mistakes I've made in my life." At the last holiday dinner, Beth saw the affection between Maegan's children and

Kate and wished Kobi could experience his grandmother that way too. If she does what Taid is asking, that chance will disappear forever.

As Beth swallows the last drops of wine, she remembers what Maegan said when she, Mike, and Kobi visited last summer. "You know it will come down to you, even if you don't want it to. You're the only one who has argued with her about Taid and the island, the last holdout, and she knows it. You hold the power. Don't let her take it from you."

Is that why Taid wrote this letter to her and why Kate delivered it personally—both urging their perspectives on her, forcing her to decide who wins this battle? Hasn't she created a new life in Chicago, where the battle doesn't matter anymore?

She's balanced in the middle of the teeter-totter between her mother and grandfather all these years, thinking she was maintaining a sense of peace within the family. How did she not see that this conflict would come down to her? If she told Taid no, the battle would be over and her mother would be the victor, if there can even be one. Beth would still have her family, her life as it is now, but she would shatter Taid's heart into a million pieces.

What of her heart? Can she let go of the past's grief and feelings of betrayal and share the island, the lake, and that part of herself with her husband and son? Is she willing to pay the price of losing her parents completely? If her father wasn't willing to stand up to Kate's demands years ago to find Dylan and keep the island, he wouldn't risk it now, even for her. Will the lake and island even feel the same after so many years?

Beth lays her head on the back of the chair and reaches deep inside to let the memories escape. She can feel the afternoon breeze in her hair as she canoes around the island with Dylan, hears his laughter when he splashes her back with his paddle. Gray jays and yellow-breasted warblers bark and whistle as she reads at her fort, and an eagle claims its territory with its staccato calls. The echo of her breath in a snorkel, the taste of whitefish and blueberry pie, the loons' heartfelt wails and trills as the sun sets. The scent of ashes that ooze into every pore and strand of clothing from the night's bonfire.

Goosebumps sprint across her arms, and she hugs herself to stop them. She tries to remember the last Christmas, the first time everyone was together in several years. Kobi was ecstatic to play with his three cousins and have a "campout" in the garage with sleeping bags from Beth, Maegan, and Dylan's childhood. Everyone around the table for dinner, raising a glass of mead from Taid's homemade collection. A stronger sense of family than she'd felt in years, even if her parents barely spoke to each other. Maybe even a sense of peace, finally. Or is she deluding herself, pretending to see something that will never be?

"Enough," Beth chastises herself out loud and returns to the envelope. Its contents fall onto the bed, and she paces as she reads: the two wills are identical except for the beneficiary for the island. One lists her, Mike, and Kobi; the other the Ojibwe First Nation of Thessalon, under the direction of Chief Makwa Akeene and his heirs. Lily. What has become of her?

Beth reaches for the letter. Her throat catches as she reads his greeting, *my dearest wyres melys,* and she drops the page to her side. She circles through the last twenty minutes to remember all she has at stake, then lifts the letter and reads.

My dearest wyres melys,

I know you are shocked and perhaps angry to receive this package without warning. I apologize. I feared you might give me an answer immediately based on everyone else's needs and wants rather than your own if we discussed this on the phone. So let me state my case, and then you are free to choose.

Life happens so fast. I woke up a young man, at lunch I was middle aged, and by dinner I could imagine my own death. I long ago finished my wine, ale, and hors d'oeuvres, the main course was mostly a grand feast. Coffee has been served, and I hope for one last, sweet taste of dessert.

The best part of me already died with Naina, and my time at the table is fading fast. I couldn't leave without doing this, without giving you the choice you deserve. You've lived with my mistakes for too long, and the guilt I feel for causing Dylan's accident and Naina's stroke and losing the one place where we—you—are most alive will live with me through eternity. That shame is why I have not defied your mother's wishes.

When we're young, disappointing our parents seems like the worst thing in the world. But it's not. It's disappointing yourself that sticks with you, robs

*you of all that you should and could be. And it's such
an easy thing to do.*

*It's time for you to decide what will finally calm
your own waves. If you return to the lake, if you lead
the way, you'll be surprised how quickly others' anger
and fight will disappear. And you will be thrilled with
what you find and gain, in return.*

*Only you can know which of the choices enclosed—
willing the island and cabin to the chief and his people
or to you, Mike, and Kobi—is right for you. Before
you decide, I'm asking you to return to the lake and
island we love as much as we do each other. Walk the
trails. See how the island and cabin have fared. Listen
to the loons with Kobi. Your brother, the island, and
all they've given and meant to us deserve at least that,
don't you think?*

*Please let yourself see this as the gift I intend.
True to our surname's Welsh meaning, you are our lake
goddess, and no one has the right to take away your
birthright. I wouldn't be loyal to myself or to you as your
grandfather if I didn't remind you of that.*

*This comes down to your life's feast, my dear, and
only you can decide what your main course will be.
Know that my love is as true, vast, and permanent as
the bluest sky and the widest sea, and I will honor your
decision either way. Choose the best part of you, and all
will be well.*

All my love, Taid

After she reads the letter three times, the last time out loud, Beth knows she can't call Mike. He'd vote immediately to go, her mother's and her feelings be damned. And he wouldn't understand her hesitation—whether she can find the strength to see where Dylan was lost, or to let someplace so precious back into her heart, only to lose it again if the Ojibwe are already living on the island. Whether she can risk seeing her life as it could be, so different and separate from the life they've created in Chicago.

The only person who will understand is Maegan. How will she feel about what Taid is suggesting? Since Maegan depends on their mother to help with the kids, will she ensure that future rather than one on the island? Is her memory of that day and her role in Dylan's death still too painful?

She dials Maegan's number and almost clicks off as her sister answers.

"Baby Sis, what's up?"

Even though Maegan has never wasted words, her directness stops Beth short.

"Is that you, Beth? Or is my gorgeous nephew playing with his mom's phone?" Still silence. "Shit, are you all right? Hello?"

Beth shakes her head, forces her brain and voice back to life. "Hey, Maegs, how are you?" Children yelling and water splashing fog the line. She presses the phone to her ear. Maegan must be in the backyard, by the pool.

"Hang on, we've got a horrible connection. Let me go inside." Maegan's flip-flops slap against the soles of her feet; the patio door slides open and closed.

"Okay, peace and quiet. Where are you?" Maegan says.

"Funny you should ask." Beth stalls as she tries to put the words together. "Mom's there, right?"

"Yep, came in yesterday, sitting under the umbrella watching the kids swim and reading another book about Bush's responses to 9/11. Should really help her anger issues."

Beth chuckles. "How do you stand her coming so often? Is she always nice to your kids? How are they, by the way?"

"Nice enough, plus they like living in a clean house—since she scrubs the toilets and vacuums every day. I figure while she's here, Dad and Taid can breathe, which is good for their brain cells." She pauses. "And the kids are fine, but that's not why you're calling." Her voice deepens, signaling to Beth that chitchat is over. "Where are you?"

"I'm in Toronto for a meeting. Mom delivered a package yesterday from Taid before she flew there, and I just read it."

"Yeah, what's it say?"

"He's worried about the island, what to do with it in his will. He's asked me to go up there, figure out if we want it."

"We or you?"

"Well, I'm assuming both of us."

"I don't think that's what it says. The will he read to me last week only mentions you."

Beth jumps off the bed. "You knew Taid was sending this, and you didn't warn me?"

"Of course not, or you wouldn't decide to go up there. That's what you're going to do, right?"

Beth paces again. It's one thing to consider a future separated from her family. It's quite another if Taid and her sister are scheming so she will cause that separation.

"So you set me up, and I've fallen for it. What's the plan? If I can handle being there again, maybe Taid can too? Or if the Ojibwe are living on the island, I get to be the one to say the final goodbye? What about Mom and Dad? I get to take the fall, be the guinea pig for their reaction?" The veins in her temples throb as she stomps back and forth.

"Whoa, take a step back on the anger and control ratings. You sound like Mom. No one's setting you up. I talk with Taid all the time too. You're not the only one who loves him."

Beth stops and drops into the chair facing the city's few remaining twinkling lights. She looks at her watch. It's well past midnight.

"Beth, he read the two wills to me because he wants to do what's right for all of us, but especially for you. He knows you've paid the biggest price all these years. He wishes he'd stood up to Mom a long time ago, told her she needs to release us from her anger and pain. Then Naina, you know, so it's taken him a while to get his strength back."

"Go on."

"He wanted to know how I felt about the island, if it was okay if he willed it just to you, and how I thought you'd respond. It's all with the best of intentions, as Taid always is with us. He wants us to be happy. And maybe get a chance to see the island once more before he goes."

Beth takes a deep breath and sighs. "How do you feel about all of this?"

"He's right, you should have the island. Even if the Ojibwe have taken it over, the lawyers claim he has the deed and other documents to uphold his rights to ownership in court. I always loved the place, but it wasn't part of me like it was and still is for you. And it's different for me, given everything with Dylan." Her voice catches as she says their brother's name.

"Why would you think it's still part of me? My life in Chicago is great. I think I've moved on pretty well."

Maegan's quiet, then responds softly, "Sure, as much as Dad has. You're both frozen. But you're never going to move forward until you face the past, Beth. I've gone through it already, to learn how to move on with just the kids. It's your turn now."

"I've never felt frozen, but maybe Mike trying to convince me for years to visit the island so I can 'get back all of myself,' as he calls it, is the same as what you're saying."

"Smart guy."

"When I told him the gist of Taid's letter last night, he thought there were clues in Taid's words for how to make peace with the past and move on—for all of us, not just me."

"So read the letter to me."

Beth lifts the letter from the bed and begins. Maegan giggles at his comparison to life as a feast—"That's so Taid, always thinking life's supposed to be a grand Lammas party"—and they agree that life without their grandfather is unthinkable. After she reads the last two paragraphs, Beth can hear chair legs scrape across the floor. Did Maegan sit down or stand up?

"Yeah, yeah, you're the perfect granddaughter, Miss Lake Goddess. Read the part over that starts with 'It's time for you to decide . . .'"

Beth reads.

"Okay, now the sentence about what he wants you to do up there."

"'Walk the trails, see how the island and cabin have fared, listen to the loons with Kobi. Your brother, the island, and all they've given and mean to us deserve at least that, don't you think?'"

Beth waits. She can hear her sister's flip-flops clapping on the floor.

"Finish the letter again."

Beth reads. "So? What do you think?"

Maegan stops pacing and speaks in a slow, determined tone. "All the reasons you need are there, Beth. I can't explain why, but you going up there may redeem my life in ways you can't even imagine."

"What do you mean? What are you not saying?"

"Listen to me. You need to do what Taid is asking, and you have to promise me you'll find Lily. As soon as you can."

"Why?"

"Just trust me. Ask her to show you a letter I sent a year after we left."

"Wait, I don't understand anything you're saying."

Maegan laughs. "You don't have to. Can you leave tomorrow morning?"

Beth plops onto the end of the bed. "I have another day of meetings, and I haven't talked with Mike. He can't get off rounds this fast, and he won't forgive me if I go without them."

"Tell him you're leaving in the morning and that he has to make it happen. He will, Beth. I know he will."

"Why are you pushing me? What's the big rush?"

"Stop asking questions and trust me for once. Trust in Taid and your own instincts. You're doing the right thing, for all of us. Even Mom. Talk again soon."

The phone line clicks off. Beth stares at her cell phone as if it will give her the answers she's missing.

Before she can read Taid's letter to Mike or repeat Maegan's thoughts, he demands that she tell him what *she* wants.

"Tell me what your gut's screaming," he says.

She stammers; he yells again. "Whatever it is, that's what we're doing. Tell me now."

"Oh, shit. *Shitshitshit!*" She jumps, runs in place, anything to release the adrenaline rushing through her. She should have known this is what he'd do. He knows her too well, and her heart swells that he's asking what *she* wants to do.

"Go. We're going. We have to at least go and see it." As she says it out loud, endorphins pulse through her bloodstream, and she laughs at her body's response.

Mike chuckles at her euphoria and his own. "This will be Kobi's first grand adventure."

His excitement halts when she tells him to pack and leave in the morning.

"What the hell? I thought we were coming up with a plan. I can't abandon rounds, tomorrow or the rest of the week." He pauses for several seconds, expecting her to relent. "Is this my wife I'm talking to? You never do anything on a whim or disregard work responsibilities."

"I know it sounds crazy, completely illogical, and I'm sorry. But I need to go now. I've opened my heart to the possibilities like you, Taid, and Maegan asked me to, and I can't stop it now. Besides, I promised Maegan." She leans against the hotel window, its chill soothing on her forehead as she waits for his response.

"Jesus, Beth, you tell me for years that you can't go up there, and now you can't wait for the right time for all of us?" She hears his heels hitting the kitchen's linoleum floor. *Stomp, stomp, stomp,* like a grandfather clock counting down the seconds.

"I can't explain it, but I have to go now. I wouldn't ask if I didn't know it's right."

"But you don't know—if the cabin's still there, what shape the island is in, if anyone's still there that you know. What if it's not good? What if you have to see it all at its worst, by yourself? Shouldn't we make some calls, at least prepare ourselves for the potential outcomes?"

She shakes her head and smiles at his foolishness. Of course it's all there—every speckled rock, every bush, every chunk of granite sprouting out of the island on the walkway from the dock to the bright red cabin door. Maybe the cabin won't be the same, maybe someone else will be living there, but the land and the lake will. Her chest pounds, her heart wild and loose, filled with longing and anticipation. Eager to move, unafraid.

"Okay, okay. Go. I'll find someone to fill in and call you when we're leaving. Promise me you won't go to the island without us. I've waited too many years to see this place and you there. At least give us that."

"I'll try. Hurry."

Even at midmorning, Toronto traffic is relentless. Cars growl and whine as they lurch along the northbound highway like impatient cattle herded through chutes, anxious to reach open pasture. Blood congeals in Beth's inner ears until the city's heat and aggression lessens. As it finally gives way to farmland, she opens the rental car's windows, the pungent aroma of fresh manure and dirt swirling through the car's interior. Only three hundred miles to go.

When Beth reaches Port Severn two hours later, where the highway meets Lake Huron's southeastern shores, the water draws her in. She stops at a small lakeside park to stretch her legs. Three mothers watch their young children dig in the sand and play in gentle waves.

"Couldn't stand another minute in the city?" one mother asks Beth, who is still dressed in her work clothes. When she jogged early that morning along Lake Ontario, her instincts pushed even stronger to go north. No choice at all. She met Harvey for coffee to offer her thoughts on the day's agenda and her apologies before she found the nearest car rental agency. She wants to save her one pair of jeans and T-shirt for when she reaches the lake.

"Something like that." She scans the open water and kicks off her heels, buries her toes in the pale grains. "You're lucky to have this for your daily playground."

"We're here almost every summer day. Nothing like water and sand to make happy kids."

Beth rolls her shoulders as she remembers the exhausted contentment she felt as a child after playing all day in and around the lake. When was the last time she felt so free, so satisfied? Almost five years ago after work, when she learned she was pregnant. They hadn't planned it—she felt too young at twenty-four to have a child—but the testing stick's positive sign made her giddy anyway. Mike wasn't expected home for at least an hour, and she had to move or she was going to explode. She jogged the dozen blocks from their home to Lake Michigan and headed south on the lakefront trail.

Almost two hours and eleven miles later, she was in south Chicago. She didn't notice the rush-hour traffic, the exhaust fumes on Lakeshore Drive, or the long shadows as she ran past downtown skyscrapers and the stately Grant Park fountains. When she reached the Museum of Science and Industry's massive columns, she realized the rhythm of the lake's waves had beckoned her on well past dark, as had the spring's evening air in her lungs and the joy of running in time with her heartbeat. She hailed a taxi and smiled all the way home.

Mike ran out the back door as the cab pulled into the driveway, a mixture of panic, anger, and relief on his face. It took him several minutes to describe what he'd been living through while she'd gone on her celebration run. He'd checked with the few neighbors they knew, called two of her friends, even considered calling the police.

A week later he bought her a treadmill for her birthday, claiming it was safer for her and the baby—no city grit or fumes to inhale inside their spare bedroom, no dangers from the elements or strangers lurking in the shadows. Convinced by his logic, she's used it ever since. She can control when and how long she runs and use television or music to drown any lingering need for the sounds of waves. She ventured to Lake Michigan to swim on hot summer weekends while she was pregnant, but never to run.

Beth watches as the women collect their children and belongings. She envies their freedom to spend days at a beach bordered by trees and grass rather than concrete and cars. Her urban claustrophobia was overwhelming when they moved from Ann Arbor—a small town with green spaces and a relaxed university vibe—to Chicago for Mike's residency in pediatric oncology at the University of Chicago, and her own job as a freshwater ecologist at the EPA.

She'd hoped to move west or north when he finished, somewhere she could smell the rich earth under her and hear the hum of dragonflies flashing across the sky on hot summer days. But after four years, the university offered him a joint fellowship to teach and practice. By then Mike had fallen in love with the city and his work, and her own career had blossomed. Her commitment to match Mike's long hours as a resident and then in his practice had paid off, and she'd moved quickly up the ladder to her current job—the best combination of science and management. And she'd grown accustomed to their quaint neighborhood in Lincoln Park, a small community just outside the city center with rows of 1950s bungalows and huge sugar maples bordering their street like overlapping umbrellas, muffling the city's noise and heat in the summer and reviving the neighborhood in the fall with their bright shades of yellow, orange, and red.

Lake Michigan was almost as cold as Wigwakobi the last time they went to the beach on Memorial Day. Mike had claimed work, so she and Kobi went with two of his neighborhood friends and their moms. She was stuck talking with the women while Kobi built sandcastles and played with the other boys in the water.

"A day spent sitting *by* the lake and not *in* it is entirely useless," she pouted to Mike when they returned home.

Kobi was a fish from the first time he tried swimming. She taught him about the lake's undertows and wave patterns as she stood in the lake and held him by his stomach so he could practice his strokes. He caught on quickly, probably etched into his DNA from the hundreds of hours she spent in the water. That is as obvious to her now as was his name, after months of indecision and twenty hours of labor. Mike was easy to convince, but her parents were taken aback—Kate resentful and Evan shocked—as if she were forcing them to remember a place and a life they were determined to banish from their memories. Her mother's face still contorts in pain at holiday dinners when she says Kobi's name, as if someone is pinching her with a vice grip under the table. Beth cringes whenever she sees how far Kobi has to come out of himself to get his grandmother's attention, let alone praise.

Beth walks to the water's edge, rolls her slacks up to her knees, and treads through the shallows. Will going back to the island make it even worse for Kobi with his grandparents? How would she tell them she'd returned to the lake and island? Her certainty of last night's decision weakens as she considers her parents, and she stares into the lake as if it can answer her questions.

A distant fishing boat's emphatic horn brings Beth back to the small beach. She focuses on the gentle waves caressing her ankles, retreating and greeting over and over. She breathes deeply, as if her lungs can absorb the lake and give her strength. This is right. It must be. *Move forward, Beth, always forward.* She returns to her car and stops at the local Tim Horton's for coffee and a muffin, then follows the signs to Highway 69 north. Two hours down, four more to go. With luck she should reach Lake Wigwakobi's south campground soon after dark and stay in one of the tiny cabins that dot the shoreline.

She checks to make sure she didn't miss Mike's call while she was on the beach, knows with certainty he will find a way to get to the island despite his frustration with her. He's proven he is the one person she can count on from the first night she saw him at a fall party during her freshman year at University of Michigan. She noticed his tall, solid build, how he listened to each person as if he was prepared to be wowed by their humor, intellect, or smile. People walked away from him on top of their game, as if he'd found the greatness he expected in them. His wide-set, dark blue eyes laughed with his voice, and he moved easily from group to group. She wondered what it would feel like to run her fingers through his loose blond curls.

They smiled at each other across the room a few times, but she was with girlfriends, and he was with a sunny blonde who knew how to interest men. A honeybee, Beth's grandfather called them.

Beth forced herself to go to every weekend football party after that. She was about to give up when she literally fell against his back by the beer kegs at the last party of the season. "Whoa, plenty for everyone." Mike turned to face her as she jumped away.

"Sorry, I was shoved from behind."

He chuckled and lowered his face to meet her gaze at the floor. "Where's your brood? You've been glued to each other all night, just like every party this fall."

Again, Beth looked away, this time to hide her happiness. He had noticed her.

"Don't tell me you haven't seen me staring at you. What an ego blow." He leaned toward her, every syllable flirting. Beth took a drink from her plastic cup. The beaten down mansion pounded with music and people.

"Too many people crammed together, I guess. Where's your blonde friend?"

"Blonde?"

"The woman with you at the party a month ago. Even I couldn't forget someone that gorgeous."

Mike stepped back, gulped his beer, and laughed, a rolling barrel sound that made his entire body shake. "Wow, what a bummer if that's what held you back. She's my sister, Isabella, dizzy Izzy to me. She's in her first year of law school and wanted a break from the library, so she hung out with her partying baby brother."

"She can't be that dizzy if she's going to law school at Michigan."

Mike shook his head. "Yeah, it's a raw deal. She has the looks *and* brains in the family, even a photographic memory. Not an ounce of common sense. Thank God I got that, at least."

"I think you did pretty well in the looks department. Hard to tell yet about the brains."

Mike grinned and leaned closer. "This is an impossible place to impress you with my intellect." He pointed at Beth's friends, watching from a far corner. "Can you bear to part with them and go for a walk? Great splash of stars out tonight."

Beth nodded and waved at her friends. She was shocked she agreed so readily, that she was willing to desert her group for a guy she'd known for five minutes, but they grinned and waved her on. As they stepped outside, both inhaled deeply and laughed at their same response to open air, then found an open spot on the Diag—a large grass courtyard surrounded by the university's oldest, most stately brick buildings, and a gathering place at all hours.

Mike seemed normal despite his upbringing, which he recounted easily. He'd lived in New York City with his father, a brain surgeon who was never home; a mom who worked equally long hours volunteering for various charities; and his sister, Isabella. They'd attended the city's finest private schools, saw their parents on Sundays, and spent holidays at huge gatherings with other families at a private multifamily compound in Costa Rica. As soon as Mike left for college, his father retired and his parents moved to London, a home he and his sister still hadn't visited. He was a senior, premed, and thought pediatrics sounded a lot more fun than brains.

She fell hard for him that night, as if she were in an elevator rushing freefall into a place that offered joy and freedom despite the terror. His openness and enthusiasm were intoxicating, as was how little he cared about his family's money or what it might buy him, and the way his curls bounced in wild abandon when he laughed. Her hands started to reach for them several times, but she pulled back at the last moment and plucked at her own hair instead. Weeks later Mike admitted he knew she had struggled to keep her hands to herself.

"I would have let you, you know," he said. "Then we wouldn't have wasted another week getting to know each other over coffee."

He asked questions that first night no one had ever asked her, in a way that felt safe to answer. He nodded at her responses without evaluation or argument, took her for who she was. Beth didn't tell him about her brother, how her family used to be, only that she'd spent summers on a Canadian island and loved being outdoors and in the wild, the same way he did in Costa Rica. He stared at her late in the evening as if waiting for her to tell him the rest of her story.

"Okay, we've got time." He smiled and stood to leave. He took her hand as they walked to her dorm; pulled her into the first of a million long, tight embraces; and whispered thank you. As she watched him walk away, her body pulsed with the same sense of desperation she'd felt that last day they left the island, a desire and need she hadn't let herself feel since.

They met for coffee on Tuesday and Thursday, when he asked her to dinner Saturday at the apartment he shared with his sister. She hesitated at such an intimate first date—she'd kept previous boyfriends at a safe distance at movies, parties, and school dances—but only briefly, her nod feeling like the most irrational and sane decision she'd made in years.

Mike and his sister greeted her with hugs at their apartment door. Isabella was even more beautiful in person. They led her to the patio and their view of the Huron River, where Isabella handed her a glass of white wine and directed her to the wood chaise while they crammed together on a wicker bench. As they shoved at each other with the easy affection of siblings who had and always would be each other's true family, Beth's throat constricted. She sipped her wine and stared at the river, willing her memories away. She had no idea how long she'd been silent when Isabella stood.

"I'm off to the library for another exciting Saturday night. You might want to avoid the bread; he used way too much garlic." Beth watched as the siblings walked into the living room, talked briefly, and hugged before Isabella grabbed her backpack and keys and was gone.

Suddenly conversation was awkward. They drank their wine, made idle chatter. After a second glass, he suggested she relax while he got dinner on the table. She focused on the river gurgling below her, but the initial sense of peace was overtaken by more bittersweet memories: lying in bed at the cabin, the lake lapping at the island's curves, her sister's rhythmic breathing next to her, the sound of Sam's pecking that last morning at her fort. Memories she'd pushed away long ago. Beth stood, recognized the second irrational yet fully coherent choice she was about to make, and walked inside.

Mike was leaning over the sink as he drained a pot of spaghetti. His forearms peeked out of the sleeves he'd pushed up to his elbows, his blond curls fell limply over his forehead in the rising steam. Beth put her hand on his forearm, and Mike set the pan in the sink. He turned to her, took her face in his hands. She stared at him, and he chuckled. "And you say it's hard to tell others how you feel."

He pulled her to him with one arm, buried the other deep in her hair and neck as they kissed for the first time. He lifted her as she wrapped her legs around his waist and kissed her neck and cleavage as they walked to the bedroom. Her hands found his curls.

"Damn, they are as great as they look."

He lowered her onto the bed and burrowed his face deep in her neck. Somehow nothing mattered except experiencing each moment together, letting the electricity flow through every cell to remind her how it felt to be fully alive. They held each other long after.

"I've been looking for you for so long, Bethie," he whispered. "I'm so glad you're here."

Every muscle and tendon froze. Only Dylan had ever called her that. Her mind tried to process the shock even as the residue of passion still flowed through her body.

Mike felt her stiffen and rolled away. "Shit, I said too much. It's too soon."

Beth sat up and dropped her legs over the side of the bed, facing away from him. "No, it's not that. It's not you. Oh God, please, not now." Her voice pleaded for understanding and to stop what she feared she could no longer keep inside. She held her head to try to regain control, but her eyes filled as the internal flood overwhelmed her.

As Mike wrapped himself around her from behind, any strength to stop the surge fell away. He held her while she told him what had happened, how she and her family had changed, how much she missed the island and her brother, the only other person to call her Bethie. How her brother's life had come and gone, and her mother and then her father moved on and away—from the island, from her, from life. She'd learned how to maneuver on her own, stay in the neutral zone at gatherings to preserve whatever sense of family remained, but with a strong shield of control to keep the emotions at bay.

"I'm so sorry, Mike. How could I do this to you, after you helped me to feel so wonderful, so cared for? I'll leave." Beth started to rise, but Mike pulled her back to him. She buried her face in her hands.

"Beth, stop. Don't apologize. I can't believe you've held that in for so long, and the last thing I want is for you to leave. Don't pull away from me, not now." He rocked her in his arms, and after several minutes she lowered her head to his chest.

She realized then that she'd gone out of herself and wouldn't get back in without bringing him with her. The thought made her heart calm.

"Even though I fell apart, it felt so right for you to call me that," she whispered. This time they moved slowly, gently, each kiss and caress confirming that they had become each other's sun, moon, rain, and stars.

Just north of Parry Sound, the car's warning light for low gas blinks. Beth checks the tiny map from the rental agency and realizes she's almost in open territory, where the two-lane highway is surrounded by trees and silence. She stops at a tiny bar—a shack, really—its silver tin walls rusting at the bottom. Three pear-shaped old men lean over the wood bar from their metal stools, their shirts barely covering the bulbous flesh pouring over their belts and jeans. She regrets not changing from her silk blouse and slacks into jeans and a T-shirt. The men lift their shoulders and heavy bellies from their legs—pregnant from years of too much fear, alcohol, laziness—and rotate on their stools toward her.

Beth stops just inside the door. "Sorry to bother. I'm looking for a gas station."

The men stare at her.

"Sweetie," one finally says, "you're out of luck. You headed back home to the big city?"

"No, north actually. Do I need to go back into Parry Sound?"

The heaviest man, his stringy black hair hanging in a greasy mess off his scalp, slides off his stool and waddles toward her. "I can give you plenty of gas if you want to come back to my place. Lots of petrol in my garage. We can arrange a fair price." He's missing three teeth from his mean grin. She takes a step back, grabs the sticky door handle as he moves toward her.

A young man carrying a carton of bottled Red Cap ale walks through the revolving door behind the bar. He looks at Beth, sets the box down, and comes around the counter.

"Harry, c'mon, back off." He steps between them, and Beth nods in thanks as the older man grunts and shuffles back to the bar. She pulls her hand off the door handle and shakes it slightly, as if the goo might slide off her fingers.

"Thanks, I'm just looking for a gas station."

When he smiles at her, Beth catches her breath. With his thick dark hair cut close to his head, muscular build, and hazel eyes, it's as if Ben's been reborn into a young man in front of her. She tries to hide her reaction by coughing, but he's already noticed.

"Sorry, do we know each other?"

"No, I apologize. You look exactly like someone I knew from east of Sault Ste. Marie. But I don't think he has any children."

"Since I never knew my dad, you could be right. My mom moved around a lot up there when she was young."

Beth hesitates; she can't imagine Ben as the type to have a one-night stand, but she never knew what he did with his time other than a few months every summer. Did he stay home every night or go to the bar in town? How could she not know more about someone who was once so important to her?

"Well, I'm probably mistaken," she says. "I'm not sure he's even alive anymore." The idea of Ben not being at the lake grips at her heart as much as looking at this younger version. "Anyway, do I need to go back into town for gas? I'm trying to get about an hour away from the Sault, and I know there's not much between here and there."

He gives her directions for a gas station three blocks to the east. "Say hi to my dad if you see him," he says as she turns to leave. After filling the gas tank, she changes clothes in the station's grimy unisex bathroom, trying but failing to hold her silks so they don't touch the floor. The cloth soaks up the urine and grease instantly, as if it's eager to tarnish its perfect appearance.

When she's back on the highway, she considers Ben—how much he meant to her and the family, and yet how little they knew about his life away from them. Her mother questioned Ben's intentions in the only conversation they had about the lake over the last fourteen years. Beth had moved home for the summer after her junior year in college to spend time with Taid after Naina's death. It was the first time she'd lived at home in three years.

"Oh, Beth, here you are. What are you doing?" her mother asked as she entered the screened porch with her mug of coffee. She perched on the edge of a middle couch cushion, her body angled sideways toward Beth, smiling expectantly at her daughter.

Beth looked up from the newspaper spread across her lap. "Same thing I do every Saturday morning after my run, Mom."

"Oh, yes, how did that go today? What a beautiful morning for a jog."

Her mother sipped her coffee, leaned back, and crossed her legs at the knees. She flicked the top leg up and down—a habit that meant she was happily engrossed in a book or had something on her mind.

"Went fine," Beth mumbled and turned the page.

"Do you have to work late this week, or will you be home for dinner?" Beth had worked with the same kids at the recycling center for three summers, and they often went to the Arboretum to hang out after work.

She stopped reading long enough to look at her mother. "No clue. Sometimes we get a late delivery and have to get it separated before we leave." She lifted the entire paper in front of her to try to treasure what was left of her runner's calm, hoping the paper wall would be her mother's final clue.

"I met with an attorney yesterday," her mother said. "About the island."

Shivers ran from the base of Beth's spine to the end of her arms and legs.

"Now that Naina's gone, we need to do something, dear. Taid can't or won't do it, but the attorney said we can. We can do it for Taid."

Naina had disappeared in a matter of hours after she fell at home and hit her head. After the funeral, her parents had demanded that Taid move in with them. "We couldn't bear if the same thing happened to you," Evan had told his father.

It still felt unreal that Naina was gone. Beth couldn't fathom how hard it was for Taid to face her passing, this woman who gave up her home and family to travel across the world to a new life so her husband could forget the evils of war he'd lived through, who'd been by his side for almost seventy years. Taid had spent those first days and months hiding in Maegan's bedroom, now his, or sitting in the backyard staring at the sky.

Beth's grip tightened on her paper cocoon. The letters blurred. "What do you mean, do something?"

"Now's the time to sell it, in case Taid needs the money for his care. Who knows what might happen?"

"Isn't that the reason you moved him out of his home, so you could care for him?"

"Of course, but Maegan needs my help with the kids, especially now that she has to work full time. I knew Brian wouldn't stick around."

Beth shook her head, willed herself not to respond. No one had been happier than their mom when Brian proposed. It saved the embarrassment of her oldest daughter having a child out of wedlock and gave a new, safe direction to Maegan's life: wife and mother.

"Well, none of us will use the place again. Someone will buy it, don't you think?"

The paper wall collapsed in Beth's lap. "I don't know, Mom, but it's not your call. Taid has the right to go to the island if he wants. It's his property, not yours."

"Yes, but he won't out of respect for your father and me. It's simply too dangerous for him physically and how he left it with the Ojibwe. They've probably taken the island over anyway. Surely his accident on the cliff and the next one proved what I said all along. It's just not safe."

Beth's anger rose from deep in her gut over what her mother did and didn't say—including Dylan's name, which Kate hadn't spoken once since his death. A few times in those first years Taid had tried to talk about the island over dinner. He'd suggest the lawyers go to court and reestablish his rights as the island's owner. Kate had laughed in a strange, high-pitched hyena sound, as if this was an outrageous reality she couldn't bear. The longer they talked, the higher her wailing laughter became. It terrified all of them to the point that they stopped discussing the lawyers or the island entirely, even when her mother wasn't around—that somehow, she would still hear and never be able to stop her wailing again.

"Taid still writes to Ben once in a while. He could take two days to drive up there, and Ben could meet him at the border to drive him the rest of the way."

Her mother frowned. "I'm not sure we can trust Ben to take care of Taid, given his family situation. To tell the truth, I never liked Ben like the rest of you did. There was a lot we didn't know about him."

Beth closed her eyes and shook her head. *Silence, please, God, give me silence.*

Her mother leaned forward, their knees almost touching.

"I know how much you love Taid, but it's time we do what needs to be done, and I'm asking you to help me. He'll listen to you."

Beth jumped from the chair and walked to the other side of the porch. *No*, she yelled to herself. *Don't say it! Don't take her bait!* She stared at the backyard until she could look at Kate and respond in a controlled, even voice.

"It's not your island, Mom. If you can't be here to take care of Taid, I will fill in, or we'll find someone else to help. But you will not say anything to him about the island, and you can't force me to discuss it with him. For God's sake, he just lost his wife six months ago. Don't ask him, let alone tell him, to also give up their most sacred place. He's already given it up all these years because of your wishes. It's the home they built together, the one place where he was truly himself. That island *is* Taid, Mother, and if you discuss this with him now, you'll kill him."

They stared at each other for what felt like an eternity, until her mother rose and walked out of the room. Beth ran out the porch door and around the neighborhood until her body stopped shaking. She'd realized, for the first time, how little her mother understood what Taid had given up all these years by not returning to the island and lake, whether it was because of Naina's stroke, her mother's demands, or his own guilt. She hadn't questioned that her parents, Maegan, or she wouldn't return, but to force Taid to leave his home in Ann Arbor *and* sell the island proved that her mother only cared about her own needs. Beth ran for four more miles.

As she drives north in the waning afternoon sun, Beth shudders again—at Kate's intentions *and* that she'd never truly considered betraying her mother to return to the island before now. Soon after they left the island, after Kate's pronouncements and Naina's stroke, Beth's father buried himself in work at the university and began to volunteer at a local youth center, teaching math to at-risk kids. Once Kate had finished her grieving and gotten out of bed, he was rarely home. When he was, his grief was resolute, an entity he carried alongside. Throughout high school, Beth pretended to study at the kitchen table until he came home. He'd envelop her in his arms, hold her chest to chest for as long as he needed to gather strength and move on, then let her go with a grateful smile.

Beth rarely saw her parents together when she lived at home. When they gathered for the occasional dinner, the air was thick from stilted conversations and tight smiles. Occasionally she could hear them argue through the thin bedroom walls, most often about Taid, Maegan, or the island. In spite of their failing marriage, Kate never changed her position on the island, believing the

Ojibwe gods had exacted their revenge, and Evan never left—most likely to stay close to Taid.

Even now at family gatherings, Beth's father maintains a mask that never breaks, just a slight glint of love in his eyes when he looks at Kobi and his other grandchildren. Can he break out of that mask and make his own choice whether to return to the island, after all these years? Or is it impossible to consider, as much for himself as for his wife? Beth's foot reflexively lifts from the gas pedal.

The car slows to a crawl, and she stops at the side of the road to consider her mother's reaction. From the first day after the accident, Kate chose anger to avoid the sadness of losing her son—anger and rage that she'd been right all along, that the lake's wildness and the Ojibwe manitous' curse were more than the family could withstand. Even when she stayed in bed those first months, her grief was vivid orange, aggressive and potent, without texture. There were no tears, no catches in her voice, just constant fire. Sometimes Beth wondered if the cloak of heat her mother wore ever made it hard for her to breathe.

Beth's grief erupted in short squalls as she tried to live through those first days and months back at home. Their urgency would weaken if she lay on the throw rug at the end of Dylan's bed, where he used to sit and draw. When her mother found her there one day after school, she shuffled Beth out and locked the door. Stand up and move on, Kate ordered.

Is Kate still refusing to return to the island or allow anyone else to do so because she's still trying to keep her family safe? Beth understands those protective instincts now with Kobi, but also how much he loses if she doesn't let him take risks he can learn from. Mike and Taid have told her that—by playing it safe, staying tightly within the parameters her mother set for the family, Beth's kept much of herself hidden, buried deep inside, and hasn't allowed that part of herself to live. When she left for college, her father told her not to stay outside of herself for too long. Back then, she didn't know what he meant, but of course he knows what she's sacrificed, because he's done the same.

She's held the island deep in her heart all these years because of Dylan, but also because of how tightly her family was wrapped together when they were there. Their family ties are stretched so thin, even though she's tried desperately to keep them connected in spite of the fraying. Like party streamers hanging from the same tree, each member of her family finds the others occasionally in the breeze, but they never reconnect into a united bond. Taid's streamer always swings near hers, the connection frequent and tight, and Maegan's flies by once in a while intentionally, for others to grab on to if they wish. If not, no worries, you can try her the next time. Somehow the most introverted, inwardly focused family member was the tie that bound them all together. Without Dylan, perhaps even a strong wind like Taid's letter can't pull them into a united bow again.

Perhaps that's what Mike has always known when he's told her she's taken the easy way out, to claim that the connection to the lake was gone because of Dylan. Mike admonished her again two nights ago after the Fourth of July fireworks.

"You don't understand," she said to him, "how much we loved it, how much I loved it. If I let my connection return to that place, to nature, I don't know how I could live another day in this city."

He raised his eyebrows and paused before claiming that was another excuse.

"And you haven't met the family that I had up there. Everyone was different, even my mom. Over the years I've grown to feel such betrayal toward the lake—that it would take Dylan and cause us to change as much as we have."

"That's nonsense. Something that deep in your soul can't be lost, just buried. Consider yourself lucky you have a place like that and those memories to hide."

Mike has one string to count on. Even though Isabella lives in Rome and they're both in their thirties, they talk at least once a day—an unbreakable bond from years of counting only on each other. She understood why after the few times his parents visited in Chicago, when it was clear they wanted a relationship with Mike as friends rather than mother and father. Drinks and dinners at expensive restaurants and stimulating conversation about world affairs are fun and interesting, but they don't provide anything to latch on to.

"You've buried that part of yourself for your family for too long," he said. "It's time to turn the page, get that part of you back, and give it to Kobi and me. We're your family now; we've earned the right to experience the island with you too."

He's right, of course. They deserve all of her, and that includes the island—even if it's without Dylan or her family—assuming it's still possible to keep it. She lets herself imagine teaching Kobi how to fish off the dock, watching Taid return to his island home, and showing her son the wonders of nature. A new family, reimagined and renewed. Maybe Maegan and her kids will come as well.

She shivers in her seat. If she lets it all in, opens that part of herself and reconnects again with that world, can she ever leave again? Will she even want to? Mike might think it's an excuse, but her body's quivering tells her what she's risking.

Beth studies the map, realizes she's almost to Sudbury and the King's Highway, when she'll turn northwest toward the lake. The scenery will become familiar, and she's relieved that dusk is settling around her. She's not ready for the rush of memories to jump out at her as she drives past the farm where she and Naina picked eggs from under the hens, or over the rivers where Taid and her father went fly fishing. She starts the car but drives slowly, trying to find a balance between her conflicting emotions.

It's almost midnight when Beth turns off Highway 17 and plods down the narrow dirt road to the south shore campground at Lake Wigwakobi. In the blackness she is protected from seeing the lake, although as she parks and gets out of the car, she can hear its soft waves against the sand. An older man, thin but muscular with white hair, jet-black eyebrows, and a kind smile walks out of the manager's office onto its small wooden deck and calls to her.

"Are you Beth?"

"Yes, how did you know?" She walks up the steps to shake his hand.

"Your sister called a while ago, wanted to make sure we had a cabin for you to rent for a few nights. It's all set: heat is on and the bed's made. Just need you to sign in."

Beth follows him inside, where his wife is waiting. As she signs the register, the couple introduces themselves as Henry and Willa, who bought the campground four years ago when they sold the hardware store they'd owned in Sault Ste. Marie for forty-five years. Now they can't imagine living anywhere else. They tell her about the lake, the boat she can rent if she wants to go for a ride, and the trails nearby that will take her to the top of a majestic cliff.

"It's a special place, this Wigwakobi. Worth it to stay a few days, if you have the time."

Beth nods and thanks them for staying up to greet her. As she walks outside, she can hear Willa say to her husband, "Henry, look at this. That girl's last name is Llyndee."

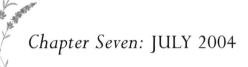

Chapter Seven: JULY 2004

The crank of an outboard engine jolts Beth awake as the frayed curtains covering two small windows lighten with the rising sun. She collapsed onto the twin bed anchoring a corner of the one-room cottage last night. The lake's subtle fragrance and the still familiar pulse of its waves lapping against the beach lulled her into stretches of blissful sleep until her body remembered where she was and shuddered awake. She hugs the pillow to her chest. The lake that stole her brother is outside the door. Can she see it in daylight, touch its cold waves? Will the sound of the seagulls and loons, the taste of blueberries, the feel of a paddle slicing through the water overcome the remains of that one horrible day, as Taid wrote to her? Or will sadness and anger prevail?

She reaches for her cell phone on the plank floor to check the time and notices Mike's text from four fifteen that morning. "Leave approved from work, K and clothes packed, on our way. Grand adventure. Love." It's quarter to eight, so they're probably in the middle of western Michigan by now and will arrive by one or two. She paces the small room, still holding the pillow. If she left now, she could meet them at the bridge between the state's upper and lower peninsulas. Their grand adventure could be a trip to Mackinac Island, and Kobi would still be happy. Mike would be mad as hell, but it would finally be over. Enough, he would say, enough.

As sad as he might be for her, he would close this door as an option in their lives and move on. If he never came here, never saw her as she was, she could keep this part of herself buried forever, and he wouldn't know the difference. But will his vision of her be tainted if she doesn't rise to this challenge?

Her pacing halts as she thinks of her grandfather. Sweet, stubborn, still full-of-life Taid, even as his body fades and his heart moans from missing Naina. And Maegan—redemption is a strong word for whatever Beth's supposed to get for her sister by finding Lily. If she leads as Taid suggests, will the rest of the family follow?

Stop thinking, she chastises herself. *You won't answer your questions inside this tiny room. Move.*

Beth throws the pillow onto the bed and reaches for her jeans and a fresh T-shirt in her suitcase. She stuffs a wad of toothpaste onto her tongue and brushes her teeth quickly; pulls her hair into a tight bun; grabs her phone, keys, and Taid's letter from her purse; and opens the door. Her eyes stay glued to the ground as she sits on the cottage's concrete step to tie her running shoes, then turns and walks away from the lake. The breeze pushes at her back as if to urge her forward, while the lake caressing the sand pleads with her to turn around. The campground owner, Henry, stands on his porch, where he greeted her late last night. He nods slightly as she walks past, as if he knows where she's going.

She drives the one-lane dirt road back up the hill and turns right at the only cutoff, which follows the bay's western shoreline around another smaller bay and stops at the southern end of Llyn-dee's Peak. She folds Taid's letter into her jeans pocket and opens the car door. *Keep moving forward. Don't think. Go.*

Her body moves in sync with the breeze weaving through the old-growth forest of birches, basswoods, cedars, and pines surrounding the trail, her memory of each turn and protruding rock reborn with every step. The air tastes damp as she folds into the deep shade, the path springy under her sneakers. Even after fourteen years, her right hand instinctively rises at the trail's first curve to push away the cedar branches still demanding attention. Her thighs know to lift higher to climb two stands of boulders, her feet stepping on the same beige plateaus and squared edges as they did when she was twelve. She smiles as she inhales the pungent scent of maidenhair ferns that edge the last large rocks before the trail returns, and laughs as she pulls the top off the tallest frond and picks blueberries from the same bushes that were her grandmother's favorite stash, the one she raced to every July to get the biggest bunches before the squirrels and deer. The fruit's energy bursts in her mouth and mixes with the fern's slight tang.

Her heartbeat quickens as the trail's angle turns steep and she passes the spot where she slipped and sliced her calf in the storm. She reaches for the smooth silver beech and the white birches' curled bark to pull her along, and stops to hug the wide trunk of the rare chestnut tree still holding court in the middle of the path. "Hello, old friend," she whispers, grateful for the break to catch her breath; inhale the aroma of pine, fir, and cedar into her heart; and hear the chatter and caw of gray jays and gulls floating across the morning sky.

Beth jogs as the trail levels out and the last turn beckons, when the darkness and quiet of trees and trail give way and the world opens up before her once again. Her chest pounds with longing and fear. As she passes the last pine, the rush of light, color, and open air blind her senses, paralyze her legs. She has forgotten the intensity of the view from the top of Llyndee's Peak—the expansive sky in every shade of blue pressing against the horizon to meet the lake's even deeper hues, with a million sparklers popping across the water from the morning sun. The same fingerlike peninsulas in greens and browns reach into the lake in uneven patterns on the south side, the crescent bays in between. She extends her arms as if to meet the peninsulas' grasp.

The air is warm compared with the woods' chill, the sky bright but sheltering. She walks slowly, taking in every familiar shrub and rock. Here is where her father's arms cradled her against his chest, in response to her five-year-old cries of fear and wonder as he inched his way to the cliff's edge. Her first experience with shivering terror from a race with Dylan when she was ten and he thirteen, as they'd both reached the cliff's top too fast and only his stronger legs had stopped them both from hurtling over. The lazy haze in her early teens when the afternoon sun baked her and Maegan as they lay on a warm rock, eating blueberries they'd picked on their way up that were supposed to go back to their grandmother to make a pie. And her potent envy as she sat by herself that last summer, legs dangling over the edge, watching young eaglets practice their swoops down and multiple attempts back up the six-hundred-foot cliff to the huge nest balanced at the base of a lone pine protruding oddly out of the rock wall, where their mother had closely observed them and her.

The waves' metronomic rhythm against the cascade of fallen rocks far below at the cliff's floor had once alternately wooed or dared her to jump. She takes the last steps toward the edge, so much more ominous now that she has her own family, and life seems even more precious and precarious. So this is what her mother felt all those years.

The last time she stood on this cliff, the afternoon sky opened up and stole everything. She searches the cliff as if her grandmother's book of poetry might still be there instead of long forgotten on the rocks below. She turns north toward the island but stops and drops to the ground a few feet from the cliff's northeastern edge. She pulls her knees to her chest, wraps her arms around them, and stares at the last spot she saw Dylan alive. The images rewind over and over in her mind as if the storm were happening again right in front of her. Her heart seizes each time she remembers turning away from her brother and sister to run down the peak.

When the ache in her chest overwhelms, Beth turns her gaze toward the north shore. The open pasture on the hill above the beach, the first place Ben and Taid looked for Dylan, is filling in with birches. Their white skins and fluttering yellow leaves are iridescent against the bright green grass. The Shepplers' dark cabin is stark against the pale sand. She knew their cabin by heart seventeen years ago, when the two families spent so many afternoons playing on the beach. They sold it the summer after Beth's family left, claiming it wasn't the same lake without them. How strange she hasn't a clue who might live there now.

Henry and Willa's campground to the south hums with kids swimming and splashing each other in the shallow teal water, their shouts and laughter echoing off the bay's walls. A small boat floats where the bay gives way to open lake, the men pretending to fish. Three lie across the boat's benches, rods still in their hands, while another leans against the boat's side, his cap angled low over his face.

Two sailboats with brightly colored spinnakers race across the open lake toward the far east bay. She recognizes one boat from its green-and-orange spinnaker and the letters jauntily pressed onto its stern: LUCK OF THE IRISH. The Byrnes were one of the first to arrive at every Lammas celebration and the last to leave, the grandfather one of the trolling crew and the lake's best sailor. He and Taid raced almost the lake's entire length a few times, both wearing their palms raw from hanging on to their mainsail's sheets for hours, neither willing to concede defeat. Beth squints to try to identify who's sailing the boat, but the distance is too great.

She leans forward to look over the edge. A smaller eagle's nest is still perched against the cliff's lone tree, above the same cascade of rocks she knows by heart. Waves drift into rocks in a casual weekend's pace, their deep bass sounds providing the low notes to the gull's high-pitched calls echoing across the water and through the trees. Everything she needs to remember who she used to be still stands in front of her, strong and true. Her heart stills, her breathing calms.

As Beth absorbs her view—the water, people, trees, rocks, and sky—her back lifts, her arms fall to her side, and her legs relax to cross at her ankles. Her palms press on the vibrant breathing earth, her fingers caress thin grass stalks magically sprouting between the granite and limestone. She inhales the rich scents of earth, water, and sky, her lungs expanding as if she were breathing deeply for the first time in fourteen years. As if the universe smells and tastes clean again, and she can choose to breathe it all back into her heart. As if everything might start over.

She closes her eyes and turns her face to the sun. Perhaps she's missed herself the most, even more than Dylan. Who she is at this lake, among nature, in the wild, is as much a part of her as her teeth or hair. How this lake smells, feels, looks, and tastes were stamped into her genes long ago, no matter how much she might have fought to forget it. No matter what has come before or what lies ahead.

Beth pulls Taid's letter from her back pocket and chuckles as she reads the line that frustrated her just a few days ago: "It's time for you to decide what will finally calm your own waves."

She stands and pulls her cell phone from her pocket to dial his number. The connection is weak, and the ringtone fades in and out, but she can hear it click to his message recording. Beth lifts onto her toes as the beep sounds, bouncing as she talks. "I'm here, Taid, on Llyndee's Peak. I haven't gone to the cabin yet, but so far it's all the same. Thank you. I'll call again soon."

Her phone says it's twelve fifteen. Mike and Kobi will be here soon. She turns slowly in a circle to pull everything into her before she leaves. As she rotates, she considers again what she might find if she walks the ten steps toward the island. Instead, she turns back to the lake and the last spot she saw Dylan in the storm. This time she focuses on remembering her brother floating in the fishing boat, huddled over a wide sheet of paper on his lap. She knows he would have used heavy pastels for the pines behind her, or watercolors to paint the sailboats as they cut through the waves. She vows to experience this place through his eyes as well as hers.

Beth turns toward the south bay and realizes that Henry and Willa are talking to Mike and Kobi on one of the thick wooden docks. She jumps and waves with both arms, but they're concentrating on a boat tied to the dock, the older man pointing toward the boat's engine. She glances at the lake one last time and turns toward the trail.

Willa is first to notice Beth running down the road toward the beach. "Over here, Beth," Willa yells from the dock and points to a small boat circling the bay.

"I bet that's the fastest you've ever run down that trail. Henry's showing your husband how to drive the boat. Course, you could have showed him."

Beth nods from her folded position, panting for air. Her thighs and shins scream. She forces her back to straighten and shields her eyes to find the boat. Mike is driving with Kobi on his lap. "Guess Mike told you why we're here."

Willa nods and touches Beth's arm. She tries not to recoil from the touch of a stranger who seems to know more about her than she'd like. "We knew as soon as we read your name last night, dear. The entire lake has been waiting for one of you to return."

Beth keeps her eyes on the boat and her family. So this is what her grandmother always complained about, that as much as she loved the lake, Naina didn't care for everyone's eyes on them when they were here—as if they were entertainment. She never noticed it as a child and certainly not in Chicago, where everyone is too busy keeping up with their own lives to notice what anyone else is doing. She never considered that others were waiting for her family to return or would watch them when they did.

She shakes her head at Willa. "I'm sure most have forgotten us by now." She steps away from the older woman, focusing on the boat. Kobi's hands are on the engine's steering arm, and they're both smiling. This needs to be about Mike, Kobi, and her, not everyone else who will distract her from the decision they need to make on their own.

"Henry trolls almost every morning. The regulars still talk about the weeks it took your grandfather to build that trail you just hiked. Even the newer folks call it Llyndee's Peak. We've heard about the grand parties your family put together every year. In August, right?"

Beth nods. "Lammas Day, the Welsh holiday for the first wheat harvest." She crosses her arms and tries to act nonchalant. "Is there a man named Ben still on the lake? He used to fish with my grandmother and dad all the time. His sister was married to the Ojibwe chief, and they had a daughter named Lily."

"We know them well. Lily lives in her family's home since her parents moved into town to be closer to the hospital." Willa pats her chest. "The chief has heart issues. They're in the Sault right now for some procedure. Ben took them yesterday. Haven't heard how it went."

"Does Ben still live in his deep woods cabin just past the cliff?"

Willa looks confused. "I'm not familiar with that place. He lives next door to Lily's cousin Amik. Did you know him?"

Beth's heart flutters, and she looks at her sneakers to hide her blushing. Her first love. "Of course. My brother and I used to go to their bonfires all the time."

The old woman watches Beth's reaction a few seconds too long, then clears her throat. "Yes, well, now you can get reacquainted with everyone here. And with your cabin. Such a lovely place."

"It's still there, then? It must be in horrible shape after so many years. Or has Lily's family taken over the island?"

Willa pats Beth's arm again. "It's all there, still waiting. Your boy will love it just as much as I'm sure you did at his age, my dear." She waves toward the boat, and Henry waves back, as does Mike when he sees Beth. She runs to the end of the dock and waits for their return.

Kobi stands as they near the dock and yells, "Where were you, Mom? We've been waiting forever!"

Beth grabs the bow to pull the boat forward along the dock and points toward Llyndee's Peak. "I was way up there. I could see you long before you saw me." She reaches for Kobi, and Mike lifts him into her arms.

Kobi wraps his legs around her and places both hands on her cheeks. "You're going to take me up there, right?"

"You'll see it all, Kobi, I promise, after you learn the rules of the lake. It's different from the beach you're used to at home." She pulls him into a hug and gazes at Mike. "I'm so glad you're here."

Mike meets her gaze for a moment, then chuckles, nods, and climbs out of the boat to embrace them. "On to the next part of our grand adventure. You kept your promise and saved the island for us, right?"

Beth nods and wraps her arm around Mike as she lowers Kobi to the dock. Five minutes later, they've rented the boat from Henry and loaded their luggage and a few bags of groceries Mike brought from home. She wraps a bright orange life vest around Kobi before he's allowed to jump into the bow's seat ("part of the rules, buddy—I had to wear one until I was almost twelve") and asks Mike to sit next to her in the back as they head across the lake. She laughs as Kobi raises his head and arms into the air as she did at his age, the wind swirling among his blond curls.

She slows the boat to point out the eagle's nest and huge granite faces still looking down from Llyndee's Peak. Have the years softened their stern looks, or could they actually be smiling just a bit to see her return? They listen as she explains Lake Wigwakobi's rhythms and tendencies, how to angle the boat through the waves, when to use the engine's speed and when to let the water do the work. Both of them take turns steering the boat.

As they round the north curve of Llyndee's Peak, she grabs Mike's hand. Tears gather in her lashes, and she knows they will fall, no matter what the island and cabin look like. Mike pulls her close, the engine's steering arm stuck between them. When the island fills their view, Beth stops the boat and lifts both hands to her cheeks. Kobi stands and points. "Is that it, Mom? Is that *our* island?"

Mike stands as if he can see it more clearly from above. "Holy shit, Beth." He spreads his feet wide and puts his hands on his hips to balance against the afternoon waves. "Holy shit. It's magnificent."

Beth stands next to him and shakes her head, speechless. The cabin sits on its island throne, its logs freshly shellacked and windows gleaming, the shutters gone that doomed them to darkness all those years ago. The Adirondack chairs encircle the stone fire pit, ready for use. New sprigs of lavender sprout among the bright yellow daisies and ruby milkweed in her grandmother's gardens by the docks. How could seeds have flown from the island's interior to these gardens? Impossible. Beth falls to the bench. She can't stop shaking her head.

Kobi climbs over the boat's benches and stares at her, his hands clasped tightly in front of him. She wipes her drenched face and pulls him into her lap.

"That's our island and cabin," she murmurs. "I don't know

who's taken care of it all these years or who lives there now, but that's it." Mike sits next to her, and they stare in silence.

A tornado of questions spin in Beth's mind as she tries to find the logic to explain the cabin's pristine condition. Lily or one of her relatives must live here. But didn't Willa say it was still here, waiting? No one would have worked this hard to keep the logs clean and preserved, the docks in such perfect shape, with only a hope that the family would return. Not even Ben.

Beth jumps as Kobi climbs out of her lap. "So are we going up there or not? Why are we just sitting here? Let's go!" He stares back and forth at Beth and Mike, bouncing on his toes.

Mike takes one of his son's hands. "Give your mom some time. This is a huge surprise after all these years."

Beth sits up and reaches for the engine's pull cord. "No, Kobi's right. We need to say hello to whoever's living there now, maybe take a tour of the island before we leave."

Mike stops Beth from pulling the cord. "Wait. I get what you're thinking, but I'm not sure you're right. Why no boats by the docks, ashes in the fire pit, or shoes by the kitchen door?"

"Taid would have told me if he'd called someone up here to do this. Willa said Ben's at the Sault with Lily's parents, something about the chief's heart. He's the only person my grandfather's talked with all these years, and Taid doesn't even know we're here. You didn't call him, did you?"

Mike shakes his head. "Would Maegan call him?"

"She might have, but that would have been late last night or this morning. No one could clean this place that quickly. Not after fourteen years." Beth shakes her head, reaches for the cord again. "Someone must be living there. That's the only explanation."

She yanks harder than needed for the engine to start and shoves it into forward gear. Kobi falls into Mike's lap as the bow lifts quickly, then drops as the speed grabs hold. Her molars reach for the insides of her cheek, and she tastes blood by the time she steers to the south dock. A painful habit she hasn't had to fight in years.

Mike holds Kobi's hand as they climb out of the boat and follow Beth up the rock-and-concrete steps to the fire pit, the north dock, and the kitchen porch. The door is locked. They peer through the windows, but there's no one inside.

"Should we break the lock?" Mike asks as he shoves the kitchen door. "Any other doors where it's easier to break in?"

"I suppose we could see if there's still a spare key hanging in the boathouse," she mutters, as her senses are overwhelmed with memories of her mother reading on the porch and her parents' looks when they saw Taid after his fall from Llyndee's Peak. When Kobi pulls on her shirt, she nods and walks to the boathouse but stops abruptly when she looks at its huge log door. The image of Taid and her father that last morning, after they'd put the boats away and the shutters up, seems as real as the three of them standing there now.

Mike holds Kobi by the shoulders behind her and whispers, "What are you seeing?"

Beth closes her eyes and gnaws faster on her cheek. *Keep moving forward. Don't think. Go.* She nods again and steps forward to open the door. The fishing boat still rests where her dad and grandfather hoisted it the last time; tools hang on their posts along the pegboard above the worktable. The key Maegan and Dylan hid in a corner—so they could get in past curfew without waking their parents—still dangles on its hook. Everything as they left it, preserved like a museum. None of it makes sense.

As she opens the door into the kitchen, a rush of smells— the wood polish Naina used every spring on Taid's furniture, the mothballs in the linen closet and huge bedroom storage trunks, the mustiness of undisturbed air—reach out and surround her. They weave around and through her like invisible threads as she opens kitchen cabinets where bowls, plates, and pans wait for use, and inspects each bedroom. Only the bedcovers in her and Maegan's room are different, Native blankets she used for her fort instead of the plaid bedspreads they grew up with. She sees Maegan lying in her bed after the accident, tears collecting in wet circles on the pillow but her eyes staring in the distance, unable to focus on the present.

Beth hugs herself and returns to the living and dining room where everything is the same except the couch fabric and curtains behind it. All but one of Dylan's paintings still hang in their respective spots—the thick acrylic painting of the lake as it stormed is gone from above the fireplace. She lifts Kobi into her arms and walks around the room, telling him where his uncle painted each scene. Mike checks the refrigerator for power and the faucets for water and meets her by the fireplace.

"No one's here, Beth. The faucets and sink are bone dry. You said there's a pump somewhere to fill the water tank, right? If someone was living here, the fridge would be plugged in; there'd be food in it, and water in the pipes. Does everything look the same?"

Beth nods. "Pretty much. But it doesn't make sense." She sits on the couch with Kobi on her lap, a slight cloud of dust wafting around them as the cushions expand. He points at the fishing rods hanging in the corner and jumps off her lap. Mike sits down next to her and smiles.

"It's got to be Ben," he says. "Taid must have told him about his letter to you, so he knew you'd come, sooner or later. It's obviously not lived in. It's waiting, just like Henry's wife said."

Beth allows herself to smile slightly, but the urge to run away from her memories is as strong as her hope that this is still her family's home.

"It just doesn't seem possible, or right," she whispers.

"Does that mean we can go fishing, Mom? Which one of these should I use?" Kobi unhooks the shortest rod and plays with the knob on the reel. "I like this one."

Mike pulls Beth to her feet. "We'll ask Henry when Ben will be back and find Lily tomorrow. Let's take today to enjoy all of this together. Show it all to us, Bethie. Let's have fun."

It could have been just last summer that Beth helped to open the cabin with her grandfather—each step comes back to her without hesitation or thought. She teaches Mike and Kobi how to grease the pump and fill the water tank; turn on the gas for the stove, refrigerator, and lights; pull the kayaks and canoes out from under the cabin to the north dock; and open the boathouse's lakeside doors to winch down the fishing boat. She hears her father's and grandfather's directions as if they're standing next to her. Would her father smile or cringe if he knew she was here?

They hike across the island, the paths faint but still there. Pine and cedar aromas mingle in the air with the hum of dragonflies, the sun glimmering off their iridescent wings. Her body moves as if it never left this island of rock, just as it did on Llyndee's Peak. When Kobi stops hiking to spin in sunbeams that seep through the forest canopy like spires from the heavens, Beth is shocked that he hasn't experienced this before. How much he's missed in her determination to stay away from this place.

When they reach the Native pictographs, two signs explain the rock paintings, and a large box of clear plastic displays the drums and sticks. A worn pathway leads to a small dock at the island's far end with a sign providing directions to the site, as well as warnings not to trespass past the pictographs. Taid would be pleased. Subtle yet respectful.

Before they trek back, Beth stops where she created her fort every summer. Two pine seedlings sprout where she used to sit. "Nature abhors a vacuum," Ben once told her. She smiles and turns to Kobi.

"When I was a few years older than you, I scoured the island to find the perfect place for a fort. I wove branches and sticks between these trees to create walls. It was my special place, where I could feel part of the island and read, sleep, watch the clouds—whatever I wanted."

"No way."

"Yes, way." They sit by the seedlings, and Beth places Kobi's hands on the ground to feel the earth living below him. They close their eyes and try to identify what they hear and feel —woodpeckers poking holes in the trees, chipmunks digging in the downed pine needles, the breeze across their faces. "Maybe tomorrow Dad and I can show you how to build your own fort, wherever you'd like."

Their walk back to the cabin takes twice as long so Kobi can circle and sit among every group of trees. Along the way, they eat blueberries and run their hands through stalks of lavender. Her grandmother's smile, Sam pecking at her elbow, the peace of living in the moment, among nature, rises again from deep inside. She fights back the tears and the joy.

As soon as they get back to the cabin, Kobi runs for the fishing rod. "Now?"

Beth looks at her watch. "Perfect time. There should be plenty of bass and perch coming up to search for bugs on the water's surface. We'll have Wigwakobi fish for dinner!" She chooses another rod for Mike and grabs the bucket, fork, and bowl from the boathouse to dig worms out of the garden soil. They squirm as she weaves a worm onto a hook, its tail wiggling in violent circles under her hand.

Kobi's face pales. "That's gross." He opens the toolbox she brought from the boathouse and lifts a large lure with brightly colored feathers attached to a gold oval. "Can't we use this?"

"That's for the big fish out in the deep water. We use worms to catch the little guys. Then we have to clean the fish so we can eat tonight."

Mike steps back and grins. "I never imagined I'd see you do any of this. A whole new side. I like it."

Beth shows them where to drop their lines. Within minutes, Kobi's rod arcs downward, and they cheer as he reels in his first bass. Beth teaches him how to wrap his hand around the fish to get the hook out of its mouth and drop it into the bucket filled with water. Six more follow, Mike as excited as Kobi when he nabs his first catch. She jogs to the boathouse to retrieve the fillet knives and fish pan, again right where they were fourteen years ago.

When she returns, a dark brown fishing boat with a Native man and three children is floating at the end of the dock. Mike turns to point to her, and the man's grin spreads across his face. She slows, peers at him, then laughs. Amik.

"Howdy, stranger, long time no see," Amik shouts as she reaches the end of the dock. He stands and grabs her outstretched arm to pull him and the boat toward her. They embrace and quiver in each other's arms but avoid the other's gaze as they separate. She points to the three children sitting in the boat.

"Are these all yours? Of course they are. They look just like you, Amik."

"The boys are mine, Keme and Tadzi. Nadie's their mom."

"I knew she had something for you, even back then."

"I only had eyes for someone else, but after she left, Nadie made her presence known."

Beth blushes and tries to hide her reaction by saying hi to his boys.

"And this is Amelia, Lily's daughter."

Beth smiles and takes in Amelia. The girl looks a bit older than Kobi, exactly as her mother did as a young girl except for the eyes: light brown, deeper set than most Ojibwe eyes.

"Willa at the campground told me Lily lives in her parents' home now, since they moved into town."

Amik shakes his head. "That's Willa, the lake gossip queen. We live three doors from Lily and her family, but all of her brothers moved to Iron Bridge six or seven years ago." He nods at the cabin. "Hope you're finding everything in good order."

"*You* kept this place in perfect shape?"

"I'd call it a family affair. We've all taken turns to make sure it's safe. That's why we rode down here. Keme saw activity in his binoculars and wondered who was here." He grins as he sits by the engine. "I'll tell everyone all is well again."

Beth steps forward. "Wait, I'd love to hear about your family. We saw the dock at the west end and the display. Thank you, Amik—it's . . . it's lovely. Will Lily be home tomorrow?"

"She owns the Circle Barn now. Best to find her there. Amelia can show your son her prized goats while you talk with Lily. She'll be thrilled to see you."

Mike and Beth wave as Amik turns the boat to the west. "So that's the famous Amik, huh? Not bad." Mike turns to her. "Where and what is a circle barn?"

The dirt road is as parched as the last time Beth went to the Circle Barn. Dust from the car's tires creates a blank slate of beige behind them. Overgrown pastures the color of ripe wheat hug the road on both sides, while the underlying clover's violet and red blossoms wait for August's warmth to explode. She knows the healing plants are there, since Ben brought her to pick the budding flowers after Taid's fall from Llyndee's Peak. He swore their detoxifying, relaxing tea would help her grandfather to heal faster, and he was right. It worked last summer to calm Kobi too, with his scraped palms and knees after his first bike crash.

Everything looks as Beth remembers it—even the basswood and birch trees dotting the landscape, their oval leaves skipping in circles in the midmorning breeze. The barn's wide sign spans the top of its curved, three-story wood frame and sparkles with a fresh coat of red and white paint. A new field next to the barn holds rows of corn, beans, peas, and sunflowers, while several jet-black goats and a few bushy white lambs graze in a separate fenced pen at the front. Lily's worked hard to keep this place going. Mike parks beside two other dust-coated sedans and a beat-up red pickup.

"Can we see the goats first?" Kobi says from the back seat. He opens the door and jumps out, his excitement trailing behind him as he runs toward the corral fence. "Baby sheep too!"

Beth smiles at Mike. "One new adventure after another up here for that boy. Do goats bite?" A few were already leaping across the pen to greet him.

Mike grabs Beth's left hand as she reaches for the car door's handle. "I've got Kobi. You go inside."

Beth stares at the barn's huge open doorway. "Maybe she's not here, or she won't even recognize me. Maybe that would be better. I don't want to dredge up her pain."

"Could be, or she might love to see you, like Amik said. Either way, she's the best person to tell you what's happened since you left, and how to find Ben."

Beth steps out of the car and stops by the front bumper, clamps her hands on her hips and kicks at the gravel driveway. Mike shakes his head and points to Kobi, who's giggling as he jumps in tandem with two baby goats on the other side of the fence.

"Do you really think you're going to keep that kid away from this place after everything he's done the past twenty-four hours? Get real, Beth." He points at the barn. "Taid's leading you in the right direction; you just need to give yourself permission. It's time to move on."

She watches Mike's back as he strides toward Kobi, lifts him onto his shoulders, and walks around the outside of the pen, the goats skipping behind. Her teeth gnaw at the inside of her right cheek as she digs harder at the gravel with her sneaker. She remembers the last time she saw Lily, when they ran into each other in the woods above the north shore, both sure Dylan was there somewhere, dazed and injured, and the search team had missed him. They cried in each other's arms, Beth for the brother she adored and Lily for her first love, and promised each other they wouldn't stop until they found him. How long did Lily keep looking for him before she gave up?

Another car parks beside her. She watches a young Native woman and four small children walk toward the barn's entrance. Here's her chance to walk inside without being noticed. She matches the kids' shuffles up the steep drive and into the barn.

The same jars of maple syrup, candles, and leather sacks of tobacco or herbs fill the front tables, a new mixture of basil and sage hanging heavily in the air. Partitions divide the barn's back in half, the left side open and the right obscured. She meanders around the front tables to keep her focus away from the women talking at the counter. One laughs softly, and Beth stops, picking up an herb bag to read its label. Sounds just like Lily.

She moves toward the back left, to shelves filled with shoes and beaded purses. Leather belts and vests dangle off hat racks. She searches for moccasins in Kobi's size, chooses a light caramel pair with multicolored beading, and positions herself behind a tall rack to glance across the room. The young woman is buying candles from a much older woman behind the counter while her kids pull carved wooden toys across the plank floor. Two couples wander among the front tables. Beth exhales. None of them could be Lily.

Tables of clay pots, mugs, and plates lie between Beth and the barn's third section. As soon as she turns the corner, the separate space feels intimate even though it's larger than the small gallery that was there before. A thick sculpture of two fighting horses, their front legs flailing in the air toward each other, sits on a table just inside. She admires the textured detail of the horses' manes, then turns to scan the first painting to her right. She moves to the next, a watercolor, and stops in front of the third. The moccasins fall to the floor as Beth clenches the sculpture table behind her for balance and circles its perimeter to take in the paintings surrounding her. Every piece whispers its familiar hellos: the dark evergreens and bright white birches on Bailey's Point; the purple, gold, and black iridescence of Llyndee's Peak at sunrise; Lake Wigwakobi's hundred shades of blue, from the surface to its deepest depths. Even the island looks back at her in all its beauty, drawn in her brother's perfect silk lines and colors so vivid they seem peeled from the earth, water, and sky.

Beth fights the vertigo threatening her senses by focusing on a large knot in the floor. *Think, dammit, how can these be here? How did Lily find these?* She glances at a watercolor before the room spins again and she's forced to look back at the floor. It's obviously his but one she's never seen. Dylan never gave away his work freely, never thought they were truly done or worthy of display. Did he paint all of these over those last summers and give them to Lily? She's certainly moved on if she can sell them now.

Beth breathes in gulps, waiting for her vision to steady. When she can focus again, she stares in disbelief but knows as deeply as she does her enduring love for her brother that no one could have painted these pieces but Dylan. The watercolor pulls her closer. She caresses the brush strokes in the air just above the paper, his same technique but with a finer touch than his early work, and pictures Dylan's hands making the brush and paint dance across the page. She moves to the next painting, then the next, mimicking each stroke and smiling at every brilliant color and hue. Her heart pounds with pride that her brother created such beauty in his short life.

"Excuse me, please don't touch the paintings," a stern voice calls from behind. Beth jerks her hands back and clasps them in front of her chest. She turns to apologize and recognizes the woman's dark almond eyes, smooth olive skin, and long graceful fingers. She seems taller and thinner in a long black sundress, except for the round, full belly promising new life. "Lily?"

"I'm sorry." Lily takes a single step toward her. "We have so many visitors to the barn each summer; I don't always remember—"

Beth waves at the paintings. "Where did you find these?"

Lily steps closer, peers into her eyes. Beth waits until Lily's face erupts with a brilliant smile and she pulls Beth into a tight embrace. "I knew you'd come, Beth. I knew it would be you."

They rock in each other's arms, Lily matching Beth's tears with her own. "So many years, so much to say," Lily murmurs.

"I've brought my husband and son. I'm so glad they can meet you." Beth steps back and looks around the room. "Where did you find his paintings? I don't remember any of these."

Lily's eyes glisten with pride. "Aren't they lovely? We sold several pastels this summer through galleries in Toronto and Vancouver." She touches Beth's arm. "I can't begin to tell you how happy Dylan will be to see you. It's been so long; we'd almost given up hope that everything would work out. But you're here now. The world will be right again."

Beth spreads her arms as the floor flips on its side, and she falls against the table. The two horses still fight as they hover in midair, the panic in their eyes even more appropriate as they hit the thick planks and explode into chunks of heavy clay and dust. Her head and heart spin in their own orbits she can't control, pushing her into oblivion even as Lily holds her upright. She stares at Lily's silver necklace, a common loon resting against her upper chest, its rich black head and white neck proud and strong. "You're okay, Beth," Lily whispers. "Just breathe."

The woman from the register enters the room with a broom and dustpan. "I heard something break. Oh crap, not the horses. What happened?"

Beth focuses harder on the loon.

"It's okay, Bertie, you can return to the counter. Leave the broom and dustpan here."

Lily caresses Beth's arms and back while she fights to regain reality. She tries to pronounce the words but can barely hear her own voice. "Dylan?" She glances at the paintings and looks back at Lily. "These . . . are . . . new?"

"He's here, Beth, painting behind the barn. This is our store now. Didn't Taid tell you?"

Beth tries to yank her upper arms from Lily's grip as the shock and anger rise from deep in her gut, but Lily grasps even tighter. "But how—?"

"It's wonderful, isn't it? He has missed you deeply and worked hard to make everything right so you could return." Her huge smile confuses Beth even more. "But I'll let him tell you everything."

Beth's jaw opens but nothing comes out. She stares at Lily, trying to understand what she's saying.

"Perhaps you'd like a moment before you see him. Come with me." Lily pulls her into a storage room just past the gallery and to an old wicker chair between shelves filled to the ceiling with Native gifts waiting to be sold. "We just got a fresh shipment of my brother's best ale. New brew, pretty good." Lily pulls a jar out of a rusting yellow refrigerator and pours the golden drink into a small mug.

Beth waves it off. "Where is he?" she whispers.

"In his greenhouse studio behind the barn. Says he needs to see the shadows as the sun rotates to paint, but I don't know how he stands the heat in there."

Beth focuses again on her breathing as Lily waits silently. What she heard can't be true. When she looks up, Lily's leaning against the refrigerator with a calm smile. How can she act that way, after what she's just told Beth? The rage rises again.

"I don't understand." She tries to control her voice as she stands, failing with each word. "You're telling me that my brother has been alive all this time, and he never tried to contact us? Never thought about how devastating it was to lose him, how much we'd change because of his supposed death? You, Ben, Dylan—no one thought to call or even write?"

Lily holds up both hands. "I understand your anger, Beth, I really do. Dylan went through his own hell, which I'll let him tell you about. It's been a very long road for us as well."

Beth turns away, unable to control the hurt, anger, and confusion gripping her. How could Dylan let her think he was gone all these years, that the lake had betrayed them? How could he do that to their parents, to Taid and Naina? To Maegan, who has blamed herself for Dylan's death all these years?

"Tell me, Beth, what changed so you finally came back?"

"My grandfather asked me to come back to decide whether to give the island to my husband and me or to your family. My grandmother passed away a while ago, and he wants to have everything in order before he goes." She looks up at Lily. "But you already know that, don't you? Didn't you say 'Taid' a few minutes ago?"

"We were so saddened to hear of her passing," Lily says. "Ben and Taid have written to each other over the years, but Ben never shared their conversations other than her death. It was Ben who suggested that it was the best time for Dylan and Taid to reconnect. I'm surprised Taid didn't tell you about Dylan."

Beth sits again and covers her face with her hands. Another betrayal, this time from Taid. Does Maegan already know too?

She hears Lily walk across the room, kneel in front of her, and gently pull Beth's hands away from her face to hold them between hers. "I know this is a shock, and you must have a million questions. We have questions too, but perhaps we should do this with Dylan. You both deserve that, don't you think?"

Beth shakes her head, lost in confusion and hurt, until enough of Lily's kindness seeps from her pores into Beth's palms. She tries to push away the shock and focus on this moment—that Dylan is alive, that he's near. All she has to do is walk to him. The reality rushes through her, and she squeezes Lily's hands. "I will have a niece or nephew soon?"

Lily grins and stretches her graceful fingers across her blossoming belly. "You will. You already have a niece, Amelia, who's probably feeding the goats their afternoon snack. She's six."

Of course those eyes were familiar—they're the same light brown as Dylan's. "My husband, Mike, and son, Kobi, are outside somewhere too."

Lily laughs. "Amelia is very outgoing and proud of her farm, as she calls it, so I'm sure they already know each other. Let's find Dylan, and you can introduce us to your family. Are you ready or would you like more time?"

Beth points to the mug, and Lily hands her the ale. "I can't believe any of this is happening. I can't believe Taid didn't tell me." She downs the ale, trying to swallow the anger and hurt and accept the possibility of seeing her brother alive. After several minutes of pacing the small space and drinking more ale, Beth sets down the mug and turns to Lily. "I think I'm ready, but . . . you'll find him first?"

Lily nods and opens the barn's back door. They walk down a stone pathway bordered on either side by white-and-yellow daisies amid clumps of lavender. Beth caresses the stalks to inhale the loving heritage of her grandmother's plants as bees hover and dive into the wealth of pollen. She looks toward the sound of children's laughter. Kobi is chasing Amelia around the tall stalks of corn and sunflowers. Mike watches as he leans against the fence, his back to her.

As the path winds down a small hill, the greenhouse comes into view. Dylan is just outside, watching the children play as he cleans his brush with a filthy cloth. Beth's breath catches, and her body halts as she sees him. He still stands as if he's firmly rooted in the land, even with his hips forward and knees slightly bent. His lanky body and sharper profile are fully grown into those of a man, his hair still wavy but already striped with gray. He wears the same loose chinos, a dark T-shirt instead of white, but still smudged with various shades of paint. She watches him wave at Amelia and Kobi, then turn slightly as Lily walks up. He wraps his arm around her, lowers his head to meet hers as she speaks and points toward the field. His head springs up and he stares at Kobi, listens to more of Lily's words, turns toward Beth. Every nerve and muscle freeze as she sees his shocked face head on.

Dylan steps away from Lily and takes in all of Beth. He walks toward her slowly, his eyes connected with hers. She can't move. The closer he gets, the more her disbelief, love, and anger compete, and she's not sure whether she will run or stay. He stops a few yards away and smiles. "That boy looks just like you except for the blond hair. I should have known you'd be right behind."

In an instant they fold into a tight embrace.

Beth buries her head to his chest, breathes him in. "It's really you," Beth whispers.

"And you're all grown up, Bethie." They search each other's eyes, sharing in turn their wonder, sadness, anger, shock, confusion, and joy, all without saying a word. Dylan pulls Beth to him again, and she feels his heart pounding against her chest as much as hers thumps against his.

"We'll figure it out together. I've been waiting so long to make this right, just like I promised."

They hold each other as they release more years of grief and pain, then step back and stare at each other again, this time more in amazement and joy. Her brother was dead, lost to her forever, and now he stands in front of her, and with Lily, as he always wanted. She feels her balance tilting again, this time starting to shift back into place.

Mike stands next to Lily with the same mixture of confusion, hurt, and anger on his face that Beth felt a few moments ago.

"I'm not sure I believe it yet either, that I can say these words to you," Beth says as she walks up with Dylan. "This is my brother."

Mike wraps his hands around the back of his head and nods at Lily. "Wait, so what she just said is really true. This is Dylan, and Lily? And that girl running around out there is Kobi's cousin?"

Beth nods, encouraging Mike to believe her.

Mike lowers his arms and walks to Dylan. "So, you're the infamous Dylan," Mike says as he shakes his hand—first politely, then with a forcefulness and speed to match his words. "I never thought when I agreed with Beth to return here that I'd be doing this—shaking your hand and then asking you what the *hell* you've been doing all these years while your sister has fought with *all* she has to keep your family together *and* stay away from the one place she loves as much as she loves her son, because it took *you* away from them."

Dylan holds Mike's hand in both of his, nods, and listens while Mike releases his anger and absorbs their new reality. "I'm eager to explain everything and for Beth to tell me her and your story too. For now, please know that I've waited for this day more than you can ever imagine. And I'm glad you're responding this way, because it tells me how much you love my sister."

Mike tries to let go of Dylan's hand, but Beth's brother holds fast. Mike looks to her.

"Yep, that's Dylan," she says. "A man of few words, but he says it all, if you listen."

Lily laughs, and Dylan shakes Mike's hand once more before he lets go.

Mike turns to Beth. "I'm in shock."

Her own shock, hurt, and confusion are still simmering inside, but for now happiness overwhelms. Beth puts her hands on her husband's chest as her eyes fill again with tears. "I am too, that and all the other emotions you're feeling. But that's my brother—right there, standing next to us."

Mike looks at Dylan and Lily and back at her. "I know it's crazy to feel so much anger when you're right, this is amazing."

"What's so amazing?" Kobi yells. All four adults turn toward the field, where he and Amelia are perched on the lowest rung of the nearby fence, watching their parents. Beth waves Kobi over. She lays her hands on his shoulders and chest from behind as she introduces him to Dylan. "He's your uncle and my brother, just like Aunt Maegan is my sister and your aunt."

"Cool. My Uncle Brian went away, so now I get one back."

Dylan looks at Beth and rolls his eyes. "What was she thinking, marrying him?"

Beth nods. "Another long story."

Lily walks to Kobi and shakes his hand. "And I'm your Aunt Lily, which means Amelia is your cousin."

Amelia squeals, jumps off the fence, and runs to Kobi. "Wanna see my rock collection at my house?" She turns to Lily. "Can we have a sleepover? Can we?"

"We'll see," Lily says. "Let's give Kobi's parents time to tour the farm and barn, and then take a break until dinner. Dylan caught a ten-pounder this morning, and we have plenty of beans out there. Amelia, grab the buckets and show your cousin where to pick. We expect full loads when you return."

Amelia grabs Kobi's hand, and they run toward the barn.

"I hope you will join us for dinner. Beth, you remember my family's place, right?" Lily says. "That's our home now."

Beth looks at Mike, then nods. "Amik rode by yesterday afternoon and told us where you live, that Lily would be here."

"You've already been to the island?" Dylan says.

"We arrived yesterday. I can't believe you were so close to us last night, and I didn't know it." Beth pauses. "Thank you for keeping everything so perfect all these years."

Dylan takes Lily's hand. "It hasn't always been that way, and it wasn't me doing the work for a lot of those years." He pauses, looks off in the distance, then back at Lily. "But it's a family project now."

Dylan shows them the greenhouse, barns, and fields while Lily relieves Bertie inside. Beth stands back, listening and watching her brother and husband talk about the barn's round design and structure, crop rotations, and the goats' finicky eating habits. At the huge stalks of sunflowers, Dylan explains how they extract the plant's oils for cooking, use the remaining dried cake to feed the animals, compost the stems for fertilizer, and roast the seeds to sell.

Her brother still carries himself with the calm assurance of an introvert not afraid of the extroverted world. She always thought Taid was the family's talisman, their North Star, his outgoing nature and love of life leading the way. But watching Dylan, perhaps it was his quiet intensity, his ability to feel completely at home within himself, that provided the family with a guiding star, as well as that essential tie that bound them together. When he disappeared, fear and grief took over, and the crevices between each of them grew wider and wider until it seemed as if they'd each crack from the pressure of even pretending to be united. She's amazed they haven't all fallen into darkness, just like the chunks of granite and limestone that break from Llyndee's Peak and disappear into the lake's indigo depths.

As she fought to keep the family connected, what was Dylan doing? She doesn't know anything about his life for the past fourteen years, or what Ben has told Dylan about her and the rest of the family. The realizations prickle, like a nagging rash that might fester and spread.

Kobi looks exhausted but happy when he and Amelia surprise them between the six-foot-high sunflower plants.

"We have a ton of beans, Mom. Except I ate a bunch, cuz we never had lunch, you know, and I was starving." He turns to Dylan. "Can we go fishing tonight? I know how to do my own worm."

"How about you show me tomorrow morning? You'll need to get up really early, though. Think you can handle that?"

Kobi nods.

"Maybe your folks will let you come with Amelia and me, and they can meet us for dinner later. I could use some help cleaning the fish for dinner. Have you done that yet?"

"Yep, we played with the eyes too. That was you, right?"

Dylan chuckles and looks at Beth. "That's a memory I'd forgotten, until now. Guess we have a lot of those to remember, and a lot more to catch up on." He pauses, still staring at Beth. "For now, though, okay with you if we take Kobi with us?"

Beth looks at Mike, who shrugs and kneels in front of Kobi. "Okay, as long as you behave yourself, young man. Follow what your uncle tells you about the lake, the rocks, and especially his filleting knife."

"Yeah, Dad, I remember everything Mom told me. Don't worry so much." He rolls his eyes at Amelia and waves at his parents as they run to the red pickup.

"Guess that's the end of the tour," Dylan says. "Lily has her own car. She'll close up at five, and we eat at six." He shakes Mike's hand again, wraps Beth in a deep hug and whispers, "See you soon," and jogs toward the truck. He stops after a bit and looks back at them, his eyes matching the grin spread across his face. "Nice name for my nephew, by the way."

They wait until he backs out of the driveway to wrap their arms around each other and walk to the car. Neither speaks as they drive back to the lake, the silence safer until feelings can be put into words.

When they get to the island, Mike falls into an Adirondack chair by the fire pit and stares at the lake. "Wow. I can't believe that just happened. The gall of the guy to live his life up here and never think about any of you."

The prickling starts again. Beth needs to move. "It's hard to decide which reaction to believe—I have so many. Let me go for a walk to sort everything out, and when I get back, we can make sense of it." She turns toward the rock stairs, but Mike jumps in between.

"You're not disappearing on me again. Now that Kobi and I are here, now that we've seen *you* here, we've got a stake in this too." He turns toward the stairs. "Race you to your fort."

They reach the island's peak in fifteen minutes. She's impressed at how he handles the slippery pine needles and sharp rocks, how comfortable he's already grown on the island. She tags the boulder with the Native paintings just seconds ahead of him.

Mike reads the board with the healing site's explanation: why it was chosen, what the Ojibwe believe about the medicine manitous, how their people play the drums and sing to ask for guidance and help. He stares at the paintings, visible but more faint than Beth remembers.

"I have trouble believing that this caused everything," Mike finally says. "I can see why Taid feared losing something as beautiful as this place. But really, why couldn't they work out what's here now? Why would he be furious enough to cause everything else?"

"I never understood it either. We were friends with Lily and her family, especially Dylan and me; we trusted them. But I don't think he could picture what the signs and dock would look like. He was so afraid of losing it all that he focused on protecting his family and what he thought was rightfully ours."

"And Dylan?"

"Taid's fight with Lily's family terrified Dylan more than

any of us, because he knew even then that she was the love of his life and that this was where he needed to be." She wraps her arms across her chest as she remembers Dylan's shocked look every time Taid threatened to kick him off the island if he supported Lily's family instead of his own.

Mike walks around the site, looks at the rockslide and back at the paintings. "Nope, anger and a hell of a lot of resentment are still winning out. Maybe it's in defense of you, but I can't imagine what Dylan can say for this to make sense. Why didn't he tell your family years ago that he was alive? How can he justify what he put everyone through, especially you? All those family dinners, your awkward conversations with your mom, trying to keep a sense of peace with your family."

Beth gazes at the north shore where they searched for Dylan. Somehow Mike expressing his feelings helps her to focus her own. "You're right. Part of me can't believe that he's been living here without us. How could he do that, knowing how much we loved him and this island? I couldn't think about breaking ties with the family, as much as I might have wanted to defy Mom's edict that we not return. For me, for Kobi and you, and for Dylan's memory, I thought I had to stay loyal to the family."

She kicks at the loose rocks with her sneaker and turns back to Mike. "In some ways, though, I'm even angrier at myself. I convinced myself that family was more important and that I could will this island and lake away if I didn't spend time here or in places like this. But I was wrong. These trees, this land and water, all of this is my family too. I know that after only twenty-four hours here. You and Kobi deserved a chance to make this a part of you so much earlier than now."

Mike stares at the lake, a pale mirror reflecting high clouds and the late afternoon sun. His eyebrows meet in the middle of his forehead, as they always do when he doesn't agree with her. How can she expect him to understand what she's feeling?

"Imagine if this had happened to you and Isabella, how you'd feel to have her back."

Mike's eyebrows shoot up as he considers what Beth's said. "My instant reaction is I can't imagine ever being separated from her."

"Exactly."

"Don't get me wrong, she'd have a lot of explaining to do. But in the end? Probably nothing else would matter." He taps the plastic box with his fingers, and she waits for him to find the connection. "What hurts the most is to see you up here, how you walk and move and think—I feel like I'm meeting you again for the first time. I get it now why Chicago is confining, why any second it's felt like you might run away. You've had all of this and this part of yourself to run back to, but you couldn't all these years—because of *him*."

Beth nods. "When I climbed up Llyndee's Peak, it felt so right to be back. The rocks and woods, the loon calls we heard last night, even the water I thought had stolen Dylan—everything was telling me what I needed to know. Then Lily told me Dylan was alive and that Taid knew, and it all felt wrong again."

"Wait, what?"

"Dylan wrote a letter to Taid, which prompted him to write the letter to me. I don't know what's in it, his explanations or apologies. Lily said Ben told Dylan it was time to reach out, so he did."

Mike steps back, turns, and walks across the flat opening. She can hear him swearing at Taid and Dylan until he returns to her. "So, more lies, and Taid's still keeping secrets."

"The betrayal I felt when I found these relics all those years ago came rushing back with Lily's words. I was excited back then to show all of this to Ben, Dylan, and Lily, thinking these relics would cement the bond between our families. But everyone else took control, hid things from me, made stupid decisions until the lake or these manitous had their final say. So yes, I'm angry too. Furious."

Mike reaches for her, but she steps away. "But here's the thing. Before everything happened, Dylan was my Isabella. So, I must believe he didn't try to hurt us on purpose. Something must have happened to keep him away, and he's probably wondered all these years why no one came back to find him or to claim the island. If he's still the person he was when we were young, there are reasons for what he's done. Just like Taid thought he was doing the right thing to fight the Ojibwe for this land. Maybe all of us had the best of intentions, but together our actions altered all of our destinies in the worst of ways."

She walks to the rock wall and places her palms on the paintings. Mike leans against the boulder, facing her. She closes her eyes to remember the parts of Taid's letter that convinced her to come: ". . . decide what will finally calm your own waves . . . return to the lake and island we love as much as we do each other . . . all they've given and meant to us deserve at least that . . ."

"Maybe this rock and these manitous did conspire against us and force us away. Or maybe life happened up here too, just like Naina's stroke, Maegan's marriage, Mom's anger, and Dad's unending grief. Taid and Dad intended to come back and find Dylan, but they never did. I suppose I could have forced the point, but I never did. Instead, I buried my anger and need to be here out of family loyalty, grief, anger, cowardice—take your pick. Maybe something like that happened to Dylan. He and Lily said it's taken this long to make things right—whatever that means."

Mike pulls her into his arms. "Okay," he whispers. "Okay."

They hold each other in silence. She touches the landing in the rock wall where Sam used to build his nest. "Did I tell you I had a one-legged pet gull?"

"You are full of surprises."

She tells him that story and several more. She doesn't pick memories with Dylan intentionally, but somehow, he's part of every adventure she shares.

"The painting you hung in the hallway? I was sitting here when he drew it."

Mike smiles. "You look like that girl right now."

Amelia and Kobi's laughter carry the two families through dinner, the adults polite but quiet. Beth absorbs every photo and memento in Dylan and Lily's home, searching for answers about Dylan's past. She can see his exhaustion, sadness, and perhaps resentment in earlier photos, but others confirm that Lily's parents and siblings have served as her brother's family in place of his own. Her heart screams at the birthdays and holidays they haven't shared, the strained holiday dinners she's endured, the guilt that's consumed Taid and Maegan, her father's withdrawal to survive his grief. How will she explain all of that to Dylan?

After the conversation wanes and they've cleared the table, Lily fills a small cooler with ale and pushes Dylan and Beth toward the door. "The lake is calling," she says.

Beth's face flushes as panic spins through her veins. She's not sure she wants to leave Mike and Kobi or is ready for what's to come. Mike walks to the front porch with her and squeezes her hand. "Remember, he's your Izzy," he whispers.

A thousand stars light up the ink sky as they walk to the dock and climb into the maroon fishing boat. Beth takes her normal spot at the bow, and Dylan starts the boat's engine and plods east at a relaxed, measured pace. Even as her mind races through all the questions to come, the moon shimmering on the water, the moist, sweet breeze caressing her face, and the rhythmic pulse of boat meeting gentle wave lull Beth into a familiar stillness. Her heart calms, as it did yesterday on Llyndee's Peak, ending its relentless pounding at a speed faster than her spirit has wanted all these years. No matter how hard she tried to control everything, her heart never obeyed.

Dylan puts the engine in neutral when they reach the island. He points to a clump of birches reduced to ugly stumps two summers before by beavers eager to erect fresh homes. Beth asks when they built the dock, sign, and display case for the Ojibwe artifacts.

"When no one returned the summer after you left, they put private property signs at both docks and around the edge of the island. They assumed Taid had abandoned his fight, but they never took over the island. The dock on the west end was built then too, so everyone could get up to the manitous. We finally convinced Lily's dad to put the artifacts in the case and build the signs this spring so it could officially become a sacred site. They've had a steady stream of visitors. Amelia loves going up there."

"Does she know what happened? Why we haven't been here all these years?"

He looks away. "No reason to pass on that history. She asked this spring when we opened the cabin if you're coming back this summer. We told her that what she hopes for will happen. And now you're here, just as we promised."

Beth starts to speak, but he turns the steering handle's throttle and follows the north bend of Llyndee's Peak around to the lake's wide center. He cuts the engine in front of the massive granite wall, the Milky Way spreading out above them and the full moon eager to light their faces and the night sky. He opens two ales and hands one to Beth. They sit at either end, deep in their own memories, until she realizes they're in the exact spot where she last saw him in their father's antique boat with Maegan—and the last time he saw her, before today.

"Do you relive it every time you go by here?" she says.

"I used to, until I realized that to have any kind of future, I had to give up hope of ever changing my past." He looks from the rock to her. "We've all paid a big price for that day."

Beth bolts upright and grabs the boat's thick iron walls to keep her feelings of betrayal from flying out of her mouth. A price? How can he quantify the grief and pain since they thought he died? How everyone is going to feel once they know he's been living a full life up here all this time?

She lifts her beer to her lips and swallows several gulps before she dares to speak. "How do we want to do this, Dyl? You want to go first, or should I?"

Her brother takes a long slug of ale and sets the bottle by his feet. He gathers his hands together as if praying. "Let me start, and maybe some things will start to make sense." When he looks at her, his eyes are full—with tears, remorse, love.

"First, I didn't stay away because I don't love you and Maegan, our grandparents, Dad, even Mom. Most days I've missed you so much that my heart feels like a violent drum on my ribs, as if it's pounding at me to change my ways. Every time I look at Amelia, she stares back at me with your brown eyes that penetrate straight into my soul. She runs like you, gangly legs that want to gallop instead of trot. And she knows only love and kindness, just like you did at her age.

"You alone should have been the reason I didn't stay away, and however your life has changed, however you've changed, I'm sorry beyond what you can imagine. But I also know the promise I made to you to make things right, and I was determined to do that. To have any of you come back before that was accomplished, to see what the island and I became for years after you left—" his voice catches, and he rolls his hands, waiting for it to return "—would have broken your heart even more. But I want to go back and pick up where we left off. Is that okay?"

He looks at her, pleading for patience. She wants to hear what became of the island and him but forces herself to nod. She pulls her legs to her chest in the same pose he painted her all those years ago.

"Those last two summers, Mom's demands that Maegan and I live the life she wanted for us felt like she was going to bury us alive. I avoided her needs for years, but college was another story. No matter how I worked it out in my mind, I couldn't find a solution. Then the fight between Taid and Lily's family. How he showed so little respect for another culture when he expected everyone to honor his. I knew they wouldn't agree that day, that it wouldn't end."

"All I wanted was to get rid of the relics, but I couldn't figure out how to fix what I'd screwed up," Beth says.

"You didn't screw up anything. The rest of us are to blame." He edges forward on his seat. "I knew you were scared; that's why I tried to shield you from my fears with Mom. But Maegan knew. All those times you found us together, talking and arguing? You were shocked and hurt to see us like that, but we were trying to come up with a plan. Not about the island—I knew what had to happen to resolve that, and it took several years before the chief trusted me again to let me anywhere near Lily, let alone talk about the island and my family's rights to it. But I'm jumping ahead again."

Dylan stands and shoves his hands into his sweatshirt pockets. His body sways to the water's soft current, and his voice slows.

"Maegan thought I should write a letter that she would give to Mom and Dad when I supposedly left for college. I would explain that I needed to lay claim to my life, take responsibility for my successes and failures, and that I hoped they would respect my choice. Maegan knew if I tried to say it in person, Mom would explode, and I would back down and drown in her plans. But I thought the letter sounded cowardly. I was sure I could get Taid and the chief to resolve their issue if I was with them at the meeting, and Lily and I could tell everyone our plans at the same time. But Maegan knew it wouldn't work, and was adamant that I stand firm or she wouldn't be able to either. Because she didn't want to go back to Northwestern—she wanted to transfer to Michigan. She married Brian the next year, right?"

"Yes, she did."

"Shit. That wasn't part of her plan. You heard Mom, Naina, and Taid. They were so proud of her going to Northwestern. But she knew if she was home, Brian wouldn't come to see her like he did in Chicago, and she could get away from him for good. She thought my letter would give her the right time to explain that to them. By the time the family came up the next summer, I'd have worked out the island dispute with Lily's dad, and we'd all have calmer perspectives. We could reconnect and get past all the conflicts. At least that was the plan we eventually agreed on."

"Did she think you'd already written the letter? Because I found her looking through your things a bunch of times before we left. When I asked her what she was doing, she said she thought you two had a plan, but she must have been wrong."

"Probably wishful thinking at the time, to save me and her. We'd talked about it a lot, but I hadn't written anything down. Has she wondered all these years if I left on purpose? You have to know I could never be that cruel."

She nods slightly but shifts in her seat, still not knowing what to think.

Dylan swallows more ale. "You saw us that day in the storm, when we were on our way back. The squalls surged after you ran down the trail, and the waves flipped Taid's sailboat around like it was a toothpick. I climbed back to right it with the ropes. The front end was getting pummeled, and the back of Dad's boat was low, so I knew we were taking on water underneath. I was afraid we'd lose both boats before we got back to the island, so I jumped onto the sailboat and untied the ropes. Without me in Dad's boat, Maegan was sure to get back. At worst, if the sailboat sunk, I could swim until she came back for me in the fishing boat."

"Where did you go? Because we looked for you for days. Lily and I went to every place we'd ever hiked or where you had painted, and everyone on the lake helped in the search. The police even brought divers."

"Yeah, Lily told me. I used the centerboard to paddle, and we were both moving okay until a series of huge waves hit the Carling. Maegan hit her head on the windshield and fell onto the steering wheel. I had almost reached her in the sailboat when she got control of the boat again and the engine kicked in. I could tell she'd make it back, but the big waves kept knocking me off the sailboat. Every time I climbed back on, another chunk of the boat broke off. I realized I had to grab onto whatever was left and float with the waves, or I was toast."

"That's why we looked all over the north shore. Pieces of the sailboat kept washing up along the beach."

"I thought that was where I was going to end up too. But when the front of the bow broke off, the mast came down on my head and shoulder. I was out of it, which probably was a good thing because I didn't fight the storm. When I woke up, the lake was calm, it was pitch black, and I didn't have a clue where I was. My brain was a mess; it wouldn't stop pounding. I crawled up the rocks to hide under some trees. The next time I woke up, my eyes wouldn't stay open in the sun. I couldn't even focus. I still don't know how long I was out. Eventually, I realized I was at the lake's east end, near the sacred site at Round Lake. I hiked over there and passed out again. I figured someone would come there sooner or later and find me."

"Who finally found you?"

"Lily's oldest brother, Kawen, who worked at the steel mill in the Sault. He didn't know who I was. He took me to Lily, but the chief refused to let me come near her or their property because of the last argument with Taid. Ben took me in until my head healed, at great cost to him with his family."

The boat turns as it floats so the full moon is at his back. Beth narrows her gaze to take in Dylan's face. His eyes are distant, perhaps reliving what he's recounted. "So, you knew we thought you were dead? Why didn't Ben tell us you were alive? Why didn't either of you call?"

"He told me why you had to leave, and that Dad and Taid were coming back for me and for the island. It took three months for my head to heal, when I could finally get out of bed, and they still hadn't come. By that time, I was sure that all of you blamed me for everything that had happened, like the chief—that I wasn't wanted anywhere. Ben wasn't writing to Taid yet, but he told me I had to go home to make things right."

He sinks onto the bench, elbows on his knees and head in his hands. His body shivers. Beth closes her eyes, hugs herself, and waits, unable to stop her own memories of listening to her father's calls to the Ontario police every night, and her own grieving.

When Dylan sits up and starts again, his voice has a renewed strength. "I got on a bus and started home, but when it stopped in Gaylord, I decided to call first so everyone wouldn't freak out. Mom answered the phone, and the pitch of her voice terrified me. I couldn't shake the hurt that no one had come back to find me, and I knew if I took a step in that door, with all we'd gone through and the guilt I felt, I'd cave in to Mom. She'd win, and I'd drown all over again, this time for real."

Beth nods. "I never thought you would go to college. I understood more than you thought I did. Dad called the police every night, but they called off the search a week after we left and wouldn't open it again. Then Naina had a bad stroke, which became Taid's sole focus, since he felt he'd caused it. As soon as we left the island, he blamed himself—for Naina's health and your death."

Dylan ponders what she's said. "So, no one came because of Naina? Not because they thought I'd ruined everything?"

Beth unlocks her legs and leans forward. "No, of course not. It took months of rehab before she could even come home. When the police came to the cabin to evict us, Mom decided then and there that you were dead, that the Native gods and the lake had exacted their revenge. She closed up after that, focused just on Maegan, and told Dad she'd leave if he came back up here. That's how certain she was that you'd died. It broke Dad not to come back up, and then Naina ended it all for him. He pulled away from all of us, focused on teaching and volunteering at a kids' center. It was never about blaming you—we were all doing that enough for ourselves."

Dylan finishes his ale, opens another, and drinks.

"Where'd you go after you called home?"

"I had enough money to ride the bus back to the Sault, and I found Kawen. He let me stay with him and got me a job in the steel mill until I could get up the courage to come back to face Ben and approach the chief about the island and Lily. I thought I could at least make that right by the time all of you came up the next summer."

Dylan's hands shake as he shoves them through his hair several times and stares at the hull. "I worked there for six horrible, fucked-up years. No hiking, painting, drawing, nothing. Just working in that stinking hellhole and drinking myself to sleep. Every time Kawen came here for holidays, he'd ask Lily if I could come back, and she'd say no, that nothing had changed. I borrowed his car every July and drove out here, sure the family would come back. But you never came. And every summer the cabin fell apart more. After a while, I was glad you didn't come so you wouldn't see it like that—or me. I figured it was better that you thought I was dead. And most of me was, except for the few times Lily found a way to meet with me when I came out here, or we talked on the phone. I called the home number a million times, usually when I was really drunk, just to hear your voices."

"Why didn't you say anything, Dyl? Let us know it was you?"

"There was a dark, cynical culture at the mill, and Kawen encouraged me to join it. I really believed he was the only one who cared."

"How did you finally get out?"

He grabs the bottle opener, steps over the benches to sit across from Beth, and hands her another ale.

"Ben and Lily, of course. She figured out how far I'd fallen and asked him to come get me. He nailed me to the wall on the drive back here—for my lifestyle, for not contacting you, for everything. First and last time I heard those swear words come out of his mouth. He put me to work building cabins and trails to get the alcohol out of my system and had art supplies waiting for me. When I was finally sober, he brought me to this spot and told me I had to stop blaming myself. That some of us need to step outside what man creates and does to one another to find peace and clarity in the woods, water, and sky. That I'd always known that Lily and this lake are my home, and that I needed to accept it and move on.

"I didn't leave this lake for two years. Ben's never had a phone, so I couldn't think about calling home, which helped me focus on the future instead of the past. Over time, as the chief saw how hard I worked and that I didn't try to do anything about the island—going to it or approaching him about it—he let me see Lily occasionally. She wouldn't cross her parents for us to be together. But being with her again brought so much of me back. Then Ben shared one of my paintings of the chief at the island's healing site, and that changed everything."

"How?"

"He finally saw that I respect their heritage. He invited me to a bonfire, and everyone slowly welcomed me back in. It wasn't easy, and some people still shun me, but Lily was always supportive behind the scenes. I hated seeing the island and cabin in such bad shape, but I had to wait for their acceptance before I could start rebuilding it. I'm glad you and Taid never saw it that way. I would have felt like a total failure."

Beth drinks her ale to stop from grunting. "You're wrong, Dylan. We never would have thought that way if we'd known what was happening to you. Besides, all of us were too full of our own shame about what happened and what we'd become as a family. Taid most of all."

Dylan sighs and looks up at the stars. "Shit happens, right? Days became months, months became years, I guess for you and for me. I focused on Lily's family, our marriage, then Amelia. Her family's rituals and beliefs have felt so right, especially their connection to nature and this place. They've even incorporated some of our Welsh traditions. We hold Lammas parties every August, and most of the lake's residents come."

He slides forward on the bench, so his face is close to hers. "But as great as my life may be now, I *never* stopped planning for your return and talking to the chief. When he agreed to share the island two years ago, we started rehabbing the cabin. Ben, Amik, Henry from shore, and a few others helped. Squirrels had invaded the inside, just like the cabin on Bailey's Point, and we had to replace the roof, most of the north deck, and the water tower. As soon as that was done, I wrote to Taid, explained the chief's agreement to share the island, and asked for his forgiveness."

Beth pushes Dylan away from her. "That's the part that galls me the most, that Taid knows you're alive and didn't tell me. As always, I'm the last one to know, betrayed again. Why didn't he tell me about you, and why didn't you write to *me?* Do you have any idea how hard I've had to fight to keep the family together all of these years, to resist the urge to run away from all the tension and pain?"

Dylan leans back to take in her anger and points to the island. "That is still Taid's island. I had to write to him first. We thought you might not come if you knew about me, that my deceiving you all these years would push you into Mom's camp for good. Then you would never get back up here."

"I don't buy it. I'm always the last to know everything. Do you still think so little of me?"

"We think that *much* of you. We knew everything depended on you. If we'd left it up to you years ago and you'd shown the chief what you found, we wouldn't have gone through all of this hell."

Beth pulls her knees to her chest again and turns sideways to the faces gazing at her from Llyndee's Peak. In the moon's glow they look pensive, but the hint of smiles she'd noticed yesterday is still there. She tries to ignore the angry, hurt energy burning through her gut.

Dylan leans toward her again. "You always thought I was the one leading this family from behind, but it's you, Bethie. Always has been, always will be. From what Taid's told me, there wouldn't be a family anymore without you."

"How many times have you talked?"

"Just a few. Blew me away to hear how weak his voice is now—but his mind is as sharp and clear as ever."

Beth tries to connect what Dylan is saying with Taid's letter.

"Taid asked me to lead the way and come back here, but he didn't say anything other than how important it was to—" She stands and pulls out the letter from her shorts' pocket. "Give me the flashlight."

Dylan climbs to the back, grabs it off the floor, and returns. He stands next to her and points the beam so she can scan for the right lines.

"Here. Here they are. Maegan had me read these paragraphs to her twice when I called her from Toronto."

"Why were you in Toronto?"

"Work meetings."

"Work and city life, huh? The only thing Ben would tell me is that you live in Chicago. How can you stand it there?"

Beth waves his questions away. "First Taid says, 'If you return to the lake, if you lead the way, you'll be surprised how quickly others' anger and fight will disappear. And you will be so thrilled with what you find and gain, in return.'" She scans the rest of the letter and swallows hard before she can read again. "Then he says, 'Your brother, the island, and all they've given and meant to us deserve at least that, don't you think?'"

She swats her thigh with the paper and shakes her head. "Those were the clues Maegan heard that I didn't. She said I had to come back for her, as much as for Taid and me. That I had to find Lily, and if I did, it would redeem her life in ways I couldn't even imagine."

Dylan chuckles. "We all thought Maegan was the flaky, selfish one, but her stubborn strength is what I thought of when I was fighting to find my way back. Even if it didn't turn out like we planned, I knew she had believed in me, and I had to accomplish my part of it."

Beth falls back into the bow, amazed to recognize the strength behind her sister's actions. The water's gentle rhythm gives Beth a simple pattern to relax her stomach's churning.

Dylan sits, empties his bottle, and lays his wide palms on her knees. "So, tell me, Bethie, how could you stay away this long, even without me here? This lake is the best part of your heart and bones, the best part of all of us. Did you forget to look in?"

Beth stares at the Milky Way spreading across the sky in brushstrokes of white and silver as she tries to mesh what she's learned about Dylan's life with her own. He lets go of her legs, and she reaches for his hands. He entwines his fingers in hers, gently rubs his thumbs on the top of her palms and waits.

How does she tell him everything that happened, how hard it was without him, how she felt abandoned too? Finally, she decides to trust Mike's advice: her Izzy. She releases his hands to take a final swig of ale; places her hands on her knees, where she can still feel his strength; and looks into Dylan's eyes to reassure him of their connection before she begins.

"First, Dyl, so much of this is like you said, shit happens. Mike and I went back to the healing site this afternoon after we saw you. As you could tell, he has a lot of anger because he knows how hard I've worked to keep the family together. If I didn't, I was sure the entire family would disappear. I'd already lost you *and* this place, so I couldn't consider life without all of them. I convinced myself that Mom and Dad were right that we couldn't return to the island—that the lake itself and the people didn't want us here. I shoved aside my hurt and anger toward Mom's behavior, how she held herself so tightly in check and never even considered that anyone might want to come up here again, and toward Dad and his disappearance. He slid away from us before we could realize it. Kobi's the only thing that brings him back for a bit.

"I knew you were still alive those last days we were up here. I slept in my fort almost every night because I thought I could feel your energy if I was outside, closer to you. Maegan had a bad concussion, so she didn't talk much for the first few days. After that she was racked with guilt, even said she deserved a life with Brian because of what happened. As soon as Mom forced her to go back to Northwestern for winter term, Brian showed up, and she got pregnant. I think they moved to Arizona to be far away from anything that reminded her of here. He left four years ago, and Maegan's carried on, raised three great kids.

"Don't ever think that Mom didn't grieve your disappearance. She spent the first days we searched lying in your bed, willing you to return. When the police officers came to evict us, she flipped to anger. Her life has been fueled by that and her grief ever since, and believe me, that's worse than her loving demands when we were kids. She spends a lot of time taking care of Maegan's children. We keep hoping the Arizona sun will bake some of the anger out of her, but no luck so far.

"Dad couldn't stand up to her coldness, Naina's stroke, and the police saying you were gone, so he retreated. Taid's guilt that he caused everything because he was so stubborn with the chief made him focus even more on Naina and her care."

"So, who took care of you?"

Beth looks away, surprised that tears spring to her eyes. Dylan always knows how to get to the heart of the matter. "I wasn't home much in high school. I worked and hung out with friends. Lived in dorms and apartments for college, except for the summer after Naina died, and Mom and Dad forced Taid to move in with them.

"We all kind of crumbled after you disappeared. None of us could equal Mom's anger, so we went along and avoided reality, just like we ignored her fears up here. Dad worked, Taid and Naina burrowed in together, Maegan disappeared to Arizona with Brian and babies, and I buried my needs to maintain a sense of family, as weak as it was. I just couldn't cut the ties.

"The spring I decided I was ready to lay claim to my life and come back up here, I went to Taid and Naina. They were all in, ready to pack their bags and never leave the island again. Then Naina fell, hit her head. We lost her instantly, Dyl."

"Ben told me. He never gave up any confidences, but he shared that. I pretty much gave up hope of ever seeing any of you up here after she died."

"Taid folded, couldn't bear to come up here without her, and honestly neither could I." Beth gazes toward the island. "The more I fought being like Mom, the more I became her. I even decided I didn't want to spend time anywhere in nature anymore, since it was what had taken you from us. Taid found his own way to connect to you and to here. He took up painting, watercolors and oil. All of the island, of course."

"Nice. Tell me more about you, Bethie."

"I met Mike about a year before Naina died, and I buried this place even deeper inside, because he was something good and honest in my life. Someone to count on. I opened up a few times about you, our summers here, but it was easier to keep it all separate. We moved to Chicago for his medical residency, and Taid and I started writing letters to each other. Kobi was a total surprise but magic all the same. It became harder to deal with Mom's distance, because I wanted Kobi to have a strong family structure he could count on, like we did. Or at least what I thought we had. And he reminded me so much of you. I'd disappear into memories a lot, which frustrated Mike because I wouldn't talk about it. But he's understood the space I needed to deal with things my own way."

Dylan smiles. "Just like I warned Amik way back when."

"I can look back on all of it and say that I wish you'd stood up to Mom, taken a stand against college and for Lily and your life here. But who knows what would have happened if you had? Do I wish you'd called or written? Yes, but I could have written to Ben or Lily, or come back on my own, once I was in college or with Mike. I *never* imagined that you might still be alive and think we'd blamed you for everything or abandoned you. If I'd known, I would have come back immediately.

"Given how all of our lives have gone since that day, I'd say we've paid more than enough of a price to get to now. I was the Pollyanna back then and for a long time afterward, believing that family should always come first. You knew even then that you had to be loyal and true to yourself and what you needed and wanted."

"Thanks to Maegan. I hung on to her words a lot over the years, trying to believe that I was doing the right thing."

She pulls out her cell phone, taps Maegan's number, and turns on the speaker phone. "It's only eleven in Arizona. Shall we tell her her instincts were right?"

Dylan stands and bounces on his toes. "Oh God, I've been waiting so long for all of this to happen." He paces the length of the boat until Maegan grunts into the phone, half-asleep.

"Maegan, it's me. You were right." Beth's voice catches as she tries to say Dylan's name. "It's all here, perfect just like always, and Dyl . . . he's here. You figured it out, didn't you?"

Maegan laughs. "Of course. Why do you think I'm in a hotel in northern Michigan?"

Beth jumps off the seat. "What?!"

"I hung up on you the other night because I had to make plane reservations. Mom's with the kids. I told her I was approved at the last minute for some work training."

"Did you call Taid?"

"Again, duh. He's sleeping in the other bed, snoring like a banshee. We should be there by ten if I can get enough coffee to drive that early. You'll pick us up on shore?"

"Of course. Just you two, right?"

"Yep. We'll figure out what to say to Mom and Dad, but that job will be Dylan's."

He drops to the bench, his shoulders heavy from what's to come. Beth finishes the conversation with Maegan and sits next to him.

They reach for each other and hug with the same intensity as earlier in the day. Only this time Beth feels relieved, almost giddy. "Maegan told me Taid was giving me the last chance to save each of us. I had no idea she guessed it meant you too. We may catch Mom and Dad, or we may not, but we'll try."

"Most important is saving yourself, Bethie, just like Taid says in his letter. Thank you for never giving up on the family, for coming back to yourself and to us."

"Thanks for never giving up on making it right, Dyl."

Beth holds on to her brother and breathes the island, rocks, trees, and sky back into her heart. All these years she trusted in their beauty and endurance, that they would live on forever, just as they lived somewhere deep inside her. She looks at her brother and realizes how much he's always been with her, how much she counted on his love and strength to get her back to herself and to this place, even though she never thought they'd see each other again.

Perhaps nature stole Dylan, or the manitous exacted revenge. Maybe everything had to happen for her to look in and remember that a place can be as much a part of her as the air she breathes, that it matters as much as the people she loves, and when she honors her own path is when she is truly home. That she can return to this lake, land, and air and to herself with the people she loves may be more than enough payment for the past. The moonlight glimmers off Llyndee's Peak; the faces beam back at her. Stars dance in the sky. She finds Cassiopeia, Andromeda, and Cepheus and smiles.

Acknowledgments

For most of my professional life, I've lived in the fact-based world of environmental communications—how every living thing is connected to another, how our lifestyles impact the majestic planet we live on, and the sometimes simple but often complicated and expensive choices we must make to restore and protect the health of our water, land, air, animals, and ourselves. The messaging focuses first on getting people outside, because the benefits of spending time in nature are well documented: it feeds the soul, reduces stress, and makes us more aware of the world around us as well as within. The vast majority of us seek out these benefits on vacations, whether it's at a family cottage, a national park, or in a backyard garden. Even short, everyday connections—from noticing the sunset to listening to a birdsong—have been proven to heighten our psyche and reinforce nature's value in our lives. What we value, we act to protect.

The Best Part of Us tells the story of a woman who must decide whether to save herself and her connection with nature in order to explore the same choice humanity faces—for Earth will survive and heal over time, but our values and actions will determine whether humans and other species can as well. When we decide to understand and value our connections with everything else on the planet, we will act to prevent further devastating impacts of climate change or even the next pandemic.

I started this novel as part of Stanford University's certificate program in fiction writing. I am deeply grateful to Angela Pneuman—award-winning author of *Home Remedies* and *Lay It on My Heart*, Stanford professor, and director of the exceptional Napa Valley Writer's Conference—who went above and beyond to edit the complete first draft in my final semester. Thank you to every teacher and fellow student for enriching the program and this book, and for their continued friendship. Special thanks to Carrie Doyle, Carol Luther, Swati Sikka, and Julie Ushio. Our calls are treasured gifts of friendship and encouragement for each other and our writing lives.

When I finally asked others beyond my Stanford professors and colleagues to read this story, I reached out to two longstanding friends. Many, many thanks to Deb Hamel, who provided the honest, straightforward assessment I knew she would. To Libby Harris, who understood the story's central message and stood true to it and to me through her generous brainstorming, edits, patience, and friendship, I am eternally grateful.

Sincere appreciation and thanks also to Dave Dempsey and Carol Luther for providing additional clarity and depth to the story's themes; to She Writes Press authors Barbara Stark-Nemon, Jenni Ogden, and Donna Cameron for their advice and encouraging words; and to many dear friends—especially my book club, Julie Reed, and professional colleagues—for their excitement and support for the novel and its release.

I'm especially grateful to everyone at She Writes Press and BookSparks for helping to create and publicize a novel that is infinitely better because of their insights and direction: Brooke Warner, Shannon Green, Lauen Wise Wait, Julie Metz, Krissa

Lagos, Tabitha Lahr, Kirstin Andrews, Crystal Patriarche, Keely Platte, and Hanna Pollock Lindsley. Thanks also to Fe Wyma for bringing Lake Wigwakobi to life in the novel's map.

My husband, Ron, and son, Emerson, have cheered me on throughout and enriched my life beyond measure. For my love of our natural world, I owe everything to my grandparents, Frank and Dora, and to my parents for the gifts they provided then and now.

Thank you for choosing to read Beth's story. I hope it helps you to consider the unique connections you have with others and with the natural world, and how you can act to protect what you value. To learn more, please visit sallycole-misch.com.

About the Author

photo © RCM Photo

Sally Cole-Misch is a writer and environmental communicator who advocates for the natural world through work and play. She holds a bachelor's degree in journalism from the University of Missouri, a master's degree in environmental education and international water policy from the University of Michigan, and a certificate in fiction writing from Stanford University. Throughout her career, she's focused on communicating our essential connections with nature—particularly the Great Lakes—and the role each of us can play to restore, protect, and enjoy all that nature gives to us. Sally lives in Michigan with her husband and son and enjoys hiking, skiing, kayaking, sailing, reading, and gardening, a hearty laugh with friends, the wonder of surprise, and the optimism that nature's beauty always provides.

Learn more about Sally and access the **Book Club Discussion Guide** for *The Best Part of Us* at www.sallycole-misch.com

SELECTED TITLES FROM SHE WRITES PRESS

She Writes Press is an independent publishing company founded to serve women writers everywhere. Visit us at www.shewritespress.com.

Magic Flute by Patricia Minger. $16.95, 978-1-63152-093-8. When a car accident puts an end to ambitious flutist Liz Morgan's dreams, she returns to her childhood hometown in Wales in an effort to reinvent her path.

Eden by Jeanne Blasberg. $16.95, 978-1-63152-188-1. As her children and grandchildren assemble for Fourth of July weekend at Eden, the Meister family's grand summer cottage on the Rhode Island shore, Becca decides it's time to introduce the daughter she gave up for adoption fifty years ago.

The Belief in Angels by J. Dylan Yates. $16.95, 978-1-938314-64-3. From the Majdonek death camp to a volatile hippie household on the East Coast, this narrative of tragedy, survival, and hope spans more than fifty years, from the 1920s to the 1970s.

Bittersweet Manor by Tory McCagg. $16.95, 978-1-93831-456-8. A chronicle of three generations of love, manipulation, entitlement, and disappointed expectations in an upper-middle-class New England family.

Things Unsaid by Diana Y. Paul. $16.95, 978-1-63152-812-5. A family saga of three generations fighting over money and obligation—and a tale of survival, resilience, and recovery.

Stella Rose by Tammy Flanders Hetrick. $16.95, 978-1-63152-921-4. When her dying best friend asks her to take care of her sixteen-year-old daughter, Abby says yes—but as she grapples with raising a grieving teenager, she realizes she didn't know her best friend as well as she thought she did.